They're ri...
they're imp...
the...

Millionaire's Club

and they're yours!

*Go on…'pick up' these two
wealthy bachelors today!*

Dear Reader,

Happy New Year!

Welcome to this month's selection of two-in-one Desires—two full length novels for one great-value price.

This month sees the start of a new mini-series THE MILLIONAIRE'S CLUB with *Millionaire MD* by Jennifer Greene and *World's Most Eligible Texan* by Sara Orwig, both books are together in one volume entitled **Millionaire's Club**. If you think you can handle a double dose of some of the richest, most sensual men around then this is the series for you!

You definitely won't be out in the rain and cold with our second volume—**It's Raining Men!** including *Reese's Wild Wager* by Barbara McCauley and *The Temptation of Rory Monahan* by Elizabeth Bevarly. These stories are just hot, hot, hot!

Completing the month is *Baby at His Door* by Katherine Garbera and *Cheyenne Dad* by Sheri WhiteFeather in a volume entitled **Dads in Demand**. These bachelors are about to find out that fatherhood—and marriage!—is exactly what they've been searching for.

We hope you enjoy them all!

The Editors

Millionaire's Club

JENNIFER GREENE
SARA ORWIG

SILHOUETTE® DESIRE™

*First published in Great Britain 2002
Silhouette Books, Eton House, 18-24 Paradise Road,
Richmond, Surrey TW9 1SR*

MILLIONAIRE'S CLUB © Harlequin Books S.A. 2002

The publisher acknowledges the copyright holders of the individual works as follows:

Millionaire MD © Harlequin Books S.A. 2001
World's Most Eligible Texan © Harlequin Books S.A. 2001

Special thanks and acknowledgement are given to Jennifer Greene and Sara Orwig for their contributions to The Millionaire's Club series.

ISBN 0 373 04737 1

51-0102

*Printed and bound in Spain
by Litografia Rosés S.A., Barcelona*

▼ SILHOUETTE®
DESIRE™

is proud to present

Millionaires Galore!

Rich, renowned, ruthless and sexy as sin

Millionaire's Club - January

MILLIONAIRE MD *by Jennifer Greene*

WORLD'S MOST ELIGIBLE TEXAN *by Sara Orwig*

Millionaire Men - February

LONE STAR KNIGHT *by Cindy Gerard*

HER ARDENT SHEIKH *by Kristi Gold*

Millionaire Bachelors - March

TYCOON WARRIOR *by Sheri WhiteFeather*

MILLIONAIRE HUSBAND *by Leanne Banks*

Millionaire Marriages - April

MILLIONAIRE BOSS *by Peggy Moreland*

THE MILLIONAIRE'S SECRET WISH
by Leanne Banks

1201/SH/LC26

MILLIONAIRE MD

by
Jennifer Greene

JENNIFER GREENE

lives near Lake Michigan with her husband and two children. Before writing full-time, she worked as a teacher and a personnel manager. Michigan State University honoured her as an 'outstanding woman graduate' for her work with women on campus.

Jennifer has written many romances, for which she has won numerous awards, including three RITAs from the Romance Writers of America in the Best Short Contemporary Books category, and a Career Achievement award from *Romantic Times Magazine*.

To my fellow Millionaire's Club authors, Sara Orwig, Cindy Gerard, Kristi Gold, Sheri WhiteFeather—you were all so wonderful to work with! I hope we have another chance to commit murder, mayhem and jewel thefts together.

One

Ask Dr. Justin Webb, and "The Tennessee Waltz" was a downright ridiculous—if not insulting—song to play at a Texas bash, but what the hey. He didn't care what it took to get his arms around Winona. Never had. Never would. He didn't even mind having to wear a tux and be on his best starched behavior for an exhaustingly long evening, as long as he could catch some private moments with her now and then. Like this one.

"I swear, honey, you look good enough to marry."

"Why, thank you, doc." Wearing spindly tall dress pumps, Winona almost reached his cheek in height, but she still had to tilt her face to make eye contact. He marveled. Those eyes of hers were the same soft, wistful, breathtaking blue of a dawn sky—but her smile, so typically, was full of the devil. And that was when she was being reasonably nice to him. "You haven't proposed marriage to me in, what, two weeks now?"

Twelve days and six hours, but who was counting. "Give or take a few days."

She nodded demurely. "And how many times do I have to tell you? If I'm ever in the mood to marry a hard-core womanizing bachelor with way too much money, I'll let you know."

Justin grinned, since there was no point in taking the insult to heart. In the past, she'd dished out far, far worse.

Come to think of it, so had he.

Tightening his grip, he whirled her past the banquet table, the fiddlers, the receiving line of dignitaries and Asterland royalty. He wanted to waltz her past and out the tall balcony doors and into the star-studded night—where he'd have Win to himself—but the idea just wouldn't fly. Unfortunately, the January night was typical of west Texas, the temperature colder than a witch's heart, and the wind twice as bitter. "Well, shoot, darlin'. If I can't talk you into marriage to-night, how about a nice, immoral, amoral, down-and-dirty affair?"

"I'd love to, doc—with anyone else. But you've already done that with so many women in town that I'd just be one in a long line. Thanks, but no thanks."

He winced—not from her comment, but because she'd just stepped on his foot. God knew, Winona was adorable, but she *did* have the grace of a coyote on a dance floor. A hand at the small of her back coaxed her physically closer to him. Close enough for him to feel the tips of her nipples beneath the monk-black dress that zipped straight and plain, right to her throat. Close enough so that he could see her light blue eyes dilate when her tummy rubbed against his satin tux cummerbund. Close enough to see the spare, soft gloss on her small mouth.

Close enough to see her scowl.

"Behave yourself, you dog."

His eyebrows arched, trying out the charmingly innocent expression that had always worked on the softer sex. With one exception. "Now, Win, you know I'm just trying to help. I'm afraid you're going to trip and fall. And I know you're not fond of advice, but if you'd just quit trying to lead, I swear you'd have a lot easier time on the dance floor."

"You're trying to help? Said the wolf in the fox den. And *what* do you think your hand is doing on my butt? You think I won't punch you?"

Actually, he *knew* she'd punch him—in public, in private, in church, at a black-tie gala or anywhere else. She'd been doing it ever since she was a furious, bad-tempered twelve-year-old, and he'd been a suave, worldly seventeen who'd known everything—except why the hell such a squirt-age girl had managed to wind his heart around her finger. "I've had my hand on your butt before," he reminded her delicately.

"That was significantly different. I was hurt, I'd fallen on some broken glass and you were playing doctor—"

"And I'm so glad you brought that up. I never had a chance to tell you before how much I always loved playing doctor with you," he said fervently.

There now. She had to choke back laughter. Winona never could keep that terrific sense of humor under wraps for long—but this time, she turned serious again all too quickly. "Cut it out, you. And this time, I mean it. The point is, you know I'd never be attending this fancy shindig if I weren't working. Just because I'm not in a cop's uniform doesn't mean that I'm really here to play. I'm here in a professional role—which means that you either put your hand where it belongs, or I really just might slug you—and I'm not kidding, Justin."

He heard her. And he not only believed her, but he'd never have done anything to publicly embarrass her in a million years. A teasing pat was one thing, an inappropriate grope in front of others, another—not just because he respected Winona and her job, but because if he ever got a shot at really getting to Win, he wanted no audience around. Anywhere. Preferably for a several-hundred-mile radius.

Temporarily, however, it seemed that he was incapable of removing his hand from her fanny. It wasn't a choice. Normal honorable, ethical standards of behavior simply couldn't apply. His palm slid down the silky dress from the hollow of her spine to the fullest slope of her rump. He squeezed several times, because hell, he had to.

Said squeezing produced the obvious biological response in him—he was hard as a hammer in three seconds flat. Above the neck, though, his forehead produced a frown darker than a Texas thunderstorm. "What in God's name are you wearing under that dress?"

He would never have asked the question, except that the answer seemed to be nothing. Absolutely nothing. There wasn't a woman in the Club—except for Winona—who wasn't dripping diamonds and sequins. Jewels winked from ears, throats, wrists and fingers, all across the dance floor. Win's ears were naked and so was her throat; the long, soft black dress made all the pricey designer gowns look overdone and fussy. To Justin, she stood out as a hopeless beauty. Always had, in his eyes.

It was just…he couldn't feel any underwear. He certainly hadn't put his hand on her fanny *expecting* to feel underwear. But the silky dress was a thinnish material, so that his hand instinctively expected to find panty lines, a sense of fabric. And when they didn't, alarm bells clanged in his mind on a par with a fire truck's siren. There weren't too many reasons a woman would neglect to wear underwear to a very public, very fancy gig—especially Winona, who didn't reveal nuttin' to no one—normally. When it came down to it, Justin could only think of one reason she'd be running around sans panties. There had to be a lover she was trying to turn on.

A lover.

A man.

A man—who wasn't him.

"Justin, what the Sam Hill is the matter with y—"

He sensed her right fist clenching, preparing to punch him.

"Get your hand off my... The dress showed lines," she hissed. "I couldn't wear anything underneath it. Not that I owe you any explanation, you low-down, overprotective, bossy son of a gun. Now you've got five seconds, max, before I—"

He was removing his hand. Really. Right then. It just took a couple seconds for relief to catch up with him, and for those few seconds he really couldn't seem to breathe. In the meantime—possibly because Win didn't realize he was sincerely getting around to behaving better—that small right fist of hers was still aiming straight for his solar plexus. That is, until a tall, handsome, dark-haired dude showed up on the scene, winked at Win, and smoothly lifted her clenched fist to his right shoulder.

"I'm cutting in," Aaron Black announced, "before either of you come to blows. Besides which, I dance a ton better than he ever will, Winona. *And* I'm better looking."

"Well, hell," Justin grumbled. But he let Aaron take off with Winona across the dance floor. For one thing, the orchestra changed tunes to a rousing, foot-stomping bluegrass, so any cheek-to-cheek opportunities had abruptly disappeared. For another, Aaron was not only a fellow member of the Texas Cattleman's Club, but a friend that Justin would trust to the wall—and had. And for yet another reason, damn Aaron, but he was a diplomat in his professional life as well as his private one, and when he motioned a thumb toward the bar, Justin picked up the subtle, tactful clue that, just possibly, he needed to get out of Winona's sight for a minute or two.

He loped over to the bar, all right...but watching Win whirl off in Aaron's arms still gave him a case of the glums that a whole well of whiskey couldn't cure.

They'd always bickered like two toddlers in the same sandbox. Justin didn't specifically mind that, because they mutually enjoyed teasing each other. But she'd always treated

him like a friend, a neighbor, a loved but insufferable big
brother. Never as a man.

He must have asked her to marry him fifty times—and all
fifty times, she'd cracked up laughing, as if the idea of marrying him was the best joke they'd ever shared.

He got it, he got it. It didn't matter if half the women in
town chased him nonstop. Winona just couldn't seem to
imagine him as a lover. For several years now, Justin kept
thinking if she could just *need* him. If he could just get a
chance to show her a different side of himself. If something
could jolt her into looking at him differently, maybe, just
maybe, he'd have a serious shot with her.

"Hi, Dr. Webb." Riley Monroe, the Club's longtime caretaker, had a smile waiting even before Justin reached the bar.
"You guys sure outdid yourself with the party tonight. This
is quite a shindig. What can I get you?"

"Whiskey. Straight. And thanks, Riley." Justin didn't
have to wait thirty seconds before the glass of liquid gold
was in his hands. Riley might be the Texas Cattleman's Club
night caretaker, but he'd subbed as a bartender for formal
functions for as long as Justin could remember. The ladies
loved him—likely because he had a dose of flimflam in his
character. Occasionally he could spread on the Las Vegas-
type charm too thickly for Justin's taste, but that didn't matter. Riley was as dependable as the sunshine and as loyal as
a hound. Good qualities in any man, and normally Justin
would have chatted for a few minutes.

Tonight, he gulped down a big enough sip to feel the whiskey burn some new holes in his tonsils, then leaned back
against the bar.

He spotted her, still out there, still high-stepping with
Aaron…and damnation, looking like she was having a hell
of a good time.

He looked around, determined to get his mind off Winona—and to keep it off. The party was in full swing, and
although good taste had to be an issue with so many royal

guests, so was having fun Texas-style. Messy, finger-dripping lobster and Texas barbecue was set up on the same table as the fragile hothouse roses and elegant ice sculptures. The formal orchestra was all dressed in black tie—but naturally, it had a damn good fiddling section. The giant boar's head hanging on one wall looked down on more diamonds and rubies than the bugger had ever seen in the wild, for darn sure, but the blaze of firelight winked on the iron-studded plaque over the entrance door. Leadership, Justice and Peace was burned into the wood—the long-term logo for the Club that had a uniquely special meaning this night.

Justin gulped down another slug of whiskey, trying to ignore the short-haired brunette dancing past him yet again. He winked at a blonde instead. The Princess Anna von Oberland of Obersbourg—at least that'd been her title until she'd married Greg, who was plastered against her on the dance floor in total oblivion to the foot-stomping, sassy rhythm of the current song being played.

The whole purpose of this black-tie shindig was Anna. An outsider would surely find the situation confounding—what could a bunch of Texans possibly have in common with royalty from the small European countries of Obersbourg and Asterland? But months earlier, Princess Anna had been in grave trouble, and the Texas Cattleman's Club had stepped in to rescue her. Two days from now, twelve citizens from both Asterland and Obersbourg were returning to Europe via private jet—without Anna, of course, who was head over heels for her bridegroom and Texas both. But this party was it. A chance for Anna's family—and government—to say thank you to the Texas Cattleman's Club boys…and a chance for the Club to strengthen the ties between the governments.

Justin finished the last gulp of whiskey, thinking how unusual this whole shindig was. Not the party itself. Truth to tell, the Texas Cattleman's Club used any excuse to throw a formal brawl—and the bigger the better. But the group generally kept a low profile about their "quieter" activities. The world was pretty damn lousy at protecting its innocents. It's not like the Club stuck its nose in a hornet's nest if there was any choice, but sometimes an innocent's life could hang in the balance—a situation where diplomacy either failed or where politics were so ticklish that tuning to normal channels simply didn't get results.

An edgy thought needled through Justin's mind, stealing the jubilant party mood and making him shift uneasily on his feet. He was the only Club member who didn't own a gun. He used to. His grandparents were big in ranching and oil both, and anyone owning a big spread who lived in that kind of isolated country knew how to handle a gun. So did Justin, but that was years ago. At this point, he was starkly aware that he was the only member who never shot anything but a hypodermic. The others had strong military skills in their background. He did his rescuing with a scalpel.

And there was nothing precisely wrong with that, but suddenly his mind was whirling, spinning down dark roads. He'd come home from Bosnia to abruptly and completely change medical specialties. No one had asked him why he'd switched to plastic surgery. No one had noticed that there were certain medical cases he no longer touched. And so far it hadn't mattered, because none of his private work with the Texas Cattlemen's Club had forced him into situations that he couldn't handle. But it could, Justin knew, and he feared letting his Club members down.

So far, thank God, the only one he'd let down was himself.

The orchestra suddenly changed to a slow dance. Swiftly, Justin lifted his head. A redhead winked at him as she sashayed past. Moments later, an elegant blonde wagged him a hello over her dance partner's shoulder.

He winked back and smiled back, but his heart wasn't in it. Tarnation, where had Winona disappeared to? Invariably he got a lot of female attention at these gigs, and that was nice, real nice, but primarily the reason he got such a rush from the single females in town was because of his wealthy, jet-set reputation.

The wealth was real enough—his grandparents had left him a ton, on top of what he hauled in as a plastic surgeon. But believe the social columns, and he only did tummy tucks and nose jobs when he wasn't taking off on impulsive, lavish vacations.

He not only didn't mind the stupid image. He catered to it. Since people expected him to disappear on a whim, it made his projects and missions with the Texas Cattleman's Club easier to pull off. In this particular situation, though, the media had been led to believe that some good old Texas boys had "accidentally" become involved in Princess Anna's dilemma. Justin had never kept his association with the Club a secret. He never kept secrets. Nothing in life got out faster or caused more trouble than a secret. But he *did* believe in keeping quiet when....

There she was. Win. His narrowed gaze soldered on her brilliant smile. Who was the blasted woman smiling at *now?* She wasn't still dancing with Aaron Black. This guy had lighter hair, broader shoulders, wasn't quite so tall...Justin's stomach muscles suddenly unclenched. It was Matt. She was just dancing with Matt Walker, and although God knew the rancher was known to turn more than one single woman's eye, he was also a member of the Club. A friend.

Still, that didn't mean Justin had to like the way he was holding Win. Or smiling at her, for that damn matter. There was a limit to loyalty and friendship. Come to think of it, there was a limit to loyalty and friendship and honor and ethics.

And that damn limit was Winona Raye.

Aw, hell. He was losing his mind. It was her. She'd always made him lose his mind, and every year it was getting worse. He was beginning to sound like a lovesick cow. More pathetic yet, he was beginning to act like one.

"Hey, Dr. Webb, can I get you another?"

Justin's head snapped around. "Sure, Riley. I'd appreciate a refill." Well aware he'd been acting—and thinking—way too soberly for a party, he offered a companionable grin for Riley Monroe and another for the stranger next to him.

The short gentleman offered his hand. "I believe that we met on one other occasion, Dr. Webb. My name is Klimt. Robert Klimt."

"Oh, yes. Of course, I remember." Actually Justin had no memory of the man whatsoever, but he scrounged his brain for some connection. Klimt, Klimt...he was almost sure somebody'd told him that Robert Klimt was a minor cabinet member in the Asterland government.

"I was just asking Mr. Monroe about the sign over the entrance door." Klimt motioned to the Leadership, Justice and Peace logo. "I heard someone say that slogan came from a historical story about the town. I gather that there's some kind of romantic legend about Royal, Texas, and some jewels?"

"Oh, there is, there is." Riley topped off Justin's glass with a flourish, then reached behind the bar for Klimt's poison—imported schnapps. "Next door to our Texas Cattleman's Club here is a park. You probably noticed. In the early 1800s, there was a mission here, an old adobe church. It's just part of the park now, but back in the War with Mexico, 1846 or so, there was a Texas soldier found a comrade fallen in battle, tried to save him...."

The fiddlers had picked up the pace for "The Yellow Rose of Texas." Justin, half listening to Klimt and Riley, researched the dance floor for the black, bouncing curly hair again. She wasn't with Aaron, wasn't with Matthew. In a sense, she really *was* working this evening, even if she was wearing formal attire. Win had never been a carry-a-gun kind of cop—she normally worked with juveniles, kids in trouble, kids at risk. But everyone on the local police force had been quietly coaxed to attend the gathering tonight, because the whole town wanted this shindig to go well, and Winona was always pulled into special problems like this. She was ideal. Everyone knew her. Everyone trusted her. And that was just great, except that she was so damned beautiful, Justin figured some guy, sometime, was going to zip down those cool defenses of hers....

"... So anyhow, this Texas soldier was just trying to save a wounded comrade, but it was just too late. Our Texas soldier had no idea the guy was carrying these three fancy jewels until he's caring for the body, trying to bury him. Anyway, the old guy was gone, no identification on him, so he took the jewels back to Royal—"

"And this is a true story?" Klimt asked.

Justin yanked his gaze off the dance floor and looked at Klimt again. The man couldn't be five foot five, but for a little guy, he sure had the puff of a banty rooster. Everything about him was starched—posture stiff as a ramrod, linen shirt perfectly creased, hair perfectly brushed, smile perfectly appropriate. Even his shoes shone like mirrors. Justin's glance strayed to the smaller man's left temple. There was a mole there, right by his eye. There were beauty marks, and then there were moles. This happened to be a plain old ugly mole—Justin immediately looked away; it was just second nature as a doc to notice a precancerous physical condition. And in this case, the minor flaw was particularly striking because everything about the guy was so spiffed-up-perfect in every other way.

Riley was laughing. "Aw, none of the story is true. Or maybe it is. The truth is that none of us seem to care. The town loves the legend, so we've been passing it on for years."

"So tell me more about these jewels," Klimt requested.

"Well, to start with, each of the jewels refers to the motto on the Texas Cattleman's Club sign, see? Each of the gems is really unusual, partly because they're so rare as to be priceless. You couldn't buy one for love or money, not then and not now. Which made it all the more interesting and mysterious, why this Texas soldier was carrying them—but we'll never know that answer. The point is that he had them. And one stone was a red diamond—''

"I never heard that diamonds came in a red color."

"They don't, they don't," Riley said. "Except once in a real rare while. And you study some gem lore, now, and you find red diamonds were the stones of kings, because they were that rare. So you look up in our motto sign, and that's what the first word—*leadership*—is about. That's what the red diamond is a symbol for. Right, Dr. Webb?''

"Right, Riley." The orchestra had switched tunes to an old-fashioned waltz. Aaron Black glided past with a tall, plain young woman in his arms. Justin thought he recognized her. Pamela something? A teacher? Very shy, very proper— and how typical of Aaron to pick out a wallflower and make sure she wasn't pining on the sidelines.

Even better that he wasn't dancing with Win. Justin searched the crowd again. He saw Aaron, he saw Matt, he saw... *Finally,* he caught a glimpse of her again. This time she was partnered by a man with coal-black hair and striking gray eyes, teeth shining stark white in a face that so rarely smiled—the Sheikh. Ben. And another Texas Cattleman's Club member, thank God, so it wasn't like Justin had to worry she wasn't in a gentleman's hands.

Exactly.

He trusted Ben the same way he trusted Aaron and Matt. With his life. But trusting them with a single, attractive woman was a different story—particularly when the men had no idea how much he cared about her.

Nor would they.

"Dr. Webb, Mr. Klimt was asking about the other stones...." Riley prompted him.

"Yeah? Well, the legend has it that there's the red diamond...and then a black harlequin opal...and then an emerald.''

"Yeah, yeah," Riley agreed, and settled on his elbows on

the bar to keep spinning the tale for his willing listener. "See, technically the opal's the least valuable of the three stones. But a black harlequin opal—she's a rare mother. And those who get into the magic of gems tend to see the harlequin opal as both having healing power and as somehow having the inner light and power to bring justice—so that's where the second word in the Club motto comes from. *Justice.* As an ideal, you know?"

"Yes, Mr. Monroe, I believe I know what an ideal is," Klimt said impatiently. "And the third stone, the emerald?"

"I'm coming to that one. Around the world, for centuries, emeralds were always considered the stone of peacemakers, and this particular emerald was said to be one giant stone besides. So *peace* was naturally the third word they put in the Club motto."

"Leadership, justice, peace," Klimt echoed. "That's quite a story. But it seems such an elaborate legend if the stones never really existed."

"And there's more to it than that," Riley said happily. "Our guy brought the stones back to Royal after the war with Mexico. He was gonna be rich, you know, sell 'em, buy a big spread, put up a fancy house and all? And he meant to, only he got home, and oil was found on his homestead. He had black gold coming out of his ears, so he never did need to sell those stones to have his fortune made."

"So what happened to them?"

Riley peered over Justin's glass, then Klimt's, then ducked down to bring up bottles again. "I don't know. Nobody knows. The Texas Cattleman's Club…well, there were some men formed this group, back even before Club founder Tex Langley's time. Some say they first got together to guard the jewels. Some say they were just the leading citizens of Royal, who passed on responsibility for the town's security from generation to generation. Some say they just used the legend of the jewels to create that motto, because, well, it was a good motto. Those are our values around here. Leadership. Justice. Pea—''

"You think the jewels exist?"

Riley fingered his chest. "Me? Oh, you bet. I think they existed for real, back then, and they exist somewhere now."

"So what do you think happened to them?"

"Well, everybody's got a theory...."

Someone cut in on her with the Sheikh. Dakota Lewis. Justin's eyes tracked the two of them on the dance floor, and he almost had to smile. Dakota wasn't much on dancing. Win'd be lucky if she left the floor without broken toes if she stuck with him long. Dakota looked what he was—no uniform, but the retired military status was obvious from his unyielding posture and scalped haircut. On the surface he looked tough and hard—and truth to tell he was—but Justin couldn't worry about Winona with Dakota. Since his divorce, Dakota had shown no interest in any women.

"Well, if the jewels *did* exist, where is your best guess they'd be hidden?" Klimt asked Riley.

Again Justin turned his head to the other two men. Klimt could only seem to march to one drummer. The town loved its legend. Actually, outsiders seemed to love it just as much; tourists consistently ate it up. But Klimt was pushing it beyond anyone's normal interest. "If the jewels really existed, they'd be under heavy lock and key," he said mildly. "We only encourage the legend because it's good fun for everyone. And who'd want to be the one to break hearts by confessing that Santa Claus didn't exist? I sure plan to believe until I'm 110."

Riley chortled appreciatively. "You saying you believe in Santa or the jewels, Dr. Webb?"

"In Santa, of course. You can have the jewels. I'll take the loot Santa carries around any day."

Riley laughed again. Klimt even threw him a sour smile, and, temporarily, Riley seemed to be off the hook for entertaining Mr. Banty Rooster. Klimt, carrying a fresh schnapps, wandered off into the crowd.

And Justin was about to do that, too…until Winona caught his attention again. She was still on the dance floor, but dancing with a stranger this time.

A non-Texan. One of the Asterlanders that Justin didn't know. He watched the dude's big hand sift down to her fanny.

She smiled at the guy. And then reached back and removed his hand.

Justin shifted on his feet. Something kicked in his pulse. Not just jealousy—God knew he knew all the shades of green there were in that particularly annoying emotion. But Winona was clearly handling the guy—no matter how protective Justin felt, the truth was, he'd never seen a man that Winona couldn't handle with both hands tied.

That was, in fact, why she so often got conned into attending these kinds of shindigs. Regular cops were always around for security, but it wasn't the same. The few serious crimes in Royal tended to be robbery. Sure, there was a crime of passion now and then, a fight at the Royal Diner occasionally, domestic dispute problems and that sort of thing. But basically this just wasn't a high-crime community. This was oil country. Those who'd made it, made it big. And those who hadn't made it were paid well, simply because there was ample to go around. The school systems were top-drawer, the whole area supported with fine services. The only "risk" prevalent in a small, ultrarich town like Royal was its being a draw for thieves.

Which was exactly why and how Winona was irreplaceable at these galas. She always showed up in the same evil black dress, the same sassy high heels. It wasn't that she showed off anything—ever—but there just didn't seem to be a man born who wouldn't talk to her. On top of that, she sensed things. She had an intuition when someone or something wasn't right.

And Justin frowned again suddenly. No guy was eyeing her at that specific moment—and her dance partner had quit trying to put the make on her. But her gaze was roving the room. She tripped in her partner's arms—which wasn't that much of a shock, because unless a man let her lead, she couldn't dance worth a Texas jumping bean. But it was the way she suddenly moved—stiffly, warily—that had Justin suddenly alert and pushing through bodies to get to the other side of the room.

Maybe she didn't know he was in love with her.

Maybe she'd never think of him as anything more than the old friend she'd grown up with.

For damn sure, maybe she'd never realize that his offers to marry her were sincere.

But if Winona were in trouble, Justin was going to be there for her—whether she wanted him there or not.

Two

Winona was in such trouble.

She'd slept with the same dream two nights running, replaying the evening of the Texas Cattleman's Club gala. She *knew* it was just another dream, because the same details kept getting embellished. In the dream, she was breathtakingly gorgeous—which was a lot of fun, but not remotely realistic. She'd been whirling and swirling on the dance floor, not tripping, being graceful—which was another reason she knew it was a dream. And she kept dancing with different men—man after man after man, all of them adorable, all of them charmed by every word that came out of her mouth, fighting to have another spin with her around the floor....

Okay, okay, so these were pretty ridiculous dreams. But they were *her* dreams, and she was having a great time with them.

Only in this particular night's version, Justin pulled her into his arms. For "The Tennessee Waltz"—which had to be one of the schmaltziest songs of all time, a song doomed

to bring out romantic feelings in even the toughest of
women—such as herself—and suddenly she was naked.
Whirling around the floor. Waltzing. Without a stitch on.
Only being naked was okay, because there wasn't a soul in
the room who realized that she was naked. Except for herself.

And Justin.

Alarm bells started clanging in her ears, but Winona determinedly ignored them. Obviously this wasn't real, and
since this happened to be her personal, wicked dream, she
didn't want to let go of it until she had to.

Justin couldn't take his eyes off her. She whacked him
upside the head—which was such a real, logical thing for her
to do that for a second, Winona freaked that this wasn't a
dream—but he didn't seem to mind, and the whack didn't
seem to stop him from looking, either…a long, slow look
that began with her naked toes, dawdled past long slender
legs (this was a dream, for sure), past hips without a single
spare ounce of fat on them (and a damn *good* dream), up,
his gaze a caress that took in waist and proud, trembling
breasts and white throat, then up to her vulnerable, naked
eyes.

Yeah, she wanted him.

She'd always wanted him.

Another alarm bell clanged in her mind—but for Pete's
sake, in the privacy of a dream, a girl should be able to be
honest with herself. Justin looked like a young Sam Elliot.
Tall. Lanky. With a slow, lazy drawl and a lot for a girl to
worry about in those sexy eyes. Cover those broad shoulders
in a tux and a woman just wanted to sip him in—correction—
sip him in and lap him up both.

A vague memory surfaced in her dream. She'd been
twelve. Until she'd been fostered with the Gerard family,
she'd never had a bike, and she was new to the family, still
waiting for someone to hit her, someone to scold her. It'd
happen. She just didn't know when yet, but she was wary
this time, prepared to protect herself. She didn't need any-

body to watch out for her…it was just the bike. Oh man, oh man, she wanted to ride a bike so badly, and everybody assumed she knew how, at her age. But she didn't. And the first time she took it out, it was almost dusk, because no one was on the street then, no strangers to see her.

And Justin had been there when she'd crashed into a tree. Helped her up. Righted the bike. A gorgeous heartthrob of a seventeen-year-old—with a chivalrous streak—enough to make her tough, hard, mean, cold heart go *hoboyhoboyhoboy.* He'd touched her cheek. Made her laugh. Then she'd had to punch him for helping her, of course. What else could a twelve-year-old do?

More alarm bells clanged in her mind. The same, annoying, insistent alarm bells.

Winona's eyes popped open on a pitch-black bedroom. She wasn't twelve and falling into a sinking-deep, mortifying crush with Justin Webb. She wasn't dancing naked with Justin at the Texas Cattleman's Club, either. It was just her bedroom, and the telephone was ringing off the hook, at seven in the morning—according to the insane neon dials on the bedside clock.

The instant she read the time, though, she snapped awake fast. There was only one reason for a telephone call at this crazy hour. Trouble. And although technically she was a nine-to-five cop, working with at-risk teens, reality was that kids never got in trouble at nice, convenient hours.

She fumbled for the lamp switch, then hit the ground running, shagging a hand through her tousled hair as she grabbed the receiver.

"Winona?"

Not a kid. An adult's voice. Her boss, from the precinct. "You know it's me. What's wrong, Wayne?"

"You know the jet that was supposed to take off last night for Asterland? The hotsy totsy flight with all the royalty and dignitaries and all?"

"Yes, of course." So did the whole town.

"Well, something went wrong. She lifted off, barely got in the air before they were radioing in some garbled, panicked message about a problem. Next thing, they're making an emergency landing about fifteen miles out of town, middle of nowhere, flat as a pancake. Fire broke out—"

She got the gist. The details didn't matter. "Holy cow. How can I help?"

"Truthfully, I don't know." Winona could well imagine Wayne squinting and rubbing the back of his head. He didn't like trouble in his town. The way Wayne saw it, Royal belonged to him. Anyone took the crease out of those jeans ticked him off. "I'm calling from the scene. Everything's a mess. This all just happened less than a half hour ago. First thing was getting everybody off the plane safely. Only a couple seem badly injured, the rest are just shaken. But what the hell happened, I don't know. And I don't want every Tom, Dick and curious Harry messing with my crime scene. It's still dark. Only so much I can get done until daylight—"

He was talking more to himself than to her. Winona knew how her boss's mind worked. "So where could I be the most help? At the hospital? The plane site? The office?"

"Here," Wayne said bluntly. "You gonna kick me straight to Austin if I admit I just want a woman here?"

"Probably." Holding the phone clamped to her ear with one hand, she reached for the deodorant on the dresser and thumbed open the lid. Applying deodorant one-handed was tricky, but she'd done it before.

"Well, then, you're just going to have to kick me. To be honest, everything's being handled that needs to be. It's just, that ain't good enough. Not for this. Dad blame it, we seem to have the makings of a major international incident. First, we have a plane that I'm told is top of the line, perfect, nothing can go wrong—but it still crash-landed. Then we have embassies calling. We have Washington calling. We've got fire trucks from Midland to Odessa joining in to help us. Then half the town—naturally—is starting to show up as the sun comes up, it's like trying to stop an avalanche. Next thing the women'll be bringing casseroles. It's a madhouse. We *got* to find out what caused this plane crash and to do that, we have to get everybody out of here and get some kind of order. I just want my whole team here, that's all. Even if—''

"Wayne?"

"What?"

"Stop talking. Give me directions." He did. "I'll be there in twenty minutes." She hung up and started moving. Plucked white panties from the drawer, pulled them on, then hopped into low-rise, boot-cut jeans. She stood up, head scrambled. Not by Wayne's call in itself. Maybe she was hired to work only with juveniles, but this wasn't some big eastern city. This was Texas. People pitched in whenever there was a crisis, and no one gave a rat's toenail over whether helping fit a job description.

But a plane crash-landing was big news—and troubling. She knew every single face that had been on that flight— they'd all been at the Texas Cattleman's Club gala two nights ago—and a few of them were personal friends of hers besides. Pamela Miles had been flying to Asterland to be an exchange teacher. Lady Helena had made herself known around town because she was the kind to involve herself in caring causes. On top of that…well, the whole world was troubling these days, but not Royal. Things just didn't happen here. Sure, there were some thefts and squabbles and people who lost their screws now and then, but nothing unusual. Nothing happened there that would ever draw attention from outsiders.

Suddenly she heard a sound—a sound odd and unexpected enough to make her quit jogging down the hall and stop for a second. The sound had seemed like a mewling baby's cry— but of course, that was ridiculous. When she heard nothing again, she picked up her pace.

In the peach-and-cream kitchen, she flicked on the light, started her espresso machine, then peeled back toward her

bedroom, mentally cataloguing what she still had to do. She
needed coffee, her hair brushed, an apple for the road, and
yeah, something to wear above the waist. She never wore a
uniform—if you were going to dress for success with kids,
you wore jeans and no symbols or labels to put them off—
but that wasn't to say she could arrive at a crash site topless.
There were times she fantasized about giving Wayne an attack of apoplexy—God knew her boss was a hard-core chau-
vinist—but not today.

She pulled a sports bra over her head, burrowed in a
drawer for an old black sweater…then jerked her head up
again.

Damn. Somewhere there *was* a sound. An off-kilter,
didn't-belong-in-her-house sound. A puppy crying? A cat lost
in the neighborhood somewhere nearby?

Silently, still listening, she straightened the sweater, pulled
on socks, shoved her feet into boots, grabbed a brush. Her
hair looked like a squirrel's nest, but then that's how it
looked when it was freshly styled, too. A glance at her face
in the bathroom mirror somehow, inexplicably, made her
think of Justin again…and that dream in which his gaze had
been all over her naked body.

She scowled in the mirror. First, strange dreams, then
strange sounds—she'd seemed to wake up in la la land today,
and on a morning when she needed to be her sharpest.

Swiftly she thumbed off the light and started hustling for
real. In the kitchen, she poured coffee, then backtracked to
the hall closet for her jacket, scooping up the stuff she
needed: car keys, an apple, a lid for her espresso, some
money for lunch. Almost the minute she finished collecting
her debris, her feet seemed to be instinctively making a de-
tour. One minute. That's all she needed to check all the
rooms and make absolutely positive that nothing was making
that odd sound from inside the house. It wasn't as if she lived
in a mighty mansion that would take hours to check out. Her

ranch-style house was downright miniscule—but it was hers. Hers and the bank's, anyway.

She'd put a chunky down payment on it last year. She was twenty-eight, time to stop renting. Time to start making sure she had a place and security and in a neighborhood with a lot of kids and a good school system. Her bedroom was cobalt-blue and white, and, since decorating choices scared her, she'd just used the same colors in the bathroom. A second bedroom she used as a den, where she stashed her TV and computer—and anything she didn't have time to put away. The third bedroom was the biggest, and stood starkly empty—Winona wasn't admitting the room was intended for a baby, not to anyone, at least not yet. But it was.

The kitchen was a non-cook's dream, practical, with lots of make-easy machines and tools, the counters and walls covered with warm peach tiles that led down into the living room. A cocoa couch viewed the backyard, bird feeders all over the place, lots of windows...*damn*. There, she heard the sound again. The mewling cry.

Either that or she was going out of her mind, which, of course, was always a possibility. But she unlatched the front door and yanked it open.

Her jaw surely dropped ten feet. Her ranch house was white adobe, with redbrick arches in the doorways. And there, in the doorway shadow, was a wicker laundry basket. The basket appeared to be stuffed with someone's old, clean laundry, rags and sheets...but damned if that wasn't where the crying sound emanated from.

The car keys slipped from her fingers and clattered to the cold steps. The apple slipped from her other hand and rolled down the drive, forgotten. She hunched down, quickly parting the folds and creases of fabric.

When she saw the baby, her heart stopped.

Abandoned. The baby had actually been abandoned.

"Ssh, ssh, it's all right, don't cry...." So carefully, so gingerly, she lifted out the little one. The morning was icy at the edges, the light still a predawn-gray. The baby was too swathed in torn-up blankets and rags to clearly make out its features or anything else.

"Ssh, ssh," Winona kept crooning, but her heart was slamming, slamming. Feelings seeped through her nerves, through her heart from a thousand long-locked doors, bubbled up to the pain of naked air. She'd been abandoned as a child. She knew what an abandoned child felt like...and *would* feel like, her whole life.

A crinkle of paper slipped out of the basket. It only took Winona a few seconds to read the printed message.

Dear Winona Raye,
I have no way to take care of my Angel. You are the only one I could ask. Please love her.

Winona's cop experience immediately registered several things—that there'd be no way to track the generic paper and ordinary print, that the writing was simple but not uneducated, and that somehow the mother of the baby knew her specifically—well enough to identify her name, and well enough to believe she was someone who would care for a baby.

Which, God knows, she would.

As swiftly as Winona read the note, she put it aside. There was no time for that now. The baby was wet beneath the blankets, the morning biting at the January-freezing temperatures. She scooped up the little one and hustled inside the warm house, rocking, crooning, whispering reassurances...all past the gulp in her throat that had to be bigger than the state of Texas.

God knew what she was going to do. But right now nothing mattered but the obvious. Taking care of the child. Making sure the little one was warm, dry, fed, healthy. Then Winona would try to figure out why anyone would have left

the baby on her doorstep specifically…and all the other issues about what the child's circumstances might be.

That fast, that instantaneously, Win felt a bond with the
baby that wrapped around her heart tighter than a vise. The
thing was, as little as she knew—she already knew too much.

She was already positive that the child was going to get
thrown in the foster-care system, because that's what happened when a child was deserted. Even if a parent immediately showed up, the court would still place the child in the
care of Social Services—at least temporarily—because whatever motivated the parent to abandon the child could mean
it wasn't safe in their care. A change of heart wasn't enough.
An investigation needed to be conducted to establish what
the child's circumstances were.

Winona knew all those legal procedures—both from her
job and from her life. And although she knew her feelings
were irrational—and annoyingly emotional—it didn't stop
the instinct of bonding. The fierceness of caring. The instan-
taneous heart surge—even panic—to protect this baby better
than she'd been protected. To save this baby the way she
almost hadn't been saved. To love this baby the way—to be
honest—Winona never had been and never expected to be
loved.

There were several coffee machines spread through Royal
Memorial Hospital, but only one that counted. After he'd
switched from trauma medicine to plastic surgery, Justin had
generally tried to avoid the Emergency Room, but by ten that
morning, he was desperate. Groggy-eyed, he pushed the
coins into the machine, punched his choice of Straight Black,
kicked the base—he knew this coffee machine intimately—
and then waited.

He wasn't standing there three minutes before he got a
series of claps and thumps on his back. It was, "Hey, Dr.
Webb, slumming down here?" and "Hi, Doc, we sure miss
you" and "Dr. Webb, it's nice to see you with us again."

As soon as he could yank the steaming cup out of the machine, he gulped a sip. Burned all the way down. The taste was more familiar than his own heartbeat. Battery acid, more bitter than sludge, and liberally laced with caffeine.

Fantastic.

He inhaled another gulp, and then aimed straight ahead. Down the hall, through the double glass doors, was his Plastic Surgery/Burn Unit. The community believed that the wing had been anonymously donated, which was fine with Justin. What mattered to him was that in two short years, the unit had already developed the reputation for being the best in the state. He couldn't ask for more. The equipment was the best and the technology the newest. The walls were ice-blue, the atmosphere sterile, serene, quiet. Perfect.

Nothing like the chaotic loony bin in the ER. Royal Memorial was a well-run small hospital, but a crisis stretched the capacity of its trauma unit—and the crash landing of the Asterland jet earlier that morning was still stressing the trauma team. Nobody'd had time to pick up towels and drapes. Staff jogged past in blood- and debris-stained coats. A kid squealed past him. A shrieking mom was trying to chase the kid. A nurse trailed both of them, looking harassed and taking mother-may-I giant steps. He heard babies' cries, codes on the loudspeaker. Lights flashed; phones rang; carts wheeled and wheedled past. Somebody'd spilled a coffee; someone else had thrown up, so those stinks added to all the other messes and noises. Just being around it all made something clutch in his chest. Something cruel and sharp.

Justin loved his Plastic Surgery/Burn Unit. He made a difference in his Burn Unit, for God's sake. He wanted nothing to do with trauma medicine anymore. Nothing.

He sucked down another gulp of sludge, and this time aimed down the hall and refused to look back…but he suddenly caught sight of the top of a curly-haired head coming out of a side room.

"Winona?" He wanted to shake himself. One look at

her—that's all it took—and his hormones line-danced the length of his nerves and sashayed back again. At least he promptly forgot his old hunger for the ER. "Win?"

Her head jerked up when she heard his voice. That was the first he noticed that she was carrying a baby—not that there was anything all that unusual about Winona being stuck with a kid in the Emergency Room. Her job often put her in the middle between a child and school or parents. But something about her expression alerted Justin that this was nothing like an average day for Win.

Her smile for him, though, was as natural and familiar as sunshine. "I figured you'd be in the thick of this," she said wryly. "What a morning, huh? Were you out at the site of the crash landing?"

"Yeah, first thing. I'm not one of the doctors on call for something like that, but you know how fast news travels in Royal. I got a call, someone who'd heard there was a fire associated with the crash—so I hightailed it out there, too. I'll tell you, it was a real chaotic scene. But any outsider was just in the way, so all I did was the obvious, help the trauma team get patients routed back here. Particularly those going into my Burn Unit."

Her eyes promptly sobered. "I haven't heard anything about how many serious injuries there were yet. Was it bad?"

Something had happened to her. Justin had no more time for idle chitchat than he suspected she did, but he kept talking, because it gave him a chance to look her over. His gaze roved from the crown of her head to her toes—the way the jeans cupped her fanny, the boots, her wildly tousled hair, the way her cheeks had pinked from the slap of a cold morning wind—none of that was unusual. But there was something different in her eyes. A fever-brightness. She stood there, rocking, rocking the bundle in her arms—the baby made no sound at all—but that liquid softness in Win's eyes was rare. Vulnerable. And Winona just never looked vulnerable if she could help it.

A blood cart pushed between them, but he wasn't about to stop their conversation just because all hell was still breaking loose. "Things could have been a lot worse. At least no one died. In a crash landing, that's pretty much a miracle in itself. Robert Klimt—one of the minor cabinet members from Asterland? He was knocked unconscious, head injury—I don't know how he is right now, I took care of some minor burns and left him to the neurologist. Pamela Miles was also on that flight—"

"I know, I know! She was headed overseas to be an exchange teacher in Asterland—did you see her, Justin? Do you know if she's okay?"

"I didn't take care of her myself, but I heard she was basically fine. Lady Helena, though—"

"Serious injuries?"

"Well, not life-threatening. Complicated break in her ankle. And once she's done with the bone man, for sure she's going to be mine. She did get some burns—"

"Oh, God. She's such a beautiful woman."

Justin couldn't say more on Helena. For him to discuss a patient, any patient—he just never did. Not with anyone, even Winona. But he still hadn't taken his eyes off her and didn't want to give her the excuse to shoot past him. "Well, at this point, I think everyone on the flight's been through here, checked out, even if they seemed to be fine. And the whole town was as shook up as the passengers on that flight, it seems like, because people were flooding in right and left."

"You didn't hear what caused the emergency landing, did you?"

On that he had to lift his eyebrows. "I was just going to ask *you* that, Ms. Police Officer. If anyone had answers, I figure it would be the cops first."

"Well, normally I'd be elbowing my way to the middle of the mess from the start," she admitted wryly, "but I got sidetracked."

When she lifted the corner of the pale pink flannel blanket

for him to get a peek, Justin finally figured out what the emotion was in her eyes. Fierceness. The fierce protectiveness of a mama lion for her cub, or a mama eagle for her eaglet. There was nothing strange about thinking of Win and motherhood, or of her wanting to be a mom, but it just hadn't crossed his mind before what a major thing it might be for her. His knuckles—almost accidentally—brushed her hand when he touched the baby's cheek.

"Don't tell me anyone hurt this darling, or I'll have to go out and kill someone," he said gently.

Her voice melted. "Oh, God. Justin. That's exactly how I felt. Isn't she beautiful?"

Considering she was swaddled up with nothing showing but about two inches of face and some blond spriggy hairs, Justin was hard-pressed to use the word *beautiful.* On the baby. "What's the story?"

"Her name's Angel. I ran out my front door this morning, headed for the crash site—Wayne called me around seven in the morning—and there she was. In a basket on the doorstep. With a note saying her name was Angel and asking me, specifically, to take care of her."

Justin felt his pulse still. "This isn't the first time you've had to handle an abandoned kid," he said carefully.

"No, of course not. But this baby's so young that obviously I had to bring her here first. I'm sure you know the beat. This day and age, a deserted baby could mean drugs or AIDS or all kinds of things in the child's background—so before we can do anything else, we have to know the state of the child's health for sure."

"And…?"

"And Dr. Julian gave her a terrific bill of health. Just under three months old, he thought. "

"So, the next step is…?" He was watching her face, not the baby's.

"Finding the mother, of course. It's not like Royal is that huge. And if anyone has a bird's-eye view to kids in trouble, it's got to be me in my job. So if anyone can track down the parents, I've got the best shot.''

''Uh-huh. And where will the baby go in the meantime?''

Her head shot up. Blue eyes blazed on his. ''I spent years in foster care,'' she said belligerently.

''I know you did.''

''The system's overcrowded. Even in an area this wealthy, there's no answer for it. Adoption is at least a possibility for a blond, blue-eyed baby—but not for this one, not for some time. Even if I run a hundred miles an hour and get answers zip-fast, there's still no way to rush a—''

''Win, you sound like you're fighting with a judge in a court of law. You're just talking to me. What's the deal here? I take it you want to keep the baby?''

Her shoulders sank, losing all that tough stiffness. And again her eyes got that softness, that terribly fierce vulnerability that he'd never seen before. ''No one's going to let me keep her. I'm single. And I'm working full-time besides. But right now—especially today—the town's in chaos because of the Asterland jet crash. So the only thing that makes sense—''

Justin heard his code paged on the loudspeaker. An orderly pushed past both of them to clean up the examining room. Bodies were still hustling in both directions, they were blocking the hallway—and the baby suddenly opened her rosebud mouth, yawned, and blinked open sleepy, priceless, exquisite blue eyes.

He looked at the baby…and then at Winona again. ''We've both got our hands full right now,'' he said casually. ''How about if I stop by for a short visit right after dinner?''

''You don't have to do that.''

Oh yeah, he thought, he definitely did.

Three

Just as Winona lifted a fork to her mouth, she heard the baby's thin cry. Somehow there'd been no time for lunch. Now it looked as if the odds weren't too hot on sneaking some dinner, either. Not that she minded. Who needed food? Dropping the fork with a clatter, she charged toward the living room. "I'm coming, Angel! I'm coming!"

Well, shoot. It wasn't quite that easy—as a woman or a temporary mom—to deliver on those optimistic words. Although it was only the distance of a fast gallop between the kitchen and the living room, reaching the baby was becoming more challenging by the hour.

She'd only called a couple of neighbors that afternoon, but it seemed that the news about the baby had spread and help had been pouring in nonstop. The whole neighborhood was kid-studded—which was one of the reasons she'd chosen to buy her house here—and almost everyone had some baby gear stored in their garages or back rooms. Buying anything would have been silly: Winona had no idea how long she would be allowed to keep the baby. But her neighbors' loans had been extravagantly generous. She had to dodge a half-dozen car seats, a couple of high chairs, several playpens and walkers, backpacks, front packs, diaper bags, toys, enough blankets to warm a child in the Arctic, and heaps of baby clothes. Finally she reached the white wicker bassinet with the pink quilted lining.

Inside was the princess, who happened to be garbed in her fifth outfit of the day. Winona figured they surely wouldn't go through quite so many clothes tomorrow. She was getting close to mastering disposable diapers.

"There, there. There, there...." She picked up the precious bundle, and started the crooning, patting and rocking movements that seemed to be the eternal song of mothers. But on the inside, panic started to ooze through her nerves.

"Are we hungry, sweetheart? Wet? Do you want the TV on? Off? More lights, less lights? More noise, less noise? Are you cold? Constipated—no, come to think of it, I'm positive that's not a problem. Are you mad? Bored? Sick? Sad? Whatever it is, I'll fix it, I swear. Just don't cry. There, there. There, there, love...."

The panic was new. All day, she'd been in seventh heaven. Babies had been on her heart's agenda for a long time, and no, of course Angel wasn't hers and wasn't likely to be for long. Winona was trying her best to be completely realistic about that. It was just...carrying the little one around had seemed as natural as breathing. There'd been a thousand things to do, starting with taking the baby to the hospital for a checkup, then carting her back to the station, talking to Wayne, then claiming some computer time, then calling some moms in the neighborhood before stopping at a store for supplies. The busier she was, the more the baby seemed to love it. But then they'd come home.

Alone.

And Angel had lived up to her name tag all day until, it sure seemed, the point when Winona realized she *was* alone

with the baby. And knew nothing about child care. The baby
had barely let out a peep all day, but now she seemed to be
scaling up every few minutes. The darling either desperately
missed her real mother, or Angel had suddenly figured out
that she was stuck with a complete rookie.

The doorbell rang. Winona whipped around, thinking,
please, God, not another car seat or another well-meant baby
blanket. Hunger was starting to set in. Exhaustion.

A nightmare-strength panic.

Before she could reach the front door, the knob rattled and
Justin poked his head in. Her pulse promptly soared ten feet.
There was no stopping it. So typically, even after a long
workday, he looked as revved as the satin-black Porsche in
her drive. He stepped in like a vital burst of energy, his face
wind-stung, his eyes snapping life, his grin teasing her before
he'd even said a word. "Win? Are you there—well, I can
see you're there. And a little on the busy side, huh?"

"I never thought you meant it about coming over! Come
in, come in!" She wished she'd had a chance to brush her
hair and put on lipstick, but what was the difference? It was
just Justin. And no matter how mercilessly he ended up teasing her, she was thrilled to see him. "What do you know
about babies?" she called over the caterwauling.

"Nothing."

Never mind. She didn't care what he knew or didn't know.
She closed the door with him firmly on the inside. He was
still another body. She wasn't alone. "You're a doctor, you
have to know something—"

"Yeah, I've been trying to tell my patients that for a long
time." He peeled off his sheepskin jacket, took a step toward
her living room and froze. "Holy cow. Did you have a cattle
drive in here this afternoon?"

"Very funny. It's just baby gear. Loans from the neighbors. Now listen, Justin, whether you know anything or not—
you could hold her for a second, couldn't you? I just need a

minute. Time to get some dry diapers and fresh clothes and a bottle warmed up—''

"Okay."

"It won't take me long to do any of that stuff—"

"Okay."

"Don't panic because she's crying. She's really a darling. I just have to figure out what's wrong. That's all there is to it. You figure out what's wrong, you fix it, she quits—''

"Hey, Win. Could you try and believe it's okay? I really did come over to help."

It's not that she didn't believe Justin. It was just that his offer to help seemed so unlikely. The town may have labeled Justin a devil-may-care bachelor, but Winona had always known better than that. Something had happened to him in Bosnia, because he'd come back a different person—quieter, more closed in, and he'd left his once-loved trauma medicine specialty in favor of plastic surgery. But his reputation as a surgeon spanned the southwest. His participation with the Texas Cattleman's Club was another unrecognized involvement. And she'd never forgotten meeting him back when she was twelve, on the first day she'd been fostered with the Gerards. To her, he'd been the best-looking teenage guy in the universe. Even that young, he'd had the sexiest eyes. The laziest drawl in Texas. A way of looking at a woman. And a way of picking up a little girl—and her bike—from the sidewalk, and somehow making her skinned pride feel better in spite of impossible odds.

Most of their relationship, though, he'd been an inescapable, nonstop tease. He'd shown up to check out the guy who'd taken her to the senior prom, had a conniption fit when she sunned in a bikini, regularly asked her to marry him as if he thought that was funny, taught her to drive stick shift, and damnation, held her head when she'd come home from a party after her first (and last) experience with rum-and-colas. Short and sweet, he'd been a friend in her life for-

ever—when he wasn't being insufferable. And it was for-
getting that "insufferable" adjective that was tough for her.

"What do you mean, you came over to help?" she asked
suspiciously.

"Just what I said." He scooped the baby out of her arms.
"Right now, though, we don't have a prayer of talking over
the sound of Ms. Bawler. Go. Do the bottle thing. And I'll
try and figure out the diapers if you'll steer me toward the
supplies."

Her hand shot to her chest. A mere twenty-eight and she
was almost having a heart attack. "You're volunteering to
change a diaper? Have you had these symptoms long? Are
you suffering from fever? Brain tumor? A history of lunacy
you never mentioned before?"

For those insults, he tousled her hair—as if it wasn't already a royal mess—before walking off with the baby. The
phone rang six times over the next hour, and two more neighbors stopped by bearing car seats and blankets. But somehow
all the confusion and running wasn't the same with Justin
there. The terror factor had disappeared. Contrary to his
claims of inexperience, he acted like a veteran with both diaper sticky tabs and burping. And Angel seemed to forget
that she was ticked off at the world in general. At the first
sound of his voice, she started blowing bubbles and drooling.

"Just like all the other women in town," Winona muttered.

"Pardon?"

"I said the baby fell in love with you from the first instant
you picked her up."

"Yeah, I noticed she quit crying. You think she recognizes
a good-looking guy, young as she is? Someone with class
and taste and brilliance—hey!"

As hard as she'd tossed the couch pillow at his head, he
just pushed it aside with a grin. By then it was around eight
o'clock. Angel had not only been fed, burped and changed,
but she'd settled down in the bassinet. Winona couldn't quite

remember when Justin had ordered her to sit on the cocoa couch and pushed a hot plate of food in her hands, but she finally seemed to have caught some dinner; she was slouched down like a lazy slug and one stockinged foot was keeping the bassinet-rocker in motion.

Justin—for the first and likely only time in the universe—was kneeling at her feet. She'd felt obligated to mention, several times, how much she approved of his kneeling position. "It's really where all men belong. In a submissive position to their superiors—meaning we women, of course. Waiting on us. Obeying us. Working to please us—"

"If you don't cut it out, I'm going to have to get up and tickle you. Then you'll start laughing and screaming. Then you'll risk waking the baby—"

"All right, all right. You're so right. I don't want to wake her up," she agreed. Still, it was tough, not pushing his tease-buttons, when he looked so adorable. He was trying to bring one of the borrowed baby walkers back to life, which was why he was hunkered down on her peach carpet, surrounded by nuts and bolts and tools. She usually saw him flying around town in his Porsche, or looking like Mr. Drop-Dead-Handsome Doctor at some gathering. And maybe these were images that Justin chose to cultivate, but Winona had still had the feeling that finding a place where he could kick off his boots and just tinker wasn't something Justin got to do often.

The TV was on in the background, but neither was watching the sitcom. They just wanted the chance to click up the volume if any further developments were reported on the Asterland plane emergency landing. Temporarily, though, they might as well have been on an island alone together—except for the sleeping baby.

"So...what'd your boss say about the Angel situation?" Justin asked her.

"Well, deserted and neglected kids generally come under my bailiwick, anyway, so Wayne didn't have to give me permission to handle the problem. It was automatic. He did seem a little startled when I showed up at the station this afternoon with the baby in a front pack. But no one at the station right now has time to worry about anything but the plane crash. Everyone's descended on Royal today, if not in person than through the wires—from state cops to feds, TV and press, the aviation safety folks, diplomats and state people—"

"I know." Justin motioned toward the TV. In the hour they'd had the tube switched on, the local news had interrupted every few minutes to provide an update on the circus. "My Texas Cattleman's group was especially involved with the citizens from both countries. We've offered to help, and I hope the authorities take us up on it. I realize that they have to sweep for evidence and prints and all first...but you can see how much this crisis is driving the town nuts. Everyone wants to know the same thing. What caused that emergency landing? Fine, if it was a mechanical failure, but could it have been terrorists or sabotage?"

"From what I've heard, that specific jet has an outstanding history for being one of the safest planes in the air. And she was deluxe to the nth degree, no expense spared for security or comfort. It's pretty hard to swallow that it was just a plain old mechanical failure—at least if the problem was carelessness." Winona pulled a couch pillow on to her lap, finding it hard to take her eyes off Justin. Last she knew, he'd long reached the multi-millionaire status...which made it all the more fun to watch him bumbling with a screwdriver.

"So what was the buzz at your station house? Your cops find any reason to think there was foul play connected to the emergency landing?"

"There was no evidence leading in that direction this afternoon...but really, it's way too soon to say. They may have collected all the relevant evidence, but it will still take weeks of testing procedures before we have complete answers. The whole world knows how much tension there was between the two countries of Asterland and Obersbourg, though…and that Texas party was the first and only thing that brought those two countries together and talking in more than a decade. I really think you're right, Justin. You and the Texas Cattleman's Club guys should be brought in, both to question and get some advice, and I'll be surprised if you don't get that call."

"I wasn't as involved as some of the other members. But I still want to help, if there's any chance. And I did know all of the people involved." Justin righted the baby walker, pushed it around the carpet. Sighed. And then turned it upside down to work on it again. "Frightening. To think you could eat dinner with someone, shake their hand, make a joke and laugh with them…and that they could deliberately have had something to do with a near-fatal plane crash."

"Or that someone could intend harm to so many good people." She leaned forward to peer over the edge of the bassinet. She cared about the plane crash. She cared about her job. But at the moment—all day really—only one thing dominated her mind and heart.

"You're not going to wake her up again, are you?"

Winona's jaw dropped. "Are you out of your mind? I may have only been a mother for a day, but I learned that hours ago. Never wake up a sleeping baby. And if *you* do, I'll have to kill you."

His chuckle tickled her into a smile, but then he shot her a more serious look. "So, what's the deal on your squirt there? What's the legal process—what happens to her now?"

"Well, the first thing you already know. An abandoned baby starts out with a medical checkup, no matter how healthy the child appears to be. In this day of AIDS and drug use and all, there's no placing a baby—even temporarily—without knowing the health picture. But that was a piece of cake. She couldn't have gotten a cleaner bill of health."

"Yeah, so you said this morning. So, then what?"

"Then, normally, she'd be turned over to Social Services,

and they'd find a foster-care arrangement for her." Winona's arms tightened around the pillow. "The court will get more directly involved as soon as something more definitive is established about the parents. And that's my job. Finding the parents. Especially the mom. I have to find out what their story is, and why the baby was abandoned."

"And how do you go about doing that?"

It seemed odd that she'd never told Justin any details about her job before, but then, there'd never been a reason for this kind of thing to come up in conversation. "There are lots of ways for me to pick up clues. Now that I have the baby's age pinned down—at least ballpark—I can start checking hospital records, see if I can get a lead into young women having babies at that time. Then I can check the papers, same reason. Check the 911 calls, emergencies, abuse, deaths, anything called in around the time the child was abandoned, to see if there could be any obvious connection."

"Uh-huh. What else?"

"Then…well, after that, I zoom straight for my at-risk kids. You know how it is in Royal. This is a wealthy community, so on the surface it'd seem we wouldn't have that many kids in trouble. But I keep finding that the very rich and very poor have a lot in common. In both types of families, there are kids raising themselves. Alone a lot of hours. Parents moving near an edge with drugs or alcohol. Divorces, absentee adults. Any way you cut it, it's the lonely kids who tend to sleep around—and look for trouble. So one of the things I always do is run a computer check for runaways."

"And—?"

"And then I'll check the truancy lists. The arrest lists. Then I'll call the high schools and junior highs for girls with a high absentee record. Talk to the counselors about girls who were pregnant. I started some things in motion this afternoon, but it'd be pretty unusual to land answers overnight. It almost always takes some time."

"Okay, Win...but what if you don't manage to locate the mother after going through all that?"

She frowned, suddenly aware that she was clenching and unclenching her hands—and that Justin was watching her. "That's not an issue. It's early days yet. Believe me, I'll find the mother. I've done it before."

"But what if you don't?" Justin righted the baby walker again, and this time, it seemed to push along without lurching like a drunken sailor. He set it aside, heaved to his feet and shook his legs as if to shake out the kinks—but his eyes never left her face.

"Well, then, there are other possibilities. A girl in trouble is the most logical choice for the mother. And frankly, I'm about as qualified as anyone in this county to find that kind of girl." For some blasted reason, her fingers were trying to clench into fists again. She folded her arms across her chest, aggravated that she couldn't seem to control the nervous movements. It wasn't like her.

"I know you are, Win." Justin's voice was low, caring. "You know what it's like for a kid to be abandoned. I was never surprised when you aimed to work with juveniles when you decided to be a cop. But you can't possibly find the parents every time there's a problem with a child."

"Well, no, of course not. And as far as Angel...possibly her mother is a married mother with an abusive husband— or that kind of story—which means that she isn't likely to show up on any record. In fact, someone like that can be almost impossible to trace. And another possibility..."

"What?"

"...another possibility is the kind of girl who's kept a pregnancy hidden for nine months. It seems impossible, but we all know that it happens—you've heard those stories surface on the news every once in a while. This one, though, had to do more than just hide the pregnancy, because the baby's already a couple months old. But the problem is the same. There has to be a record of something for us to be able to trace it. And if someone is absolutely determined to keep a pregnancy secret—and has some enablers somehow, someway—we really may never know who the mother is.''

"Okay. So we've covered most of the possible scenarios, good and bad. But in the meantime, what's supposed to happen to our miniature princess here, while you're going through all those record searches and waiting?''

Instinctively her hand shot to her stomach, as if to quell the sudden churning going on in her tummy. Normally she could eat red-hot chili, follow it up with an O.D.-size hot fudge sundae, and never have a digestive problem. But all day, she'd been thinking about what "was supposed to" happen to Angel next…and making herself sick every time she let those fears surface. "Well, the court usually places her in foster care, through Social Services. Like I already told you.''

"I know what you told me, Win," Justin said gently. "That's why I'm asking you for the details. So I can understand the situation better.''

Again she pressed hard on her stomach, then met his eyes. "Potentially, down the road, she's adoptable. She's a young baby, healthy, and though it's not fair, her being blond and blue-eyed makes her extra desirable in the adoption market. But for that to happen, we have to find the parents—and find that they deliberately abandoned her, really don't want her and will legally sign off. Or we could find that the parents are dead. But otherwise…''

"Yeah. It's that 'otherwise' that happened to you, wasn't it?'' Justin had been standing, but now he plunked down on the couch next to her. His gaze prowled her face with the quiet, determined intent of a hunter. "You were in the foster-care system from the time you were six, right? But there was something about how you couldn't be adopted. I remember the families and neighbors talking when the Gerards brought you home. I just don't remember the details.''

"There weren't a lot of details. It was pretty cut-and-dried.'' She glared at him, not in anger, but in self-defense.

At twenty-eight years old, it was about damn time she quit letting this past-history crap bother her. "I wasn't adoptable because my mother was alive and could have come back for me at any time. So I was basically stuck in the foster-care system until I was eighteen."

"You never mentioned your mom before. Or anything about what you remember from when you were real little."

She shrugged, but she could feel an old, aching sense of haunting from the inside out. "My parents' story was older than time. They were two young kids, hot in love—too hot to keep a lid on their hormones. When my mom got pregnant, they both dropped out of school. Two sixteen-year-old idiots with no money and no job skills—undoubtedly thinking they could live on sex and love. The fun part didn't last long. My dad died, some kind of car accident. I have no memory of him at all. But I was with my mom until I was six."

"And that's when she took off."

She shifted restlessly, not meaning to move closer to Justin. She just never liked talking about feelings or the past. "I keep thinking one of these days I could find her. I still run a search every once in a while. But the point is, back then, she couldn't handle me. I certainly didn't realize it then—but I do now. She was in trouble in every way a woman can be in trouble. Alone, broke, a small child to take care of, thinking a little drug here and a little alcohol there would take the edge off the worry, no skills, getting more desperate with every loser she took up with."

Justin fell silent for a moment. "Win...why didn't you ever mention any of this before?"

"Because there's nothing to say. I work with girls like her every day—girls in trouble because they've gotten over their heads, made one mistake and watched the rest of their lives fall down like a stack of dominos. The only thing my mom ever really did wrong was fall in love—or should I say, fall in lust—too young. Cripes, Justin, you know all this—"

He shook his head. "No, actually, I didn't. I remember

my mom talking to my dad. I knew you'd been abandoned when you were a kid. And that your mom had left you with a note, that she'd be back for you as soon as she wasn't so broke, something like that. And I remember the Gerards being furious—"

That made her blink. "The Gerards were furious? About what?"

He lifted a hand. "I was seventeen, Win. I wasn't listening that much to neighborhood stories. But there was some story about when Sissy Gerard first saw you...I don't know what foster family you were with, but it was at a county fair, something like that. Something about the way the family treated you that infuriated her. She came home, told Paget that he was hiring a lawyer and they were getting you away from those people and bringing you home—and that it was going to be your last home until you were grown."

"I didn't know that. I didn't remember any of it, either," Winona admitted. "I just remember the Gerards. Sissy and Paget's faces in this sterile Social Services office. She just wrapped her arms around me as if she'd known me forever. God. They are such good people."

"Yeah, they are." Justin scratched his chin, his eyes suddenly lightening up. "And you were a pistol and a half back then. Clawed anybody who was nice to you. Spit at all the boys. Fought on the playground—"

She had to grin. "Hey, you dog, whose side are you on?"

"Yours. Always yours." His tone turned so quiet that she had to quit chuckling and suddenly looked at him. Really looked. But he was already talking again. "So this baby is going into foster care? In fact, pretty immediately?"

"No." The single syllable was out before she could stop it.

"What's this No? Isn't that what you pretty much told me happens to an abandoned child?"

"The baby has to go somewhere—a place that's honored by Social Services and the court—until something is determined about her parents. Whether they're around and fit, or whatever. And that place is usually foster care. But if the foster-care system is crowded—and right now it's disastrously crowded—then someone else can be assigned temporary guardianship, if they fit the criteria.''

''Win.''

''What?''

His voice wasn't a whisper, but melted butter couldn't have been softer. ''You don't want to give her up, do you?''

''I don't want her going in foster care. Lost in the foster-care system, like I was.'' Her own voice came out fierce and sharp. She couldn't seem to help it. ''I fell for her the minute I laid eyes on her. I admit it. And I admit that's stupid. A good cop never gets emotionally involved. But whoever left her on my doorstep, Justin, must have known me somehow. It's hard to pretend that doesn't matter. It does, to me. I just want to know that if she goes back to her parents, they're in a position to take good care of her. And until then…''

''You want to keep her.''

''I don't want her in foster care,'' she repeated. A thousand memories were in her head. She didn't have the words for any of them. She only knew that they added up to one thing. She didn't want—she refused to think about—this baby living the childhood she had, flip-flopped between homes and people who neither wanted her nor had room or time for her. But damnation. Somehow, totally unlike her, she could suddenly feel so much emotion welling that her eyes were actually stinging. It was ridiculous. She never lost control like that—not with Justin, never with Justin.

Obviously she had to find an immediate way to lighten things up. She forced a grin—her infamous snappy grin—and cocked an eyebrow at him. Considering all the times he'd joked about marrying her, this should be a guaranteed way to get a laugh out of him. ''Normally, the court wouldn't consider a single working woman to be a good bet for that temporary guardianship business. You wouldn't like to marry me, would you? It would really up my chances.''

Four

Justin felt his heart stop, then start galloping at breakneck pace.

Winona wasn't *really* asking to marry him. He realized that. Completely. Marriage had become a ritual tease subject between them, because he'd asked her to marry him so many times. She'd always assumed he was joking, so it was perfectly natural that she would joke back with him the same way.

There were just a few tiny differences in these circumstances, though.

He'd always meant those offers.

And the sudden advent of the baby in Winona's life was obviously deeply affecting her. She'd never admitted that she needed help with anything—and for damn sure, she'd never given him the opportunity to come through for her in any way. Justin didn't quite comprehend all the emotional ramifications for her with this baby, but he was dead positive of one thing. He'd been waiting for a chance—any chance—with her for years now. And he wasn't about to let it go.

"Okay, let's do it," he said lightly.

For the first time all evening, the haunted tension left her eyes and she laughed. Really laughed. "Sure. Nothing to it, right? Just get a license and hit the Justice of the Peace. Just what you were dying to do this week."

"Actually, it sounds like a lot of fun to me." He leaned back, as if he could find nothing more important to do than stretch out his long legs.

She was still laughing. "I can just see the headlines in the social column on Sunday. Royal's Most Eligible Bachelor Finally Cuffed By A Cop. And I'm sure there'd be some comments about the bride having to give up her six-year-old Jeep and suffer driving your Porsche—not to mention having to face up to all the trials of suddenly being filthy rich—"

"Shut up, Win. I know you were joking, but why don't you think about it? You sounded really serious to me about wanting to keep this baby."

"I was. I am…but holy mackerel, Justin, I never meant it about getting married. It was just a joke. It wouldn't even solve anything, because Angel's mother could show up at any time. Today, even. Or tomorrow—"

"And maybe she won't ever show. But even if she knocks on your door in a matter of hours, the courts wouldn't just let her have the baby back. Isn't that what you were just explaining? That it's not automatic that the mother would get Angel back—not after abandoning her the way she did." It wasn't hard for Justin to fill in the blanks when Win's fears were right in her eyes giving him easy clues what to say. "So no matter what, Angel is going to be 'housed' somewhere for a while—and that could be a long while. Long enough to make a difference in her life, if she's in a good situation. Or a bad one."

"I know, I know. That's exactly what's driving me crazy." She scraped a hand through her hair, making the curls spring up in tufts. She faced him, her eyes so fierce. Soft-fierce. "I can't stand worrying that she'd be put in a bad place for her. All I really want is to be able to take care of her until we know for sure what's what in her life. I *know* that I'll love her. And that almost anything's better than being thrown into the limbo of foster care. The overcrowding. The never knowing how long you can stay in one place or another. I can't stand it. I know that's irrational and emotional and stupid, but I've *been* there, Justin. And I hate it that that could happen to Angel, to this baby. I know it's nuts, I—"

"Win, I don't really give a damn if it's nuts or not. If I understood what you told me earlier, they'd consider you for temporary guardian, if you were married. Is that true or not true?"

"True. Actually, it's true that they would consider me anyway—but I'd almost certainly get turned down right now. I don't know of any circumstances where a single woman's been allowed to foster. Not here. It's always a two-parent family—"

"So let's get married."

She tried to answer and ended up sputtering on another bubble of laughter. She laughed harder. Then quit. Then hiccuped.

He'd never seen Winona undone before. Had no idea she could be—at least by him.

When he lifted a hand, he knew he intended to kiss her. When his fingers touched her cheek, pushed back, so gently, into her hair, cupping her head toward him…he knew what he was doing then, too. Sort of. He sure as hell knew how to kiss a woman.

But he'd never kissed Winona before. Any kind of kiss. Any way. Possibly because he'd known that even one small kiss was never going to be simple. Not with her. Not for him.

She wasn't expecting the kiss, because her forehead puckered in a frown and her eyes widened in surprise and confusion when he kept coming closer. But when his fingers laced in her hair, she didn't move. When his mouth honed in on hers, she didn't pull away. She went as still as a statue.

But nothing about Win resembled a cold statue. She tasted fragile. Soft. Warm. Alluring.

She made a small sound when his mouth touched hers, tasted, came back for more. Win rarely wore perfumes, yet he suddenly felt surrounded by her scents. Her tongue still carried the echo of the vanilla cappuccino he'd made her. Her hair was a tumble of springy, unruly curls, threaded with that hint of strawberry shampoo she used. And she was always slathering cream on her face and hands because her skin was so dry, and that was the other scent. Almonds. Vanilla. Strawberry. All edible stuff.

Like her.

She made another sound, and her fingers suddenly clutched his arm, as if to push him away. Only she didn't push him away, and beneath his mouth, her lips were suddenly moving, trembling like a whisper, her eyelashes swooshing down as if the light in the room were suddenly too bright. The TV flashed on a news interruption, which technically they'd both been rabidly interested in earlier. Now, he didn't look up, and neither did she.

Those first exploring kisses turned deeper, silkier, sexier. The fingers clutching his arm suddenly wound, tight and hard, around his neck. Tongues tangled, tangoed. He kissed and kept on kissing, but now he could feel her skin heating, feel her body yielding, bowing to his on an angry groan of a sigh. He heard the anger in that groan, and a thousand years from now—when he had time—he'd want to smile. Win had had no idea she'd feel desire with him.

Neither had he. He'd been pretty sure, for years now, that his panting after her had all been one-sided. Yeah, there was a kind of love. The way you could love a brother at the same time you smacked him upside the head. The way you loved an old friend who knew your childhood secrets. It was good love. All love was good love. But it wasn't man-woman love.

It wasn't heat like a volcano, and a hurricane rush, and wanting that could claw you from the inside out, if you let it.

He wanted to let it. He wanted to peel that big sweatshirt off her and bow her back into the couch cushions, into the shadows, and dunk her in sensuality so deep, so hot, that neither of them could get up until it was over. He wanted to see her naked. To touch her naked. To have her naked.

But there was a sleeping baby only three feet away. And these few potent kisses were suddenly raising questions that Justin never thought he'd get the chance to ask. Fire or no fire, need or no need, he was afraid of losing the answers he wanted if he moved too fast.

So he eased up on that last kiss. Tried to remember how to breathe normally. Smoothed his hand back up above her neck. Pressed his forehead to her forehead, eyes closed, loving how she was huffing like a freight train, too.

And that helped him relax. And smile. "Hey, Win…I'm richer than Croesus. You did know that, didn't you?"

Her eyes were still more liquid than a lake, but she gave him a short frown, expressing confusion. "Am I supposed to care about that?"

"Yeah. Because it matters. It matters because I can put a marriage together faster than most people. And get those temporary guardian papers going through the legal system. You want this baby? We can make it happen."

"Justin…" She swallowed, hard, when he lurched to his feet.

He'd already heard the baby stir. He pushed into shoes, glanced around for his jacket, but then he met her eyes again. Those soft, liquid-as-a-lake-blue eyes. Liquid for him. For the first time in all these years, liquid for him. "I don't know about you and me. But we've known each other forever, Winona. And again, I've got the money, the resources to put this together fast. The resources to make it easy for both of us—to get in, to get out, to do whatever we both want to do. There's no woman in my wings. Is there a man in yours?''

She blinked. ''No.''

''Come on. I need you to be frank with me. There has to be some guy—''

''No.''

Well, hell. He couldn't hold back a grin. He ruffled her curls, grabbed his jacket and let himself out. And yeah, he'd left the proposal hanging between them. But there was no way Winona Raye would ever—in this life—give him a yes on the spur of the wild moment like that.

By his leaving right then, he'd given her no chance to say no.

That wasn't just progress. As far as Justin was concerned, it was damn close to manna from heaven.

Snuggling the baby more securely on her shoulder, Winona paced the house from window to window. Justin's satin-black Porsche had disappeared from her driveway an hour ago, but she kept looking out anyway. Maybe his visit had been a mirage. Or maybe he'd put a drug in her coffee— because something had dropped her off in Oz for a few hours, for darn sure.

Angel let out a sleepy burp, making Winona smile. Still, she kept on pacing and patting, pacing and patting. Really, her brief sojourn into Oz was downright funny. She'd actually imagined Justin seriously asking her to marry him. Not joking this time. But low-down serious.

Boy, was that funny.

So funny that even after the baby fell asleep big time— for the night, she hoped—Winona still couldn't think, couldn't breathe, couldn't sleep. She was as tired as a worn-out hound, yet still pacing the floors in the dark.

He'd asked if there was a man in her life. And simply couldn't seem to credit her avowal that there wasn't.

At midnight, she prowled to the refrigerator for some

milk—poured out a half a cup, all she had in the house—
and carted it back to her bedroom. She climbed in between
the cobalt-blue sheets and mounded the pillows behind her
head, sipping, staring out the windows at a lover's moon and
a sky full of stars.

There'd been men. But not in a while. Once she'd realized
that she'd been the one screwing up the relationships, she'd
backed off from trying. She wasn't any good at getting
close—not in the sack or out of it. Sex wasn't the only problem, but it was a nuisance of a big one. She had no objections
to intimacy, getting naked, big inhibitions, nothing like that.

She'd just figured, a long time back, that her sweat with
intimacy was about abandonment. Being abandoned once in
a lifetime was enough. If you had your soul ripped out once,
most sane people didn't volunteer for a repeat experience.
But when that translated into a relationship...well. She could
lie there beneath a guy. Smile. Make the right movements.
Make the right groans.

In fact, she had.

Frankly, she thought she was pretty good—if not downright outstanding—at faking it. But there didn't seem much
point. She wasn't that unhappy alone. She liked her job, her
life. She had friends, respect in the community. She *liked*
feeling contained. Safe. So maybe she had a hard time trusting others at a gut level. So what?

But she hadn't liked that kiss from Justin. Her lips still felt
bee-stung, her nerves sharp-stung even more. She didn't let
go like that. Ever. She never went loopy, dizzy, spinning high
with any man—and certainly not for a few ridiculous idiot
kisses.

What the Sam Hill did Justin think he was *doing?* Kissing
her? Offering to marry her?

Something was wrong with him, she concluded. Bad
wrong. Seriously wrong. The idea soothed her. She set down
the empty milk cup and curled up under the covers, immediately starting to relax. She simply should have thought this

through earlier. If Justin was acting bananas, there had to be a reason for it. Whatever it was, she'd talk to him. Help him. Like the friends they were.

And she'd reassure him, of course, that she realized he'd never meant that offer of marriage.

Two mornings later, as Justin drove to the site of the Asterland plane crash landing, his mind was on Winona, not business. Weddings, not plane crashes. Love, not problems. But the closer he got to the scene of the accident, the faster his mood turned grave.

As of hours after the crash landing, the sheriff had set up a roadblock, both to protect the evidence and to discourage strangers and gawkers. The cop immediately recognized Justin's black Porsche, though, and waved him on.

The road ran out within yards, and turned into a desertlike hard pan surface. After spring rains, possibly the land was more forgiving, even decent grazing ground, but right now it definitely wasn't the most hospitable spot in Texas. Most vehicles could undoubtedly traverse the hard surface, but with his baby, Justin had to slow to a crawl. Finally, the plane loomed in sight. And when Justin finally stopped the car and climbed out, a witch-bitter wind bit his cheeks and stung his eyes.

"Justin!"

He'd already recognized the other two members of the Texas Cattleman's Club—and their practical, sturdier vehicles—but for a second, the look of the private jet had stunned him into staring. At the sound of his name, though, he promptly pivoted and hiked toward his friends. Typically, Dakota Lewis didn't seem to notice that the January morning was mean-freezing; his jacket was gaping open. At least Matthew Walker had a red nose and cheeks like his own.

"I'm sorry to be late," he grumped. "I started out early enough, but the Porsche does what the Porsche wants to do.

One of these days, I'm going to turn into a grown-up and get a serious car."

"We've only been waiting a few minutes," Dakota assured him.

Again, Justin looked around. "Hell. If this isn't enough to put chills up your spine."

Just like the others, he'd hightailed it to exactly this site when the plane had first gone down, but it wasn't dark now; there were no flames, no crying passengers...there was no sound at all but the shriek of a winter wind. Acres of Texas flatland stretched in all directions, bleached of all color and life at this time of year, and in the middle of that ice-gray desert was the mirror-silver of the plane, just sitting there. She was listing a bit, but she didn't look as if she'd crashed or had an emergency landing. She just looked like an alien vehicle in the middle of a Star Trek episode. Big. Silent. A scream of high technology in a land of rattlesnakes and coyotes. And the door to the small jet gaped open like a mouth waiting for a dentist's probe.

"I'm still surprised that the cops called us." Matthew brought up the rear as they all strode toward the metal plane stairs.

"I don't believe it was the cops' idea that we were called in. I suspect it was Princess Anna's family. No one in Asterland or Obersbourg has any real contacts in America except for the Texas Cattleman's Club, so I think it's pretty natural they'd want us as part of the investigation. They know us. They trust us." Dakota led the way inside the plane. "It'd be different if some clues had surfaced as to the cause of the emergency landing. Of course, a fire's the best way in hell to destroy evidence. But right now, I think everyone's still worried about sabotage. If some answers don't surface real soon, I'd be surprised if Asterland doesn't send over its own team of investigators."

"Well, I hear you, but you're retired from the Air Force," Matthew said to Dakota. "If anyone belongs here, you do.

God knows, I'm willing to help, but I can't imagine anything I can really do.''

"Same here," Justin said. "But I think the point is to get a fresh pair of eyes on the site. Experts have already been over the place with a fine-tooth comb, but we're the only ones who knew all the people on board. I think they're hoping we'll find something that no one else had any reason to notice." He frowned. "But I thought Aaron and Ben were going to join us?"

Dakota nodded. "Ben is. In fact, he should be here shortly. He cell-phoned a few minutes ago just to let us know he'd been tied up. Not Aaron, though—Aaron took off for Washington a couple days ago and he isn't back yet."

"He went to Washington? Related to this problem?" Matthew asked.

Dakota shook his head. "I don't really know what Aaron's doing there, but when he was home over the holidays, I knew there was some problem with his job. I understood that he'd taken a leave of absence from his diplomatic work, so I figure he's at the embassy in Washington—but all I really know was that he was really unhappy and worried about something."

"I had the same impression," Justin agreed. "In fact, I tried to talk to him at our Texas Cattleman's Club shindig." But then he'd gotten caught up watching Winona dance. Watching Win smile. Watching Win breathe. And that fast, she stole into his mind all over again. Memories snapped into his mind, of her holding the baby, and then of her holding…him. Kissing him. Coming alive in his arms in a way he'd never believed could happen.

The plane-crash scene, though, slapped him back to reality. And Matthew was still talking about Aaron Black.

"I tried to talk to him the night of the party, too, but then he got dancing with that plain-faced teacher with the sweet smile. What's her name? Pamela?"

"Pamela Miles," Justin affirmed. He remembered her, not

from the night of the party so much, but from treating her the morning after the plane's emergency landing. "She was on this plane flight, in fact. Headed to be an exchange teacher in Asterland—at least before the crash."

"Well, she sure didn't have her mind on teaching that night. I'd never guess that Aaron would go for that kind of gal, but they were sure glued closer than peanut butter and jelly for a while there. Anyway, I never got a chance to ask him anything about his job. He left early the night of the party. And in the meantime..."

In the meantime, all three of them fell abruptly silent as they slowly walked through the plane. Justin glanced at the other two men, but the view seemed to disturb all of them the same way. The whole group had been here the morning of the crash landing. Justin remembered it well. He'd gotten the phone call, driven here like a bat out of hell, saw the smoke billowing out, hurled out of his car and started working. He'd been a doctor that morning. Nothing else. Trauma medicine used to be his adrenaline flow, his heartbeat.

It wasn't anymore.

He couldn't let it be.

But the morning of the crash, for damn sure, all he'd seen were the passengers, their injuries, their frightened faces. Now the silence was eerie and the devastation inside the plane as frightening as a bomb site.

"Hell. What a mess," Matthew muttered.

"It could have been worse."

"A ton worse." Dakota's gaze riveted on the cockpit, with which he was obviously more familiar than either of the others. "You saw more of this than any of us, Justin."

"Because I was inside right after the crash? Yeah, I suppose. But I only saw people. Patients. It's all I was looking for or looking at. I never gave a second look to anything about the plane."

"Well, let me fill you both in on what I know. This is where the fire started..." Dakota motioned, and then motioned again, "Robert Klimt was sitting here. And Lady Helena across the aisle there. Not surprisingly, those two were hurt worse than anyone else on the flight."

The three of them had a passenger list and a diagram showing where each person had been seated, but Justin couldn't keep his eyes off the plane's interior. The overhead compartments were all yawning open, debris spilled all over the aisles and seats. No one had been allowed to recover their personal belongings yet. The fire had left a gaping hole with black char climbing the walls and the carpet still seeping and stinking from the water and extinguisher chemicals.

"As bad as it is, it's still like looking at a miracle," Matthew said soberly. "I don't know how anyone walked away from this. It's too damn easy to imagine everyone being killed, the whole thing up in flames."

"Yeah. If this was the act of a terrorist, I hope to hell we get him. And soon."

For a moment Justin couldn't speak. His fingertips went ice cold, the way they did when he woke up from nightmares sometimes, memories of Bosnia still moaning through his mind. This kind of crisis was exactly why he'd accepted the Texas Cattleman's Club's invitation to join their group. Maybe outsiders thought they were a male bastion social club, but Justin knew how committed the men were to saving innocents. Too damn often, neither the law nor any government could protect innocents. Not in any country.

He sucked in a breath, forcing those old nightmare memories to fade. At least there'd been no small children involved in this plane flight.

His gaze swept and reswept the plane's interior. He saw an overturned romance paperback on the floor. A woman's red high-heel shoe lying on its side. A black driving glove. A small carry-on had upended, revealing a spill of lingerie that looked like a bride's trousseau—Matthew muttered something about Jamie Morris and what he'd heard about her marriage to some higher-up dignitary in Asterland's government. Down the aisle a little farther was a snakeskin purse, also lying open, with lipsticks and combs and what all strewn down the aisle. There was a sweater here, a coat there. The acrid after-smell of burned plastic and chemicals.

The door to the pilot's cabin stood ajar, the cold morning sun streaming through the windows. It seemed crazy to notice the dust spinning in the sunlight, as if anything about this scene were remotely normal.

But then a sharp, bright glint caught his attention. On the carpet, near where Lady Helena had been sitting on the flight, Justin hunkered down, frowning.

"Matt. Dakota."

"What?" Matthew bent down, too, but Justin raised a cautious hand to prevent him from touching anything.

Dakota pushed closer, sensing from the sudden excitement and seriousness of the other two that they'd found something important. He looked over Justin's shoulders. "That *can't* be what I think it is," he breathed.

The two stones were just lying in the carpet, not noticeably separable from all the other debris. A handkerchief wasn't far. The black driving glove. Ash and messes from the fire. But the two stones were a startling contrast to everything else.

One was a black harlequin opal.

The other, a three-carat emerald.

Justin exchanged glances with Dakota and Matthew. Matt's face had bleached white. Probably his own had, too.

None of the men could give a holy hoot about gems—but all of them recognized these two stones. The jewels were too rare and distinctive to be mistaken for anything else, even by lay people such as them.

The whole town knew the legend of the Texas Cattleman's Club's three jewels. And Justin distinctly remembered the old story being retold at the last Texas Cattleman's Club party— Riley Monroe recounting the old yarn to one of the Asterlanders. The townspeople never seemed to get tired of the jewel tale, even if they never believed it was true. It just didn't matter. It was a great story, and specifically a story with a message about the values of leadership, justice and peace—the Club's motto.

Two of the stones in the old legend, of course, were a black harlequin opal and a great big green emerald.

Just like these two.

Amazingly like these two.

Exactly like these two.

Matthew wildly shook his head. "I don't get this. Someone tried to steal our stones? But I didn't think anyone really believed they existed—much less that anyone had a clue where we had them locked up all these years."

"Neither did I. In fact, none of this makes any sense. If there'd been a break-in at night, Riley Monroe would have immediately contacted one of us. And obviously nothing happened during the day, when people are around, or we'd have easily known about that, too." Justin was already lurching to his feet. So was Dakota. "But the frightening thing is…if those two gems *were* stolen—then where is our red diamond?"

All three men swore at the same time, even as they were pawing and prowling around the plane, searching every nook and cranny and sifting through all the debris. All three stones were priceless, but the red diamond was so rare it was literally beyond price, beyond even a collector's dreams. "It doesn't make sense that anyone would have taken the other two stones and left the diamond," Dakota grumped.

"It doesn't make sense that any of them could have been stolen to begin with," Justin shot back, and then sucked in a swear word.

"What?" Dakota demanded. "Did you find it? The red diamond?"

No, he hadn't found the stone. He'd found a creased sheet of paper that would never have drawn his eye if the word *emerald* hadn't been written on it in a big, slashing scrawl.

Frowning, he noted the Asterland stationery. "I don't know what this is," Justin told the others. "It's not a letter. It doesn't seem to be written to anyone specific—at least there's no name on the stationery. But someone jotted down the town legend about the jewels. The whole history. The Texas soldier who found the stones on a fallen comrade in the War with Mexico, took the stones home to Royal, then made it rich on oil before there was any reason to spend them...."

"What else?" Matthew couldn't see at the same time as the other two men.

"The whole thing about the jewels. That red diamonds were traditionally called the stone of kings because they stood for leadership. There's a scrawled history of black opals here, specifically black harlequin opals, and how, symbolically, they were credited as being healing gems as well as allowing their owners to 'bring justice' to those around them. And the emerald is described as a symbol of peace and peacemakers." Justin looked up.

"Leadership, justice, peace," Dakota echoed. Again, the men exchanged quiet glances. They all knew why those words had been chosen as the Texas Cattleman's Club motto—and what each man had vowed to protect when he'd been asked to become part of the group.

"I still don't understand any of this," Matthew said irritably. "The whole world knows about the legend. But who could possibly have known that the stones were real, much less know where we had the jewels locked up? Where's the damn red diamond? And...for God's sake...do you two think the jewel theft had anything to do with the crash landing of this plane?"

Justin lifted a hand helplessly. "I don't know how it could. But the coincidence is pretty hard to ignore."

Dakota said swiftly, "We need to get together—as soon as we can get hold of Aaron and Ben. But even sooner than that, at least one of us needs to get to the Club. Find out if the red diamond is still there. Talk to Riley Monroe. And find out what happened to our safe.''

Justin pushed a hand through his hair. ''I'll volunteer to do anything you want…but to be honest, I'll have a hard time meeting until later tonight—say, eight o'clock, earliest. I have patients back-to-back until then. I realize how critical this is, and I *can* cancel patients if I have to, but—''

''No, it's all right, Justin. I'd rather wait until after dinner tonight, too,'' Matt concurred. ''We've got a better chance of Ben joining us. And if Aaron isn't back, we could at least have consulted with him by phone before then. Because of his diplomatic connections and knowledge, I really think Aaron should be brought into this before we make any decisions.''

''Yeah. Agree.'' Dakota nodded. ''But I'll hit the Club this afternoon—or as fast as I can. I have to cancel a meeting to get freed up—but I'll try, because I think we'll all go nuts worrying whether the red diamond's been stolen until we know for sure. But as far as a meeting time for all of us to get together, I agree with you, too. Let's aim for tonight. Justin?''

He'd already turned toward the plane door, as the other two had. ''You want to take the emerald and the opal back with you?'' Justin asked, assuming that was why Dakota had signaled him out.

''No. Hell. If the safe's been broken into, we all need to decide together what to do with these two stones for security in the meantime. But you hold them until then. No, that wasn't the issue. I was going to suggest that you be careful what you say to Winona Raye.''

Justin's expression had to reveal his astonishment. ''Why on earth would you think I'd be seeing Winona?''

''Because we all saw the way you were looking at her at the party.'' Dakota slapped him on the back, then hiked past him. So did Matt. ''Far as I'm concerned, you couldn't get involved with a better lady. I think the world of her. Far as

I know, so does this whole town. So mostly I was just trying to get a rise out of you—but it does keep occurring to me that this situation is getting seriously complicated. Right now, the police don't know about the jewels or the theft—much less that there could be any connection to the problem with the Asterland plane. Maybe that information has to come out? There may be no choice.''

Justin nodded. ''But we all know what's at stake—the reason we've guarded our privacy all these years.'' The Club members could hardly have taken off on their private causes across the world if their comings and goings were regular headline news.

''Hell, doc, I'd trust you with my life. You already know that. For that matter, I couldn't think more of Winona. It just crossed my mind that we could be putting her on the spot if she knew something that was being kept from the local cops. At least until we know more facts about the jewel theft and decided what we need to do.''

Justin had no trouble agreeing. The three split up swiftly. Everyone had their own lives and work to attend to. But as Justin headed for his car, the wind whipping a burn on his cheeks, his plan to see Winona for an early dinner went on a front burner.

He'd left her alone for two days now—except for phone calls—to consider marrying him. He'd known she needed time to think. More than likely, she'd had enough time to have a cow and a half over his proposal.

He never intended to put her on the spot about the jewels. He only wanted to put her on the spot about a relationship between them. And nothing as annoying as some priceless stolen jewels was going to keep him from her. Not today. He'd waited as long as he could stand.

Five

"**W**inona!"

Winona had barely pushed open the door to the Royal Diner before the waitress shrieked her name. Sheila abandoned her customer and bustled straight toward her.

"I been hearing all over town about you and that baby! Let's have a look!" Although it was barely the dinner hour, the diner was already filling up. This was not a crowd worried about eating at a fashionably late hour—more likely they were worried about how fast they could get the kids home to bed. Sheila popped her favorite Juicy Fruit gum as she herded Winona and the baby carrier toward a booth in the back, talking the whole while—loud enough, of course, for the whole town to hear.

"Dr. Webb called. Said to put you in a spot away from the drafts and get you started, he'd be here, but he got held up with a patient for a little bit. So you're seeing Dr. Webb, huh? God, he's such a hunk. Could make a girl think about getting a breast reduction just to get his hands on her...but

I guess that's a little tasteless, huh? If you're seeing him and all. But you don't have to worry about me, honey, he'd never look my way…and I can't wait to hear the whole story about that baby. Let's see her, let's see her…well, aren't you a beauty, darlin'.''

Sheila tugged down her waitress uniform, which tended to ride up her thighs with every other step. Years ago, Winona had realized that buying another size uniform wasn't a possibility—not for Sheila. She'd been fighting to stay in a size twelve for half a decade now, and there was no way she was going to let a fourteen win. But right then, she peeled back Angel's blanket and picked up the baby with a long refrain of oohs and aahs.

Because the baby chortled happily for the attention, Winona decided to let Sheila live. Actually, she was too tired to kill her and too old to feel embarrassed at the waitress's loud personal gossip. Still, she pushed off her jacket and sank onto the booth seat, wishing for a long, tall whiskey instead of straight water—and she didn't drink. The thing was, over the last two days, Sheila wasn't the only townsperson who'd made wild, presumptuous assumptions about Winona's relationship with Justin.

It didn't make sense. Folks should have been gossiping ten for a dozen about the plane crash. That was the crisis in town. That was the big news. Who Winona happened to be seeing—or not seeing—shouldn't have mattered to a soul.

And the really crazy thing was that she wasn't even seeing Justin. At least not exactly. Yeah, he'd offered to marry her…and for damn sure, that was why she'd insisted on seeing him right now, today, over dinner, and specifically chosen this public place for the occasion…but there was still no reason from here to Austin that anyone should leap to the conclusion that she was "seeing him." Heaven knew he'd proposed to her fifty times before this. And most folks in Royal had seen her slug him probably that many times—or more.

"Well, okay, honey, if you want to keep it quiet, I won't tell a soul," Sheila boomed, as she settled the baby back in the carrier. "But I hope you realize that no one's curiosity is intended in a mean way. We all love you. We all know you. Anyone who's had a kid in trouble, for years you were the one who stepped in. This here baby, though…" Efficiently she slapped down two paper place mats that read: The Royal Diner—Food Fit For a King! and then extracted her pen and pad from her front hip pocket. "She doesn't look Spanish or Indian or Mexican. Not with that blond hair and blue eyes…but you haven't found the mama yet?"

"Not yet."

Sheila motioned with her pen. "So, what'll you have? Dr. Webb, remember, he said for you to order."

"Really, I'd rather wait for him—"

"No, no. He said you'd be tired from working and from carting the baby around all day. He'll be here. Just ten minutes late, he said. But he wanted you to start eating. Manny—" she motioned toward the grill cook in back "—he says the pork chops are extra tender today."

"I was thinking a salad—"

"Now, you can't build up your strength on leaves and rabbit food, honey. Much less can you build up a bust, and men do tend to like a substantial woman, you know. Did you see my pies up front?" She motioned toward the revolving pie stand near the front door. "Strawberry rhubarb today. And I got a banana cream to die for. You need me to warm up a bottle for the baby? You sleeping with Dr. Webb?"

"Cobb salad. No dessert. Yes, thank you on the bottle, I have one in the diaper bag here. And none of your business."

Sheila cocked up an eyebrow. "Now, hon, with the Gerards gallivanting on vacation the winter months, who'all's gonna give you advice if your friends in town don't? But I don't see the question made you blush, so I'm thinking, no, not yet. Ask me, I'd nail that man fast and any way I could. There's some men you can string along, they like the hunt and chase. But him, I wouldn't risk nothing like that. Too many girls got their eyes on him. He's too cute and too rich. You get a chance, you get that boy in the sack and you don't give him a chance to even look at anyone else.''

"Thank you so much." Winona swiped a hand over her eyes. "Is there anything else you want to offer me advice on? Deodorants? Hemorrhoids? Constipation?''

"There now. You won't be so crabby after you have some food. I'll bring you the chops and my cheddar cheese mashed potatoes. Trust me. You'll like them. And the whole town's been asking whether Wayne's gonna actually let you bring that baby to work right in the police station.''

"It's only a temporary circumstance, my having the baby. It's worked out for a few days. But obviously, I wouldn't have the baby around any situation that could be dangerous. It just takes time to find an answer for—''

"Yeah, yeah." Sheila waved off the politically correct answer. If she couldn't have dirt, she didn't want anything. "So, did you tell the Gerards about the baby yet?''

Winona sighed. To a point, it was easier to answer the questions than exert all the energy it took to duck them. "Yes. They're still vacationing in Japan and having an outstanding time. But I talked to them on the phone two nights ago.''

"They love you." Sheila set out the silverware, working around the baby's carrier in the middle of the table. Two other customers waved hands to get her attention, but she clearly didn't want to move quite yet. "And I just know they'd be happy if you were involved with Justin, because the Webb and the Gerard families were always so close. And really, at your age, hon, I think they'd expect you to be, how should I say it, physically involved—''

Winona propped her chin on her knuckled hand. "Okay. I give up trying to deny it. I'm having wild, unprincipled sex with Dr. Webb. If it'll make y'all happy, tell the town, tell the whole universe—''

She was stunned into immediate silence when she suddenly saw another face appear behind the waitress's—and Justin was grinning to beat the band.

"Now, darlin'. Please don't be giving all the wild details of our sex life to Sheila. You didn't tell her what we did two nights ago in the Porsche, did you?"

Smoothly, as if they'd been a couple for a hundred years, he bent down, bussed the top of her head, chucked the baby's chin, and then plunked down on the opposite side of the booth. "Sheila, I've only got forty minutes, max. I want the greasiest hamburger you've got back there, heavy on the barbecue, and a ton of fries—"

"Like you need to tell me this, sweetheart?" Sheila whirled around, clearly delighted with him, and sashayed off to deliver their order.

Winona needed a second to recover her equilibrium. Five minutes ago, she'd had no equilibrium problems, but suddenly her heart was flopping in her chest louder than a beached whale and her nerves were suffering hiccups. She didn't have nerves. She'd certainly never suffered from arrhythmia—at least until Justin walked in. And that kiss from two nights ago seeped back into her mind with a twinge of guilt.

She felt his gaze on her face. Nothing new, their looking at each other. They'd known each other for five million years, for Pete's sake. Only, nothing was the same since that kiss. He'd never—never—looked at her this way before. As if she were a woman, instead of an old ragtail-younger-neighbor friend. As if she were a woman who sexually interested him. As if he didn't have all that much trouble imagining her in bed. And was enjoying that imagining.

Her gaze frittered around the diner. The red barstools were all taken, the long Formica counter filled up with locals. Booths lined the walls, mostly spilling over with young families, but, traditionally, medical personnel popped over here to grab the counter seats because the hospital was so close by. No one in the medical field ever seemed to eat healthily. On the jukebox, someone was wailing about losing somebody. There was a truck and a cup of a coffee and a dog in the song, so no question it was a country-style wail. Manny, the cook, was visible from the open window of the grill kitchen. He was wearing his beefcake-style white undershirt that showed off his shoulder and upper arm muscles, and he was wielding a black spatula. Sheila patted his butt every time she went by.

The diner was familiar. Comfortable. The teasing was a pain in the keester, but what could Winona expect from a small town where everyone knew her, and, damnation, everybody cared? Hell, she cared, too, and could pry with the best of them when she was in the mood. Normally it was as easy to be in the Royal Diner as at home.

Except tonight.

She felt a sensation of panic, as if her whole world were shifting on her. It wasn't exactly that she *minded* his looking at her in that new way. That intimate, hot, unnerving-damnhim way. But she'd always known what to say to Justin, how to behave, what to do around him, and suddenly all that comfort level was lost.

Finally he got around to saying something. "You look tired, Win."

"Thanks, Doc. That's just what a girl wants to hear."

"And not just a little tired. You look just plain whipped."

Immediately she bristled. What had happened to all the sweet talk he'd used when Sheila'd been around? "Are you looking for a sock right in the *labonza?* I'm not the least tired," she snapped.

The insult went right over his head. "What's wrong?"

Her shoulders sank. The feeling of strangeness disappeared. This was, after all, Justin, who she'd known forever—and who already knew all about Angel. "Everything."

"So. We'll fix this 'everything.' But that's a little tough to do unless you're willing to be a little more specific."

Out it poured. All the frustrations from the last time she'd seen him. Even though technically Angel should have been promptly turned over to Social Services, no one really had a sweat with her temporarily baby-sitting. Still, the whole world, and especially her boss, kept reminding her that the baby showing up on her doorstep didn't mean she had any dibs—or legal rights—on Angel. And she *knew* that. But for the same reason, one of the first things she'd done was check out what was going on with foster care.

"Okay." When Sheila served dinner, Justin didn't even look up, just kept his eyes on hers, encouraging her to keep talking.

"There's no great foster-care family waiting in the wings. The court finds a place when it has to. That's the way it is. So there are the Barkers, who've already taken in two kids, even though they barely had room for the second one. They can take in a baby for a couple of weeks if there's no other place. They're good people, but they don't *want* Angel, Doc."

"Okay."

"And there's another family on the foster-care list...." She pushed her fork around fretfully. "On paper, they're qualified. In reality, we've never put a child with them. He...smells. She dresses vintage Victorian to scrub her bathroom. I'm not saying anything's that terrible, but there seem to be some raisins missing in their bran, you know? They claim to desperately want kids, that they can't have their own, be happy to foster. But I'm telling you—"

"Angel isn't going there." Justin, God love him, didn't waste time phrasing the comment as a question.

Again, her shoulders eased. He understood. "I realize that doesn't mean that I'm the best choice to take care of the baby. Or that I'm entitled. In any way. But—"

"Oh, shut up, Win. You don't have to justify anything to me." He peeked at the snoozing baby as he started wolfing his burger. "So keep on talking. What's happened so far with the parent search? I take it you haven't found the baby's mother?"

"God knows, I'm trying."

"But…?"

She started filling him in. Leading her mom-suspect list were a couple of teenage girls. Both troubled. Both had histories of drinking and truancy. Both came from rich families where the parents had recently shipped them off to residential ranches. "You know the kind of place I'm talking about. They have a dry-out program, but it's also a live-in school, all the academics. The idea is to remove the kids from the environment that was contributing to their trouble, see if professionals and positive peers can't help turn the kids around."

"Actually, I don't know anything about those places, but it's obvious you do."

"Yeah. And some of them are excellent. Kids *do* take a wrong turn sometimes. Especially if they can't get away from bad peer influences on their own. The only thing that ticks me off is how expensive they are, it's not like everyone can take advantage. But, anyway, on those two specific girls—neither of them was pregnant, according to their parents."

"Which means…?"

"Which means nothing. The parents could be lying, thinking that they're protecting their daughters. So I can't be sure until I've checked that out, and that's going to take longer than overnight." She lifted a forkful of cheddar cheese mashed potatoes, but then let it drop again. "In the meantime, I picked up news about another kid. Parents live in a trailer park, dad works in the oil fields, girl got pregnant at fourteen, supposedly had the baby in the family trailer and it died. Only maybe the baby didn't die. Maybe that's what the girl said to avoid trouble, and if so, and if her child was Angel, then it could well have fetal alcohol syndrome—at best. But right now, I have no grounds to haul in the girl and force her to take a medical exam." She glared at Justin. "I'm almost positive that this girl isn't Angel's mother. But if she were…then either of those foster-care families would be the worst place to put a baby with those kinds of special problems.''

''I hear you. You're saying you'd want to take in Angel even more if you thought she had special problems. Not less. But in the meantime, how come you're so positive that that one girl isn't Angel's mom?''

''Well, I can't be *positive*—but whoever is the mom of that baby knew me personally. She had to. I mean, she not only left the baby at my house, but left a personal note to me. And I didn't know that kid in the trailer park from Adam—or anyone in her family.'' Sheila stopped by the table, delivered the warmed bottle and two gigantic pieces of pie, but when she couldn't get another conversation going, moved on again. ''I spent hours in the schools today. And on the computer. Found three runaways. Six truant cases. I'm still trying to follow up on all of them. Then I hit the docs, the clinics, the obstetricians, Planned Parenthood. I swear I could smack 'em all upside the head. None of those people talk. They'd guard the confidentiality of a kid in trouble no matter what. It's like trying to get blood out of a turnip. So then I tried calling ministers and priests and rabbi Rachel—''

He glanced over at her plate, and stole some of the chops she wasn't eating.

''They've all got worry-lists of girls or kids they think are promiscuous. But whether any of those girls were for sure pregnant at the time Angel's mom had to be—no one knows. One minister gave me a couple of names to check out. So did one of the vice principals at the high school.''

''But…?'' He held out a tidbit of pork chop on a fork, until she bit into it and chewed.

''But it could be an adult woman. It's not like the mother *had* to be a teenager.'' She swallowed, only to have the exasperating man nudge another bite toward her mouth. ''So I called the women's shelter. Asked if anyone was pregnant at the time Angel's mom had to be. Since this woman knew my name, I keep thinking that if I could just get some clues, some ideas, I might recognize her in some way. And I'm looking for a grown-up now, a woman with the means to hide a pregnancy, but for some reason feels she can't keep her baby. Unfortunately, the people at the shelter were as bad as the doctors. Angel's mom could have been right there, but no one was about to tell me. I understand confidentiality. I believe in it, for Pete's sake. Only it's been days now, and I can't get a solid lead to save my life.''

"Win,'' Justin stopped trying to coax her into more food. "Are you positive that you want a lead?"

The question startled her. "Are you asking me if I'd drag my feet because of wanting the baby for myself?" She shook her head, fast, fiercely. "I admit I've fallen in love with her. I know it's only been three days, but I swear she already feels like she's mine. But there's only one way I can make this right, Justin. To find the mom. To know what the whole story is. Then to legally go after doing whatever's right for Angel. I admit, I want her. But there's still only one way to drive down this street, and that's the right way. You know how it is. The truth'll come back to bite you in the butt if you don't face it down to start with.''

"Um, is that a Texas saying?"

She grinned. "No, but it should be, don't you think?''

"What I think, Ms. Raye, is that you've got too much on your plate—and that's a problem that you'd be really, really stupid not to let me help you with. What the hell good is it to have a friend with a ton of money unless you use him now and then? You know my house. You know Myrt, my housekeeper. And while you're trying to work full-time—"

"No," she interrupted firmly.

"No? No? This 'no' is in reference to what? I never asked you a question."

Since Sheila was nowhere in sight, Winona got up herself and carted their plates to the old Formica counter, out of their way. The baby was still snoozing, but starting to stir. With a little more space, she could use a hand to keep the baby carrier in a gentle, rocking motion, but her gaze stayed glued on Justin's. "Somehow you managed to get me talking all this time about Angel and my problems, Doc. But that isn't why I wanted to see you today."

She could see him brace, his eyes pick up a wary glint. "Yeah. I suspect you wanted to talk to me about weddings."

She nodded. "You're not going to bamboozle me into a marriage, Doc," she said gently.

"Do you think you're announcing something I didn't know? Why on earth would I want to bamboozle you into anything?"

But she was all through being fooled by that easy, lazy teasing tone. "That's exactly what confounded me for the last few days. Trying to understand. You've asked me to marry you a gazillion times, but I always knew you didn't mean it. I mean, it's one of our favorite private jokes together. But this time—you sounded serious. So then I started thinking. Maybe something was really bothering you." She watched his eyes. "I know something happened to you in Bosnia."

He stilled. "What is this? A guy can't ask a woman to marry him without her thinking he's mentally ill or has some deep dark problem?"

"Don't even try throwing feathers in front of my eyes, Doc. You know perfectly well that's not what I meant. Answer the question. Or is Bosnia something you can't talk about?"

She'd seen that exasperated look on his face before—and that unwilling hint of humor in his eyes. Somehow, some way, they'd always been able to talk honestly together. Even when Justin fought it tooth and nail. He threw up a hand. "How Bosnia got in this conversation beats me. But yeah, of course things happened to me there. I went through a year of real hell."

She nodded gently. "I know you did. And you've always pretty openly admitted that…but I meant, was there something that happened that you didn't talk about? Or couldn't? I know you saw horrors. I know you went through hell. But you came home and changed from trauma medicine to plastic surgery."

"So?"

"So…when I realized that, I tapped into my memory banks and it seemed like that was around the time that other things changed for you, too. You picked up a reputation as a devil-may-care playboy. It's stupid."

"I don't know about stupid. More, hard to avoid. I've got money and I'm single, so the press naturally—"

"Don't try to sell me cow patties, darlin'." Winona leaned forward, feeling better now. In fact, feeling downright good, now that the subject was off her and on him, and Justin was no longer looking at her as if she were whipped cream. "I'm talking about how the media regularly pegs you, Doc. I'm talking about the kind of reputation that you've let happen. And it isn't at all true."

"It's not exactly a *lie* that I'm single. Or that I have the means to—"

She snorted. Not particularly delicately. "You make out like you spend all your time on tummy tucks and boob implants. Nothing wrong with boob implants, mind you—but why is it that no one in town realizes you're the reason we have that fancy Burn Unit at Royal Memorial?"

"Who told you that?" Justin yanked on his ear, a clear clue that he was feeling edgy. "And for the record, I do my share of tummy tucks and nose jobs. If you think I'm apologizing for that—"

"No one's suggesting you need to apologize. If anything, you should take a bow. Some idiots think tummy tucks and boob jobs are about nothing but vanity. You've always been a women's supporter for real, Justin. Reconstruction after cancer or a tumor can make a difference to a woman's esteem...." Abruptly she stopped and waved that subject aside. She could have ranted on, but he was obviously trying to distract her. "Anyway, the point is—I'm not knocking the work you do. I'm only asking why you give the community the impression that you only take on spoiled rich women for patients, when in reality you donate a ton of your time to some of the worst burn cases over three states."

"Hell." He tugged on his ear again. "Who told you *that?* Someone's been spreading vicious lies and slander about me."

"Shut up, Justin. I'm just trying to tell you...I know something's wrong. Maybe it's not my business. But once I started realizing how much you've changed since Bosnia, it just kept hitting me in the face. Obviously something serious has been bothering you. Something you don't talk about. And I don't know whether that wild-assed idea about marrying me could be part of that, but..."

As if she hadn't been right in the middle of an important, serious conversation with him, Justin suddenly bolted to his feet and grabbed his jacket. Some instinct made Winona turn around in bewilderment, seeking some reason for his sudden behavior.

At the door to the diner, Willis Herkner was just ambling in. The jerk was still working for *American Investigator,* which, as far as Winona was concerned, was the belly-buster of all the sensational media rags. Willis was dressed to impress, wearing a long white aviator scarf with his ultracool jacket. Still, even though the smarmy investigator was a major nuisance, Winona couldn't fathom why his appearance would bother Justin enough for him to be hustling double-time out of there.

"Justin..." she began, intending to question him, but just then Angel's baby-blue eyes fluttered open and her rosebud mouth opened in a squeal. The first squeal was fairly sleepy and friendly sounding. The next one, Winona knew, wouldn't be. The baby needed to be fed, bathed and rocked to sleep. Come to think of it, after this long day—so did she.

Justin, in the meantime, had lunged out of the booth and was zipping up. "You know what? Even when you were a belligerent, aggravating, sullen twelve-year-old, I realized this odd thing about you. You were never fooled by people's bologna. You always saw past the cover story to the truth. I could never lie to you, Win, even when I wanted to."

"Well...that's good," she said forcefully, and then hesitated. He'd seemed to mean a compliment, didn't he? Only he'd managed to confuse her by the side comment. She organized the thoughts in her mind again, determined to get back to the point—there was something wrong, something bothering Justin, and she was determined to get him to talk about it.

Instead, faster than she could get the words out, he leaned down.

Half the town—maybe more—was sardine-packed in the Royal Diner, most of them familiar, the baby squawking louder now, children screaming from another booth and Sheila shrieking something to Manny in the back. Yet he kissed her. Just bent down, and softer than the stroke of a petal, brushed his lips on hers.

Like a rose hungry for sunlight, her whole body strained upward for the touch of him. Her throat arched at the same time her eyelashes swooshed down. It wasn't dark behind her closed eyelids. If anything, there were fireworks of light and soft, silver flames. Her closed eyes just cut out the riffraff sensory images in the restaurant until there was nothing in her mind—nothing in her sight, sound, touch, taste, but Dr. Justin Webb and his wicked, wicked mouth.

Her conscience scrambled for some common sense. Some inhibitions. Some sanity.

Nobody home behind any of those doors.

Oh my, oh my. She didn't let go. Not with men, not with anyone. You get too close to people, then if they abandoned you—even if they never meant to or wanted to—your heart broke. You didn't die. Your heart just hurt and ached and never stopped aching. Nothing was worth that. She was sure of that yesterday, and she was sure of it today.

But her lips clung to Justin's and wouldn't let go. Her hands didn't touch him. Her breasts, her legs, her tummy— no body part was connected to him except her lips. And tongue. His warm, silky tongue touched hers, gentle as a spring breeze, not demanding, not taking, just…offering. Touch. Taste. The intimacy of himself.

Heat flushed her body head to toe.

The baby revved up the volume of tears. A child galloped past toward the rest room. A plate clattered on the floor. The jukebox twanged out another song about pickup trucks and getting up in the morning. Neon lights flashed on, off, on, off into the dark winter night street outside. Winona saw. She heard. She just didn't care.

And then Justin lifted his head, eyes suddenly darker than a midnight sky. "It's a good idea, don't you think? Kissing in public."

"What?" He might as well have suggested rolling naked in a mud puddle. It would have made as much sense.

"Everyone in town realizes that we know each other, Win. But just in case…this way they'll get the picture that we're close…that we were thinking about getting married even before Angel entered the picture. This way we'll look like a couple. So it won't seem contrived or hokey when we tie the knot."

"Tie the knot," she echoed.

"And you're damn right. There was a very serious reason I asked you to marry me. It's because I thought we could make it together. And I thought that ages before you ever laid eyes on our beauty here."

He touched Angel's cheek, which was enough to startle her from whimpering into a gurgle for him. And then he strode for the door.

All that noise, all that chaos, but there suddenly wasn't a sound in the restaurant but the scratched tape from the jukebox. Some folks were being polite. But the others were either outright staring at her or at Justin's departing figure.

Swiftly, Winona gathered up the baby, patting, soothing, trying to grab her jacket and car keys at the same time. He put a drug in his kisses. Well, what else could she possibly think? Maybe she didn't recognize the controlled substance, but it was there. In the taste of him. The mood. The look in his eyes. And whatever was in that damn chemical went straight to her head.

And it was still going straight to her head.

Blasted man—richer than a tycoon—yet he'd forgotten to pay for their dinners. So she had to finagle that money out of her pocket, get her jacket on, get Angel and all the baby paraphernalia, all under the watchful, smiling eyes of everyone in the whole darn diner.

But when she finally hurtled into the night a few moments later, she sucked in a lungful of frigid winter air and, out of absolutely nowhere, smiled, too.

There was nothing funny about her situation. Nothing. She needed to figure that man out, and pronto. Somehow there still seemed to be a marriage proposal hanging between them. More worrisome yet was the stunning, startling thought that he actually *wanted* to marry her. But boy…

That man sure could kiss.

Six

———

Justin drove to the Texas Cattleman's Club, but when he parked the Porsche, he turned the key and sat there, motionless. His meeting with the guys was at eight. It was already a few minutes after. He could see lights on within the building, recognize some of the other members' cars in the lot. His mind needed to be on the plane crash and the missing jewels and serious business. Instead, all he could think about was Winona.

He was so in love with her.

Technically, loving her was old news. Heaven knew, he'd figured out his feelings for her long, long before he'd kissed her in the diner.

But that kiss was the first time he'd really dreamed, thought, *believed* that she could come to feel the same way about him. The baby was the first need he'd seen in Winona, the first dent in her emotional armor, the first emotion that she'd willingly revealed to him…but that kiss wasn't anything about Angel. It was about *them*. About something new and strong and powerful building between the two of them.

Justin tapped his fingers on the steering wheel, thinking that when a man got a taste of heaven, it was tough not to want it all. Both the problems and the joys. It was possible that Winona wanted to adopt every abandoned kid in the county for the rest of their lives, and God knew the woman was stubborn, closed in, too independent to lean on him even when he damn well wanted to be leaned on. But he really didn't care. Justin was also well aware that she was confused about the emotions suddenly exploding between them, but just as Shakespeare had said, all was fair in love and war. She'd been doing a lulu act on his heart for a long time. It wouldn't kill Win to be off balance for a bit.

Not when the cause was right.

Whistling, he finally climbed out of his classy chassis, and hiked toward the building. When he stepped inside, his mood promptly sobered.

He had to quit thinking about Win. For that matter he had to quit thinking like a cockeyed dimwit in love. This was no time to be singing in the rain.

He could hear a game of poker going on in the far room, saw a few men putting on their coats, leaving the card room where cigar smoke gushed out in a fog. From old habit, his eyes shot to the Leadership, Justice and Peace motto on the far wall. The actual sign wasn't that intrusive or large; most strangers ambling in rarely seemed even to notice it. But for him, it was like making eye contact with an old friend, and abruptly he charged toward the east rooms, expecting to find the others in the standard meeting area off to the right...and he did.

The room was as comfortably overloaded with testosterone as a room could get. A fire blazed in the hearth. A boar's head hung over the stone mantel. The pool table stood under a Tiffany chandelier, untouched, rack ready. The furniture was all leather, couches and big chairs, with ottomans to put your boots on—but no one was sitting tonight. Justin braced, feeling how much tension the others were giving off. Matt was pacing like a caged cougar, Dakota standing in the window, pensive and still. Aaron still wasn't back from Washington, but Ben was here now…typically, the sheikh had on his proper kaffiyeh for a serious meeting, and any other time Justin would have smiled. Ben was an extraordinary man who'd become a special friend, but he *did* have a way of looking like a desert warrior, between his kaffiyeh and those fierce dark eyes and rigid posture.

"For someone who's usually never late, I can't seem to catch up with a clock today to save my life. I'm sorry if I kept you waiting." Justin strode in, feeling guilty as a shamed hound. "And hell, you're all looking as dark as a thunderstorm. Are we talking more bad news? Dakota, I take it you looked for the red diamond—"

"No. I came here earlier, intending to do just what we said—check on the red diamond and report back to the rest of you," Dakota said. "Only when I got here, I discovered there was a problem. The wine-cellar door was unlocked."

Justin swore under his breath. Dakota continued, "So I could have called you all, but it made more sense to wait until I informed Hank Langley as he is the owner of the Club. He said he'd inform the other members, but we five, including Aaron, would take the lead and handle the situation. So now we need to discover what's wrong together. Decide what to do together. And earlier, there were just too many people here. It made the most sense to hold up any further investigations until after dark, now. Once the poker game breaks up in the other room, we'll be the only ones here. I only wish we'd managed to get hold of Aaron before now, because I have a feeling we're going to need his advice."

Matthew rolled his shoulders, obviously trying to shrug off the tension kinks. He also helped fill Justin in. "In principle, finding the wine-cellar door unlocked shouldn't be that much of a shock. We already know someone stole the two stones. Obviously they got in here somehow.''

"Yes." Ben stepped forward. "Except that the night watchman should have caught an unlocked door and reported something about it.''

"There was nothing in Riley Monroe's log in the last two nights?" Justin asked.

"Nothing written in any way," Dakota said with frustration.

"Well, that's odd." Justin knew, as they all did, that the older night caretaker was a hundred percent dependable. Riley may never have been the sharpest knife in the drawer, but he was both reliable and loyal. "In the meantime…we haven't been able to track down Aaron?''

"No." Matthew's tone expressed more frustration. "We know that he's still in Washington—which wouldn't have to be a problem if we could just reach him at either the embassy or his hotel room. But the embassy acts like he's not expected, and if he's getting messages from the hotel, he's not calling back.''

"But we left word for him to contact one of us, ASAP," Dakota affirmed.

"Well, we know he'll call as soon as he can. It's just that with so many people involved from Asterland and Obersbourg on that downed plane—and now we presume potentially involved with our theft—well, we all know Aaron's the one with the diplomatic expertise and background." Justin half turned. All of them could hear voices in the hall, men's laughter, louder as they moved toward the door. On a mean cold night like this—and a weekday night besides—it was unusual that the weekly poker game hadn't already broken up. But they should be alone within minutes, judging from the departing sounds of the group in the hall. Right then Justin was just as relieved to have a few more moments to study the others, anyway. "You all seem to sense that something's wrong. I mean—obviously—besides the crises we already know about.''

Matthew nodded immediately. "There is."

Dakota concurred. "Something badly wrong."

Ben nodded, too. "I think we should wait until we are alone in the building for sure, but this is hard. Like waiting for a tornado. I feel there should be a sword in my hand. A gun. As if something were menacing in every shadow."

"Sheesh. You guys are giving me the willies. Come on now," Justin said reassuringly, thinking that the group would calm down if they reviewed what they knew. "We had a theft. How or why that happened, none of us know. But whoever took the two jewels was on the flight to Asterland for sure. And since we recovered two of the jewels, we're not only ahead of the robber, but he—or she—is very likely out of the country by now. In fact, as far as I know, there's almost no one still in Royal who was originally scheduled on that flight—"

"Robert Klimt," Ben said.

"Who's in a coma."

"Lady Helena—" Matthew reminded him.

"Who's still in the hospital, between her broken leg and the burns."

Matthew frowned. "There was someone else. The teacher. Pamela something—"

"Yeah, Pamela Miles, the teacher who was dancing with Aaron the night of the gala." Justin threw up his hands. "You guys saw her, didn't you? Even if you don't know her. I mean, she's a thief like Walt Disney was a secret terrorist. There's no way she could have been our jewel robber. And another local person on the flight was Jamie Morris, but she was going to Asterland to be a bride, so she's hardly a likely thief."

"Yeah, yeah." Dakota suddenly cracked a slow smile. He knew what Justin had been doing. He always did. Dakota never hesitated to take charge of anything—actually, no one ever had to sell any of the Club members tickets. But he'd mentioned before how naturally Justin took the healer role, somehow diffusing the stress from a situation so all of them could work together better as a team. "I haven't heard a sound since the door closed the last time a few minutes ago. I'm positive those were the last guests in the place. Lay on, Macduff. Let's get this search party in motion and find out what's what."

Ben led the way. Actually, there was nothing mysterious about the passageway. Justin, like the others, always felt that secrets were dangerous. The best place to guard something important to you was out in the open, being honest about it— the way they'd always been honest about the three priceless jewels in the town legend. Everyone knew the legend of the jewels. No one believed it.

Although one person, Justin realized from the weight of the two stones in his pocket, obviously had.

Down a hall, past the cloakroom and rest rooms, was the giant kitchen. Beyond the kitchen was an anteroom, a spacious pantry. Inside the pantry was a door leading down several steps to the wine cellar. And at the far end of the wine cellar was a spring-loaded door. Neither the door nor the door lock was hidden from sight; they just appeared to be a natural part of the cellar wall unless someone looked closer. But the door was where the key should have worked—the key they each had.

Unfortunately, as Dakota had already warned them, the lock was already open. The door click-sprang open with the simple pressure of his hand. Inside was a stone passage. Narrow, cold to iciness, dry. Illuminated by bald lightbulbs strung from the ceiling at regular intervals. The passageway wasn't as cold as the wind-bitter night, but chilly enough to make Justin shiver uneasily.

Back in the War with Mexico—when the original Texas soldier carrying the jewels had died—an adobe church had stood on this site in Royal. The church was the original mission to the area, which was why Tex Langley had bought the land next to it and formed the Club—to protect the area's heritage. The law itself wasn't so dependable in those old days.

Not now either, Justin thought. Which was really the core reason the group had originally formed and persisted in staying together. Laws in themselves had no way to right all wrongs—or protect everyone. There always seemed to be abandoned babies like Angel. Things that went wrong in peoples' lives. Things the law couldn't fix. Things no one could fix if someone didn't step in and make a commitment to trying.

"Oh hell, oh hell, oh hell," Dakota muttered.

Justin surged forward. His vision was blocked by the other men's broad shoulders, but he sensed this was a problem specifically for him from something in Dakota's tone of voice. From one heartbeat to the next, he became a hundred percent doctor. The instant he caught sight of the crumpled body on the floor, he recognized Riley Monroe. He crouched down and felt for a pulse, but from his first look, he already knew.

There hadn't been a pulse in a long time. Probably a few days. Too damn long to do anything for the Club's old caretaker.

Over his head, the others had started moving. "Check the box for the other jewel," Ben said in a tone full of grit.

Matthew responded, "No, the red diamond's gone, too. Nothing here."

Then Dakota spoke, his tone as quiet as a winter night. "Justin?"

Justin understood that Dakota—that all of them—were counting on him to come up with some answers. No one had said the word *murder*. But they all knew that's what had taken place. "Well...there's a blow on Riley's head, but I don't think that's what caused his death. I think he was knocked out, then something else done to him. Not a gunshot or a knife wound. There's no blood. My guess is, an injection of some kind—which would imply planning on the part of the murderer. And it's so cool down here that I can't guess for sure when this happened, but I would think a couple of days ago—''

"A couple of nights ago. You mean, the night the Asterland plane tried to take off?" Ben asked.

Justin used his own jacket to cover Riley's face, and then looked up. "Yes. That's my guess."

All of them exchanged glances, but it was Matthew who sucked in a breath and summed it all up. "What a mess. We've got a dead body, a stolen red diamond, a plane crash. Tell the cops, and we risk an international incident—the worst thing that could happen when Asterland just achieved an uneasy peace with Obersbourg. And we'd risk that without knowing if our jewel thief/murderer was an American or one of the Asterland people."

"We also have no actual reason to believe that the plane crash has any relationship to the jewel theft," Dakota said. "The two events could be completely coincidental."

Slowly Justin stood up. "That's really true," he said thoughtfully. "In fact, if it weren't for the plane crash, we might not have known about the theft of the jewels for quite a while. Which makes me believe that the two incidents really might have had nothing to do with each other. But right now, I'm afraid none of that matters. We have to deal with Riley. We don't have any choice about calling in the authorities."

"I know." Matt cocked a foot forward. "But the question is, which authorities? Riley's been murdered. Obviously we have to call the cops. But does that mean we have to tell them everything related to the Texas Cattleman's Club and the three jewels and our whole history of missions around the world? The thing is, it's one thing to tell the cops about Riley—and another to make the whole situation public. I wish we had someone to give us advice from the inside. There are bigger problems here than just Riley's murder.''

"I agree," Ben said. "I doubt any of us would want to withhold information. That is not the issue. But if we get embassies involved here, we have a new nightmare. And unless we guard some information on our past Texas Cattleman's Club history, we jeopardize all our goals and all we've tried to do. I think we need a cop to know the whole story. But it has to be someone we can trust. Any too-fast decisions could make the situation even worse.''

Immediately Winona's face sprang into Justin's mind. "Well...the first thing we have to do is take care of Riley. But on the subject of someone we could trust in the police department, I have a suggestion—''

Just then, though, his hospital beeper went off. Justin mentally swore. He couldn't be in three places at once, yet it was one of those nights when he *had* to be.

Winona had the telephone plugged to her ear when Wayne's beefy face showed up in her office doorway. Her boss cocked a leg forward while she finished the call. With one hand, he scratched his chin as he surveyed the wreckage.

Back when, Royal had had no juvenile department—which had meant there'd been no office for Winona when she'd been hired, until she converted a supply closet. At the best of times, there was turnaround room for a small man. Right now, apart from files stacked chin-high and a desk whose surface hadn't seen light since the millennium, the room was draped ceiling-to-floor with baby paraphernalia—and Angel herself took up no small space between blankets and rattles and bottles. She blew an excited bubble just for Wayne, though.

Wayne sighed, heavily, from the doorway. "First time I've been able to catch up with you all morning. You heard? About Riley Monroe being murdered?''

"I sure did.''

"I don't like trouble in my town, and this whole week, there's been nothing but." Wayne scratched his jowly chin. Again. "How long you keeping that baby in the office, Raye?"

Wayne was one of those dogs where his bark was bad, but his bite was far worse. "The baby hasn't stopped me from pulling a full load," she said defensively.

"I didn't say it had. But it will. I got two of those at home. I know how full-time they are. Now, where you think you're going with this, Winona?"

"You know where I'm going with this. I'm searching for the mother."

"That's not what I'm asking and you know it. You're already so attached to that kid it shows in your face. She's not yours. And you're skating a line—you know you are— on not releasing the baby to Social Services."

"They haven't pressed."

Occasionally, Wayne could be annoyingly logical. "Because this is Royal. And because it's you and everyone knows and loves you." Wayne grunted. "That doesn't mean that this is by the book, though, and you know how I feel on that. If a cop doesn't behave by the straight and narrow, how can we enforce a law for anyone else?"

"I'm not breaking any law."

"I know that. I didn't say you were. Quit ducking the issue."

She nodded. "I'm sorry." She *was* sorry. As difficult as her boss could be sometimes, Wayne had always been on her side, and she could see he wasn't enjoying this discussion any more than she was. "Okay. As far as where I'm going with this—I'm expecting to find the parents. And I'm not even close to being done with the parent search. But if that turns up bad news, I'd like to adopt Angel. Or if not adopt, foster."

"All right. At least that's a straight answer." Wayne washed a hand over his tired face. "You need something filled out about what kind of character you got, what kind of foster parent you'd make, that kind of thing, you come to me, Raye," he said gruffly.

She couldn't kiss the boss. It would be completely inappropriate, and he'd hate it besides. "Thank you," she said sincerely.

"Yeah, well. That's not the only reason I stopped by. Did you happen to know Riley Monroe?"

"I knew he was the night watchman at the Texas Cattleman's Club. And he bartended for them at a lot of parties. He always seemed like a nice man. I can't imagine him involved with any trouble. But I didn't know him personally."

Wayne nodded. "Well, your impression's like everyone's. He's the last person anyone'd think would get murdered. The thing is, there's no keeping the death out of the papers. Folks'll want to show up to show respect and all, especially because Riley had no family. But I want all details kept out of the media until the investigation's over. I want a lid kept on this. Tight. And I know nothing in homicide's directly your problem, but I still want everyone in the station on the same page. If the press hound you, don't say anything."

"No problem." Someone screeched that there was a phone call for Wayne, and he hiked back to his office, four-letter words spilling from his mouth like drool. It was one of those mornings when no one could catch their breath. She was just reaching for the phone herself when it rang, and she grabbed it.

"Winona?"

"Yes?" She was positive that she recognized the feminine voice—only not exactly.

"I'm at your house, dear—"

"I beg your pardon?"

"And I just wanted to know if there was anything that you're allergic to."

"Well, no, but—"

"Fine. I just didn't want to risk cooking something that

didn't suit you. And Justin didn't feel that you'd want me baby-sitting until the two of us had a chance to sit down and talk, but it's not like we're total strangers. So I did want to say right up front, I'm available. And I adore children. And I'll be here, helping in your house, anyway, so there's no problem if the baby were here, too. And that's all, dear. I realize that you're at work and probably aren't supposed to be getting personal calls. No problem.''

The woman abruptly hung up. Winona stared at the buzzing phone for several moments, feeling completely befuddled. Yes, the woman's voice was familiar, but she couldn't place it. And the whole conversation, covering cooking and allergies and baby-sitting—made no sense to Winona whatsoever. She might have been alarmed, particularly at the idea of a stranger being in her house—if someone's telltale name hadn't come up.

Justin.

A series of bubbles were cooing from the baby carrier on her desktop. "Angel," Winona said, "I think we'd better go home for lunch today. Is that okay by you?"

Angel kicked her feet, clearly thrilled at the thought.

At ten minutes after twelve, Winona took one last bite from a fast-food hamburger as she pulled into her driveway. An unfamiliar car was already parked there—an Olds. Gray. And the model was older, but the car was still kept up to within an inch of its life, with paint gleaming and white-walled tires cleaner than brand-new.

Feeling even more bewildered, Winona grabbed Angel from her car seat and whisked the diaper bag to her shoulder. The baby wasn't fussing, but she was going to any second. Angel was such an ultrasmart baby that she could already tell time. At 12:12 p.m. she was going to want a bottle. Not 12:14 p.m. Not 12:13 p.m. But at precisely 12:12 p.m., and as long as she got exactly what she wanted, Angel was possibly the most miraculous, perfect, congenial baby ever to have been born. And Winona would have loved her no matter what, but right then it seemed a good idea to run for the door.

As swiftly as she juggled the baby and her purse and the diaper bag and the back-door key, however, she abruptly discovered that the door was already unlatched. Her door. Unlocked.

One peek inside almost gave her a new reason for a heart attack.

There were no dirty dishes piled in the sink. The kitchen tile was scrubbed within an inch of its life. A sponge cake was cooling on the counter, and something savory was brewing on the stove. Winona didn't bake. And she sure as hell didn't make—or know how to make—French stews.

She tiptoed in a few more steps. Both the washing machine and dryer were churning in the utility room. More shocking yet, there were folded clothes on top of the dryer. Folded. Not heaped or hurled willy-nilly.

This was all pretty terrifying. Still, she unwrapped Angel from her jacket, then pushed off her own, and carried the baby through the rest of the house. Clearly there was an intruder. Clearly no good mother would risk her child when there was obviously a stranger in the house, but there was building evidence to Winona that this particular intruder was mentally ill. Not in a dangerous way. Just in a distinctive way.

There wasn't a single towel on the floor in the bathroom. Not one. There were no stockings, no slips, no jeans piled on the floor in her bedroom. The bed was made. *Made.* With clean sheets. Like real people lived.

Holding the baby protectively close, she tiptoed toward the living room—where she already knew the intruder was, from the violent roaring sound. Sure enough, there was a woman's rump, bent over her couch, pushing the vacuum cleaner beneath it.

As if finally sensing there was someone else in the house,

the woman suddenly jumped, whirled, slapped a hand on her chest and turned off the roaring vacuum at the same time.

"Don't be frightened," Winona said warmly. "I can help you with this. I know there has to be a recovery program for cleaners. There is for every other problem. If nothing else, I can be your support group. Trust me, I can teach you to live with dirt. I know. I do it every day—"

The woman dropped the hand from her chest and let out a guffaw…followed by a second guffaw and then a full belly laugh. "Justin always said you were full of the devil. You do remember me, don't you? Myrt?"

"Of course I do." Even if all the clues hadn't come together, Winona would have recognized Justin's housekeeper when she finally got a good look.

It wasn't as if they really knew each other, but Myrt wasn't the kind of person anyone forgot. The jeans and T-shirt fit the figure of a thirty-year-old, but the worn, leathered face looked more like sixty, creased with both life and laugh lines. Huge silver earrings dangled from her ears when she leaned forward to catch a glimpse of Angel.

"So that's our baby, huh? Just for the record—I had four of my own. And seven grandkids now. But I hardly get to see the children. Everybody moved so far away with their jobs and all. I get so hungry to hold a baby."

Winona was slowly picking up the picture of what was going on here—but she wasn't completely sure. "Our baby," she echoed.

"Uh-huh." Warm brown eyes met hers. Winona was smart, but she had a bad feeling that Myrt was smarter. "Justin said you had your hands way too full, trying to work full-time and take care of the baby, too. Said you were getting worn out. His house is big, but it's nothing to clean, pretty much because he's never there. Truthfully, he has so much room that it would be much easier to set up you and the baby at his place—"

"Whoa." Winona could feel her knees giving way.

"—but it doesn't matter to me. He's paying me a ton—which, of course, is only half of what I deserve—because I'm the best grandma you'll ever hire. I bake like a dream. Never lose patience with a child. And I love to clean—"

"You're frightening me," Winona said baldly.

"Now, now. Pretty darn silly for you to look a gift horse in the mouth, isn't it? You need the help. I'm here. And Justin's paying my salary, so it's not like you have to worry about it. I can sleep over any time you want—"

"Whoa. Double whoa."

"Truthfully, I wish my nights weren't so free, but since Ted died…well, there's still heat in this old furnace, but I just can't seem to look at another man. I've tried. The point being, though, that I can stay all night with our Angel if you need me to. It's no problem at all. Truthfully, it's better for the baby to be in her own environment than taken out to a baby-sitter's. Now, let's get down to the important stuff. How often does she want a bottle? When's her bath time? Her fussy time?" Myrt waggled her fingers, signaling that she wanted Winona to fork over the baby.

Winona carefully handed her Angel, then stood as rigid as a school principal, watching every movement the other woman made. She didn't hold Angel the way Winona did. Didn't pat her exactly the same way, either. Nothing was remotely perfect. But the woman was clearly enamored big-time the instant she touched the baby, and Angel was cooing right back.

"Myrt?"

"Hmm?" The woman had dropped the vacuum cleaner and sat down with the little one. Clearly work and cleaning were forgotten. Winona's respect for her upped ninety notches.

"She gets cranky around dinner. Actually, it's no set time. Just whenever I'm trying to eat. And other than that, she almost never cries unless she's got a good reason. On food, though, she wants a bottle every four and a half hours, and I do mean pronto—and she's a minute overdue right now.''

''Well, then, I'll get it. We're going to have a great time together, aren't we, precious?'' Myrt seemed to have lost all interest in paying attention to Winona.

''Well, I don't want to leave you, but as soon as she gets this bottle, she's likely to drop off for almost a two-hour nap. And I really need to have a talk with Justin. Would you mind if I took off for just a bit?''

''Well, of course not, dear. That's what I've been telling you. I'm here for you. And the baby.''

Winona grabbed her jacket and car keys and hightailed it outside. As soon as she climbed in her car, she cell-phoned her boss so Wayne would know she wouldn't be at her desk for a while.

Possibly ''a while'' was an understatement, she mused, as she shot out of the driveway. When she caught up with Justin…well, when she caught up with Justin, she wasn't quite sure *what* she was going to do to him.

But she was going to do it *good*.

Seven

When Winona pushed open the door to Royal Memorial Hospital, her pulse was hurtling at a hundred miles an hour. Heaven knew why she was so nervous when the chances were slim that she'd even find Justin. He could easily be tied up for hours in surgery, and it wasn't as if she would ever interrupt him when he was busy with patients.

She didn't *have* to see him this instant, Winona kept telling herself. For darn sure he shouldn't have sicced Myrt on her without asking permission, but being good to her was hardly a murdering offense. She could yell at him about that any old time, and, yes, it troubled her that they still hadn't settled the proposal question, but that was part and parcel of the same problem. Something was wrong with Justin. He was behaving in very odd, very troubling ways. She wanted— needed—to get to the root of all this nonsense, but grabbing him at work for a snatched conversation was never going to resolve any of that.

She should be home. Or at her own work. Anywhere but

clipping down the hall toward the Plastic Surgery/Burn Unit hell-bent for leather—and still she kept bounding along at the same breakneck pace. Although a number of familiar faces called out a "Hey, Winona!" she avoided making eye contact or anything but a brusque return greeting. Everyone in town knew she was a cop, and she roamed the hospital floors at all hours without anyone ever saying boo, so she had no fear that anyone would stop or question her. Nerves were hammering on her conscience, though. She knew perfectly well that she had no excuse in God's great earth to be here. She just wanted to see him.

And for some unknown reason, she wanted to see him *now*. Not later. To yell at him for being manipulative and bossy, she told herself virtuously.

But even having given herself a good, sound, self-righteous excuse didn't seem to stop her heart from hammering.

She paused at the nurses' desk right inside the Plastic Surgery unit. "You haven't seen Dr. Webb, have you?" she asked a nurse in ice-blue scrubs with Mary Jo on her chest badge.

The blonde recognized Winona with a tired smile. "He's been in here off and on since last night. You know, the accident with the two teenagers on Cold Creek Road? Stevie really got his face cut up."

"Aw, hell," Winona said. "Stevie Richards?" As if there were more than one Stevie living on Cold Creek Road.

"Yeah. Parents called Dr. Webb right away last night. The whole family was just a mess. Dr. Webb finally kicked them all out, sat with Stevie himself after the surgery, got him calm, kept him calm...." Normally Mary Jo would never have told a patient's business, but Winona had known her for years. She generally knew more about an accident or a kid's problems than ever made it on a hospital's records, so the two frequently exchanged notes and information. "Anyway, I knew he wasn't in Stevie's room an hour ago, but I can—''

Winona could see her hand reaching for the phone. "No, don't call him. I don't want to bother him if he's with a patient. This wasn't that important." If Justin had been up all night, he had to be exhausted. That changed things. Her need to see him was some kind of emotional thing, but that was foolishness. Win was an ace pro at putting emotions in the bank when she didn't absolutely have to spend them.

"Well, he's still in the hospital, I know." Mary Jo tapped a finger on the desk. "I'm pretty sure he was headed up to Lady Helena's room. At least, he mentioned wanting to do a consult with Dr. Harding and Dr. Chambers. That was about a half hour ago, so I'm guessing you might have picked a good time to catch him."

"Thanks. I owe you."

Outside, she heard the whir of a helicopter. Royal Memorial was hardly a metropolis-size hospital, but the Burn Unit had begun earning a stellar reputation from the day it opened, and these days patients were often flown in from other cities. Still, the minute she walked into the Burn Unit, it was like wandering onto another planet. All the noise and hustle of the Emergency Room disappeared. Here, it was quiet. A gentle place, with pale blue walls and soft lighting. Nobody sneezed here, no one coughed—Winona had always figured that no one would dare. Justin would shoot anybody who came in here with a cold, because even bitsy germs could be a serious threat to a burn patient. The smells were the same old hospital smells—alcohol and bleach and antiseptics—but somehow neither the quiet nor the stinks made for a cold atmosphere. If you were a patient here, you were in big trouble. You needed peace and serious healing. And that's how Winona always felt here, as if she were in a place designed to soothe the spirit as well as heal the body.

Somehow, for a while now, she'd intuited that Justin needed that kind of healing place as well—that he hadn't created the Burn Unit just from studies of how a good one should be, but from something inside himself. Some sore that he hid from sight.

That thought was still on her mind when she located him.

Lady Helena's room was supposed to be a secret for security reasons—she was one of the most seriously VIP patients the hospital had ever had—but every cop in town knew where she was. When Winona rounded the corner, she recognized Dr. Harding and Dr. Chambers. They were both standing in the doorway, and she could hear Justin's voice from inside the room.

Dr. Chambers was the bone man. He wasn't the chattiest guy in town, but Winona had taken him busted-up kids before, knew he was an okay guy.

Dr. Harding was a woman and impossible not to like. Her specialty was burns, and the compassion in her eyes created its own kind of beauty. Justin never took credit for a damn thing, but Winona'd heard through the grapevine that he'd stolen Dr. Harding from Boston because of her innovative work with burn patients.

Winona hesitated at the far end of the hall, wary of coming closer and intruding. Because the town rehashed every ounce of news related to the plane crash every morning at the Royal Diner, she basically knew what had happened to Lady Helena. Helena had suffered burns as well as a severely broken ankle in the crash. Justin had been a consult on her medical team from the get-go, even though she wasn't in his direct hands yet. The break had to be healed and so did the burns, before he could do plastic surgery for the scars. Winona remembered exactly how beautiful Lady Helena was, how graceful and elegant she'd come across to everyone at the Texas Cattleman's Club gala. Now, her voice inside the hospital room was pale and groggy and frightened.

"When can I go home?"

"I'm afraid you're stuck with us for a while. Weeks yet.

But I promise, we'll do our best to keep you entertained,'' Dr. Harding teased gently.

"I'll have use of my hand? My leg again?"

The two doctors in the hallway exchanged glances. "We believe so, Helena." And then they walked out, down the hall in the other direction, leaving Justin alone with Lady Helena.

"Doctor Webb, what am I going to look like? Please tell me the truth. No one else seems willing to answer a direct question. I can't deal with the truth if I don't know what it is. How bad are the scars going to be?"

Right then, Winona almost spun around and took off. She completely changed her mind about talking to Justin. It would wait. It was just selfishness, her wanting to see him, to be with him. And it was now obvious that he'd had a harrowing night and was having an even tougher day—Lady Helena's careful, softly voiced questions could darn well break any woman's heart—and Winona just couldn't imagine bugging him right now.

Still, she lingered, just for a few more moments. Not to bug him. Not even to wait for him. But even though she couldn't make out his specific words to Helena, she could hear him talking, the cadence of his voice like the refrain of an old love song, gentle, familiar, soothing. And then he was striding out, his head bent as he stuck a pen in his white hospital coat, the smile for his patient still plastered on his face…but that smile disappeared the instant he moved out of Helena's sight.

He clearly believed that he was alone in the hall for that second. Winona could see those proud shoulders of his sag, the starch go out of his posture. His good-looking face was darn near chalk-white from exhaustion.

There was no way she was walking away from him.

"Justin?"

Even before his head whipped around at the sound of her voice, he had his normal expression back in place. His spine

automatically straightened; his mouth tipped in that Sam Elliot, lazy, almost-smile; the virile vitality clipped back in his
step. And those gorgeous eyes looking her over were—naturally—opaque as far as revealing any of his own feelings.

"Sheesh, Win. You prowling the bad neighborhoods
again, looking for trouble?"

That was the whole problem with his teasing. She either
wanted to smack him—or kiss him. The bottom line, as she
was coming to realize, was that no matter what, she had
always been tempted to touch him. How could she have
failed to notice that for so long? "You had to know I'd track
you down, after what you did," she said severely.

"What, what? I didn't do anything."

"Don't try that innocent routine on me, Doc. You're in
trouble—and most people know better than to get in trouble
with a cop. It's time to face the music. Exactly what do you
still have to do this afternoon?"

"Well, I'm done with patients for the day, but I think I
was supposed to meet with some insurance woman this afternoon. And I've got a good two hours of paperwork." He
shot her a wayward grin. "I can cancel that stuff. I'd rather
get in trouble with you any old time. But I have to admit,
Win, I can't promise to be any kind of great company. I'm
a little on the tired side."

A little? That wayward grin couldn't fool her in a month
of Sundays. The more she studied him, the more she realized
that he'd be lucky to drive himself home without falling
asleep at the wheel. "Well, I promise, I only want a few
minutes of your time—"

He frowned abruptly, as if suddenly remembering some
terribly serious thing. "Actually, I need to talk to you. Serious talk. In fact, I wanted to call you much earlier, but stuff
kept happening at the hospital and I just couldn't get free to
make the call. I'm glad we ran into each other—"

Winona was afraid it was weddings he wanted to talk
about. That wasn't going to happen. Now that she realized

how completely wasted he was, his fate was sealed as far as how this encounter was going to go. "Okay, I'll tell you what. Let's swing by your house. Grab a sandwich. We can talk while you're eating and then I'll hightail it home."

His eyebrows raised. "That plan works great for me, but it doesn't seem very convenient for you. Since when do you want to go to my place?"

Since never. She'd been there; she knew where he lived, but she'd never felt comfortable alone with him in his house. It wasn't a matter of not trusting Justin—in any way—but of always feeling edgy with the feelings he stirred in her. But right now none of that mattered. The only issue was getting Justin fed, comfortable, and asleep, which she figured would be a lot easier to manipulate on his own turf.

She followed his Porsche, which gave her a chance to use her cell phone to call Myrt. "How late can you stay?"

"I told you, I told you. All night, if you need me to. Any time."

"Well…how's Angel?"

"Just like her namesake."

"Being good?"

"Happy as a clam."

Winona's worry nerves detangled. "Well, the thing is, I just caught up with Justin and he's really whipped. What I'd like to do is take him home and make sure he gets some rest, but I know he won't go along if I tell him that plan. I can't believe I'm going to be at his place for very long, but I just can't give you an exact time when I'll be home."

"So this is easy. I know where you are, I'll call you if I need you. Otherwise, take the evening off, mom. Go play. If you're not back by the time I get tired, I'll just bunk down in the spare bedroom and leave the door cracked so I can hear the baby. Now, do you have a key?"

Winona blinked at the phone. Even her foster mothers had never asked if she'd had a key. Myrt was like having an honorary mother—whether she wanted one or not.

But her humor suffered a fadeout when she pulled up behind Justin in his drive. Her house was only a couple miles
from here, but it might as well be another universe. His place
was white stucco with a Spanish red-tile roof, two stories tall
with pillars framing the front door. A covered patio stepped
down in layers to water gardens. Her yard had a clothesline.
His had a marble fountain and a jetted pool.

When he unlocked the door, he ushered her in first. Possibly it was the sudden silence that made her so oddly nervous. She scuffed off her jacket, pushed off her shoes, tried
to brazen past her nerves with some normal conversation.
"It's been a while since I've been here. In fact, I don't think
I've ever been upstairs—how many rooms up there?"

"Four bedrooms and three baths, I think—but I can't
swear to that," he said wryly. "I haven't been up there myself since I can remember."

She shot him a bemused smile. "And that's another question I never got around to asking you before—why on earth
did you buy such a big house?" The downstairs alone was
a maze of room choices. Past the dining and living areas were
a den and office, a sunroom and game room, and somewhere
on the first floor was the master bedroom as well.

"Beats me. At the time, it seemed to make sense. I wanted
a house in town, close to the hospital and my office. But I
didn't want a place in the same neighborhood as my parents—I love 'em, but that'd be too close. And as much as
I'm crazy about my grandparents' ranch, I couldn't see living
in the country. It's just too far from my work."

"But you didn't need anything this monster size!"

"Well, I know. But Myrt and the gardener both came with
this place. And the closed staircase made it easy to shut off
the upstairs, so I have all that extra space for company, but
it doesn't get dirty or messed up if I just stay out of it. I
really do like the room, though. And that brothers and sisters
and family can pile in here over the holidays."

She took a breath, but Hell's bells…there was no way to

get a question answered if you didn't ask it. "Were you thinking about a house big enough for a family when you bought it?"

His head shot up. For a moment, she forgot how tired he was. The look of awareness kindling in his eyes seemed as electric and wide-awake as a charge of lightning. "If you're asking if I can imagine you and our kids living here—yes, I can. And yes, I have been. Although imagining you and I practicing how to make those kids is mostly what's been on my mind."

She was a cop. Too old and too life-smart to blush, but blast the man if she didn't feel warmth surging up her cheeks. No matter how close they'd become—no matter that there was a marriage proposal between them. She still couldn't seem to believe that he wanted her. Or that she hadn't realized how much fire had been simmering between them for so many years without her knowing. "Justin, I wasn't asking about us—"

He grinned, but he also quit teasing. "Yeah, I know, you were asking me why I bought the house. But the truth is…I don't know, Win. At the time, I just liked the place. It wasn't that practical a decision. I fell for the two fireplaces and the unbeatable pool table in the game room. And the two trees in here."

There were. The two fringey trees in his great room stretched at least ten feet tall. He flipped on switches as they walked through. Recessed lighting immediately softened the darkness, illuminating the picture windows and vaulted ceiling, the hardwood floor, the giant furniture—couches, chairs, cushions—all upholstered in a thick, white cotton duck. Most of the color in the room came from true-life greens—not just the trees, but also bushy plants in tubs.

Her gaze swept from the plants and white furniture to the occasional splashes of contemporary art on the walls. "Did you choose all this yourself?"

"Are you kidding? Mostly the house came this way. All

I had to do was water the plants and pick out some stuff for the walls.''

"Men," she murmured dryly.

"Hey." Still headed for the kitchen, he pushed on more switches. A gas fire suddenly sizzled in the great-room hearth, adding warmth and light. They passed a hall table heaped with mail. A door opening onto his office. The downstairs bathroom looked more like a sitting room for a sultan than a practical john. She only caught a fast glimpse of the lapis lazuli tile, the square tub with whirlpool, the blanket-size towels in cobalt.

"I've got that color blue, too, but somehow it doesn't look quite the same at my budget level."

"I keep telling you to marry me, don't I? Then you could get your hands on all my money. Doesn't that sound good?"

Getting her hands on him sounded good. Too good. Particularly for a woman who had never considered herself sex-obsessed before—but just then she had other priorities. Justin was barely walking straight. He was weaving-tired, groggy-voiced tired, his teasing even sounding slurred.

When they passed by the game room—right before the kitchen—she flipped on the light switch herself, because she strongly suspected they'd end up in there. It was so obviously Justin's nest. Between floor-to-ceiling windows were floor-to-ceiling bookcases, all crammed to the gills with dog-eared volumes. The pool table sat in the room's center, and the hearth in here wasn't gas, but had real wood stashed in bins by the side. The old Oriental rug under the table was as thick as a sponge, and the far couch was red leather, a dark cranberry, as warm as the lantern lamps on the mantel top.

The look of that room lingered in her mind as she walked into the kitchen. Without giving Justin a chance to start talking, she promptly pushed her sleeves up and put her hands on her hips. "Okay, you, it's your lucky day. While you get a chance to shower and put your feet up, I'm volunteering to cook. I'll make anything you want—as long as it's no tougher than melted cheese sandwiches and potato chips. No, no, don't thank me. I realize you're used to Myrt making you riff-raff gourmet stuff, but out of the goodness of my heart, I'll even add Oreos for dessert—''

''Um, could I change my mind about loaning you Myrt and get her back?''

''No.'' She used the royal pointing figure to motion him toward his bedroom and bath. She didn't want Myrt touching the conversation. Or even teasing hints about marriage. Not until the damn man had some food and rest. For Pete's sake, he had bags under his eyes bigger than boats. ''Go. Get cleaned up.''

''Did I know you were this domineering and abusive before?'' he asked plaintively—but he obeyed and left, even if she did hear him chuckling all the way down the hall.

She prowled his kitchen for the ingredients for their make-shift dinner. By the time he emerged from the shower, rubbing a towel in his hair, barefoot, wearing clean jeans and a loose, long-sleeved T-shirt, she had a tray of food set up in the game room. A small fire hissed and snapped in the stone hearth. She'd lit the lanterns on the mantel, and the glow shone on the cheese-and-bacon sandwiches and chips.

''Hell. This is almost as good as fast food. Myrt's always making me eat nutritional kind of stuff.''

''I had a feeling that you really suffered regularly with her cooking.''

''She bosses me around worse than…'' he yawned as he plopped down on the leather couch, ''…my mom.'' He glanced at her with an owlish expression. ''Man, I'm sorry, Win. I should probably make some coffee. I know I'm lousy company.''

''Forget the coffee,'' she said gently, thinking that if he made a move toward caffeine, she just might have to sit on him. ''Just eat a little, okay? Then lean back. Watch the fire for a while. It won't kill you to take ten, will it?''

"No, but I have to talk to you. About something important. Really important."

She figured this talk was about marriage—and really, she agreed. It was time they settled that wild proposal of his. He deserved an answer. And tonight was one of the first times in a blue moon she'd had him alone to talk privately—but not right then. Darn it, he was beyond exhausted.

He wolfed down two sandwiches and a glass of iced herbal tea, leaned back with a sigh, and just like that, he was out. His eyes closed, and he dropped off faster than a worn-out baby.

With a quiet triumphant chuckle, she scooped up their few dishes, took care of those, then tiptoed back to the game room. She spotted a throw on a chairback, and gently tucked it around him, then curled up in the red leather chair at his side.

She had no intention of staying more than a few more minutes. Even if Myrt was all settled to take care of Angel, she wanted to get home, get back to the baby. But first she wanted to make sure that Justin was sound asleep, and that there was someone to field the phone or any other noises that could interrupt him for a while.

In a half hour, max, she was leaving.

For sure.

She woke up feeling disoriented. For a few moments she couldn't fathom where she was or how she'd come to be here, but gradually the details came into focus. She saw the yellow fire still sizzling in the hearth, recognized the rich Oriental carpet and the fancy pool table, finally realized that, of course, she was at Justin's...but then she felt it.

His gaze. On her face. Justin was sitting up, wide-awake but as silent and still as a secret, his dark, soft eyes on her face as if glued there.

She suffered through it again. That feeling. That feeling she never got with anyone else...of wanting to let go, of wanting to be abandoned. Not the dread-sick sensation of being deserted and alone, but the other meaning of abandoned, the kind that was a choice—a fierce desire to abandon everything familiar and safe and just feel. Him. From her toes to her chin. From deep in her belly. To explore and discover everything she might be with him if the lights were off—under the sheets.

Her throat was suddenly arid, her pulse suddenly pounding. Swiftly she tried to say something normal. "Hey, Doc. I take it we both fell asleep?"

"Uh-huh. You set me up, didn't you?" he accused her. "That's why you volunteered to come here. Because you knew I'd fall asleep the first chance I had to sit down."

"Yeah, I did set you up. But I'd heard you were up all night with that boy in the car accident. It wasn't going to kill you to be taken care of for a change."

"Yeah, well, two can play that manipulative game. I called Myrt earlier so she'd know where you were, said you'd fallen asleep. She said she already knew where you were, and the baby's fine and to stay put."

"What time is it?"

"A few minutes after two. Are you awake enough to talk about something serious?"

"Um…give me a five-minute time-out, okay?" She high-tailed it out of the room, washed her hands, brushed her hair, slapped on lipstick, and came back with two mugs of instant coffee. "Now I'm ready," she said, but as she sat back down, she felt stiff with worry. What she wanted to do as far as Justin's marriage proposal, and what she thought they should do were two different things. While she was trying to marshal her thoughts into something tactful and coherent, though, he started talking.

"Win…I need to tell you about some jewels."

"Jewels?" She asked blankly.

"Yes. You know the old town legend? How back in the War with Mexico, one of our Texas boys, Ernest Langley, came across a wounded soldier and tried to save him. The man died, but our Ernest found three jewels on the old guy, brought them home to Royal, planned to live high on them—but the way life worked out, he didn't have to, because oil was discovered on his land. So he quietly donated the jewels to the old mission to secure the future of the town. Basically that was how the Texas Cattleman's Club came to be. The original founder, Tex Langley, grandson of Ernest, brought a group of men together who were charged with protecting the jewels, using them to keep the town prosperous and for the town's greater good through the generations. They built the Club right next to the old mission.''

"Um, Justin? I was raised on that legend. Everyone in Royal knows it. Except for the part about the Texas Cattleman's Club, anyway." She was wide-awake now, but of all the things she was tensed up to discuss with him, old legends weren't remotely on the list.

"Just bear with me, okay? Those three jewels were an emerald, an opal and a diamond. Only, each of them were extraordinary jewels of their kind. The opal was a black harlequin, of a size and color that made it especially rare. It was an old tradition for judges to wear amulets of opal, because the stone was said to give the wearer the power of justice and healing.''

"Um, Justin—"

"The emerald was a particularly big sucker, and through history, emeralds were considered the stone of peacemakers. Those first two gems were priceless to a collector, because they were so unusual in themselves, but the third stone was a red diamond. You see one, you'll likely never see another, because they're that rare, that precious. And red diamonds, of course, were symbolically the stones of kings, likely because only the most powerful men could possibly own them. So that's how we chose the sign for our Texas Cattleman's Club—Justice, Leadership and Peace. Because of those stones.''

"Uh-huh. Justin—" she started impatiently.

"They were stolen."

"Ju— *What?*"

"The stones—the ones in the legend—were always real. So was the legend. It all happened. It was never just a story, it was always the truth. The soldier dying, our Texas boy finding the jewels, his grandson deciding to use them to secure the future of the town by forming the Texas Cattleman's Club. And over the years, the group has slowly, quietly taken on other kinds of protectorate roles. I'd like to think that there's always someone willing to stand up to protect the innocent. To step in when no one else wants to—or when there is no one else—to help someone who needs it."

Winona weakly waved a hand. "How about if you let me catch my breath for a second and a half? You just gave me a lot to take in. This is all related to where you disappear to sometimes, isn't it? The times you've let everyone think you're some kind of playboy doc, taking a spur-of-the-moment luxury cruise with your latest woman—"

"Nah. I don't do cruises. Every once in a while, maybe I do something for the group. But back to the theft of the jewels—"

"Yes. For God's sake. Let's go back to the theft—"

He hunched forward, looking serious again. "Someone on the flight to Asterland stole the jewels. We didn't know they were gone until four of our Club members went to examine the plane a few days ago. There was a reason we were included in the investigation. The Texas Cattleman's Club was involved in helping Princess Anna, had a leading role in getting those two countries talking again, so we were more familiar with their diplomatic problems and the personalities than any other outsiders—"

"Yes, that's why you had the whole party a few weeks ago."

Justin nodded. "And so far, no one has uncovered an explanation for the plane's mechanical problems—whether the problems were accidental or sabotage. Because there's been so much friction between the countries, obviously sabotage was, and is, a serious concern. The point, though, is that when we started searching for evidence on the plane, instead of finding clues to the mechanical problems—by complete accident, we found two of our jewels. The opal and the emerald.''

"My God." Her head was starting to reel from the implications of everything he was telling her.

Justin nodded again. "But we didn't find the red diamond. It's still missing. When the men went back to the Club—to the safe where the jewels were kept—we found the safe wide-open and Riley Monroe dead. Murdered. Apparently by the jewel thief.''

"Holy kamoly. I don't understand—"

"Neither do we, Win. That's why I'm telling you all this. The situation has gotten more touchy by the day. The group mutually determined that we need someone on the police force that we could absolutely trust...and naturally, you're it. As soon as I said your name, the others clicked with it." He scalped a hand through his hair. "I realize you're not directly part of the investigation related to Monroe's murder, but that's not the point.''

Winona stopped trying to talk. She was just listening. Hard.

"The complications just keep coming. For one thing, the last thing we want to do is publicly accuse anyone from Asterland or Obersbourg of stealing the jewels. Now that those two countries have finally achieved an uneasy peace, we don't want to fire up tempers again, or risk an international incident. But that means that the investigation into the jewel theft—and Riley Monroe's murder—needs to be done quietly. And tougher than that..." Justin stood up with an impatient sigh and rolled his shoulders.

"...tougher than that...is that the Texas Cattleman's Club has kept the jewels a secret for generations now. For a good cause. We were able to keep our little expeditions and missions quiet, for the same reason. If we blow our cover, we blow our ability to help people—at least in the private ways we've been able to do in the past. If the truth about the jewels has to come out, then that's the way it is. But we'd rather it didn't get out. It would be different if we were just positive there was a connection between the plane crash and Riley's murder and the jewel theft. We're not. We don't know that. We don't know *anything* for sure. Not right now."

Finally she could see where he was leading. "Okay. You're obviously telling me this for a reason. What do you need me to do?"

In the intimacy of firelight, his gaze seemed to glow and soften on her face. "Win...I don't like putting you on the spot. But until we sort this out, we need someone we can trust inside the police force. Someone who can help us evaluate what facts go where, help us keep things quiet that don't have to be public. Someone, for that matter, who can brainstorm with us over the clues we've got going...I don't mean that the police chief would be unaware of what we're asking you. But he's not our man, because there'd be nothing but a conflict of interest problem for him. We need someone else. Someone who's judgment we trust. Whose integrity we trust. We need the kind of person who everyone felt we could be comfortably and completely honest with—"

"Justin—?"

"What?"

She surged to her feet.

Eight

Winona wanted to wildly shake her head, as if to make absolutely positive that she'd heard him correctly. "You trust *me?*"

Justin had been pacing back and forth in front of the hearth, but now he stopped still, his brow furrowing. "Of course I trust you. What kind of question is that?" He hesitated. "The only worry I have is about putting you on the spot, Win. It's not fair. There's no reason you should feel obligated to help the Texas Cattleman's Club. This is their problem. My problem. I'm the one who brought your name up, and I should have been thinking about how this could affect you. At the time, the only issue on my mind was coming up with someone whose integrity and judgment I didn't question—and that's how all the guys felt, too. You just seemed the perfect one for us to ask. Everyone said the same thing. We all trust you, we all knew we could be comfortable and honest with…"

He abruptly stopped talking as if distracted by her sudden,

swift charging across the room toward him. Maybe she was just stumbling across the Oriental carpet, but she felt as if she were flying. As if her heart had taken flight and had the power to soar. Toward him.

There seemed to be a lump in her throat the size of…well, the size of wonder. Most of her life, she'd been careful not to react to anything impulsively. It's not as if she could ever completely forget that she'd been a throwaway kid, an abandoned child. She'd always felt that she had to carefully earn other people's regard.

And she had. Winona had long learned to value herself. She knew she was an especially good cop and did a great job with the kids. She knew that she was respected, well liked in the community—and that she'd earned respect. But she hadn't specifically realized that she had Justin's trust and regard in that way.

Someone who she valued.

Someone who she loved—even if she'd been scared witless of allowing that four-letter word to surface in her heart before now.

It mattered. It mattered like she couldn't remember anything, ever, mattering this much before. And when she launched herself into Justin's arms, he responded with a *whoomph*. Possibly he wasn't anticipating a rib-crunching hug at that instant. Possibly he wasn't expecting a hard-ball pitch of a human female from across the room. Possibly he wasn't prepared for the trembling, hard smash of her lips against his.

But it couldn't have taken him three seconds—maybe less—to figure it all out. Before she'd realized how impulsively she'd reacted, his arms had balanced her—against him—and they were both glued in a lip-lock. The fire shimmered. Shadows whispered on the walls. The night seemed to surround them in a special, private silence.

He kissed her, then kissed her again and again, as if years had gone by since the last time. As if he'd only barely sur-

vived since those last kisses. As if the taste of her were all
he needed to sustain life.

But it wasn't all she needed. Before, she'd thought it was
a fluke, the incomprehensible wildness she felt with Justin.
The letting-go. The freeing. The need trammeling up and
down her nerves like a clattering train, gaining momentum
with every motion. Her hands touched, scraped, caressed,
clenched. She tilted her head, taking in his last kiss, then
leaned into him to give one of her own.

She had been wearing jeans and a chambray shirt, but not
for long. She pushed at his long T-shirt in a frenzy, seeking
skin, more playground to explore and touch. After his shirt
skimmed over his head, Justin seemed to be slower than molasses, as he unbuttoned her blouse, one button at a time, his
lips tracking the path from the hollow of her throat to the
crest above her breasts, down to the shadow between. And
then his hands were inside, his big warm fingers splayed to
caress the span of her waist as he pushed the shirt out of his
way. His mouth ducked again, this time to the rim of her
bra.

Her breath sucked in, like a lost wave, her lungs scrabbling
for oxygen that couldn't seem to be found. She saw his eyes
opening, then closing, his face aiming toward her for another
kiss, this time on her lips again, this time taking her tongue
and her teeth in a kiss that started out sweet and ended up
wicked.

By the time he'd pushed the shirt off her shoulders, he'd
kissed her shoulders awake as if they were erogenous zones
in themselves, and then her shirt snagged at the wrists because of the tight wrist buttons. He smiled—clearly liking
that her hands were trapped. Within a millisecond he'd found
the catch for her bra, and her breasts tumbled into his hands,
her heartbeat tumbling just as fast, just as much in his power,
and he took advantage by bending down and skimming her
tight, vulnerable nipple with the edge of his teeth.

She'd invited this explosion. She wanted it. But when he

surged back up for another wicked kiss—the bad kind, the scary kind, the kind that took her tongue and her breath and tasted all her secrets—she was quivering like a leaf in a wild spring storm. Justin sensed it, lifted his head, studied her face with liquid dark eyes.

"There's nothing we're ever doing, Win, that you don't want."

"I want this. I want you."

But now he hesitated as if he meant it. "I need you to be sure you want this. Yeah, I'll stop if you say, but I'm really, really gonna be unhappy if we go any further and you *don't* want this. It's all right. Whatever you want is all right, but I don't think you came here believing we were going to do anything like this."

"Maybe I didn't expect it. But I know exactly what I want. And it's you." He didn't get it. Didn't get how much his trust meant to her; his respect. How much something he'd so freely given her, without even having to think, had turned an emotional corner in her heart that simply would never turn back again. She framed his face, kissed him again, this time softer, this time with the "please" buried inside it.

"Well, that's it," he said hoarsely. "You're in trouble now."

"Oh? Is that a promise or a warning?"

"A promise," he said thickly. He pulled off the rest of her shirt. "And I always keep my promises, Win."

A thrill whispered up her spine, an excitement that both embarrassed and unnerved her. The thing was, she believed him. And suddenly she wasn't so sure of the situation or him—or of herself. He left the lights on, the wood fire blazing, but he was suddenly kissing her in a way that made her walk backward, propelling her out into the dark hall.

"Where are we going?"

"I think making love with you by the fire'd be outstanding—another time. On the pool table might be another terrific idea. Another time. But the first time, I want you on a big, hard mattress.''

"Um…''

"Cat got your tongue, Winona?''

He was unnerving her, and he knew it. Liked it. She wasn't afraid of anything. Never had been. She'd faced down strung-out kids and brutalizing adults and even, as a child, stood up every time she was afraid—partly because there'd never been any other choice; she'd only had herself to depend on and she'd learned courage from doing just that. But somehow, right then, she was afraid of him.

Not that he'd hurt her.

Never that.

This fear was a curious thing, elemental, sharp. Thrills and adrenaline kept scissoring up her nerves, electrifying her hormones, charging heat through her whole body. She wanted to dive off this cliff. She wanted to soar without a parachute. She wanted this high-speed chase.

She wanted him.

She was just scared. Of something she couldn't name, wasn't sure of. But when she kissed him, the fear ebbed back. And when she kissed him hard, mindlessly, putting her whole self into it, the fear became something so much fun that she never wanted it to go away.

Her shoulder grazed the stucco wall in the hall. Then a doorjamb. There was no way to recognize anything in his bedroom—not just because she'd never been in there, but because he didn't seem to remember to turn on a light. She had a sense of a long narrow room, lots of space, a chill from a window cracked open. She caught scents—sandalwood and leather. She caught sights because of certain objects shining in the darkness—his metal four-poster bed, a mirror over the bureau reflecting the star-spangled night, his shadow and hers moving past it.

The room was part of him. His. But the textures spinning spells around her were his whiskery cheek, his smooth naked shoulders, the liquid heat pouring off his skin, the silk of his mouth and more of those deep, dark, wicked kisses.

He opened a bedside drawer in the dark, took something out, slammed the drawer. "I'd love your babies, Win. I'd love to make half a dozen with you. But this night, I don't want anyone in this bed—any thought on your mind—but how much trouble you're in. And what I want to do to you."

"What *do* you want to do to me?" she asked weakly.

"Love you. Like I've wanted to love you for a long, long time."

She felt a keening inside. A caving in. Maybe he didn't mean it. A grown-up woman should know better than to believe a man's words of passion…but she did believe him. She felt the truth in his eyes, felt the emotion in his touch and his voice. And that was the last coherent thought she had.

The rest of their clothes peeled off, pushed off. Jeans, socks. Cold air rushed on her bare skin, raising gooseflesh, but then his tongue and mouth covered that gooseflesh, searing kisses everywhere, anywhere. Her elbow, her ribs, the insides of her thighs…oh my, no one had ever kissed the insides of her thighs.

It was payback time. She rolled on top of him, letting him know who was in charge now. In response, she heard his throaty laughter in the darkness, more whispered love words, the hint of more wicked promises glinting in those eyes. He was delighted with her. That's what he'd have her believe. That he cherished, exulted in her letting loose and losing control.

Her being abandoned.

With him.

Finally they were both completely naked. He pulled her hands over her head, stretching them, so that the feeling of length to length was exquisitely intimate, breast to chest, belly to belly, her pelvis rocking against his aching hardness. The thrill wasn't so much fun now. Need started biting at her heels, want gnawing at the lonesome, empty place inside her. "Justin. Come to me," she said urgently.

"I don't want you to forget this."

"I couldn't forget this in a hundred million years."

"I don't want you to wake up tomorrow and think, aw hell, I'm not sure this was such a good idea."

"There's no way I'll regret this. I promise."

"I want this right for you, Winona. I mean it. We can make it right. The two of us—we can make anything right. I know you're not used to the idea of us being together—"

Holy horsefeathers…and they said women talked. She swiveled around and then bent down, thinking that words alone seemed to be completely failing to communicate to him, so she simply had to try another way. She stroked him, then cupped, then leaned even closer. Her caress was tentative because she knew perfectly well this wasn't her personal preference and she wasn't comfortable with it. She understood men liked it; it just wasn't the sort of thing that personally sizzled her toenails. But with Justin…

With Justin, none of the old rules seemed to apply. Different things were true with him, because she didn't seem to be herself. This wasn't just about herself. It was about love. And giving. And the more she tasted, and stroked, and learned him, the more inspired she became by his body's intense and volatile response to her. She heard him groan. Then she heard him growl. She gestured with a hand, trying to say, this was her party and she'd do what she wanted to…but, of course, it was dark, and he likely couldn't see the gesture.

When she failed to respond to his verbal entreaties, though, she suddenly found herself lifted in midair and smooshed into that nice, big, hard mattress again. She vaguely remembered thinking the room was cool before. Now she wondered if his furnace wasn't disastrously malfunctioning. Heaven knew there was a blazing conflagration in his eyes.

"Did you want this over before we even got started?" he demanded.

"Well, no. But I was having a good time. And since I'm the guest, I think you should do the polite thing and let me do what I want."

"How about if I let you do what you want for the next ten years, but I get my way tonight?"

"Hmm. Well, on the surface, that sounds like a pretty good deal…but the more I'm with you, Justin, the more I'm getting the impression that possibly I could get my way all the time."

"Oh, all right," he agreed. And kissed her. Then took her. She couldn't have been more ready for him, yet she was still snug, the fit still tight, and he speared slowly inside that soft, private nest, easing in until his shaft was completely inside her. Colors of sensation washed behind her closed eyes. Sparks of fire seemed to ignite along her nerve endings.

"Justin…" The teasing was gone from her voice. Her belly was filled with him now, yet only ached more fiercely, seeking completion.

As he did. He began a rocking cadence that shook the bed, the room, her universe…whether she rode him or he rode her, Winona could neither keep straight nor cared, but this was a galloping song, a rhythmic race as pagan and pure as exhilaration and joy. "I love you, Win. Love you," he whispered, and then tipped her over the edge into oblivion.

In the dark, afterward, it seemed hours before her lungs could remember that complicated task about inhaling and exhaling. She didn't want to breathe normally. She didn't feel normal. She hooked up on an elbow and just looked at her lover in the dark, savoring everything she saw. The lustrous dampness on his skin, so like hers. The dark satisfaction in his eyes, that had to be reflected in hers. His mouth, as swollen from her kisses as hers was from his.

He lay there, wasted, at least until he opened an eye and realized that she was wide-awake and studying him. She felt fingertips grazing her jaw. "Did I tell you how beautiful you are?"

"Yes, you did."

"Did I tell you how sexy?"

"Oh, yes. In fact, you went into a lot of detail."

"Did I tell you that you're the most fabulous lover and the most extraordinary woman in the universe?"

She bent down and kissed the very tip of his nose. "I'm not even going to answer that. But…if that offer to marry you is still open, Doc…my answer is yes."

She slipped into her house at 4:00 a.m., turning the key in the lock with the stealth of a burglar, carefully closing the door and then tiptoeing through the house until she reached the back bedroom/nursery. Angel was sleeping solid, her little rump in the air, wearing the yellow sleeper with feet. A rush of love hit Winona. She edged closer to the borrowed crib, careful not to make any noise, but just wanting to look and love.

"I missed you," she said in her heart. "I missed you so much. But, Angel, you're going to love Justin."

He really seemed to want the baby. After making love to her a second time, he'd talked for a long time. Both of them were grounded in reality. He understood that Angel's future was a hundred percent uncertain. There was no guarantee that Winona would be allowed to foster or adopt her. The search for the mother was still ongoing. Even if the birth mom never showed up, that still didn't mean that Win had first dibs on the baby. Being married would raise her odds, but that's all it would do.

Winona still wanted to wrap that conversation around her heart. Justin must have said it a half-dozen times. "This is between you and me. It's not about the baby." He'd really seemed to mean it. It was only the timing on the marriage that could help Win's chances with keeping Angel—the sooner she was married, the better. "So why not?" he'd asked her. "If you want a fancy wedding and honeymoon, we can make that happen. But if the baby's the first problem, then let's solve the most important thing for you."

"For me, the baby has to come first, Justin—because she's the one at risk, the one who's vulnerable. If I can make her situation more secure, I feel I have to do that."

"I feel the same way. She's an innocent in a precarious situation, and her needs can't wait."

He really did understand. Yet she'd soberly touched his cheek. "But you can't marry me for the baby's sake, Doc. It's nuts."

"I wouldn't marry anyone for a baby's sake. I agree with you. It's nuts. But just because it happens to be *helpful* for you to be married, why fight it? When it's something we both want and both believe is a good thing?"

"But you never wanted to marry me before."

"Win. You obviously don't know me at all. But you will," he said, and kissed her again.

Now, as she bent over the crib, that memory washed over her in a fresh, warm wave…including everything he'd done to her after that. "I'm crazy about him, Angel," she whispered aloud. "And he's coming over tomorrow. We'll see how you feel about him, too, okay?"

"So…" The soft soprano from the doorway had Myrt's acerbic tone. "You're finally home. Did you have a good time?"

Winona must have jumped five feet—a guilty five feet. She hustled toward the door and out into the hallway. "Myrt, I'm terribly sorry to be so late. I never meant to take advantage of you this way—"

"Lord, girl, I swear you just don't listen. I told you I was crazy about babies. And I offered to stay, how many times, a good dozen? Furthermore, it's not like I was really a stranger to you—you know how long I've worked for Justin, even if you and I never had much of a chance to get to know each other very well before now."

"I know, I know…but I just don't want you to think that—" she scrubbed a hand at the back of her neck, embarrassed "—that I…"

"That you slept with my boss? Well, I should probably say that's none of my business, not to worry—but it wouldn't be the truth. When Justin told me the situation with the baby, that you were working so hard and needed some help—I could see how he talked about you, how he looked. So, to be honest, I really wanted a chance at some matchmaking, at least a little bit—"

"He asked me to marry him," Winona confessed.

Myrt's smile beamed brighter than sunshine. "And that's wonderful, girl. But right now, I think you better catch some sleep while you can. We'll talk about schedules and babies a little later."

"Whatever you're having, I want a prescription for it." Later that afternoon, Dr. Harding happened to pass him in the corridor. Justin had been immersed in a conversation and was unaware how the sound of his laughter had echoed down the hallway until she chuckled, going by.

"She is right." Sheikh Ben Rassad—Ben—nodded with a wry half smile. "You are so buoyant today. So vital and full of spirit. It is good to see you wearing this contentment, Justin."

"Just happy today, I guess."

"Uh-huh. Woman happy, I am thinking." It wasn't like Ben to tease, but every once in a while, his sense of humor surfaced with friends.

Justin didn't confirm or deny his pal's guess, but he knew it was true. All day, he'd walked as if there was a sponge in his shoes and light in his eyes. A gruelingly long workday hadn't sogged down his mood even this late in the afternoon. It was as if Winona were with him, sitting in a place in his heart where she could make his pulse soar, just thinking of her.

Last night with her had been everything he'd dreamed of—and more. All these years, he'd never been sure that Winona would ever notice him, that he could win her, that the chemistry would ever fire for her the way he'd always felt it.

Now he knew better. They had enough chemistry to fuel a couple of planets. Big ones.

Damnation, if he wasn't daydreaming of having it all with her. Really. All. Love. A lifetime. The whole kit and kaboodle.

Temporarily, though, he had to concentrate on serious things. He sobered—as did Ben—when they reached Robert Klimt's hospital room. Both quietly entered.

Although Justin wasn't Klimt's physician, he'd been automatically stopping to check and evaluate Klimt's progress ever since the plane crash. The last time he'd seen him before that had been the night of the Texas Cattleman's Club gala. Justin couldn't say that he'd liked the little banty rooster, but it was still another thing to see the man so reduced. Silent. Helpless. He checked Klimt's pulse, touched his skin, automatically read and assessed all the tubes and machines connected to the patient.

"There is no guessing when he'll wake up from this coma?" Ben asked.

"Not really. His main doctor—Busher—is a good man. He also brought in some outside opinions, just to make absolutely sure he wasn't missing something." Because even an unconscious patient could sometimes hear and take in certain things, Justin was careful to voice his answer positively. "Let's just say that the sooner he wakes up, the more optimistic we're all going to feel. And I'm trying to think what else has happened that I need to fill you in on...."

"Well, mostly what I wanted to know was the status of the patients that were part of the plane crash and could have been witnesses, or known something. But in the meantime—is Aaron still in Washington?"

"Yes. I believe Walker finally reached him by telephone

yesterday, so Aaron at least knows about the jewel theft and
Riley Monroe's murder. I just wish he'd get home. No one
knows about diplomatic channels and problems the way
Aaron does. Obviously no one wants to run around accusing
or raising suspicion about anyone from Asterland if we can
help it. Relations with that country are precarious enough.
But the Asterlanders are naturally getting more and more
upset that we haven't found a cause for the plane crash.''

Ben stared at the silent Klimt and all the beating, bleeping
machines he was hooked up to. ''If he would just wake
up…maybe he saw something, knew something. The fire on
the plane started so close to where he and the lady Helena
were sitting. And two of the jewels were just as close. If
anyone knows anything, it *has* to be him.''

Justin nodded. ''All of us feel the same. We really have
no proof that the plane crash was related to the theft. To risk
an international incident for nothing gives us all the willies.
But I suspect that Asterland is going to send someone to
investigate on their own if our authorities don't start coming
up with answers soon.''

''I would do the same in their shoes.'' Ben shifted on his
feet. ''And in the meantime, we're still missing the red diamond. At least, we can eliminate one suspect from the list.
It's a cinch Klimt doesn't have it.''

''That's the only thing we're really sure of right now.''
Justin hesitated. ''What concerns me is that others could be
in danger. Whoever killed Monroe wasn't just a thief. He
was willing to murder. And if the killer was someone on that
plane, there are others who could be vulnerable—either because they saw something or knew something. Even if they
didn't realize it at the time.''

''You've talked with Lady Helena?''

''I've seen her every day. She's a trooper. But right now
I can't begin to guess if she saw anything. She has almost
no memory of the crash. I don't mean that she's suffering an
amnesiac condition, but that what she went through was ex-

tremely traumatic. What emotional and physical energy she has is entirely focused on her injuries and healing. And she still has months of recovery ahead of her. Maybe she could still remember something, but who knows when?''

Ben paused. ''Well, have you had a chance to talk to Winona?''

''Yes. Last night. She didn't even hesitate. She offered to do anything she could.''

''She understands why the Club wants this kept quiet? To protect the work we do?''

''Yeah. And she understands how ticklish it is, communicating between local authorities and feds and safety agencies and diplomats. It's not that she has power, but it's not power we're looking for, and for damn sure, we're not looking to impede anyone's investigation. Only to make sure the innocent are protected in this complicated mess. She'll help advise us.''

''I have always had the impression that she is a good woman. An unusually special woman.'' Ben studied his face with sudden intentness.

Swiftly Justin lifted a wrist to check his watch. ''It's after five. I have to go.''

''You're meeting her.''

''Yeah. And either you quit smiling at me or I'll have to slug you,'' Justin said wryly, as they both exited Klimt's room with a last glance at the Asterland cabinet member.

''I wasn't smiling at the serious situation.''

''God knows, neither was I.''

''But I admit I was smiling at you. One mention of her name, and you are—how do they say it?—bouncing off the walls. A sudden smile on your face that is close to blinding. Oh, how the mighty do fall.''

''Watch it, Sheikh. We have an expression in Texas. You're cruisin' for a bruisin'.''

''We have an expression like that in the Middle East, too. In fact, I think all countries have an expression like that.

We're meeting again on Tuesday night? To determine what to do with the two jewels, whatever new security measures we want and so on?''

"Yes."

"Okay. In the meantime, try to remember to eat. To sleep. To not sing in the rain. And to climb down from the clouds before you drive."

"I'm going to remember this conversation when you fall in love. And I'm never going to let you hear the end of it," Justin vowed darkly.

"Yeah, yeah." Ben smiled, but then he sobered. "Justin…you have not been happy since you came back from Bosnia. Always, there is this dark look at the back of your eyes, the silence. You work, the long hours, but it's like something is running after you, and you cannot catch it, see it, stop it. This woman…it is good to see you coming alive again. I am glad for you. I mean it."

Justin was smiling when he walked out to the parking lot. But when he climbed in his car and started the Porsche engine, a chill chased up his spine that had no relationship to the howling winter wind.

He couldn't wait to see Winona.

He couldn't have been happier with how last night had gone between them.

He hadn't thought about Bosnia in a long time now, nor had the chronic nightmares troubled him since Winona had become personally involved in his life. But now, suddenly, he felt itchy, edgy. Win was coming to care for him. Just maybe, the sky was the limit between the two of them. It was just that sometimes, he felt like Bosnia was a smudge of dirt on his face that refused to wash off. Nothing seemed to make those memories go away, not completely.

Forget it, he told himself swiftly. Think about her. Nothing else.

So he tried.

Nine

When Winona heard the knock, she swallowed hard, and then hustled to answer the door. It was just before six, so she knew it was Justin. All day she'd been higher than a kite, looking forward to seeing him again...and she still wanted to see him, but the circumstances had sure changed.

She yanked open the door, carrying Angel. The baby was dolled up to go out to dinner, wearing an ultracool pink jumper with an ultracool pink heart sweater and pink booties. She could have won over the heart of a stone; she was that adorable—if she hadn't been screaming at the top of her lungs.

"Darn it, Justin, I'm afraid—" Winona started to say.

"Eh?" He cupped a hand over his ear, as if he needed a megaphone to hear over the symphonic volume.

"I don't think we're going to be able to go out to dinner," she shrieked.

"Yeah, it does look like we'd better come up with plan

B.'' He stepped in, quickly shut the door on the draft and, as soon as he'd peeled off his jacket, waggled his fingers.

"Trust me, you don't want her," Winona assured him.

"Hey, she can cry just as good in my arms as yours, can't she? I take it we're not in a real good mood."

"She's not hungry, not tired, not sick, not anything, so PMS is my best guess. I just didn't expect it to hit before she was six months old."

"Now, don't be criticizing my second-best girl." He kissed Win first—on the tip of the nose—and then swooped the baby in his arms. Startled, Angel stopped the faucet for a second and looked him over. "I'm the handsomest guy you've seen all day, right, darlin'?"

Winona wanted another kiss. One significantly stronger and deeper and more romantic than that peck on the nose. But Angel seemed to be considering what she thought of the heartthrob with the Sam Elliot eyes in the doorway. Then she decided. First there was a heartrending sniff, and then another melodious bloodcurdling cry designed to alert all neighbors in a ten-mile radius that she was Not Happy.

"Okay," Justin said. "Get your coat and the baby's coat. We're bumping this pop stand."

"Justin, we can't take her anywhere like this."

"Well…I do think she's a little young to be blackmailing us into taking her to Disney World, but I'm almost sure we can come up with something that'll win a smile out of Her Highness."

There were circles under his eyes. There were circles under hers. Winona theorized that possibly the baby guessed what they'd been doing the night before, and wanted to make sure they never, ever, had an opportunity to do it again. But she simmered down for the ride in the car, and only let out an occasional squeal—as if to keep in practice—as Justin carried her into his house.

"I just figured it might work better at my house because I knew we didn't have to worry about dinner. Myrt made something, left it in the fridge. Corned beef, I think? I'm not sure, but I know it's something we could put together quickly. And in the meantime, there's a bunch of things I want to talk with you about.''

She wasn't sure how he managed it. Within five minutes, he'd taken her jacket, ordered her shoes off, poured her a glass of merlot, and was leading her through the house. His bossiness wasn't the surprise. It was all he was managing to do while holding Angel at the same time. And the baby had quit crying—as long as she was bouncing along in Justin's arms.

''Really, Win, it doesn't matter to me which house we choose to live in. If you want to stay at your place, that's fine. But I do have a ton of space here. And Myrt's already installed. Not that those details make this house so great—for one thing, as many bedrooms as there are upstairs, maybe they're too far from the master bedroom? We couldn't hear the baby if we set her in a bedroom upstairs? So then I was thinking, maybe this room would make a good nursery....''

He pushed open the door to his downstairs office, which was wainscoted in teak with a burgundy-striped wallpaper above. Background lighting illuminated his expensive computer setup. A couch overlooked glass doors and the view of the water-garden landscaping in his backyard.

''This is all too dark. I figured we'd throw all this junk—''

''Junk?''

''Stuff. All this stuff could go upstairs in one of the spare rooms. We could just rip out the wainscoting and dark wallpaper. Do baby colors—whatever baby colors are. There's a lot of room for a crib and rocker and all. And next door's a bathroom—although right now, that room's too dark, too. I mean, for right now, we could just make these two rooms work easily enough. It's not like Angel's crawling or walking yet. I can hire a couple of strong backs as soon as tomorrow to start moving the heavy furniture around.''

Once back in the kitchen, he tried to put Angel in her baby

carrier. She let out a prompt, furious squeal. He picked her up again.

He talked about safety gates and baby monitors. He talked about turning in his Porsche for a "grown-up car" that would more easily accommodate a baby car seat and groceries. When the telephone suddenly rang, he again tried to put down Angel. Again she squealed. Again he picked her back up again, and answered the phone call while carrying her around.

He found the bread, scooped the lettuce from the refrigerator, knifed on fancy mustard and made corned beef sandwiches on rye, holding Angel the whole time. He looked at the baby once, as if debating whether it was worth even trying to eat without her on his shoulder, and then just ate one-handed.

Before dinner was over, Winona was in love with him.

All right, all right, she'd realized that she'd fallen before this. But some of those earlier feelings were surely lust. And as extraordinarily powerful—and desired—as that lust was, this was a different kind of love. This was watching Royal's most eligible and supposedly most self-indulged and spoiled bachelor working heart and soul to charm a baby. This was watching a doc who'd put in a ten-hour day—after making love to her all night—never lose patience with a fractious little one. This was watching Justin be a father. This was seeing his patience and gentleness and giving nature without him having a clue how much he was revealing.

"Justin?"

"What?"

"You're making all those marriage and life plans so fast that you're scaring the life out of me. You've thought so many things through already, as if you were really that sure—"

"I am sure, Win. We're going to love being married. I just know it. The faster the better. If we don't get all the details resolved ahead, so what? We'll just do things as we go."

The baby blew a bubble in his face. That was it for Winona. "If you don't mind my changing the subject from marriage for just a minute. I just wanted to mention…if it's all right with you—the very minute Angel goes to sleep—I'm going to jump your bones."

Smooth as silk, Justin chucked the baby's chin. "Well, that's it. What do I have to bribe you with to get you to bed?"

Winona chuckled, but there was no hurrying Angel into doing anything. The baby had had a super day, but something just seemed to hit her wrong around the dinner hour, and she was nonstop fretful—unless Justin was holding or walking her.

"I have an idea," he announced finally.

"Ideas aren't helping us. We need a miracle," she said wryly.

But it seemed that Justin was capable of coming up with one of those, too. In the cobalt-and-marble bathroom downstairs, he started filling the whirlpool tub. While Winona stripped the baby down in the warm, moist air, he fetched candles from around the house, lit them and chose a CD to play a muted, low bluesy sax—achy, yearny love songs, one after the other.

"See how fast I managed to get your mom naked? And you thought I wasn't very bright, didn't you, Angel?"

It was a romantic setting for lovers, not for a baby's bath. The warm jetted water. The candle scents and quivering lights. The yearning love songs. The darkness and nakedness and Justin's dark, soft eyes looking at her from the far corner of the tub, his bare toes caressing her bare toes.

The baby chortled and giggled, either from the safety of Justin's arms, or hers. Angel seemed to think this party had been arranged just for her—which it had—and the little ham managed to keep both the adults chuckling…yet Winona kept looking at Justin. And yeah, she could feel the desire seeping

and building between them. But she also could see him relaxing, just as Angel was. Letting down his hair. Letting go.

Possibly because she'd always had such a hard time letting
go herself, she had always recognized how closely Justin held
his emotions. In his work, he gave freely. It wasn't as if he
were a stingy man with his heart. But what he personally
wanted and needed in his own life, he rarely showed the
world, including her…especially since he'd come back from
Bosnia.

Watching the baby try to grab his nose, hearing Justin's
gentle laughter, seeing his natural easiness with the darling,
Winona fell in love all over again. Deeply. Painfully. Irrevocably.

She rose from the tub abruptly.

"Did you see that view, Angel?" Justin teased. "Your
mom is trying to drive me crazy. And doing an outstanding
job of it."

"We can't stay here all night."

"*Why?* She's happy."

"Because she'll turn into a prune, you goose. But keep
her in here for a couple more minutes, okay? While I go heat
up a bottle and fix a place for her to sleep?"

Naturally she'd brought a diaper bag and a change of
clothes for the baby, but several hours before, it really hadn't
occurred to her that they might be spending the night. Now,
wrapped in a towel, she prowled the downstairs, spotting a
half-dozen places where she could set up a secure sleeping
arrangement for Angel, just trying to pick the best. She decided on the couch in Justin's office, where she could push
two chairs against the open couch edge to create a secure
barrier. Then there was the business of finding the equivalent
of a rubber sheet, and a real sheet, and blankets, and then
getting the bottle warmed.

By the time she slipped back in the bathroom, Ms. Prune
seemed to be out of the water and was on a thick, fat towel

next to the tub, chortling her head off while Justin tickled her.

"Sheesh. We were *trying* to settle her down," she scolded.

"She doesn't want to settle down. She likes being naked. You know who I think she takes after?"

"You. All day," Winona murmured.

"I was thinking about you. To think that you've been walking around my house that way all this time and there wasn't a damn thing I could do about it...it boggles the mind."

"Well, I admit, I'd been thinking about boggling something of yours, too, Doc. But it wasn't your mind."

She was up for flirting with Justin indefinitely...but for a second, words failed her. She caught it. The baby's first yawn. Faster than lightning, she whipped a fresh diaper and sleeper on Angel. And then there was another rosebud yawn when she settled the darling in her arms, those soft velvety eyelashes already drooping as Angel latched on to the nipple of the bottle.

She kept thinking sex and babies shouldn't go together.

She kept thinking that maybe she was nuts, because the candlelight and music hadn't turned her on nearly as much as watching Justin discover being a dad.

She kept thinking that they were teasing and flirting like an old married couple who were already comfortable with each other naked, who already knew the things to say to trigger desire.

And she fell quiet as she fed the baby. So quiet that Justin noticed. She felt his gaze on her face as she coaxed the last drops into Angel, who was all set to snuggle down and sleep deeply now—but Winona didn't want her trying to sleep for the night short on food. Finally, she lifted the little one to her shoulder—all dead weight and baby breath and smelling of powder—patting, rubbing, trying to get up that last nasty burp before putting her down...and still she felt Justin's gaze on her face.

"She's out. Really out this time," she whispered finally. "I made a bed for her in the den. I'll be right back."

Once Winona laid the baby down, though, she suddenly realized how long she'd been parading semi-naked in front of Justin. What had seemed natural before now seemed... different. It wasn't the same situation without the baby as a barrier. That had been like playing poker without ever having to ante...playing at being lovers without ever being alone.

Reality, though, was that they'd only been lovers one night...and Winona suddenly felt an attack of nerves. Technically, this was what they'd both wanted, to have the night to themselves, the baby finally asleep. Only she seemed to be suddenly standing in the hall outside the bathroom, clutched up like a ninny. Surely Justin was tired of the water by now? But would it be presumptuous to go into his bedroom? Should she be getting dressed? And then suddenly she heard his voice, as if he sensed her sudden uneasiness.

"Win? C'mere, you."

It was the lazy, easy sound of his voice that made her tiptoe back into the bathroom, and there he was, waiting for her in the tub with those sexy dark eyes. "Yeah, I know," he said gently. "We've been here a hundred hours already. And both of us need some just plain sleep, don't we?"

"Yes—"

"But how about if you just dip in here for one more minute. I'll give you a back rub."

She hurtled back into the tub with splashing speed, making Justin laugh.

"You're not just a little bit of a hedonist, are you?" he teased, but he wasn't teasing as he nestled her between his bent legs and started working his hands on her neck and shoulders. Her eyelashes drooped as if they weighed five pounds each and her head bobbed forward. She groaned and kept on groaning.

And he kept rubbing and caressing and molding any last

tension from her shoulders, but eventually she heard a different note in his voice. A quiet note. "What were you thinking, Win? When you were feeding the baby a few minutes ago, and you suddenly turned so serious?"

She'd been thinking that she finally believed him—that he really did want to marry her. It wasn't a dream. It was real. All his plan-making for the baby tonight was proof. The way he treated Angel was another kind of proof, that he had strong, tender feelings for the baby and was already taking joy in being a father. But it was the two of them where she kept feeling this rain of wonder. They'd known each other so long…but until Angel had so accidentally slipped into her life, she'd had no idea that Justin had feelings for her.

Now she wondered how he'd fooled her for so long.

And how she'd fooled herself.

She closed her eyes, struggling to offer him a kind of honesty that she never had done before. "I was thinking…well, I almost don't remember my mother. But I remember the morning when I woke up and she was gone. I was pretty young—but I knew I was alone. I remember feeling abandoned, feeling that there must be something terribly wrong with me that she'd left as if I were nothing. And as much as I've wanted a child, Justin, I think I was always afraid that I wouldn't be a good mother. That that fatal flaw in me would show up. The thing that made me unlovable. And I worried that I could do that to a child."

She watched his mouth work, as if he wanted to spill a dozen things to her. Instead he hesitated, and then he just listened. "And…?"

"And then I was watching you play with Angel. Be with her. The joy and fascination in your eyes."

"Well, hell. There's nothing surprising there. She could win a tear from a glass eye."

She smiled softly. "I think so, too. That's exactly how I feel with her. The joy. The fascination. No, I don't know what I'm doing. But this huge feeling of love wells up, this bond to her that just seems bigger than I am. And I know I can be a good mom. I just know."

"Aw, Win, I can't believe you doubted yourself this way."

"Well, I did. It's hard to explain, but I doubted…that I could let go. I was angry when I was a kid. I think I always believed under the surface that it had to be my fault—something wrong with me—that made my mom take off. And I was afraid that something-wrong-in-me could affect my being a parent."

"Winona. You'll be the best parent this side of the Atlantic. And this side of the Pacific, too. You already are. Hell. I didn't know you were worried about this…." He hesitated. "When you suddenly got so quiet, I thought maybe you'd found out something in the investigation of Angel's mother—and you just hadn't had a chance to tell me."

"I'm finding out things every day. But nothing that's helped me pin down where Angel came from, at least so far."

"Then…you're still worried about keeping her?"

"Yeah, I'm worried about that. Badly. And I'm going to keep worrying about that until we know for sure what's going to happen to her. I can't help it. Any more than I can help hoping that Angel ends up mine. Ours." She turned in his arms. "But that's not the reason I'm saying yes to you."

"Yes to…?"

"I never gave you a clear-cut answer, did I? I mean… you've been making marriage and living plans at the speed of sound. And I know we've come together. I know we've both used the *marriage* word. You especially. But I never came out before this and admitted that I'm in love with you, Doc. Really in love. Off the deep end in love—"

She never got a chance to finish the thought before his mouth latched on to hers. The whole evening, she'd been waiting for this. The whole evening, he'd been seducing her with candles and saxophones and his burping techniques and his blowing bubbles on the baby's tummy…and being in that tub, naked with him, because dark or not, he had to know darn well where her eyes were straying all this time.

She made a soft sound of longing, of want, that he sipped in during another slow, lazy, liquid kiss. His warm, slippery skin rubbed against her warm, slippery skin. His tummy rubbed her tummy. Breasts snugged against his chest, where his wiry dark chest hairs glistened and the orbs of his shoulders gleamed dark gold. His long, strong legs slid and rubbed against her slim, softer limbs. He was inside her before she could catch a breath, had her legs wrapped around his waist before she'd had time to consider whether this was even possible.

"We're going to drown," she feared.

"I already am drowning," he said, and dived for another kiss, taking her tongue. His hands splayed, clasping her fanny, melding the two of them even closer together. Inside, she felt that secret, hot pulsing between them. On the outside, there was nothing but that womb of water, the magic of him, the stars on the water surface caused from the candlelight, the stars in her eyes caused from the look in his.

"I have no protection," he remembered suddenly.

"Good," she said.

Again, his mouth tipped in a slow, intimate grin. "If you think I mind if we make a baby, Win, you must be out of yours. I hope we have half a dozen. And I'm warning you now, my plan for the rest of the evening is to love you 'til the cows come home."

"Good," she said again.

"It'll be two nights without sleep. We'll both be basket cases tomorrow."

"Good," she said again.

"If you think—"

Holy moly, how the man could talk. She framed his face with her hands to pull him closer. Then flexed her thighs to wrap him closer in that way. He didn't talk any more after that. Neither did she, although, tarnation, they made a horrible mess. Water splashed over the marble sides, onto the floor. Once they sank under and nearly drowned. He rolled with her on top, then maneuvered her right under the pulsing hot jets where the dark, silky water pulsed intimately on both of them, never separating from her for an instant, never losing rhythm, just spinning, spinning....

Spinning a magic spell, she thought helplessly, that she never wanted to wake up from. Somewhere that night, she lost all her inhibitions. The good ones. The important ones. The inhibitions that she'd cultivated so carefully her whole life because she was so absolutely sure that she needed them to survive. With him, everything was different. With him, she felt as abandoned as she'd ever imagined....

But in the most joyful of all ways.

"I love you, Winona Raye," he whispered, just as he hurled them both over the last crest and tipped them into ecstasy.

The next day, as Winona was driving to lunch with Angel propped in the car seat next to her, she suddenly laughed out loud. All morning, memories from the night before had been rolling through her mind, making her buoyant and smiley all over again...but this time, her sense of humor was sparked for another reason.

Last night, she'd finally said yes to him. In fact, Winona suddenly remembered how many times she'd given Justin an opening to set a specific marriage date. Only he hadn't.

For a man who'd been hustling her to the altar faster than the speed of light, it just struck her funny bone that he'd finally gotten what he wanted—and then forgotten to pin down the date.

Quickly Winona pulled into the one spare parking place in front of the Royal Diner, then scooped up Angel and all the baby paraphernalia it took to get the little one through a short lunch. "You know this place, now, don't you, darlin'? And today we're going to meet a friend."

The minute they walked in, she spotted Pamela Miles, sitting in one of the front booths. "Darn it, I didn't mean to be late, Pam. I hope I didn't keep you waiting—"

"Not at all. I've just been here a minute. And what do we have here?"

Winona smiled, watched Pamela make a fuss over Angel—who hammed up for the attention, kicking and bubble-blowing. "This is Angel, and she's the reason I asked to meet with you. But let's get lunch ordered, okay? I'm guessing that you don't have any more spare time than I do."

Sheila, cracking gum, brought her pad over to take their orders. "Hey, Pam, the bruises are starting to fade finally, huh? You look like you're doing way better, sweetie pie."

"I'm fine, except still having a little trouble getting an appetite."

Winona shot the second-grade teacher another, sharper, look. For a moment she'd forgotten that Pamela had hoped to be an exchange teacher in Asterland for the winter term, and had been traveling on the plane that crashed. "You really are feeling okay?" she asked.

"Fine. Honestly, compared to some of the others, I didn't go through anything. Just some bangs and bruises. Although I have to admit that I was really shook up for the first few days after the crash. It was quite an experience. I still can't seem to eat much."

"I take it that your plans to go over there and teach were put on hold?"

"Yes. I'd still love to, but it'll have to be another time. They couldn't hold the job and leave children without a teacher, obviously, and right after the crash, I wasn't sure how fast I could get there and be functioning. It just made the most sense for both sides for me to cancel out. So I've got a little unexpected time off. It won't kill me to relax until next term—but please, Winona, I don't want to waste your lunch hour on just catching up. I know you said you needed to talk to me seriously about something."

"Yes," Winona said, but then she hesitated. The two women knew each other through their respective jobs. Several times, Pamela had asked her to come in and talk to her second graders, and Winona had loved the opportunity. Before that, all Winona had ever heard was that Pamela's mother had quite an unfortunate reputation in town—which was always a complete surprise to anyone first meeting Pam. She was plain, inclined to wearing dowdy Peter Pan collars and demure, concealing styles. She wore her black hair short and simple, and never seemed to bother with much makeup. Her features lit up around children, though, showing off dimples and big blue eyes. She seemed to be a quiet, genuine person in a way that Winona had always liked. She just didn't quite know how to approach this subject, but she had to start somewhere.

"I'm guessing you've heard through the gossip grapevine about Angel. Someone abandoned her on my doorstep a couple weeks ago. I've been trying to track down the mother ever since."

"You bet, I heard. The whole town's charmed at you running around doing your cop thing with a baby in tow."

Winona nodded. "I know you work with the younger kids, rather than be exposed much to teenagers. But I'm really having trouble finding leads to Angel's mom. I don't know for sure that her mother was a teenager—but it has to be someone from town, because if she didn't know who I was, she'd have had no reason to leave the baby with a note to me specifically. So I was hoping—"

"You were hoping I'd know something?"

"Yeah. I figured it was a long shot to ask you—but all the standard routes I've tried have ended up dead ends. Everyone says that kids all ages just naturally talk to you. So I was hoping you might have heard something about a girl in trouble…."

"Well, darn. There is someone." Pamela tapped her fingers on the tabletop. "I'm trying to remember the woman's name. She was at the Texas Cattleman's Club party early this month—someone said she'd lost a baby before Christmas, but at the time, that struck me as odd. You know how it is in Royal. The whole town would have turned out for a funeral, anything to help someone going through a loss like that. Only there was no funeral—'' Pamela suddenly shook her head. ''This is nuts. I really don't know anything. That was just vague gossip I heard at the time, and to tell you the truth, I was only paying attention to one thing at that party—''

''Uh-huh.'' Because Angel started fussing, Winona picked up the baby and plugged in a bottle, although she shot a woman-to-woman grin at Pamela. ''I saw you dancing with Aaron Black, girl.''

Color bloomed on Pamela's cheeks. ''I felt like Cinderella at the ball—and believe me, I'm not into fairy tales. I'm not usually a party person, either. The only reason I went to that gathering was because I was planning on teaching in Asterland, and I thought I'd have a chance to meet more Asterlanders there…but I just don't belong in a group like that.''

Winona sensed the other woman's insecurity and pounced. ''Hey, what's that supposed to mean?''

''Come on. You know Aaron—he looks like a fairy-tale prince. Tall and sophisticated and good-looking…''

''Well, yeah, he's a nice-looking man.'' Winona knew Aaron. Everyone did. His diplomacy work took him overseas so much that he was rarely home except around the holidays, but she remembered seeing him at Justin's shindig. It was just, compared to Justin, no man seemed hot. Not anymore.

''Hmm. I saw you at that party, too, Winona. It's no wonder you didn't pay that much attention to Aaron. You only had your eyes on one guy yourself.''

''Huh? What are you talking about?''

''Come on. I saw you dancing with a bunch of guys. But you still only had eyes for Dr. Webb.''

Winona was so startled at Pamela's observation that she

accidentally dislodged the bottle from the baby's mouth. Was it possible, that others had noticed the chemistry between her and Justin before she'd realized it?

When Angel sputtered, she popped the bottle back in, unconsciously rocking and soothing the baby at the same time…but her mind was really spinning now. She'd always had special feelings for him. She'd also always seemed to notice things about him that others never saw—like that the playboy reputation he'd cultivated was never true, and that there was a whole emotional side to him that he never showed to the world.

Maybe she'd always felt the seeds of love, Winona mused, and maybe he had, too. But still, something had triggered his asking her to marry him in a serious way. And anxiety suddenly threaded a drumbeat in her pulse. Everything had been going so well, but she still hadn't shaken the sensation that something was wrong. Something not right in Justin's life, in his heart, that he hadn't shared with her.

"Okay, I'll quit teasing you," Pamela said. "If you don't want to talk about your doctor hunk, I won't press. And I promise, I'll keep my ear to the ground on anything I might hear about Angel's mother." She motioned to the baby, and hesitated. "You want to keep her, don't you?" she asked softly.

"Yeah." Winona could feel her eyes burning. "I already feel like she's mine. But what matters is that we know what happened. It's the best way to protect the baby's future long-term. The truth. Not just wishful thinking."

"I'm afraid that's true of life, too. Unfortunately." Pamela suddenly pressed a hand on her abdomen. "I'm sorry. I have to go."

Winona saw the gesture. "Are you ill? Do you need some help?"

"No, no, I'm fine. It's just that ever since that darned plane crash, nothing seems to sit well on my stomach. Maybe it's a little post-traumatic stress or some silly nonsense like that.

It's only been a couple of weeks. I figure I'll be patient a little longer before throwing in the towel and seeing a doc. Anyway...'' She stood up, pressed Winona's hand and kissed the baby's forehead, before heading for the door.

Angel seemed to finish the bottle at the same time. Winona lifted the baby to her shoulder, patting her, burping her, still smiling a goodbye as Pamela left...but the smile slowly faded from her face. She snuggled the baby close.

She couldn't shake the feeling that there was something troubling Justin that she didn't understand. Before, it hadn't mattered. Before, it hadn't been her business, her right to know or ask or help.

But now it was.

And now her heart was hanging out there, at risk in a way she'd never risked her heart before. For a man who was worth it. But a man she suddenly wasn't sure really needed—or wanted—her.

Ten

When Justin picked up Winona for dinner, he was so close to a shambling mess that he wanted to laugh at himself. He'd never been a nervous type. Couldn't be. In his work, he had to do hours of intricate surgery without hesitation or allowing emotions to fluster his judgment. Yet tonight, his stomach was flip-flopping, his heartbeat galloping like a clumsy colt's, his palms sticky-damp, and the extremely small package in his suit pocket seemed to weigh five tons.

He counted on feeling better when he saw her—only it didn't work out that way.

For a few minutes she stood in the doorway, giving Myrt instructions and talking about the baby. And while she was standing there, she tugged on a coat, which she was definitely going to need, since the January night was frigid, the stars colder than diamonds against a black felt sky. Still, he'd caught a look at her in the black silk and heels. Even when Win dressed up, she never wore show-off clothes, nothing to toot her figure or draw attention to herself. But something had gotten into her. Something dangerous. Something worrisome. He didn't know what to make of it all—the dipping-to-trouble bodice and the smoky thing she'd done to her eyes and the subtly lethal scent she wore.

His blood pressure had been in trouble before he picked her up. Now it was threatening stroke levels.

He was tugging on his tie even before he'd parked and walked her into Claire's. The restaurant was on Main Street, past the bustling new town, past the shopping district, past the old, historic Royalton Hotel. Possibly five crystal snow flakes fell from the sky—no more, just enough to add atmosphere and magic to the night—and they stepped inside.

Although Royal was a wealthy town because of its oil, the town's personality had never been formal. Claire's was the exception. Just inside the door, there was almost an audible hush. The tables were decked with white linen, each center-pieced with a fresh rosebud. No prices showed up on the menus. The carpet was a luxurious wine, the wallpaper some type of velvet flocking in ruby-red. In the far corner, a piano player wearing a tux played muted love songs.

Once he'd taken her coat, Winona half turned to whisper in his ear, "All right. This is scary. I've been here before. You know how it is. The Gerards used Claire's for special celebrations like everyone else does—at least everyone who can afford it. But I always wondered…exactly what happens if someone trips? Or burps?"

In spite of the five-ton weight of the package in his pocket, Justin started relaxing. How could he have forgotten? Win was as natural to be with as his own heartbeat. Even if that dip in her dress was affecting said heartbeat with drumroll enthusiasm. "It's okay," he assured her. "Nothing bad is allowed to happen in here, so you don't have to worry about it."

"Ah. Is that how it works? I always have the feeling that I'm going to get a run in my stocking the minute I walk into this place. Or, more to the point, that I'll be the only woman in Claire's with a noticeable run.''

"Well, that could be. But if that happens, you could take off the stocking and hand it to me to hide—along with anything you're wearing under that slinky black dress."

"Justin! This dress is not slinky!"

"It sure is. On you." Again, he yanked on his tie. "Maybe we should go straight home. You're not that hungry, are you? I am. But not for food anymore."

Winona crackled the menu. "You are a bad, bad man and an even worse influence," she said severely, and then smiled like a saint for the waiter.

"I think we want to start out with the most decadent bottle of wine you've got in the cellar," Justin said, only to have Win bat her eyes at him.

"You mean those grapes went out and misbehaved? Created a scandal on their own?"

"You bet. You just can't trust those grapes. Some of them grow up just praying for a chance to raise hell...." And to the waiter, he said, "Don't mind us. We're out of our minds. And in the meantime—we want the best steaks you've got in the back—and I don't mean the ones you shipped in from Kansas. We want Texas steaks or nothing—and cooked more rare than a politician's promises."

"Yes, sir." The waiter had a hard time not cracking up, but then he was gone.

"Slip off your shoes, Win. You're just with me. We're going to do the gluttony and decadent relaxing thing tonight or die trying. No thinking about work or babies or worries or anything else, okay?"

Her smile was so sweet he was damn near tempted to sing her love songs. In public, yet. She raised a hand, matching his, touching fingertips to fingertips as if there wasn't another soul in the restaurant. How he'd lived without her this long confounded Justin. And that he could help ease her nerves made him feel sky high…although that moment of private peace didn't last, unfortunately.

Her soft smile suddenly seemed to wax still. "Darnit, Justin, I was really hoping to talk to you…but there are two men sitting over at a corner table by the window. They can't be local, because I'd have seen them before, and there's something a little odd about their clothes. The thing is, though, that they keep staring at you…."

Justin didn't glance over his shoulder. He'd already noticed the two men when they'd first been ushered in. "Yeah. Their names are Milo and Garth. Quite a pair, aren't they? They remind me of a poodle and a pug."

"A poodle and a pu…." Again, she glanced at the two men, and then her soft mouth worked as she tried to control a giggle. "Justin, that's terrible!"

"But true, isn't it?" Once the waiter brought the open bottle, Justin motioned him away and poured the pinot noir into her glass.

"Well, I take it you know them? Oh shoot, they're coming this way."

Well, hell. There were only two human beings on the planet Justin really wanted to see tonight—one was the baby, and the other—the only one he really wanted—was Win. But now he was forced to look up. And as Winona had warned, bad news seemed determinedly bearing down on them.

Milo, the tall one, really did resemble a standard poodle. He was ultralean, with fairly broad shoulders but no butt or body and reedlike legs. A head full of springy, wiry curls framed an angular face with small eyes and a long nose. His sidekick, Garth, was a total contrast. Built short and squat, he had a pug's flat nose and ornery expression. When Justin had first noted them eating, Garth had been shoveling in food as if he feared never getting another meal.

Both now approached their table with courteous smiles. "Doctor Webb, it's nice to see you again. We don't want to interrupt your dinner, but when we recognized you across the room, we thought we should say hello.''

"I'm glad you did,'' Justin lied smoothly, and promptly introduced Win—although there was a limit to manners. There was no way he was asking the two boys to sit down. ''Milo and Garth are here from Asterland, Winona—''

Milo turned an extra-watt smile on her. ''Yes, we just arrived yesterday.''

''—and they're here to investigate the difficulties with the plane. Hopefully, by pooling American and Asterland resources together, we're going to find some solid answers soon, right, gentlemen?''

''We all hope.'' Milo bobbed his head. ''Since you happen to be here, Dr. Webb, Garth and I have been going over the passenger list. Do you happen to be familiar with a Ms. Pamela Miles and a Ms. Jamie Morris?''

Justin felt Win's gaze leaping to his face. His ankle brushed hers, hoping that she would pick up the message that he wanted to handle this alone. ''Yes. Both young women live locally. Although I would certainly hope that you would be studying the entire passenger list, and not just the two individuals who happen to be American.''

''Of course, of course. It was just that, naturally, the Americans are the ones who are the least familiar to us.''

And it would be far handier to find an American to blame for the plane crash than one of their own countrymen—although Justin took care not to voice that thought. ''Well, to be truthful, I am in no position to answer any personal questions about either woman. And neither will Ms. Raye. But both Ms. Miles and Ms. Morris have lived in Royal their whole lives, and I believe you'll find there's no problem with them in any way.''

''I'm sure. Thank you for your time.'' Garth's flat, shiny eyes acknowledged first him, then Winona.

When they'd finally walked out of earshot, back toward

their table, Winona turned to him with a frown. "The little guy gave me the willies, Doc."

Justin shrugged. "I'm not surprised the Asterlanders sent someone to investigate their plane trouble. I don't think there's anything weird about that. But they hit on me for information right after they got here. I had a feeling they thought they could get more from a doctor than the law. Which just struck me as off base, not the normal chain of questioning...but it's not like it matters. We're going to completely forget about them now, okay?"

"Okay."

"How's my baby today?"

"Your baby started out this morning by charming the entire juvenile court. I swear, the only time she ever fusses is when she's alone with me. In a crowd she never fails to live up to her name."

"Myrt's going to be really unhappy to hear that. She was counting on you needing a nanny more during the day, couldn't wait to baby-sit for us tonight..." They both kept up a light chatter over dinner. The waiter served steak with Béarnaise sauce, snow peas and whipped potatoes. When he got around to taking those plates away, he showed back up offering crème brûlée, which was enough to make Win moan.

"Honestly, I can't."

"Sure you can." He motioned to the waiter to bring two servings.

"You don't understand. I have a weakness for certain desserts. I can't give into it or I'll be fat as a tub."

He heard her protests, but when the dessert arrived, all he heard was "Oh, my," followed by more "Oh, my, my, mys."

He said, "I'm not positive, but I'm almost sure that they generally discourage customers from having orgasms in front of the other restaurant clientele."

"Tough. That's their problem." Now that she'd quit being nervous, Win was back to being herself. Full of devilment and fearless—at least fearlessly diving into his dish of crème brûlée. She'd finished her own. "You *did* bring a wheelbarrow to cart me out of here, didn't you?"

"No. But I did happen to bring something else." He pushed a hand in his right pocket, and geezle beezle, realized his dad-blasted fingers were shaking again.

"Justin…" Maybe Win sensed that something momentous was coming, because she suddenly launched into a nonstop talking fest. "Let's talk about some problems, okay? I don't know what might be bothering you, but it occurred to me that one thing could be the house. You know what I mean. Which house we're going to live in? And it doesn't really matter to me, but my place is so small that your house seems to be obviously the best choice."

"Well, your house is too small for the three of us, but that doesn't have to limit us, Win. If you don't like my place, we could either go house shopping or build from scratch."

"Do you really want to do that?"

"I want to do whatever works for you. And the baby."

"Well…I love your house. So unless you actually want to move, I think it's ideal. Although…"

It wasn't going to work. Trying to talk about anything normal. Not while the box in his pocket was burning a hole in his mind. So when she lifted another spoonful of crème brûlée, he slipped the small black box on the table. When she lowered the spoon, she saw it.

Even though she hadn't leveled all of his dessert yet—and was obviously still hungry for it—she dropped the spoon. She dropped her hands, too. Her eyes met his, softer than lake water and more vulnerable than a spring night.

"Can I…open it?" she asked softly.

"You're going to give me a heart attack if you don't. Not that you have to like it, Win. I wanted to give you a surprise, but in the long run, I want you to have something that you really love and want to look at every day. The best jeweler

I know is in Austin. We could fly up there, and he could either make you something specific to—''

Since she was paying no attention to his monologue, he quit talking. By then she'd opened the box. It was just a ring. Not a diamond, because once he'd become part of the Texas Cattleman's Club, he'd become exposed to the value and meaning of certain gems. The sapphire not only matched her eyes, but a sapphire was supposed to be a stone for a woman who valued her individuality, a one-of-a-kind, as she was. And because he couldn't choose a huge gem, because Win was mightily against ostentation, he'd opted for a priceless one. The hue was unusual for a sapphire, not the dark blue of midnight, but the clear, deep blue of her eyes, the limitless blue of…love.

He'd prepared a speech to communicate all that, partly because he wanted to tell her…but also because he was desperate to have something to say so that she couldn't change her mind. But as it happened, he never had a chance to worry about any of that.

She hurled herself at him. Arms raised. Head tilted. She knocked over a spoon, then a saucer, making enough of a clatter to have heads swiveling from all over the restaurant to witness her throwing herself in his arms. He saw her eyes glistening and almost died to realize she was crying.

And then she kissed him.

Or he kissed her. By then, who could tell? The only thing that mattered was meeting her exuberant kiss halfway…and then more than halfway. Lips touched, and all that rough, fast hurling around was suddenly over. The kiss turned soft and silent and secret. Reverent.

The whisper of her taste was a promise. The texture of her lips a vow. God, she won his heart all over again. Every time she came to him, he felt this horrible melting from the inside. A changing. An instinctive understanding that his life could be bigger with her, his heart could be stronger, the whole universe richer—if she just loved him.

And man, he did love her. From the inside, from the out-side, to hell with where they were or who was watching. Nothing mattered but telling her how he felt, what he wanted for her, for them. Love shimmered between them like liquid gold that coated both of them in its warmth and power. And yeah, sexual desire loomed between them, too. Hot and wicked and needy. Craving her was good, too. He couldn't wait to get her out of here, get her naked, wearing nothing but the blasted ring…but it was funny. Just kissing her that instant was all he ever wanted, too.

Finally she eased away, both of them out of breath, their gazes still locked tight on each other.

"I'll be damned. I'm getting the craziest feeling you like the ring," he murmured.

"Don't you try to tease me now, Doc. I couldn't handle it."

He dropped the smile instantly. "I love you, Win. No teas-ing. No nothing. That's always been what this is about. Not the baby, not anything else in our lives. Just love."

"And I love you. Set a date. Any date you want, Justin."

In the middle of the warmest, most important moment of his entire life, Justin suddenly froze.

Two nights later, as Justin drove to the Cattleman's Club, the roads were empty of traffic—and for good reason. Ev-erybody that could be was tucked inside their houses. Sleet poured down in silver sheets; the asphalt was icy-slick and a fierce wind buffeted and blustered around every corner.

Still, when Justin parked and climbed out of the Porsche, he trudged toward the Club's front door as if he didn't give a damn if the sleet soaked him or not. And the truth was, he didn't.

Win was wearing the sapphire engagement ring. And they'd gone home that night to make love until the wee hours. But he'd also jerked awake around four in the morning from a nightmare, and nothing had been the same since. Something was wrong. Bad wrong. With him.

The crazy thing was, everything was *right* for him for the first time in his entire life. He adored Winona. And the woman he loved more than life itself had freely agreed to marry him. Nine hours out of ten, he was over the moon, feeling as if there was nothing he couldn't do or conquer or dream. Except that when it came to setting a date for the marriage, he got a lump of ice in his throat the size of an iceberg.

Guys all over the planet were petrified of commitment—but that wasn't him. Commitment to Win, forever, was exactly what Justin wanted, so this panicked reaction to setting a wedding date made no sense at all. Until he figured it out, though, he was too ashamed and confused to admit to Win that he was having this idiotic problem. Maybe he could hire someone to punch him out? Beat some sense into him? Shake the screw loose from his mind?

"Justin! Good to see you!" Matthew must have been waiting at the door, because he was right there to push it open. But his gregarious welcome changed focus when he saw Justin's face. "Hell, man. What happened to you?"

"Nothing, just running a little late." At a glance, he could see that the others were all inside, except for Aaron. Drinks had been served. Typically, Ben had his hands wrapped around a coffee mug while the others had aimed straight for the more serious blood warmers. The familiar scent of whiskey was in the air, as were the smells of leather, wool and a brisk, wood-burning fire. Walking into the Club had always invoked a comfortable male-bonding sort of feeling. It was created to be a place where a man could let down his hair.

But not tonight. Not for him.

Dakota stepped forward with a grin. "Hey, man, sure looks like someone rode you hard and put you up wet." But like Matthew, when Dakota got a good look at his face, his smile disappeared. "I didn't mean to joke—you all right? You're not sick, are you?"

"No. I'm fine, really. Sorry to be so late. Afraid I just had a few days in a row with some grueling long work hours." That's what he'd told Winona. He was afraid she hadn't bought it. And it didn't appear his friends were buying it, either.

But they had serious issues to contend with tonight, and no one was wasting time on idle chitchat. The first job on their agenda was finding a new hiding place for the emerald and the black harlequin opal. Before the robbery, they'd considered the safe under the historical mission next door to be both symbolic and as secure as any place could be, but obviously they'd been wrong.

Justin fetched a ladder from the back storage room. The others collected a toolbox and the quarter-inch drill and a broom. The job didn't have to take five minutes, but Justin figured with four men there, it would likely take a good hour.

It took a full hour and a half.

"I'll do the drilling," Ben started out by volunteering.

"I can do it." Matthew stepped forward. "I'm used to doing every type of chore on a ranch. This is nothing."

Dakota hunched fists on his hips. "Yeah, well, I think we got a good chance of running into trouble. Drilling a hole in the paneling is easy enough, but behind that is straight adobe brick. If we're not careful, we're going to end up with a hole the size of a crater."

If Justin had been in any mood to laugh that night, his friends would have easily induced his sense of humor. All the guys were so literally fearless. Men who'd step up, without hesitation, without expecting thanks or reward, to save a child or an innocent. Each of them had literally pledged to do exactly that as Texas Cattleman's Club members—and had.

But hell. Get a bunch of guys near a construction project

and naturally the four-letter words flew…along with arguments over the right way to do things.

Justin would normally have contributed his useless two cents. Tonight, though, when the small hole had finally been drilled—and the swearing settled down—he climbed the ladder in the front entrance hall. The Club sign—Leadership, Justice and Peace—was lying on its side on the ground. And all of them suddenly turned quiet.

Each took one last look at the black harlequin opal and the emerald, before the two stones were wrapped in white velvet inside a film canister. The drill had made a hole big enough to put the film canister inside, so after that, there was nothing left to do but rehang the sign.

"It couldn't be more perfect," Matthew said. "I mean, in the long run, obviously we need to find a more secure vault for the stones. But until we know what happened to the red diamond, this is ideal. Symbolic. Beneath the sign that stands for the stones. We did good."

"Now if all the other problems connected to the theft and the plane crash were only half this easy to solve," Dakota said dryly.

They swept, cleaned up, put away the broom and toolbox. Yet all of them ended up back in the front entrance hall. For them the sign had never been a corny symbol, but an echo of the very real vows they'd made to help others when they'd joined the Texas Cattleman's Club. At the moment, they were all frustrated in fulfilling those vows.

"The more we dive into this mess, the less makes sense," Dakota groaned.

"Let's go over what we know," Matthew suggested. "Nothing's surfaced to identify Riley Monroe's killer yet, has it?"

No, it hadn't—and the red diamond was still missing. As yet, the men had no evidence to link the plane crash to the jewel theft—but the jewel thief positively had to be someone on that Asterland plane flight. Klimt, one of the few who might have given them specific answers about what happened on that plane, was still in a coma. Riley Monroe's killer was obviously their jewel thief, but the cops had no leads or even ideas on Monroe's killer yet...and one of the most curious issues in the whole mess was that two stones had been recovered, and not the third. All the Texas Cattleman's Club directly involved with this—except for Aaron—had gone over the plane with a fine-tooth comb. As had the authorities. As had the two investigators, Milo and Garth, sent by the Asterlanders.

"Well, something has to break," Matthew said. "Part of the problem is that none of us copes well with frustration. We're all in the habit of going out and doing something to fix things. Having to wait is partly what's driving us nuts."

Dakota concurred. "I also doubt that there's a gem as notoriously unique on the planet as our red diamond. Which means that it can't surface anywhere without raising news. Even in the blackest of a black market, it'll raise a flurry when it shows up—if we don't find another way to find it first."

"Yes. The red diamond is really the key to solving the rest," Ben said thoughtfully, and then, "Justin?"

Justin swiftly turned toward them. "I agree with all of you. It's just going to take a little more time. None of us have ever accepted failure and we're not about to now."

The others exuberantly agreed, but Ben was still frowning at him. "Something was on your mind. You were really staring at the sign. Did something occur to you?"

"Yeah, it did."

Justin couldn't explain. Not to anyone. But this strange epiphany thing had happened when he'd taken one last look at the precious emerald and opal. Suddenly his heart had started beating like a drum, hollow, anxious, the *thud-thud-thud* of dread. The missing gem was the reason. The red diamond, for all of them, had always been the true talisman symbol of the group's cause. Not because it was the most precious and priceless, but because it represented the leadership and honor that a good man really stood for.

And the drumming in his heart kept thundering like a hollow echo. Memories of Bosnia knifed through his mind. He'd had such a heroic goal when he'd volunteered to go there. He'd wanted to help. To save people. And at the time, he'd been egotistical enough to believe that he was an ideal person to do that—that he was one of the best docs in trauma medicine anywhere.

Only he'd flown into a nightmare. Patient after patient had been suffering severe wounds from bombs and guns and shrapnel. But the conditions were petrifying. Sometimes there were no drugs. Sometimes there was no heat, no electricity— hell, sometimes not even running water. He had the skill; he had the heart, but he had no way to save them. And patient after patient died, until Justin had started to feel a breaking sensation on the inside. Maybe it wasn't his failures that caused the deaths, but it was still failure. It was still unlivable. And when he'd come home, he'd aimed straight for plastic surgery and away from any medicine where patients died.

It made sense to him then.

It made sense to him for a long time.

It had made sense to him until he'd asked Winona to marry him. All these years, he'd prayed that Winona could love him, but now that she'd admitted to those feelings…aw hell, Justin knew exactly why his heart felt hollow. Because it was. Part of him was missing, no different than that damned red diamond was missing. He was afraid of failing her. Afraid of not being the strong, honorable man that she seemed to think he was—the strong, honorable man that Justin was no longer positive he was, either.

Ben's fingers closed on his shoulder. "Something is wrong. Do you want to sit down somewhere? Find a place to talk?"

Matthew picked up on Ben's concern. "Justin, hell, you

looked like you'd been driving yourself ragged when you first walked in. What's wrong? Tell us. What can we do?''

"Nothing," he started to say. He wasn't sure if he felt more relieved—or more worried—that he'd finally figured out why setting the marriage date had been throwing him for six. At least he was finally getting his mind wrapped more clearly around the problem.

Unfortunately, that didn't mean that he had a clue what to do about it.

Startling all of them, a telephone suddenly rang. The Club, of course, was closed. A call this late was likely nothing more than a telemarketer or a wrong number. But Justin took the excuse to hike for the phone, relieved to get away from his friends' searching attention, no matter how well-meaning their concern.

The closest receiver was in the Club office. He reached the phone just as it rang for a fourth time.

"Justin? Oh, thank God I got you. I didn't know where to track you down...." He heard Winona's voice, sounding not at all like her. Win kept her cool in a thousand crises, and always for others. Yet her tone was shrill with panic and fear. "I need you. Right now. Oh God, oh God. Angel isn't breathing right. Something's terribly wrong. I'm afraid to take her to the hospital, afraid to do anything that could make it worse, I—"

No matter how messed up he was, this was easy. Justin didn't have to think. Winona needed him. That was cut-and-dried. "I'll be there in five minutes flat. I promise."

Eleven

Winona had been afraid before, but never like this. Late that afternoon, she'd discovered who Angel's mother was. At the time, she'd thought that nothing could possibly be more important or traumatic than that—but she'd been wrong.

Right now she was carrying the baby and pacing because she was too terrified to do anything else. She'd been busy, coming home from work, getting some dinner on and the baby down for the night, but everything had been basically fine—until Angel suddenly woke, making petrifying choking sounds.

She was afraid to put the baby down. Afraid to keep carrying her. Afraid anything that she did might be wrong—and yeah, of course, as a cop she'd had first aid. Intensive, extensive first aid, for that matter. But what the spit good was that? There was nothing in any manual about the emotional stakes being so screechy high and unbearable when it was *your* baby who was suffering and you were terrified of doing the wrong thing and risking hurting her worse.

Winona heard the front door open. "Justin? Back here! Hurry!"

She wanted to brace before seeing him. She knew it would hurt. Winona had no idea what was in that damn man's head, but two days ago she'd finally added up two and two. For days, he'd been pushing her to marry him. First, making out like a marriage of convenience would enable her to foster Angel. Then, making out like he wanted a real marriage. Then, not just making out—but showing her—that he loved her in every way a man could love a woman.

But when it came down to setting a date, he'd ducked one too many times now.

She'd thought they'd had something. And no, she'd never bought into that marriage of convenience malarkey. Since when in the history of men and women was a marriage ever convenient? The concept was an oxymoron if ever there was one. But then she'd started to see how much Justin cared. How much he'd hidden. How he'd be as a dad, how he was as a lover, how much love poured out of him when the door was finally opened up.

Only the blasted man had *made* her fall in love with him. Practically forced her into falling hopelessly, helplessly, deeply in love. And *then* to stall out when it came to setting a date?

Man, it bit. In fact, it hurt so much that she'd prowled the floors for two nights in a row. Right now, though, she had no time for hurt or anger. There was only one thing on her mind—the baby.

She sensed his shadow in the nursery doorway, even before he'd said anything. She heard him yanking off his jacket, hurtling it aside. She didn't look at him, because she was too sick-scared, soul-scared, to take her eyes off Angel for even a second, but she started talking. Fast. "She's been half choking like this for almost twenty minutes now. Maybe I should have taken her right to the hospital, but I didn't understand what was happening—I also didn't want to take her out in

the cold or do anything to make her worse. But I can see—
anyone can see—something's *wrong*. She's not breathing
right—''

"Keep talking. Just keep telling me everything that's been
happening to her."

"I put her down for the night about forty-five minutes ago.
All day she was fine. Completely fine. And she dropped off
to sleep right away, only it was like she swallowed something
somehow, because suddenly I heard her coughing. I ran in
from the kitchen. It seemed like she was choking. I grabbed
her, picked her up, started thumping her back, thinking that
I could help her get something up—''

"And did you see anything come up?" Justin's voice was
calm, quiet, fast.

"No. But it had to. Because she wasn't choking so bad
after that. Still, it's like now. You can see how she's struggling to breathe. Her coloring is almost blue—''

"Did you call a pediatrician?"

"No, of course not. I called you. I want you."

"Win, come on, you know I don't have any specialty with
babies—''

"You know trauma medicine like no one else. There's no
one I want but you."

"Damnation, Winona. You don't know what you're asking
me."

That was such a strange thing for him to say that her head
shot up. This moment wasn't about her and him. It was about
the baby…but somehow all her hurt disappeared at that instant. She didn't know why he'd ducked on setting the marriage date, but love wasn't the problem. She saw the way he
looked at her. His dark hair was still gleaming with melted
snow, his cheeks rubbed red from the wind, but his eyes were
soft and haunted with love, fastened on hers for one long
lonesome second—before he returned all his attention to Angel.

He'd already stolen the baby from her arms, already

moved over to the crib, where he had a flat surface to lay Angel down. Gentle fingers were firmly, swiftly, pulling off the baby's clothes, assessing her, studying, murmuring to her.

"What do you mean, I don't know what I'm asking you?" she asked quietly.

"I can't risk anything happening to Angel. Not her. I can't, Winona, dammit. I *mean* it. I don't do trauma medicine anymore."

It was confoundedly bewildering. She heard his words, but they didn't make any sense. He'd already competently, calmly, taken on Angel.

And the minute he'd walked in the door, Winona had felt herself stop panicking. Well, almost. Her head was still screaming, her knees still shaking, her hands slicker than slides. Because she'd never been the kind of person to panic in a crisis, she wasn't prepared to deal with herself when the symptoms hit so hard. For Pete's sake, it was her *job* to handle people in a crisis and she did it darn well.

But this was about a baby.

Her baby.

And it just wasn't the same.

Still, once Justin was there—no matter what the blasted man said—everything eased. Not her worry that Angel was in trouble. But if anyone could save a baby, Justin could. If anyone could help Angel, Justin would find a way to do it. If she trusted anyone in the entire universe—and there weren't many on that list, never had been for Winona—she trusted Justin.

Quieter than a whisper, he said, "Put on the overhead. Bring the black bag over here for me and open it, would you? And then get me a straw from the kitchen. Quick, okay?"

There was no panic in his voice, nothing to make her worry, yet she instinctively understood to put on the spurs. She returned quickly with the items.

"You know what's wrong, don't you?"

"Yeah," he said. "It's the whale."

"Huh?"

"The stuffed animal. The minute I laid her in the crib—there had to be a reason for the symptoms, obviously? So I looked, and I saw the hint of loose stitches on the whale, the little fuzz of stuffing coming out. I'm guessing the baby put some in her mouth. And I'll bet that's where you were patting her—" He motioned to the carpet to her left "—because she spit some out on the carpet there."

"Oh, my God. Do you think she swallowed some? Is that why she's having trouble breathing? And could it be poisonous? Could—"

"Win."

"What?"

"I need you to listen."

She gulped in a breath. "I'm listening."

"I can't make this pretty. There's still some in her throat. That's exactly what's clogging her air passage and why she's having trouble breathing. It has to come out. Winona?"

"What?"

"I love you. And I promise—I *promise*, Win—she'll be okay. But this isn't going to be any fun to look at, so I just want you to go in the other room and sit down."

She wasn't about to go anywhere—although she did take a couple of seconds to grab the whale and hurl it into the trash before coming back to his side. He kept talking, using a low, easy voice to soothe the baby, but she was the one he was communicating to, warning her that he might have to do a tracheotomy, cut the baby's throat, if he wasn't able to suck the debris with a straw. One way or another it had to come out, and now, and the baby wasn't going to like anything about this, but there was nothing else he could do.

It was an odd sensation, under the circumstances, to be more afraid for Justin than for the baby. But she kept watching him, with her eyes—with her heart. And whether it made logical sense or not, she understood that something was at stake for Justin—something more than the baby, something more than he'd known how to tell her.

And he was right. Nothing about the procedures he tried was pretty, but it was only a few minutes later when the baby suddenly choked and gagged and furiously coughed. And then it was done. Justin eased the little one to his shoulder, patting, whispering, soothing, looking at Winona with wet eyes.

"You tell our daughter *never* to scare me like that again," he said.

Winona wanted her arms around Angel, but deliberately let Justin keep holding her. She did the running, changing the sheets, throwing out everything that had been in the crib earlier in case the stuffing could have contaminated anything else. By the time the sheets were clean and the light turned off, it was past midnight; Justin had redressed the baby in a warm sleeper, and Angel was hard-core snoozing. He laid her in the crib, but both felt the same reluctance to leave her. They both stood there, watching.

Fifteen minutes later they were both still standing, weaving-tired, still watching the baby, even though Justin had said three times that there was really no longer any reason to worry.

"And she's sleeping like a log," Winona agreed. "Come on, this is silly. It's time for both of us to lie down ourselves and get some sleep."

"You go. I'll watch for just a little while longer."

"No, you."

"No, you."

At two in the morning, Winona woke up in the rocking chair next to the baby's crib...and immediately saw Justin next to her in the second rocking chair she'd carted in earlier. His neck looked as cramped as hers felt, his face as tired and drawn as hers must look.

Her mouth softly tipped into a smile, looking at him. He loved her. And he loved Angel. Whatever had been wrong with him earlier in the week, Winona knew positively what the truth was now.

His eyelashes shot up, as if sensing that she was awake and studying him. Just as swiftly, he jerked to his feet and immediately bent over the baby, assessing Angel's happy, little breathy snores, before he could relax and plunk back down in the rocker again.

He rubbed a weary hand over his face. "She really is okay, Winona. This is nuts. We both need to get some serious sleep."

"I know," she agreed, but she didn't move any more than he did. In the dark room, she kept seeing shadows and silhouettes, until the thoughts chasing around her mind finally took shape. "With all this trauma going on, I never had a chance to tell you, Justin. There's no reason that you have to marry me anymore."

"What?"

"I found out who Angel's mother is."

He swallowed, then stood up from the rocking chair and simply took her hand. In the dark, silent living room, he wrapped a throw around her shoulders and then hunkered down next to her on the couch. "Okay. Now tell me the whole story."

"She was at the Texas Cattleman's Club ball. One of the guests. Herb Newton's wife, Alicia. Herb was on sabbatical in the Far East. She was pregnant last year, but then about the time the baby was supposed to be born, she told her neighbors and family that the child was stillborn, that she'd lost it. She had a midwife instead of going to the hospital. The midwife backed up what she said. Herb wasn't part of the birth process. She told him the same thing, that the baby had died."

"But I take it that you found out that she lied?"

Winona nodded. "Yes. The midwife took the baby for the first couple of months. The midwife was caught in the middle of the story, wanting to help Alicia, but not knowing what to do. The problem was that Herb was physically abusive. He didn't stop knocking Alicia around during the pregnancy, which made her afraid that he'd hurt the baby as well. In fact, she was positive he'd hurt the baby. So she asked the midwife to put Angel on my doorstep.''

"God." His voice communicated a wealth of emotion. The fingertips brushing back her hair communicated even more. Her pulse bucked. With love and hope. But there were still things she needed to say.

"Alicia was just one of the leads I was tracking down. But when I caught up with her this afternoon, it all came out. It's not going to be simple, Justin, as far as Angel's future."

"Why?"

"Because she's afraid Herb will kill her if he finds out the baby is alive. She doesn't want the child. At all. It's going to be all she can do for a long time to get herself a divorce, get out of that relationship and start a life over again. But if Herb finds out the child is alive, she's also afraid that he'll demand custody—and because he's the blood father, she's afraid that he could both get it and force Alicia to live with him again—either that or risk him hurting the child."

"What a mess," Justin said quietly.

"Yeah. And that's the point—that it can't be solved legally, at least not for a while. If Alicia gets what she wants, she's going to give the child up for adoption, specifically to me. Or to us." She met his eyes. "But the real point is— there's no reason for you to marry me, just to enable me to foster or adopt Angel. We know the child's situation now. It's going to take a while to fight this out in the courts. But no marriage is going to help or hurt my keeping Angel. The real legal problems are between Alicia and her husband."

"Win, I wasn't marrying you for Angel's sake."

"I didn't think you were, either. But you sure ducked out when it came down to setting a marriage date—as if you really weren't that serious. You hurt me, Doc."

The lines in his face all tensed with anxiety. "That was

never what I wanted to happen. Never. And I always wanted to marry you, Win, for years. From the first time I saw you, and you were twelve and kicking every boy in the shins who dared to say 'hi' to you. God. You were so stubborn. So mean. So full of courage—"

"Quit complimenting me, you turkey, and tell me why you hurt me."

"I didn't want to. I didn't mean to."

"Justin—that isn't good enough."

Silence fell between them, raw and tense. He looked away, then down, then straight into her eyes. "It was about suddenly realizing…that maybe I wasn't the man you thought I was."

She laid her hand on top of his, her left hand, so he could see the engagement ring shining softly in the shadows. And then she clipped their fingers together, tight, so he had something to hold on to.

"I lost so many patients in Bosnia. In trauma medicine, you lose patients sometimes. That's how it is. Always. A fight, a war, against death. Emergency rooms are messy, imperfect places, where sometimes you only have a split second to make a life-or-death decision. It's impossible. But…Win, I swear that I believed I was good at it."

She clutched his hand tighter.

"But there was no medicine over there. Sometimes no electricity. No light, no water, no facilities, no drugs. You'd get patients that should have been saved. Men who never had to die. Children in terrible pain. And there was nothing I could do. Nothing."

If she could have bled for him, she would have. For so long, she'd known there was a reason for that wounded loneliness in his eyes. The emotion that didn't show. The way he fooled people about the kind of man he was. And she'd known he had secrets, because everyone did. But she didn't know it'd break her heart to hear his pain.

"I thought I was a stronger man. But I came home from

Bosnia and I got the shakes at the idea of seeing another patient die. So I switched medical fields. I see pain, but it's almost always something I can do something about. And no one's died on me. I thought the change was a good choice, but on the inside, it's just been sitting in here—'' he thumbed his chest ''—that I let myself down. Let others down. I wasn't the man I wanted to be. The man I thought I once was.''

''Damn you, Doc.'' So much for holding hands. She reached for him. ''You're so stupid. And I love you so much.'' She framed his face, tight, so that she could smack a kiss on him. A hard, mean, possessive kiss, not a sweet one. Yet somehow so much love poured into that kiss that she felt tears bunching in her eyes like salty thunder clouds. ''You're ten times any ordinary man, you cretin. Did you think you could do everything?''

''No. But…I just didn't realize how much the whole thing had weighed on my conscience. Until we started talking marriage, and we made love, and every dream I had about you and me was finally coming together. And then it just came to me, that I hadn't faced it…being a coward.''

''That's how much you know. Now write it down somewhere so you get it straight. I wouldn't love a coward. Not like I love you. Heart and soul. Sinker and clinker.''

She could see in his eyes, in the way he kissed her back, that it was going to be all right. But he still seemed to need to get more out. ''I just wasn't sure…if you knew me. You didn't know I'd had that failure. And I was afraid that maybe I was fooling you. And me. That I couldn't promise you I was the man you needed me to be.''

''You saved our baby tonight, Doc. Where's the failure? You were afraid. But you still stepped up. You're the best doctor I know. But way, way more than that…you're the best man.'' Again she kissed him, but this time softly. Tenderly. Wanting to show him her heart stripped bare. ''I love you, Justin.''

"Aw, Win. I love you back. So much. That's why I had such a hard time getting past this. Because I wanted the right to love you for a lifetime."

"We've been through a trial by fire, haven't we? But from now on…your fears are my fears. Your worries, my worries."

"And your love…my love," he said fiercely, and took her in his arms, offering a kiss flavored with all the love and promises they brought each other.

Epilogue

When Winona heard the telephone ring, she was surrounded by open suitcases. How one short honeymoon could create so many dirty clothes was beyond her—particularly when most of the garments were itsy-bitsy baby-size. Now, though, she vaulted from the laundry room toward the telephone in the kitchen, delighted to abandon the chore. As she reached for the phone, she heard the muffled sounds of splashing and giggling. Justin was giving Angel a bath—and someone was laughing uproariously. It wasn't the baby.

Winona couldn't help chuckling as she pressed the phone to her ear. To her surprise, the caller was Pamela Miles.

"How nice of you to call," Winona said warmly.

"You're probably really busy if you're just back from your wedding trip, and I hate to bother you. I just couldn't stop wondering how everything was going. If you found Angel's mother and what happened—or what's going to happen—to the baby? If things had settled down?"

"The whole world's going great. And we've just been

back for a few hours—the baby couldn't have loved the honeymoon more. In fact, I actually planned to call you tonight, so I'm extra glad you called."

"You were going to call me?" Pamela asked in surprise.

Again Winona smiled, this time a secret smile from the inside out. "Yes. Because I owe you—we all owe you—special thanks. You're the one who gave me the clue to finding Angel's birth mother."

"Oh." Pamela's voice sank, as if she feared that she had suddenly stepped in sensitive waters. "Well, I know it has to be a relief to know the truth about who she is. But does that mean you're not going to be able to keep the baby?"

"Just the opposite." Winona stretched the phone cord so she could reach the refrigerator. Still talking, she pulled out a bottle and nuked it, knowing Angel would be hungry shortly for her nighttime feeding. "We've barely had a chance to set all the procedures and legalities in motion, and that's going to take quite some time. But right now, the whole situation looks wonderful. Do you remember the lunch we had, and your mentioning the woman who you happened to see at the Texas Cattleman's Club party early in January?"

"I sure do. The one with the scary husband."

"Exactly that one," Winona confirmed. "I tracked her down. Originally my intent was just to find out the truth about the baby. But I've been around abused women before. Got her talking, coaxed her into calling a psychologist friend. I only wish I'd gotten to her sooner. She didn't get out in time—at least technically—because that son of a seadog she married took another swing at her. This time with a bat. And that was enough. Finally. She pressed charges, and because he'd tried to use that bat, we could make an attempted murder charge stick. She's free, and he's going up the river."

Pamela heaved a sigh. "I'm so glad she's away from that man. Because he had such a good job and they lived so nicely, the family always looked okay on the surface. But I kept hearing gossip. But I was worried for a long time that there was something frightening going on in that household.''

"Yeah. And she's a nice lady. About time she had some decent luck on her side. Anyway—that all happened while Justin and I were on our honeymoon. She contacted us to formally ask Justin and I to adopt Angel. Right now, she has a lot of work to put her life back together. She wants to move, she is absolutely positive that she doesn't want the baby. I have trouble believing that she won't change her mind, but she says she is one hundred percent sure that this is the right thing for Angel as well as for her. And God knows, we both want to adopt our darling.''

"Hoboy. It's so nice to have a story have a happy ending once in a while. That creep. All that money sure didn't make him a nice man. It just gave him the means to hide what he was doing. Um, Winona…?''

Winona heard the implied question in her friend's voice, but she also heard the sounds of more boisterous laughter. She craned her head to see around the corner. Two streakers were running down the hall. She caught a breathtaking glimpse of two bare fannies, one attached to an extraordinarily adorable hunk, and the other teensy, held high in his arms. Both seemed to be headed—dripping wet—toward the master bedroom.

"Winona?'' Pamela repeated.

"I'm here—I'm sorry—I was just distracted for a second.''

"I understand. You're just home from a trip and you're busy, and for heaven's sakes, you two are still really on your honeymoon. I just want to ask you one more very quick question.''

"Sure. No problem.''

"Do you happen to know…'' from the sound on the other end of the phone, Pamela seemed to haul in a giant breath "…do you happen to know if Aaron is coming back to Royal soon?''

"Aaron Black?"

"Yes. It's none of my business. In any way. But I was just hoping that you might have heard…"

"I'm almost positive that I heard Justin say that Aaron was due back in town within a few days. And that he's going to be here for a while." Winona didn't add that the men needed to get together for Texas Cattleman's Club business. She just kept her voice light, as if Pamela asking about the distinguished diplomat was an ordinary everyday question.

But once she hung up, and aimed down the hall with the warmed-up bottle, she couldn't seem to wipe the grin off her face. Memories of the Texas Cattleman's Club party whispered through her mind. Something about that party had somehow worked as a catalyst for all kinds of events—some of them dark and serious—but some fantastic, extraordinary events had been kindled that night, too. Who'd have thought that a shy, gentle schoolteacher like Pamela would end up dancing with the sophisticated Aaron Black?

Winona was dying to know why Pamela was asking questions about Aaron Black all these weeks later…but her curiosity disappeared when she stepped into the bedroom. Other events had happened the night of that party. Other extremely unlikely couples had danced together—such as a tough woman cop who'd never planned to get married and never thought she'd belong to anyone. And a doctor with a disgraceful playboy reputation who couldn't possibly fall in love with a woman like her.

Only he had.

Just as she'd fallen in love with him.

Completely. Irrevocably. Hopelessly.

Wonderfully.

She saw the two bodies, naked on the king-size bed, playing and chortling so loudly that she had to tap her foot and harrumph to get their attention. "Just what," she said severely, "is going on here? I leave you two alone for two seconds, and what happens? The bathroom looks like a flood plain. Nobody's dressed. Nobody's dry. And the sheets are all damp now, for Pete's sake.''

Justin's head jerked up, his dark magnetic eyes fastening on her face as if the lovers had been separated for hours instead of only minutes. "Don't blame me for the wet bed." Justin motioned to the fifteen-pound blonde at his side—the one currently suckling on her big toe and drooling at the same time. "It's all her fault. She didn't want to get dressed. She wanted to get her tummy tickled. She made me do it. I'm the innocent one in this story."

"You're blaming a three-month-old baby?"

"Hey, help me out here," Justin told the baby. "Tell your mom the truth. Quick. Before I get in real trouble."

"You're dreaming if you think she can save you." Winona plopped the bottle on the bedside table and dove onto the bed with the two of them. Justin was dead right. He was in trouble—an entire lifetime ahead of delicious, wicked, non-stop trouble. She straddled his waist, bent down and kissed him, good and hard.

Angel chortled when her mom's fingertip accidentally tickled her bare toe, but Winona knew the baby was shortly going to need feeding and putting to bed. The three of them just needed a few more minutes of play first. A half hour from now, however, Dr. Justin Webb was going to have more trouble on his hands than he'd ever dreamed of.

And from the look in his eyes, he couldn't wait.

* * * * *

WORLD'S MOST
ELIGIBLE TEXAN

by
Sara Orwig

SARA ORWIG

lives with her husband and children in Oklahoma. She has a patient husband who will take her on research trips anywhere, from big cities to old forts. She is an avid collector of Western history books. With a master's degree in English, Sara writes historical romances, mainstream fiction and contemporary romances. Books are beloved treasures that take Sara to magical worlds, and she loves both reading and writing them.

Ladies, what fun to join
The Millionaire's Club with you!
Thanks to Jennifer Greene, Cindy Gerard, Kristi
Gold, Sheri WhiteFeather and our intrepid editor,
Karen Kosztolnyik.

Prologue

"You're going home to Royal?"

"You heard me right. Can I get the family plane to pick me up?" Aaron Black persisted patiently on the phone, knowing his request was a shock to his brother.

"You're taking a leave of absence," Jeb Black repeated. "I don't believe it, but I'll have the plane there as soon as possible. The diplomat from Spain, my worldly brother, is going to take a vacation in our hometown of Royal, Texas. I'm finding this damned difficult to believe."

"The State Department has cleared it so I can take some time to go home," Aaron said. "Dammit, you take vacations."

"Yeah, with the family and we go to one of those countries you work in. We don't leave Houston to go back and sit around Royal."

"Maybe you should. Royal is nice."

"Yep, if you like cows and mesquite. I'll bet you last two

days and then you'll be calling me to send the plane to get you out of there. What about the embassy while you're gone?''

For the first time that day, Aaron was amused. He smiled in the darkness of his silent Georgetown house. ''The American Embassy in Spain can carry on nicely if the First Secretary is not there for a little while.''

''I'm not sure I'm talking to my brother. Aaron, are you all right?''

''I'm fine. Tell Mary and the boys hi for me. Better yet, give them a big hug. Thanks for sending the plane.''

''Sure. Keep in touch. And tell me one more time that you're okay.''

''I'm okay, 'Mom.'''

''Well, I'm your big brother and I have to take her place sometimes. And you'll have to admit, this isn't like you at all. Aaron—does this have something to do with the Texas Cattleman's Club?''

''Yes, it does,'' Aaron could answer honestly. His brother wasn't a member, but he could have been and he knew that the club was a facade for members to work together covertly on secret missions to save innocents' lives.

''Why didn't you tell me,'' Jeb said, sounding more relaxed. ''Take care of yourself.''

''Thanks, Jeb.'' Aaron replaced the receiver, breaking the connection with his older brother. Aaron stared out the window at the swirling snow. ''No, it isn't like me,'' he whispered to himself. ''Thanks to a tall, black-haired Texas gal, I'm doing things I've never done in my life.'' Mesmerized by the swirling snow and twinkling lights, he remembered early January, three weeks ago, the night of the Cattleman's Club gala.

Aaron's pulse accelerated as he recalled the moment he had glanced across the room and seen the willowy, black-haired woman in a simple black dress. When she'd turned, her blue-eyed gaze had met his and, just for an instant, he'd felt something spark inside him. She was laughing at something someone else had said to her. Seeing her wide blue eyes, dimples and irresistible smile, Aaron had a sudden, unreasonable com-

pulsion to meet her. He'd thought he knew almost everyone
in Royal, but she was a stranger.

Then Justin Webb had spoken to him and he'd turned to
shake hands with his physician friend. The next time he'd
looked back, the woman was gone from sight. It had taken
him twenty more minutes to work his way through the crowd
and get introduced. Another two minutes and he had her in
his arms, moving on the dance floor. And then later—images
taunted him of her in his arms, of the heat of her kisses, her
eagerness—memories still fresh enough that his body reacted
swiftly to them. Pamela Miles.

Breaking into his thoughts, a car slid to a stop before his
Georgetown home and Brad Meadows, his stocky neighbor,
emerged. Brad walked around the car to open the door for his
wife, and then he opened the back door and leaned inside. In
minutes he straightened up with his little girl in his arms. As
they rushed toward their front door, they were all laughing,
but then the curly-headed three-year-old looked at Aaron's
house and evidently saw him standing in the window because
she smiled and waved. Feeling a pang as he watched them,
Aaron smiled and waved in return.

Brad Meadows had a family, a beautiful wife and a precious
little girl. Aaron ran his hand across his forehead as Pamela's
image floated into his thoughts again. "What the hell is the
matter with me?" he mumbled. Since when did he envy a guy
being *married?*

Yet he thought about his own family when he was growing
up and what fun he'd had with his two brothers and sister. He
glanced around his quiet living room. Empty house, empty
life.

The thought nagged at him—why did he feel this way so
often lately? Except that night with Pamela Miles. The loneliness, the feeling that he was missing something important in
life, the hollowness he had been experiencing the last few
years had vanished from the first moment he'd looked into her
eyes. From that first glance the chemistry between them had
been volatile. It had erupted into fiery lovemaking that at the

slightest memory could make him break into a sweat. But there was something deeper than physical need. At least there had been for him.

The next morning she had been the one who'd slipped out without a word. When he'd stirred, she was gone. He had tried to shrug off the evening. When had he let a woman tie him in knots? If the lady wanted to end it that way—fine. He had to return to Washington and then to Spain and his busy life. And he knew she was going abroad to Asterland as an exchange teacher. If he wanted, he could look her up there after he was back in Spain.

He had left Royal without seeing her, flown back to D.C. and then to Spain. Two days after the ball, a private jet had left Royal, Texas, bound for Asterland with Pamela Miles on board. Not far from Royal, the plane had had to make an emergency landing. When Matt Walker, a rancher and a fellow member of the Texas Cattleman's Club, called about the landing and about other strange happenings in Royal, Aaron had tried to call Pamela, but to no avail.

The hospital had released Pamela soon after the landing and Aaron knew so little about her, he couldn't easily find her. It was clear that the lady wasn't interested in seeing him, so he tried to put her out of mind.

But Pamela Miles had a persistent way of staying in his thoughts until he was driven to constant distraction—something so foreign to his life that he decided to see her again.

As he watched snowflakes swirl and melt on the slushy narrow Georgetown street, an emptiness struck him with a chill that was far colder than the snow. He had gone into the diplomatic corps from Army intelligence, thinking he could make a difference, help change things a little in the world, but now he was losing that feeling.

Lately he had been too aware of his thirty-seven years and what little he had in his life that was really important. But the night of the Texas ball, that desolation had vanished. Pamela had brought him to life to an extent he wouldn't have guessed possible.

Play The Lucky Hearts Game

and get...
a FREE BOOK & a FREE GIFT...
YOURS to KEEP!

Yes! I have scratched off the silver card. Please send me my **FREE BOOK** and **FREE MYSTERY GIFT**. I understand that I am under no obligation to purchase any books as explained on the back of this card. I am over 18 years of age.

Scratch Here!
then look below to see
what you can claim...

D2AI

Mrs/Miss/Ms/Mr   Initials

BLOCK CAPITALS PLEASE

Surname

Address

Postcode

Twenty-one gets you
1 FREE BOOK and a
MYSTERY GIFT!

Twenty gets you
1 FREE BOOK!

Nineteen gets you a
MYSTERY GIFT!

TRY AGAIN!

The Reader Service™ — Here's how it works:

NO STAMP NEEDED!

THE READER SERVICE™
FREE BOOK OFFER
FREEPOST CN81
CROYDON
CR9 3WZ

NO STAMP
NECESSARY
IF POSTED IN
THE U.K. OR N.I.

He swore, looking at the phone in his hand as an annoyingly loud recorded message told him his receiver was off the hook.

Aaron stared out the window, no longer seeing swirling snow or the neighboring houses with warm glows spilling from open windows. He was seeing sprawling, mesquite-covered land and a willowy, blue-eyed woman.

"Dammit," he said. "Pamela, I know there was something you felt as much as I did." He shook his head. He was being a world-class sap. The lady wasn't interested. She had made that clear. Maybe so, but he was going home to find out.

The following afternoon, the last day of January, Aaron gripped the wheel of a family car left for him at the airport as he sped down the hard-packed dusty road toward a sprawling ranch in the distance. Mesquite trees bending to the north by prevailing southern winds dotted the land on either side of the road, but all he could think about was Pamela.

He was home and he was going to find his lady.

One

"Well, I can tell you what's making you nauseated, Pamela."

She sat on the examining table with her legs crossed, the silly light cotton gown covering her as she faced white-haired Doctor Woodbury who had been treating her since she was born. She tilted her head to one side and waited, long accustomed to his blunt manner.

"You're pregnant."

"Pregnant!" Pamela's head swam and she clutched the table she was seated on with both hands. *Pregnant. It was only once. One night three weeks ago. She couldn't be.*

Dr. Woodbury was talking, but she didn't hear anything except the ringing in her ears. Her teaching job—they wouldn't want her. *Pregnant! She was going to have a baby. Baby…baby…* The word echoed in her mind. Impossible! But of course, it was possible. That night with Aaron Black. She closed her eyes and clung tightly to the cold metal, feeling as if she were going to faint.

"Knowing you as I've done through all these years, I'm guessing you'll want to keep this baby."

Dr. Woodbury's words cut through the wooziness she was experiencing. *...keep this baby...*

She opened her eyes and placed her hand protectively against her stomach. "Yes! Of course, I'll keep my baby," she snapped, her head clearing swiftly. How could he think she wouldn't!

His blue eyes gazed undisturbed at her as he shrugged stooped shoulders. "After she had you, your mother had two abortions. She wasn't having any more babies."

"I'm not my mother," Pamela said stiffly, suddenly seeing how not only Dr. Woodbury, but everyone else in town would see her—with morals as loose as her mother's had been. The town tramp. That was what Dolly Miles had been called too many times. Pamela remembered the teasing, the whispers, and worse, the steady stream of men who came and went through the Miles's tiny house.

She was shocked to learn there had been two abortions. When she thought about it, though, she wasn't surprised. Dolly thought of no one except herself. Two abortions. Pamela had a strange sense of loss. She might have had brothers or sisters. She pressed her hand against her stomach as she tried to focus on what Dr. Woodbury was saying.

"I'm keeping my baby."

"I thought you would," he said complacently. "You seem in perfectly good health. I'm going to put you on some vitamins, and then you make an appointment to come back this time next month."

The rest of the hour she moved in a daze that lasted through running errands, getting her vitamins and heading to the Royal Diner to eat. It was early for lunch and the diner would be empty, which suited her fine. Right now she didn't feel like seeing anyone. Thank heavens Aaron Black had gone back to Spain. She would have three or four months before her pregnancy would show, so she would have to make her plans in that time.

The brisk wind was chilly, catching the door to the diner and fluttering the muslin curtains at the windows, following her into the diner in a gust that swirled dried leaves around her feet. The little brass bell over the door tinkled. She glanced at the long, Formica counter top, the red vinyl-covered barstools and headed toward an empty booth along the wall. The jukebox was quiet. She put her head in her hands, her elbows propped on the table, while she thought about her pregnancy.

"Hi, Pamela," came a sharp voice, and she looked up at Sheila Foster, who plopped a plastic-coated menu into her hands. The Royal Diner—Food Fit For A King! was lettered across the top. Trying to focus on the words, Pamela skimmed the menu and ordered one of Manny's delicious hamburgers and a chocolate malt, knowing she would have to start thinking in terms of healthy meals because of the baby. The baby. She was going to have a baby. She was pregnant!

She couldn't believe the news. First sheer terror had gripped her because she didn't know how to be a mother and being unwed and pregnant was still scandalous in Royal, Texas. But the terror was quickly replaced with awe. And then when Dr. Woodbury had asked her if she would keep her baby, reality had come and she'd known she wanted her baby with every fiber in her body.

A precious baby all her own. She had never once expected to have her own baby. She had rarely dated. What Aaron had found in her, even for one night, she couldn't imagine. Except she had easily fallen into his arms, succumbed to his charms, returned his lovemaking with unbridled passion.

As she sat waiting for her lunch, her mind went back to that magical night of the Texas Cattleman's Club gala.

The gala had been given to celebrate the European dignitaries who were visiting Royal from Asterland and Obersbourg and to thank the members of the local Texas Cattleman's Club for their help in the rescue of Princess Anna von Oberland, now married to Greg Hunt. It was a glittering array of diplomats and titled people including Asterland's Lady Helena

Reichard. It had been a cold, clear night, and when Pamela had walked into the light and warmth of the ballroom, she had wondered what she was doing there. Yet, it had sounded like fun when Thad Delner, her recently widowed principal, had told her he had to make an appearance and would she like to go, since his invitation included a guest.

While Thad had talked to friends and she had talked to people she knew, they'd drifted apart. As she stood in a circle of acquaintances, she felt compelled to turn. Glancing across the room, she looked into the green-eyed gaze of a tall, ruggedly handsome man. Looking dashing in his black tux and white shirt, he had stared at her too intently, a little too long to be a casual glance. Broad-shouldered yet lean, he had short, neatly combed dark brown hair. His features were rugged with a prominent bone structure, but it was his thickly lashed green eyes that mesmerized and held her.

As she gazed back at him, time was suspended. Her pulse jumped: it was as if he had reached across the room and touched her.

Then Justin Webb had spoken to him, and he'd turned away to talk to his friend.

She knew who he was. Aaron Black. Older, an American diplomat stationed abroad, he was from Royal. Everyone in town knew the Black family. Old money, but down-to-earth good people.

Trying to concentrate and forget the look from the disturbing stranger, she turned back to the conversation at hand.

And then she was looking into his eyes only a few feet from her as he extended his hand. "Fun party. I'm Aaron Black." His voice was low, husky and mellow. She'd placed her hand in his and his grip was solid, his fingers warm, curling around hers.

"I'm Pamela Miles."

"Native?"

"Yes," she'd answered, wondering how he could possibly not know. She'd thought everyone in town knew Dolly Miles, and that Dolly had a daughter.

"I haven't spotted your date hovering over you."

She'd laughed. "You won't. I'm here with Thad Delner, my principal. I teach second grade at Royal Elementary, and Thad has been recently widowed. He had an invitation for tonight, and thought he needed to attend briefly to represent Royal Elementary, so he asked if I would like to come along. I've never been to one of these balls before."

"Well, since no date will be breathing down my neck—want to dance?"

When she'd nodded, he'd taken her arm to steer her to the dance floor and then she was closer than ever to him, aware of the cottony scent of his stiffly starched shirt, his cologne. Her fingers brushed his neck as she put her arm on his shoulder to dance. His hand holding hers was warm. They moved together as if they had danced with each other forever.

His cheekbones were prominent and his lower lip full, sensual. She realized she was staring at his mouth, and her gaze flew back up to meet his. She saw fires in the depth of his emerald eyes. Once again her gaze was caught and held by his and conversation fled while her heart drummed. As the moment stretched, making her breathless, tension crackled between them. With an effort of will she looked away.

"Tell me about your life, Pamela," he said. "You're here with your principal. Does this mean there's no guy in your life right now?"

"Yes, it does. I lead an ordinary teacher's life except I'm going to Asterland in two days as an exchange teacher."

"You're the one!" Aaron's eyebrow arched, and he tilted his head as he leaned away slightly to study her. "This is my lucky day. I'm with the American Embassy in Spain. On weekends we can see each other," he said with a warmth in his voice that sent a tingle through her. "Lucky Asterland. It's a pretty place. Very different from West Texas," he drawled.

She laughed. "I'd imagined that."

She'd listened to him talk as they danced through two more dances, and then his arm had tightened and they were dancing cheek-to-cheek and her pulse was racing.

She'd danced once with Matt Walker, an old friend and one of the local ranchers, and then Aaron was back, claiming her for another dance. And she was aware of other women watching Aaron, and she knew they wanted to be dancing with him, and she could understand why they did. As they'd spun around the floor to a fast number, she looked at women in fancy gowns they had bought for thousands of dollars in elegant boutiques here in Royal or in stores in Dallas and Houston while she was in her simple black sheath she had purchased for a little over fifty dollars. She was amazed that Aaron was dancing with her—amazed and glad. And in some ways, it seemed the most natural thing in the world to be in his arms, moving with him, looking into his green eyes.

After an hour, between dances, Thad Delner had joined them. As soon as she introduced him to Aaron, Thad had turned to her to tell her he was ready to leave. Before he could finish, Aaron broke in.

"I'll take Pamela home, Mr. Delner. I'm glad you brought her."

Thad Delner's blue eyes focused on her with a questioning look. "Is that all right with you, Pamela?"

She'd nodded, breathless, amazed Aaron was offering to take her home "Yes, it's fine," she said, looking at Aaron, whose rugged handsomeness made her heart race.

"All right. You two go back to your dancing. I'll talk to you before you leave for Asterland, Pamela."

"Thanks for bringing me, Thad," she'd said and then she was back in Aaron's arms to dance again.

When he'd invited her to come by his house for a drink, and she'd accepted, the dreamlike quality of the evening continued. At Pine Valley, an exclusive area of fine homes, Aaron slowed for large iron gates to open. As a gate swung back, he drove past it and waved at the guard.

The stately mansions sobered her. The lawns were vast and well-cared-for, the houses imposing, and his world of wealth and privilege seemed light years from her world of teaching and budgeting and ordinary living.

"Why so quiet?" Aaron asked. The lights of the dash threw the flat planes of his cheeks into shadow. When he looked at her, she could feel his probing look. Handsome, dashing, he was incredibly unique.

"I was just thinking about the differences in our lives," she said, looking at the palatial Georgian-style houses with sweeping, constantly tended lawns. "We're very different, you and I," she said solemnly.

"Thank heavens," he said lightly and picked up her hand to brush her knuckles across his cheek. "If you were just like me, I wouldn't be taking you home with me now, I can promise."

She smiled at him and relaxed, but the feeling returned again when they entered his house and he turned off an alarm.

"Gates, guards and alarms. You're well-protected."

He shrugged. "This is a family home. Ninety percent of the time, no one lives here," he said, taking her arm as he switched on a low light in the entryway.

"I'm sorry you lost your parents," she said, remembering headlines several years ago that had told about the plane crash in Denmark when his parents and six other Texans had been killed.

"Thanks. What about your parents?"

"They're deceased," she said stiffly, amazed again that he didn't know about her mother. She had never known her father and wasn't certain her mother even knew which man fathered her.

Aaron had led her through a kitchen and down a wide hall into a large family room elegantly furnished with plush navy leather and deeply burnished cherrywood furniture. An immense redbrick fireplace was at one end of the room and a thick Oriental rug covered part of the polished oak floor. He crossed the room to the fireplace to start the fire and in minutes the logs blazed. Following him into the room, she wandered around to look at oil paintings of western scenes. When she glanced back at him, he'd shed his tux coat. As her gaze ran across his broad shoulders, she drew a deep breath. He removed his tie and unfastened his collar and there was something so personal in watching him shed part of his clothing, that her cheeks flushed.

As soon as he moved to the bar, he glanced at her. "Wine, beer, whiskey, soda pop, what would you like to drink?"

"White wine sounds fine," she answered, watching his well-shaped hands move over sparkling crystal while she sat on a corner of the cool leather sofa. He joined her, handing her a glass. When he sat down, he raised his glass. "Here's to tonight, the night we met, Pamela," he said softly and his words were like a caress.

While she smiled at him, she touched her glass lightly to his. "You think tonight is going to be memorable? You're a sweet-talkin' devil, Aaron Black. You're dangerous," she said, flirting with him and watching his green eyes sparkle. Yet even as she teased him, she had a feeling that his words, *tonight, the night we met,* would stick with her forever.

"I'm dangerous? I think that's good news," he said, sipping his wine and setting it on the large glass and cherrywood table in front of them. He scooted closer to her and reached out, picking up locks of her hair and letting them slide through his fingers. She was too aware of his faint touches, his knuckles just barely brushing her throat and ear and cheek. "Now why am I dangerous?"

"All that fancy talking can turn a girl's head mighty fast. Texas men are too good at it."

"And Texas women are the prettiest women in the world," he said softly, his gaze running over her features.

She laughed and set her wine on the table as she looked at him with amusement. His brows arched in question. "That is high-fallutin' talkin'! I'm too tall, too freckled and there's never been a time in my entire life that anyone told me what a beauty I am, so that's a stretch, Aaron."

He didn't smile in return which made her heart miss a beat, but he gazed at her solemnly while he stroked his fingers through her hair. "Maybe I see something others haven't seen."

"Oh, heavens, can you lay it on thick!"

"Just telling the truth," he drawled and smiled a lazy smile at her.

They were in dangerous waters and she glanced around, trying to get the conversation less personal. "If no one lives here most of the time, who takes care of your house?" she asked, looking at the immaculate room.

"We have a staff," he answered casually without taking his eyes from hers. His fingers stroked her nape in featherlight brushes that ignited fires deep within her. His voice was low. The only light now was from the blazing fire, and there was a cozy intimacy that was made electric by his nearness. "Why are you a teacher?"

"I love children," she answered, and he nodded his approval. "I feel strongly that all children should be able to read, so I like working with them, particularly in reading. I never had any family. Maybe that's why I feel the way I do about kids. Why did you want to be a diplomat?"

"Everything about it fascinated me," he said quietly, his green gaze studying her as if he were memorizing every feature. "I thought I could help save the world when I went into it."

"And now?"

"Now I know that's an impossibility. The old world will keep turning no matter what I do. There will always be wars and intrigue, and now, more than ever, terrorism."

"You sound disenchanted."

"Not tonight. Tonight is good," he said, giving her a heated, direct look that blatantly conveyed his desire.

"Behave yourself, Aaron! You do come on strong."

"You won't believe me, but I don't usually." As she smiled, he touched her cheek. "Dimples. You have to have been told your dimples are pretty."

"Maybe so," she said. "Tell me about Spain."

"I'll tell you, but soon I want to show it to you. You'll have your weekends free when you get to Asterland and I can take you to my favorite places in Spain."

Though she merely smiled at him, his words gave her a thrill. She listened to him describe Spain and Asterland, and she answered his questions about her job. Their conversation roamed over a myriad of subjects as if they had a million things to tell each other. And all the time they talked, his fingers drifted over her hands or nape or ear or played in her hair while he watched her as if she were the first woman he had ever seen.

"Your family has lived in Texas for more than a hundred years, haven't they?" she asked him. He nodded while his fingers stroked her nape and she barely could concentrate on what he was answering. While his index finger traced the curve of her ear, she inhaled deeply, tingles fueling her desire.

"Yep. My great-granddaddy, Pappy Black, ran cattle when he came home after the War Between the States. He amassed the Black fortune. Then my granddad, Rainy Black—I'm named for him—he was Aaron Rainier Black, was a Texas senator, so I grew up around politicians. I'm as Texas as you can get."

"Sure, Aaron," she said, thinking of his eastern education. His fingers trailed from her ear down over her throat and along her arm, moving to her knee. His thickly lashed eyes were filled with desire and she tingled along every nerve ending from all his feather touches. *"¿Habla Español?"* she asked.

"Sì. ¿Y usted?"

"Muy poco. Only what I've picked up from living in Royal. What other languages do you speak?"

"French, German, Arabic, Italian, Polish and Chinese. My undergraduate degree is in languages and political science and I had to learn Arabic in the military. I had to learn Polish with the State Department."

She thought again of the vast differences in their lives. "Which colleges did you attend?"

"Harvard for an undergraduate degree," he replied in an offhand manner. "Now tell me what you like to do? What's fun?"

"Playing with little children, reading. I enjoy doing pencil drawings. Just simple things. I've taught aerobics before, but not for the past year.'' Her gaze dropped to his mouth, and she wondered what it would be like to kiss him. She wanted to kiss him. Why did he have this effect on her? She felt as if sparks constantly danced between them, and her awareness level was at a maximum. With an effort she tried to concentrate on what he was saying.

They sat and talked until a grandfather clock in the hall chimed three in the morning. It seemed she had been with him five minutes, yet it seemed as if she had known him all her life.

By three he had unfastened and removed his cuff links, turned back his white sleeves, kicked off his shoes. Her nerves were tingling and raw, and she was intensely aware of him, looking at his full lower lip and continuing to wonder what it would be like to kiss him.

When the clock softly chimed the third time, she stood. ''Well, it's getting late,'' she said.

In a fluid movement, he came to his feet instantly and placed his hand on her waist, turning her to face him. One look in his eyes and her breath caught. He drew her closer.

''I feel like I've waited all my life for this moment,'' he said softly.

Her heart thudded, and she told herself not to believe what he said, but the words thrilled her as his hand slid behind her head and his arm went around her waist, pulling her against his hard length. He leaned down, his mouth brushing hers and her pulse skipped with the first contact of his lips on hers. Fire and magic. Even more, before her lashes came down, was the look in his eyes of wanting her—as if his words had been the truth and he had been waiting forever.

What was it about this man that melted her physically and emotionally? That made all barriers go down and her body and heart both yield completely? He took her breath and made her pulse race and it seemed so incredibly right, as if she were destined for this night from the day she was born. He rubbed his lips softly against hers again.

"Aaron," she whispered his name, that from the first moment they'd met had been special, irresistible.

His mouth settled on hers, opening it fully while his tongue thrust over hers, stroking it and conveying such need that she quivered in response. She wrapped her arms around his neck and returned his kisses and his passion. She felt his arousal and felt his hands slide over her and then move to her zipper. Cool air played across her shoulders as her dress fell away, and Aaron raised his head to push away the top of her lacy blue teddy. Inhaling deeply, he cupped her small breasts in his large, tanned hands. His breathing was ragged when he bent, and his tongue stroked her nipple.

"You're beautiful," he whispered. "I need you."

His words were as seductive as his kisses. Moaning with pleasure, she shook and gripped his shoulders and knew she should stop, but his every touch was magic. Sensations and desire bombarded her. Never in her life had she known passion. Never before had she found a man who ignited desire into blazing flames. She would stop him, but oh, not yet. Not yet...

His thumbs circled and stroked her taut nipples and her insides turned a somersault. Her fingers went to the studs on his shirt, and in minutes she had worked them free and pushed away his shirt and then her hands were on his chest that was lean, hard-corded muscles. Her fingers tangled in the mat of short brown hair across his chest.

Swinging her into his arms while he kissed her, he carried her to a bedroom and then they were in bed together, her length stretched against his. As he peeled away the teddy and her hose, his hands and kisses were everywhere.

Was it the wine? The man? The magic of the night? His beguiling words that made her feel an incredible need in him for her alone?

A dim voice within her urged her usual caution, but it went up in smoke in minutes as he moved lower, trailing kisses to her thighs. His hand slipped between her legs, stroking her, driving her over a brink and making her want what she had never known, want it all with this man who was so special to her from the first moment she had looked into his eyes.

She helped him peel away his trousers and briefs. He moved over her, hard, ready, breathtakingly handsome as she wrapped her long legs around him and pulled him to her. She heard him whisper, asking if she was protected, and she answered yes, yes, wanting him with a desperate urgency in a manner she hadn't ever dreamed possible while desire demolished all her wisdom and caution.

His mouth covered hers, taking her cries of passion as he slowly entered her. When he raised his head and frowned, she arched her hips, tightened her legs, and pulled him to her.

"Please, Aaron," she whispered, knowing this night was more than magic for her and she wanted him as she had never wanted anything. She gave her virginity to him eagerly, wanting him and lost in the roaring of her pulse, only dimly hearing him cry out her name as she gasped, carried out of the world into pure ecstasy, finally tumbling over a brink of release.

In the quiet of the fading night he showered her with kisses, and then he held her tightly against him while they talked. His other hand caressed her, and his voice was a deep rumble that she loved to listen to.

"What do you like best in the world, Aaron?" she asked, wanting to discover everything about him she could.

"This night. You in my arms. Long, slow hot kisses, people who care, Switzerland, the ranch. What do you like?" he asked in a lazy voice while he languidly drew his fingers over her hip.

"Tonight, too. Being with you. Little children. Books." She ran her finger along his jaw that had a faint trace of stubble now. "What do you want out of life?"

"Ahh, that's an easier question. I want a family, a woman who is my best friend and lover. I want to do some good for people, to settle on the ranch—"

"You want to live here on your ranch?" she asked, interrupting him and surprised by his answer.

"Sure. I grew up on the ranch and love it. I want some

more years in the diplomatic service, but then I want to come home to ranching. What do you want out of life?'' he asked, gazing into her eyes while she caught his hand to kiss his knuckles lightly.

''I don't think about it much. I want to be a good teacher. I don't want any child to ever pass through my classroom and not be able to read when moving on. They should all learn in first and second grade and never go on until they master reading.''

''No yearning for marriage?''

She was glad it was dark and he couldn't see her blush, because she could feel the heat rise in her cheeks. ''You know now, Aaron, that you're the first man in my life. I've never dated much and never thought I would marry.''

''I'll bet the ranch you do.''

When she laughed, he touched her dimple. ''Are you a gambling man?''

''Actually no. But I don't think that would be much of a bet. You'll marry, lady.''

''Right now, I'm thinking about going to Asterland. Tell me some more about Europe.''

''Asterland is a beautiful little country. You're going to like it.'' She listened to him talk for another twenty minutes and then while she was talking, she heard his deep, regular breathing and realized he was asleep. Hugging him, knowing she would carry memories of this night with her the rest of her life because she had fallen in love, she settled against him and closed her eyes.

She lay in his arms and listened to his heartbeat and his deep steady breathing. He held her tightly as if afraid of losing her. The wonder of the night left her dazed. Aaron was a marvel. Their lovemaking was ecstasy she had never expected to experience. She'd slept, then stirred as dawn spilled into the room, and along with it, reality.

Memories assailed her, and in the light of day, they held clarity and a shocked realization of how he must see the night.

How could she have fallen into his arms and given all to

him the first night she'd met him? She closed her eyes in pain, thinking of her mother and the taunting cries she had been teased with when she was young—"...your mom's the town tramp," "trash mama," "she's cheap," "easy lay"—even worse names.

Shame, shock, fear of what Aaron would think of her, all ran through her mind. Was she that much like her mother after all? After all these years of being so circumspect, so careful, the moment a dashing, worldly man had turned his charm on her, she had thrown prudence over instantly.

Wiping at tears that stung her eyes, she slid out of bed. She could only imagine how Aaron must see her. Then her gaze fell on him and, momentarily, her feelings shifted and longing shook her. He was sprawled in bed, the sheet down below his narrow waist. His body was lean, muscled and looked like the body of a runner. The mat of dark brown hair across his chest tapered down in a line to his navel. Her gaze traveled lower to the sheet covering him, but her memories conjured up visions of Aaron last night when he was hard, ready and so incredibly male and appealing.

Giving a little shake of her shoulders, she knew she didn't want to see those probing green eyes open and look at her in a demeaning manner. Nor did she want to hear him make excuses or make light of an evening that had taken her heart. Again, she wondered how she could have succumbed so swiftly. Was it in her genes? She had fought that notion all her life, treating boys coldly, keeping barriers around her when she was older, barriers that turned guys off quickly.

As quietly as possible, with shaking hands and tears stinging her eyes, she gathered her things and dressed. Then she slipped downstairs and called Royal's only cab.

In minutes she was standing on the drive, praying that Aaron wouldn't waken. Today she was supposed to go to Midland to see her closest friend, Jessica Atkins, a fellow teacher. Aaron probably couldn't find her if he wanted to. She suspected he wouldn't even care. Yet he hadn't seemed that way last night.

"Of course, he didn't, ninny!" she whispered to herself. "Get real. He seduced you—it was a one-night stand and you fell into his arms eagerly. Practically jumped into his arms."

The cab whisked her away, and when the tall iron gates began to swing shut behind her she was certain she was closing a part of her life away. From this time forward, last night would only be a memory, yet she knew she had given Aaron much more than just her body.

Embarrassed and saddened, she had ridden home, packed for the weekend swiftly and rushed to her car to drive to Midland and the haven of Jessica's small frame house. No matter how many miles she put between them, she couldn't get Aaron out of her thoughts. The realization that they hadn't used any protection came to her. Aaron had asked if she was protected, and, totally lost to the moment, wanting him as she had never wanted anything in her life, she had whispered yes.

"You know better than that!" she said aloud to herself.

Realizing she was sitting in the Royal Diner, talking to herself, Pamela took a deep breath. Aaron had asked if she was protected. She couldn't blame him. And if he learned about her pregnancy—that must never happen. She wouldn't even consider the possibilities.

She thought about the Blacks. Everyone in town knew that his parents had been into missionary work; his brother was a minister, channeling funds to worldwide missions, his older sister was a doctor in a third-world country. She didn't know what his other brother did, but they were good people and used their enormous wealth to help others. Aaron had told her how he had gone into the diplomatic service because he thought he could try to do something to help world situations.

She ran her fingers across her brow. Aaron Black must never know he was the father of her baby. He would be a man to marry out of a sense of duty and doing the right thing. Aaron...

Such a pang hit her she clutched her middle. Longing rolled up through her like a tidal wave. Along with her body, she

had given her heart to him. She knew that. But she was realistic. She was a veteran of watching pillars of the community
sleep with her mother, give Dolly tokens of appreciation—or
much more than tokens—cars, jewelry, but always they eventually turned their backs on Dolly and went their own way.
And out in public she had seen them meet her mother and
seen the furtive glances, the coolness, the lack of respect they
had treated Dolly with.

She couldn't bear that with Aaron. Aaron Black's baby.
Again, she pressed her hand to her flat stomach and felt a
surge of maternal joy. She already loved this baby with her
whole heart and she would devote her life to her precious
child.

She would have to move from Royal because there would
be too much gossip here, but that was something she didn't
have to worry about today. She just had to keep her condition
a secret until her plans were made. It was a secret to be kept
most of all from Aaron Black. He had already gone back to
Europe, so there was little chance of his finding out unless
Justin Webb or Matt Walker or another one of those buddies
of Aaron's learned about it and told him. And if he did find
out, Matt was a good enough friend to respect her wishes. She
could trust Matt to be the friend he always had been.

Once again the enormity of what she had done struck her.
How could she have been so like her mother? How could she
have thrown over all her caution when she had spent a lifetime
being cautious? The man could charm the proverbial birds out
of the trees, but that was no excuse. She had met charmers in
college and had managed easily to say no. What was it about
Aaron Black that twisted her into knots, melted her reserve,
dissolved all barriers she kept up?

She clutched her middle again, aghast when she thought
about how easy she had been, how careless, and what Aaron
must think about her.

"Are you feeling better, Pamela?"

"I'm fine, thanks," she said, aware of the waitress approaching the table. Sheila's pink uniform was bright and her gaze was sharp.

"What happened was scary. I guess you'll get over it as time goes by. Sorry you won't get to go to Asterland to teach this semester. I heard the program was suspended."

"That's right, but with my ankle hurt, I wasn't able to teach right after the crash," Pamela said, wishing they could stop talking about it.

Sheila turned away, and Pamela stared at the giant burger and golden fries on her plate and knew she couldn't eat a bite. Nor could she leave the entire burger and fries without stirring up a storm of comments. She sipped some of the chocolate malt, ate two bites of the burger, and then she couldn't get down another morsel. She wrapped the burger and a few fries in her napkin and jammed them into her purse. Her purse would reek of hamburger, but she didn't want any gossip starting now. No one ordered one of Manny's juicy burgers and then left it with only a couple of bites taken out of it.

Thank heavens, so far, both she and Thad Delner led such straight and square lives that no one could conjure up gossip about them going together to the ball. And everyone in town knew he went to represent the school. Also, everyone in town was sorry about the loss of his wife, whom he had deeply loved. But once word got out that she had left the ball with Aaron Black, that would be another matter.

She slid out of the booth, paid and rushed from the diner before she had another conversation with anyone else. A few people were beginning to appear for lunch and she greeted them perfunctorily without even seeing who they were.

She drove home, her thoughts still churning, but an absolute determination growing within her that Aaron Black should never know about the baby. Their baby. She would call Jessica to tell her to watch for teaching jobs in Midland. The teaching position in Asterland was suspended this semester and by the next term, she would be very pregnant and she wouldn't want to go to Asterland even if it were possible. She wanted her baby born here in Texas where she had friends.

Midland was larger than Royal, far enough away that her life would be her own, yet close enough she could get back to see her friends in Royal when she wanted to.

At least she didn't have to worry about running into Aaron. He was halfway around the world and most likely had forgotten about her by now. She could imagine the kind of women in his life and wondered whether, while home in Texas, he had simply been amusing himself with the country girl that she was. In many ways Royal wasn't a typical small Texas town because of oil money and all the wealth it produced. Basically, though, Royal *was* a small West Texas town and she was pure country.

She turned onto her street and saw her two-story brick apartment complex. She drove through the open wooden barriers that never closed and turned down the row to the back of her tiny apartment and her carport. As she approached her carport, her heart thudded. Seated on the tailgate of a shiny black pickup was Aaron Black.

Two

Her throat went dry and it was difficult to breathe. She felt hot, embarrassed, as if she were nine months pregnant instead of only weeks. There he was, and more than that, he looked marvelous. Her pulse raced like a shooting star. He looked as good in jeans and a plaid woolen shirt as he had in a tux. He wore scuffed boots and slid casually to his feet with his hands hooked into his wide, hand-tooled leather belt. A lock of brown hair fell across his forehead.

His green eyes were just as she remembered—going right through her. How could she keep her secret? *Why was he here and not halfway around the world?* What was she going to say to him? What did he want?

A cynical voice answered *that* question in a flash—another easy night with her. Her chin raised and her lips compressed while she tried to breathe deeply and wondered if she was going to faint right in front of him. Except she wasn't given to fainting. It might be a lot easier if she could.

"Go away, Aaron Black," she mumbled as she parked, and

knew he was watching her every move. And then he was at the door, opening it and holding it for her.

When she stepped outside and looked up at him, her heart skipped beats. Gazing at him solemnly, she wrestled with her feelings because she wanted to walk right into his arms.

"Hi, Pamela."

She couldn't say a word.

"Well, hi, there, Aaron, it's good to see you," he said in a teasing voice while he ran his finger lightly along her cheek. "Cat got your tongue? Some reason I developed the plague and you want to avoid me?"

At his touch, tingles flashed through her, and she knew she was hopelessly lost unless she got her wits together and her defenses up. She drew herself up. "Hi, Aaron. I thought you were in Spain."

"Well, I was," he drawled in that mellow voice that was like a stroke of his fingers. Darn, if he would just quit looking at her like she was a bit of steak and he was a starving man. "But I came home because I wanted to see you."

"You came home to see me?" she whispered, shocked and unable to believe she had heard correctly. Did he *know?* She rejected that notion instantly.

He looked around while a gust of cold wind buffeted them and spun leaves into the air. "Could we maybe talk inside?"

"Oh! Of course. Come in," she said, feeling ridiculous and knowing the women in his life knew how to handle moments like this smoothly and casually, while she was acting like a twelve-year-old with her first crush. She moved ahead of him, reached out to unlock the door and dropped her keys. He scooped them up, reached his long arm around her and unlocked the door, pushing it open and waiting for her to enter. Too aware of how close he was behind her, she stepped inside. He made her fluttery and overly conscious of him and of herself and her condition.

She glanced around her tiny kitchen and thought of his palatial family home in Pine Valley. Her whole apartment would fit into his kitchen.

She opened her purse to drop her keys inside and the smell of the hamburger wafted into the air. His brows arched and he reached down to pull the wrapped burger from her purse. She could hear the laughter in his voice. "You carry hamburgers and fries in your purse?"

"Not usually," she said, snatching her lunch from him and carrying it to the counter to set it down. "I wasn't hungry. Do you want anything to drink?"

"No thanks, but help yourself."

She shook her head. "Let's sit in the living room."

He looked all around as they entered her tiny living room with its white wicker furniture, red, blue and yellow throw pillows, colorful prints on the walls—an attractive room to her, but a far cry from his lifestyle.

"Nice place."

"Thank you."

He prowled around with both the grace and curiosity of a cat and stepped into the bedroom that opened off the living room. "This is your bedroom," he said, and she wondered how she had left her room that morning when she had dressed for the doctor's appointment. She ran her hand across her forehead, watching him as he returned to the living room and moved across the room to the sofa. He tilted his head again.

"Are you going to sit down?"

"Yes," she replied, knowing she was acting ridiculously, but he had jolted her with his sudden appearance when she'd thought he was in Spain.

When she perched on the edge of the sofa, he sank down near her, looking relaxed and as if he owned the place. He leaned closer, and she realized she should have sat across the room from him. He ran his finger along her cheek. "Big blue eyes just like I remembered," he said softly, and she wondered if he could hear her heart thudding.

"Why are you here?"

Again, he looked as if amusement danced in his eyes. "Glad to see me?"

"Yes," she said cautiously. This time there was no mistaking the laughter in his eyes.

"Uh-huh," he drawled. "Can I ask you a question?"

"Sure," she said, bracing up and wondering what was coming.

"Why did you disappear the next morning?" His voice was quiet, his words innocuous, but his eyes nailed her and a flush heated her cheeks.

With an effort she looked away from those damnable green eyes that made her feel as if he could see every thought in her head. "I was supposed to leave town and I needed to get home."

"Oh, yeah," he drawled in a voice that indicated he didn't believe that answer for a second.

She knotted her fingers in her lap. "I don't usually sleep with a guy the first night I meet him," she whispered stiffly, feeling her cheeks burn, but there it was, the flat-out bald truth.

"I know you don't," he said in such a tender voice that she wanted to fling herself into his arms. His fingers lifted her chin and turned her to face him, and when she looked into his eyes, she felt she was melting and all her resistance was slipping away.

"Go to dinner with me tonight."

"I can't be—"

"That's why I came home," he interrupted.

Shocked by his statement, she stared at him. "It isn't either! You didn't come home to take me to dinner."

"Did so," he argued quietly. "To my way of thinking, we have some unfinished business between us," he said, and beneath his soft voice, she could hear a steely determination.

She thought about her condition and shook her head. "I think it is finished," she said. "You move in one world and I live in another. I'm just a country girl, Aaron, so let's be realistic. You couldn't have come home to take me to dinner!"

"Yes, ma'am, I surely did," slipping into a West Texas drawl that she knew he didn't usually have. "And what's all this about a country girl? Where do you think I grew up?"

"Right here, but don't give me that ol' country-boy routine. You were educated in the east and you live abroad and you move in circles that I know nothing about and the women in your life—"

"Bore me witless," he said, scooting a little closer. "I wouldn't pursue this if I didn't feel like there was something between us."

His words devastated her, and she clutched her fingers even more tightly together. *Resist the sweet talk, resist…*

She scooted away from him a few inches, keeping the space they'd had, but now she was pressed against the end of the sofa.

"We had sex between us, but—"

"That was lovemaking, Pamela," he interrupted with such solemnity that her heart did another lurch. "It was good and fine and important." He studied her. "Maybe we need to take some time now to get to know each other."

"No, we don't!"

"Why the hell not?"

Her mind raced on how to answer him. *Why did he have to sit so close?* It was difficult to think. "I told you, I'm country and you're not and don't say you are. Our worlds are really different, and there is no way you can convince me that you're here because I'm so fascinating."

"You don't think so?"

"No. How'd did you get off work in the middle of the week?"

"I asked for time off to come home to see you."

Her jaw did drop. While she stared at him, he gazed back steadily with no amusement in his features now.

"This is important," he announced solemnly.

Her heart stopped. Missed beats and then picked up. *No. Not now,* was all she could think. *Not now. Don't do this. He mustn't know.* Her head swam. *This can't happen now. It's too late. Much too late for us.*

She shook her head. "You need to pack and go back to Spain. This is ridiculous. We're in different worlds, Aaron.

That night was special, but it was just a night. Now I need to—''

He moved closer. ''Pamela, I want a chance to show you that our worlds aren't that different. There are some basic things about people that match up, and I think we ought to get to know each other a little and see how much we match up. Maybe you're right and it won't be the magic it seemed, but let's get to know each other a little better and give a relationship a chance.''

''I just don't think we should.'' She could barely get out the words.

''What will it hurt?'' he persisted softly, lacing his fingers in hers and running his thumb across her knuckles and scrambling her thoughts.

If you only knew, you would run like crazy. She stared at him, her heart pounding, knowing that she had to send him on his way.

''You're sitting close.''

''I'm glad you noticed. What will it hurt?''

I will be in love with you more than I am now, she thought, *and you'll find out I'm carrying your baby, and then you'll want to marry me for all the wrong reasons.* She knew she could never, ever let him know about the pregnancy. Send him on his way back to Spain.

''One little dinner date,'' he said softly, leaning forward to brush his lips against her throat. ''Just go out with me tonight, okay? Come on. I'll bet we'll have a good time getting to know each other a little better,'' he coaxed. He was close enough that she could feel his warmth, smell his woodsy aftershave.

''We shouldn't—''

''You'd rather eat alone than with me?'' he whispered.

''No, but—''

''Good. It's settled.'' His lips trailed kisses lightly along her throat, and she ached to turn her head and kiss him fully. With that first brush of his lips, she was lost. He leaned back. ''I'll pick you up about seven. I made reservations at Claire's.''

Her eyes opened. What had she done? How did he get his
way so easily with her?

"Aaron, you couldn't have come back from Spain to take
me to dinner."

"Yes, I did."

If he was lying, he was doing a magnificent job of sounding
convincing, but then she knew in his job he must be accustomed to some slick talking to get what he wanted.

"But what about your job? You can't just leave on a
whim."

"I have so many vacation days piled up, I can take off for
a long time. When I started this job, I was in love with it. I
guess I thought I was doing my part to help save the world. I
gave it my everything. I didn't take vacations very often, so I
have a lot of days coming. Besides, I asked for a leave of
absence and they granted it."

Appalled, she stared at him. "Leave of absence! You're in
Royal for more than tonight?"

"Don't sound so thrilled," he drawled, and his eyes were
full of questions. "You keep looking at me as if I'm some
kind of monster."

"No! Oh, no! I just am shocked about your leave of absence. It takes some adjusting to think of you in Royal instead
of Spain."

He placed both hands on either side of her face while his
gaze probed hers. "Why does it take some adjusting to have
me here? That's not too flattering."

"I'm sorry," she said, heat burning her cheeks. Why
couldn't she control her darn blushes! "I'm just surprised."

"Well, get used to it, lady, because I came home for us to
get to know each other a little better," he said in a husky
voice.

She pulled away from him and stood, her knees bumping
his knees. He was on his feet instantly and his hand rested on
her waist, stopping her from moving away from him.

"Pamela, I don't know what's going on in that pretty head

of yours, but yes, I want us to get to know each other better. I've been thinking about you constantly since that night."

"Oh, my heavens! I don't believe it."

He frowned. "Well, you better believe it, and I'll do my damnedest to convince you because memories of you have played hell with my work. You've got some notion in your head about the kind of woman I want in my life, but you're wrong."

"Oh, Aaron," she said, his words tearing at her.

"At least, let's just take a little time. Maybe we're not compatible, but let's give ourselves a chance to find out."

She didn't have that option. In spite of her longing, her feelings for him, his charm and persistence, she knew she had to keep her secret from him and send him packing back to Spain.

"I don't think that's a good idea."

"You promised dinner tonight. I'm holding you to that." She gazed up at him, aware of his hand on her waist, his nearness, his green eyes filled with determination and a look that kept her pulse racing.

He brushed her lips lightly with a kiss and moved away. "I'll see you at seven, darlin'." He strode through her tiny apartment and opened the back door. "I doubt if that hamburger is fit to eat now. I'll feed you tonight."

And then he was gone, and she stared at the closed door, frozen in shock over how once again she had capitulated to what he wanted. She heard the roar of the pickup. A pickup and cowboy boots and jeans. He had looked at home in them, but she knew better. He was a diplomat who lived in Europe and had spent nearly all his adult life abroad. He was First Secretary at the American Embassy in Spain. She could imagine the women he knew, beautiful, sophisticated—they didn't drop keys and carry hamburgers in their purses. She rubbed her temples and moved restlessly around the room. When he'd asked her out, all her resolve had just melted away. She was jelly where he was concerned, and she was going to have to do better tonight.

Why was she going? What would she wear? Was he doing this to sleep with her again? That question brought her up short and a flash of shame and anger burned in her.

She turned to a small mirror and shook her finger at her reflection. ''Pamela, you were easy. Get a backbone where he is concerned! You'll have to send him packing tonight and stay cool, cool, cold.''

She thought of guys who had called her frigid. Where was all that coldness she could turn on so easily with others?

She looked down at her flat stomach and splayed her fingers against it. A baby. Aaron's baby. He must never, never know. But in spite of the foolishness of getting pregnant in her first night of lovemaking, in spite of how it would turn her life upside down and in spite of all the struggles of being a single mother, she couldn't stop being thrilled and awed. Her own precious baby. Aaron's baby.

She knew from teaching the struggles the young single mothers and dads had, how they had to be everything for their kids and juggle jobs and schedules, but she would do it. Her own baby. Aaron's baby. This baby had a wonderful father.

Aaron has a right to know about his baby.

That thought was an unwanted one. He might have a right to know, but if he did, she knew he would want to do the right thing, and out of duty he would insist they marry. His family would hate her and think she had trapped him. No, he wasn't going to know, and he would marry some beautiful woman who was the right kind of woman for him and have his own family someday. She was certain of that. This was the only way it could be because Aaron would never be happy married to a woman like her. Not ever. And she didn't want duty or pity or charity. She couldn't bear to see him feeling trapped.

''Go to dinner and send him back to Spain. You know how to turn men off,'' she said and wondered when she had started talking out loud to herself and realized it had been since she met Aaron.

She threw up her hands and went to find something to wear

tonight. Her life had changed forever today—pregnant, dinner tonight with Aaron. He had come home to take her out! To get to know her better. A pang of longing made her tremble. Why did it have to be this way! "Because of my own carelessness," she answered herself.

Long ago she could remember Dr. Woodbury asking her if she wanted a prescription for the Pill and her turning him down, saying she wasn't dating and there was no need. When he had lectured her, she had turned a deaf ear. She should have listened, but then she touched her stomach again and knew she really had no regrets. She adored little children and this would be her own baby, something she had never dreamed possible.

Dinner with Aaron. If only— She shut her mind to following that line of thought, but she couldn't resist touching her throat and remembering his lips brushing against her.

Aaron whistled as he drove. He was excited, eager and he had to laugh at that hamburger stashed in her purse.

"No, darlin', I don't know any women like you and that's what's so wonderful about you. I like a country girl," he said out loud. It was refreshing to know she was going to tell him what she thought and not twist things all around or play games with him.

She couldn't believe he was here to take her out, but he would convince her. And maybe they wouldn't get along as well as he expected, but he had to find out. Maybe this was a bunch of foolishness on his part, but he knew he was excited, happy, and felt better than he had since the night of the gala.

At seven that evening his pulse raced while he stood at her front door and punched the bell. The door swung open and she smiled at him. His pulse jumped another notch at the sight of her. Her shiny black hair was short, straight, hanging loosely with the ends curling under just below her ears in a simple, uncomplicated hairdo that was like the rest of her. Her dress was an indigo sheath that clung to her slender figure. She didn't wear jewelry and had very little makeup, but she took his breath away, and, for an instant, he saw her without the dress, as he remembered her from that first night, slender, curvaceous, supple, warm, so damn giving and open to him.

"Hi," he said, his husky voice betraying what he was feeling.

"Come in," she said quietly, her blue eyes pulling him into their depths, and he wanted to say to hell with dinner and take her into his arms and straight to that tiny little virginal bedroom she had. Instead, he watched her as he walked inside. As soon as she closed the door, he turned to face her. He inhaled her perfume, a scent of lilacs, and it was an effort to keep from reaching for her, but he knew he'd better keep some kind of distance. The lady wasn't overwhelmed with eagerness to go out with him tonight.

"You look gorgeous."

"Thank you," she said, smiling with her cheeks flushing and a sparkle coming to her eyes that made him feel better. Why was she so solemn? She hadn't been that way that first night. He felt like he had done something wrong, but he couldn't imagine what.

"I'll get my coat. You look nice, too, Aaron, very elegant in your navy suit," she said shyly, and he couldn't keep from reaching out to brush her cheek lightly with his fingers.

"Thanks, darlin'. I've been getting ready for this date since I drove away from your place this afternoon."

She gave him an I-don't-believe-you look and turned to get her coat. He watched the gentle, sexy sway of her hips and tried to get his thoughts elsewhere because the slightest little thing with her could turn him on in a flash. For the first time he noticed the small elastic bandage that wrapped one slender ankle and he wondered if that was a lingering result of an injury during the rough landing of the Asterland jet.

His hands trembled slightly as he held her coat, brushing his fingers across her nape and trying to keep from taking her into his arms. She couldn't have any idea how badly he wanted her.

"You have a bandage on your ankle," he said when she

turned around to face him. Unable to keep from touching her, he smoothed the collar of her coat.

"I had torn ligaments in my ankle because of the plane's rough landing. I'm supposed to wear this bandage two more weeks. I thought about leaving it off tonight and seeing how I get along, but that might not be a good idea."

"Bandage or no bandage, your legs are beautiful. You wear it as long as you're supposed to," he said quietly, looking into her eyes while she gazed back at him and tension coiled between them.

"We should go, Aaron," she reminded him solemnly. He took her arm, still wondering about the barriers she had thrown up between them. When they left, she locked her apartment. He took her arm to walk to the car, looking at the flash of her shapely legs again as she slid into his black car.

When he entered the stream of traffic in the street in front of her apartment complex, Aaron glanced in the rearview mirror out of habit. He had spent years abroad, sometimes involved in intrigue, sometimes residing in countries that didn't welcome Americans, so he was accustomed to checking his surroundings and did it without thought. And, through habit, he noticed the black car turning into traffic a few cars behind him. When he got to Claire's, Royal's finest restaurant, instead of driving up immediately for valet parking, he circled the block.

"If you're looking for a parking spot, they have plenty in the back of their lot," Pamela said.

"Just driving around," he answered casually, aware she was watching him. In the rearview mirror, he saw the same black car turn the corner behind him, just as he turned another corner.

"I think we're being followed," he said, glancing at her to see what her reaction would be.

"Have you brought someone all the way from Spain to follow you around Royal, Texas?" she asked, her voice filled with disbelief. "Surely not!"

He turned back toward Main Street and slid to a stop at the

curb, knowing he was squarely in front of a fire hydrant, but he would be there only briefly. She didn't guess she might be the one being followed.

"No, darlin', I don't think so," he drawled, waiting. The car swung around the corner and had to pass him. He watched and pulled into the street behind the car.

The sedan had darkened windows, but when he drove behind it, he could see the silhouettes of two men. He noted the license tag, memorizing the number. At the corner they turned away from the restaurant and he turned toward it, driving up in front to let a valet park his car, but the incident worried him. He took her arm to walk to the front door of the restaurant.

"If they weren't following you—no one would be following a second-grade school teacher, Aaron. That's absurd."

"Maybe." He remembered talking to Justin about the site of the forced landing of the Asterland jet and all the questions the plane's malfunction had raised. Was Pamela in any danger? He reached out to open the door for her.

"You've spent too much time involved in European intrigue. You're in Royal, Texas, with a teacher from Royal Elementary. Nothing exciting here."

He stopped to face her, suddenly blocking her way. Startled, she looked up at him. *"Au contraire,"* he said solemnly, brushing her hair away from her cheek. "Being with you is the most excitement I've known in a long, long time."

"There you go again, pouring on charm thicker than molasses," she teased, making light of his statement, but her words sounded breathless and pink filled her cheeks.

"I mean it, lady," he said and moved out of her way, following her inside. He passed her to talk to the maitre d' and then they were ushered to a table with candlelight, a red rose in a crystal vase and a white linen tablecloth. When he ordered a bottle of French white wine, she interrupted.

"Aaron, I'll just drink water. I'm not much into wine or drinks."

She had been that night. She'd had wine at the gala and

another glass at his house. Maybe that had been a once-in-a-year thing. He knew so little about her, but he wanted to know everything. He ordered the wine for himself and water for her, wondering why everything she liked or said or did was so important to him.

"Do you like French food?" he asked. "If not, Chef Etienne does broil steaks—a concession to the steak-eating Texans. I know because I'm one of them."

She studied the fancy menu. "I see salmon that I'd like."

When their waiter returned for their order, Aaron said, "The lady will have the *saumon fumé avec pommes de terre primeurs au beurre de persil,*" he ordered in what sounded to her like flawless French. "I'll have a steak, medium rare, and a baked potato."

"You really do speak French fluently, don't you?" she asked as soon as they were alone.

"You make it sound like I rob gas stations often," he answered with a twinkle in his eye.

"Sorry. It's just another difference between us."

"Well, I won't converse with you in French, darlin'," he said, lapsing into a West Texas drawl.

She smiled slightly, but she didn't look happy.

"Believe me, we wouldn't be out together if there weren't differences between us," he said and she shrugged her shoulders slightly.

All through salads, his sizzling steak and her smoked salmon and new potatoes, he sensed a reserve in her that she hadn't had before. Something wasn't quite right, and he didn't know what it was. But when he looked into her guileless blue eyes, his heart raced. In their depths was desire.

He could feel that same volatile chemistry between them, that urgency that made sparks dance between them and kept him touching her lightly as often as possible. He wanted her in his arms, as close as possible. He wanted another night with her like the one they'd had. And he knew she was responding to his touches and looks. No matter how coolly she seemed to act, he could see her fiery response in her eyes. Buddies

who knew he had taken her home the night of the gala had
teased him unmercifully, talking about the ice maiden, the
woman no man could touch. He'd learned about her mother.
Justin had clued him in on that one, and he dimly remembered
hearing things about Dolly Miles and the men who slept with
her. Did that have something to do with Pamela's reserve? But
Dolly Miles was of his parents' generation. Growing up,
Aaron had paid little attention to rumors about Dolly Miles.
He hadn't even known she'd a daughter, but Pamela was much
younger than he was.

Over candlelight, he gazed at her, and for once couldn't eat
much of a delicious steak. All he wanted was to devour the
woman, looking regal and poised, sitting across from him. He
even loved the smattering of freckles across her straight nose.
And she was country in all the best ways, down-to-earth, practical. Except there was something she was holding back. He
could sense it and there was no mistaking the cool reserve that
held her in check most of the evening. Occasionally, he could
bring forth a laugh and then the reserve was gone, and once
she seemed to forget herself and reached over to grasp his
wrist while she told him about a little boy in her second-grade
class.

While he laughed with her, he was far more aware of her
fingers holding his wrist. He twisted his hand around and
grasped hers, raising it to his lips to brush a kiss across her
knuckles. Instantly, she drew her breath and fires flickered in
her gaze.

"Let's go home," he said in a husky voice and after a
moment's hesitation, she nodded.

When she slipped her hand away from his, he motioned to
their waiter. As soon as the waiter left them alone again, as
Aaron put away his wallet, she touched his hand.

"Aaron, we rushed things before. I don't want to do that
again."

He knew instantly what she was telling him, and he could
not keep from being swamped with longing and disappoint-
ment. He wanted her in his arms again, bare to him, loving

him totally, but lovemaking had to be the lady's choice. When he nodded solemnly, she looked relieved.

Was it her past? Her mother's reputation that she feared? Surely not. That was long ago. It had been her mother, not her. Pamela had a reputation for being circumspect and untouchable. Aaron certainly would do nothing to change that reputation either. He hadn't said a word about her spending the night at his house. His friends just knew they'd left the gala early together. Aaron had said he had taken her home and as far as townspeople were concerned, she was still Miss Untouchable, so how could it be that?

During the drive to her house, they both were quiet. He felt as if she was withdrawing from him, and he couldn't figure out why. While he thought about her, he was also watching to see if they were being followed. He couldn't pick up a tail, but when he went around the car to open her door, he thought he saw a movement in dark shadows to one side of her apartment building. He had a prickly gut feeling they were being watched, and he wished she had let him take her to his house, but he knew she wasn't going to.

Then, when he closed and locked the door behind her, he forgot about danger or being followed. As they entered her tiny living room, he reached out to slide her coat from her shoulders, letting his hands brush her neck.

He tossed her coat over a chair, placed both of his hands on her shoulders and studied her.

"What is it, Pamela? Something's changed."

"I'm shocked at your being here just to take me out," she answered, unable to look him in the eye, too aware of him, fighting her warring feelings. She wanted to close her eyes, stand on tiptoe and kiss him wildly. The evening had tightened the golden bands that bound her heart to him. She loved this tall, charming Texan desperately—and just as desperately, she knew she couldn't let him ever know about his baby.

He was a charmer, and she only half believed all his glib compliments. She knew she was out of her depth with him. She had to keep up her guard, but looking into his thickly lashed eyes, filled with intense desire, she knew keeping up barriers would be impossible with him.

"I asked you before, but I didn't get much of an answer so I want to ask again. Why were you gone before I woke that morning?" he asked quietly.

Three

Sooner or later she had known the question would come up again. She'd dreaded it, yet knew she had to face it and give him a reason for her flight. She met his questioning gaze squarely.

"I realized we had rushed into being intimate. That isn't like me, Aaron."

He stroked her hair away from her face. "I know that. You have a reputation for being very cool, very proper." As his voice dropped, his eyes darkened with desire that was so blatant, she could feel all her resistance melting away. "You gave me your virginity. I hope you don't have regrets. I don't have any. Far from it. I don't think we rushed anything—I think we followed our feelings. Mine haven't changed."

"Oh, Aaron," she whispered. How could she argue with him? How could she avoid telling him the truth? His questions were probing, difficult, and there was one way to end them. She moved the few inches closer to him, slipped her arm around his neck, stood on tiptoe and kissed him.

His arm banded her waist instantly. There was a husky growl deep in his throat as his mouth opened and his tongue thrust over hers, kissing her hungrily, pulling her tightly against him. He was rock hard, strong, lean and marvelous. She felt his arousal, felt her own body ache and tingle with longing.

Winding his hand in her hair, he tilted her head back, tightening his arm around her waist and bending over her so she had to cling to him while his kiss curled her toes and blocked out the world. Her pulse thundered in her ears, and she was aware only of Aaron and his kisses that scalded. Each stroke of his tongue over hers fanned the fires already blazing within her. She wanted him absolutely. Her hips thrust against him, need driving her and demolishing all her intentions of being cool.

He slid his hand down her back and his other hand slipped lower over her buttocks.

"Aaron," she whispered against his mouth, drowning in ecstasy and agony over being in his arms again.

"Why have you avoided me since the gala?" he asked, raising his head a fraction and studying her.

"I told you. I think we really rushed things."

"There's something you're holding back from me."

"Not this," she whispered and kissed him again, too aware that he knew something was dreadfully amiss. She had to keep him from learning the truth, but how could she hide anything from him?

Driving away her worries, his mouth covered hers and his kisses heated, conveying clearly that he wanted her. He swung her into his arms and moved to the sofa, sinking down with her cradled in his lap. One arm held her close while he kissed her. His other hand slipped lightly along her ribcage and then brushed across her breasts. She moaned softly, arching her back, and tightening her arms around his neck.

"Ah, lady, how I've dreamed of you, wanted you!"

The words were seduction; his kisses rapture. His fingers drifted over her nape, and then cool air brushed her back as he slowly tugged down her zipper. The coolness brought back a rush of resolutions and remembrance of her condition. She broke free and slipped off his lap, reaching around to try to pull up the zipper of her dress.

Aware of his heavy breathing and his piercing scrutiny, she slid to the other end of the sofa. "I want to stop," she said, knowing that wasn't what she wanted at all. She saw the desire in his eyes, and the questions. She had to get him out of her life. He was only amusing himself. Whatever drew him back to her was beyond her, but she knew, in spite of his smooth talk, it wasn't anything lasting. It couldn't be. Men like Aaron Black did not fall head over heels, instantly in love with second-grade school teachers from small West Texas towns.

"All right," he said, running his fingers along her knee and starting more tingles that battered her resolutions. "We'll just talk."

She couldn't tell him to go. She loved being with him and she gazed at him in silence, totally aware of his fingers moving on her knee.

"I think we were followed tonight. I don't suppose I can talk you into staying at my house—even in another bedroom. Just so you'll be safe."

Momentarily, her tension eased. She laughed and couldn't resist touching his hand lightly. He sat facing her, one long leg drawn up on the sofa. "No one is following me! And I'm perfectly safe here in Royal. No, I'm not spending the night at your house."

He gave her a long, direct look that erased her amusement. She realized he was in earnest. "No one knows why the Asterland jet had to make a forced landing."

"You think someone deliberately caused the plane's malfunction?" she asked, astonished. No question of sabotage had been raised in the papers. No one knew the cause of the jet's difficulties yet, but she had assumed an engine malfunction. "Surely not!"

"We don't know."

"I'm sure I'm safe. But I'll be careful."

"Promise you'll call me if there's anything that disturbs you."

"I promise," she said without giving it much thought, more focused on his steadfast gaze, aware of his fingers trailing above her knee now. "One thing that disturbed me since the crash, was the Asterland investigators. They came to ask me questions about the flight."

"They bothered you?"

"Don't look so fierce," she said, smiling at him and touching his cheek. "They were just too persistent with their questions."

"What did they ask you?"

"About what I was carrying on the plane, what my plans were for Asterland, if I had valuables with me. Forget it, Aaron. I don't want to think about them."

They talked until half past three, and then, when he rose to go, he pulled her into his arms again to kiss her long and hard. More kisses that conveyed that he wanted her with all his being. Kisses that made her melt and tremble and burn with need. His arms held her tightly against him and his tongue thrust deeply into her mouth, stroking her tongue. Suddenly he stopped and raised his head a fraction, bending down again to nibble kisses along her throat.

"Have breakfast with me," he said, trailing kisses to her ear, his tongue flicking over her ear. "Say yes, darlin'."

"Yes, oh, yes!" she said, her hands drifting over his back, wanting to touch him all over as she had that last time, wanting to feel his weight over her, feel him inside her again.

How she wanted him! He was as sexy and wonderful and exciting as she had thought he was that first night. Then she realized she had agreed to have breakfast with him, and that he had stopped kissing her. She opened her eyes to find him watching her with stormy green eyes.

"Pamela, anything your mother ever did doesn't have a damn thing to do with us," he said, and her heart thudded.

"I'm not like her," she whispered, wondering what he truly thought.

"I never once thought you were like anyone except your own special self," he said, leaning down to brush her lips lightly with his. His mouth was warm against hers, tantalizing. His words even more dazzling.

"I'm glad," she whispered. "So glad," she said, turning her mouth up to his for another long, searing kiss that she wanted to last forever. Too aware of her racing heart, his hot kisses, his long, lean body and strong arms, she clung to him until she knew she had to stop or there would be no stopping. She pushed against his chest and he raised his head. His breathing was ragged, and she could feel his heart pounding.

"I can be patient. I'll pick you up about eight. It was wonderful tonight, Pamela." He brushed another kiss across her lips and turned to the door and then paused. "Be careful, and if you want me anytime, just call. When I stay in town, I'm not that far away."

She nodded, barely hearing him, just wanting him so badly, memorizing everything about him. He shrugged into his coat and left. She stepped forward to slip the lock into place and leaned against the cool, hard wood, remembering Aaron's hot kisses, his hands moving over her.

"I want you, Aaron Black," she whispered, knowing she did want him with her whole heart. And knowing it was impossible to tell him.

She switched off lights and went to her bedroom, turning on the light, but standing frozen, lost in memories of the night. He knew something was amiss and not the same. He was too perceptive, too attuned to her feelings, and she wasn't accustomed to hiding the truth. He drifted in and out of that West Texas accent of his, reminding her there was another side to him and he wasn't a good ol' country boy. He was worldly, sophisticated, wealthy—everything she wasn't. She had to avoid being taken in by charm, glib words, hot sexy kisses.

"Aaron," she whispered. "Aaron."

Driving away, Aaron was hot, hard, tied in knots. Frustrated, still puzzled about Pamela's mixed signals, he wondered what was holding her back. Again, he wondered about her mother's reputation—if Pamela feared getting one like it. That seemed absurd, given that all the males who had ever mentioned her had talked about how cold and untouchable she was. Aaron drove out of the apartment lot, but on impulse, he went around a corner, cut the motor and climbed out. He turned his coat collar up and did as much as he could to hide his white shirt.

Moving into the shadows, he cut across yards until he was back at Pamela's apartment building. He circled one side of the building and, as he turned the back corner, he saw several things at once. She had a ground-floor apartment, and a light burned in her bedroom windows, escaping around the edges of the blinds. The dark silhouette of a tall man in a cap showed against the windows.

As Aaron moved forward, the man spun around and burst into a run.

Furious the bastard was window peeping or spying on Pamela, Aaron stretched out his long legs, but the man had a head start. Aaron was a runner, and he was closing the gap swiftly when the man vaulted a fence. As Aaron leaped over the fence after him, the man jumped into a black car parked only yards away on a driveway.

When the motor roared to life, Aaron was just steps away. He lunged for the car, sprawling across the front fender.

The car raced backwards and Aaron couldn't get a grip, his fingers sliding over the smooth hood before he spilled off to the ground, but he saw two faces, one narrow with a long nose. The other face was a pale blur, much more square-shaped. The car whipped down the drive, turned into the street and, with a squeal of tires, was gone.

Aaron stood, brushing off his suit. He was certain it had been the same black car that had been following him before, and he'd got a dim glimpse of the two men inside. Total strangers. He worried about Pamela's safety. Someone was watching her, but who? And why?

Lost in thoughts about her and about the man he had chased, Aaron drove home, checking his rearview mirror for a tail, but seeing no car trailing after him. Tomorrow he would trace the tag number on the car that had tailed them. It was Pamela who was being followed, and she obviously didn't have an inkling why.

At his Pine Valley house, Aaron stripped down and stretched out in his king-size bed. It would soon be time to get up, but sleep was as elusive as ever.

Lying awake in the dark of the large master bedroom, he wondered about the men following Pamela. Midmorning tomorrow, actually today, he had an appointment to meet with his friends, other members of the Texas Cattleman's Club. He thought about the old legend of Royal.

During the War with Mexico, jewels had been found and hidden in Royal. In 1910 when Tex Langley decided to establish the Texas Cattleman's Club, he and the founding members made a pact that only members of the Cattleman's Club would ever know of the jewels' true existence and members of the club would be the guardians of this town treasure, jewels that, according to the legend, were supposed to be the reason Royal prospered. The stones were kept in a treasure box, accessible to the club members via a secret passage under the original adobe mission built when Royal was founded. Now the mission was in Royal's large park by the Cattleman's Club.

Shortly after the Asterland jet had had to make the forced landing, four members from the Cattleman's Club had gone to the crash site, and Justin Webb had found two of the jewels—the black harlequin opal, the most valued of opals, and a two-carat emerald. All three jewels had to have been on that plane, but the third and most valuable, a red diamond, was still missing.

So far, the club members had kept things quiet, giving some of their information to Winona Raye, who was marrying Justin. A policewoman who worked with juveniles, Winona had agreed to be their contact with the authorities so they could keep things as quiet as possible and out of the media. The facts marched through Aaron's thoughts, taunting him with puzzle pieces that needed to be put together as quickly as possible. Someone out there was desperate. A trusted bartender, Riley Monroe, had been found dead near the mission where the jewels had been hidden. A scrap of a burned note found at the landing site didn't have enough written on it to piece together answers to questions. Robert Klimt, an Asterland cabinet member on the plane, was in a coma in the Royal Memorial Hospital, and the Cattleman's Club members wanted to talk to him to find out what he knew.

The priceless red diamond entrusted to the care of the Cattleman's Club members was missing and a man had been murdered. Two men were following Pamela. Plagued by concern for her safety, Aaron wished he had been more persuasive about her staying at his place. He wanted to let his friends know that Pamela was being followed. Others must be searching for the missing red diamond. Why were the jewels on the Asterland jet? Was it solely a jewel theft? The jewels were worth a fortune. Or were the jewels to be sold and the money to be used for some nefarious project? Who had killed Riley? Too many questions with too few answers, yet Aaron and his friends were dedicating their efforts to finding out.

He shifted restlessly. If he were staying out at the family ranch, he'd saddle up and ride because sleep wasn't coming anyway, but he couldn't do that here in town. And he wanted to be in town to be closer to Pamela and to his friends at the Cattleman's Club.

When they were needed, the members of the Texas Cattleman's Club worked together secretly to save innocents' lives—and now they seemed needed here in their own home town. Five of them were working on the jewel theft and the murder of Riley Monroe. Aaron stared into the darkness and ran through the list: Justin Webb, one of the Southwest's finest surgeons. Aaron's friend Matt Walker, local rancher. There was Sheikh Ben Rassad, rancher and horseman, and there was another longtime friend, retired Air Force, ex-Special Forces man, Dakota Lewis. Dakota gave him pause.

Aaron was a friend to both Dakota and his estranged wife,

Kathy Lewis. He had known Dakota most of his life and then had got to know Kathy when they were both in Washington, D.C., just starting in their careers. He had introduced Kathy to Dakota and the two had fallen wildly in love. Aaron had been shocked to hear of their breakup.

Once again, Aaron thought about all the men working on the theft. They had diverse occupations and backgrounds, but they all had had military experience, and now they were all able to take the time to solve the disappearance of the jewels and try to learn who murdered Riley Monroe—and why.

Aaron moved restlessly, his thoughts shifting to Pamela, memories taunting him. She was fighting her feelings, but the feelings were there and they showed sometimes. Like when she had stood on tiptoe and pulled his head down to kiss him. Just remembering made him respond physically as he became aroused.

Her true feelings were revealed in her responses to his kisses. All that cool reserve had gone up in flames, and she had all but come apart in his arms. But then she would become tense, pull back, and the barriers would come up again. Why?

The first gulf between them had opened that morning when she had slipped out of his house without his knowing it. The only reason he could figure had to be her feelings about her mother's reputation and shock over how swiftly she had yielded to him.

Yet he didn't have regrets. Far from it. That night had changed his life, and he felt to his bones that it had been important to her, too. And he intended to show her and try to get her back to that openness with him, that complete giving and honesty they'd had with each other the night of the gala. One step at a time.

Every time he searched his own feelings about her, he knew she was special. He was as tied up in knots as when he'd arrived in Royal. She had done nothing to alleviate that, far from it. He ached with wanting her. He wanted to make love to her all night long. The desolation he had lived with the past few years was gone now that he was home and seeing her again. Whatever it was that had come between them, he didn't think it would last or that it ran deep.

At least, come morning, he would have breakfast with her. Maybe he could talk her into staying at his place until they knew who was following her and why. Yeah, right, buddy, a cynical voice said. *You want the lady as close to your bed as possible.* So maybe he did, he admitted to himself. She felt something for him; he could see the longing in her eyes. She all but quivered at the slightest of his touches. And he really was concerned with her safety. He would bring his worries for her safety up again at breakfast, but the lady had a mind of her own.

What was disturbing her and holding her back? There was something going on in that pretty head of hers, some reason for the wall she was keeping between them. Before long he would have his answer. He intended to learn the truth about what was worrying her.

Promptly at eight the next morning, Pamela heard a motor and looked out to see a black pickup swing into the drive. A pickup during the day, a black sedan last night, a home in Pine Valley, one in Georgetown in Washington, one in Spain, the Black ranch here—while she rented a tiny apartment. Their lives were poles apart and she couldn't believe he was deeply interested in her. It seemed completely impossible.

As if unable to contain his energy, Aaron bounded out of the pickup and his long strides ate up the distance to the door. He was in boots, jeans and a plaid wool Western shirt and he looked like the other cowboys who lived around Royal. Only he wasn't like the other cowboys. In spite of his appearance and the West Texas drawl he could slip into so easily, she needed to remember that he led a far different life.

When he knocked on her door, she opened it and motioned to him to enter. She was too aware of his assessing gaze and the pleasure in his eyes as he took in her jeans and blue shirt. "Mornin', darlin'," he said quietly and stepped inside, bringing cold air in with him. "You look prettier than a prairie rose."

"Thanks, Aaron. I almost overslept."

"Wish I had been here to see you oversleeping," he said with a devilish twinkle in his green eyes.

"Well, it's best you weren't," she answered primly.

"Want to go back to catch a few winks?" he asked, swinging her up into his arms.

Startled, she yelped and put her arm around his neck. "No! Put me down, Aaron Black!"

"If you didn't get a good night's sleep, we can remedy that quickly." He headed toward her bedroom. "Just leave it to me, and you'll sleep like a baby."

"Don't you dare set foot in my bedroom. Put me down!" she said, laughing and knowing he was teasing as he headed toward her bedroom. He grinned and stopped.

"See—we can have a good time together."

"I know we can," she said, sobering, too aware how irresistible he was to her. She kept saying yes she would go out with him when she needed to avoid seeing him altogether. Yet he would be back in Spain so soon. She didn't really believe him about a leave of absence. And looking into his green eyes now while he held her in his arms, she tingled as he studied her in return.

"You handsome devil," she whispered, unable to keep from flirting with him.

He slowly lowered her feet to the floor, holding her so she was pressed against him. "Good mornin'," he whispered, and leaned down to kiss her, his mouth opening hers, his tongue stirring instant fires and driving all thought of sleep away. His strong arms held her tightly and in seconds her breathing was as erratic as his, her heart thudding violently.

Finally she broke away, pushing against his chest. "Aaron—you promised to take me to eat."

"Yeah, I did," he said in a husky voice, his gaze going over her features, his hand stroking her throat. He leaned down to kiss her throat and push open her shirt slightly to trail kisses lower. "I'd like to eat you," he whispered against her throat. "Kiss by slow kiss until you let go all that reserve." His warm fingers twisted free the top button of her shirt and he pushed it open, trailing kisses over the curve of her breast.

"Aaron," she whispered, her body growing taut, trembling with wanting to just let go and step into his arms and make love with him. Instead she put her hands against his chest that was as solid and hard as the wall. She pushed slightly.

He straightened up to stare at her solemnly. "I will, too, Pamela. Maybe not this morning, but you're going to be mine. You're pushing against me and saying no, but your blue eyes and your kisses are telling me something else."

"No, no!" She stepped back and buttoned her shirt. "Aaron, it's just impos—"

"Shh," he said, placing his fingers on her lips and then trailing them featherlightly over her mouth, teasing her while he stopped her argument. "C'mon, we'll go eat. We have time."

He helped her into her denim jacket, took her arm and they left to climb into his pickup. Dazed, all she could think was, no, they didn't have time. Time was against them. Definitely against them. They didn't have anything together. *You have a baby together,* a voice within her argued. She glanced at Aaron as he drove, looking at the angles and planes of his face, his prominent cheekbones and straight nose.

She should tell him about his baby. Yet she knew if she did, he would want to marry her because it was the right thing to do. Aaron Black was the kind of man honor bound to do his duty. She couldn't bear that. That night had meant something to him, too, but she couldn't believe it had really meant anything lasting or that she could begin to interest him like the other women he knew. Not even remotely. A second-grade teacher from Royal, Texas, being fascinating to an American diplomat stationed in Spain. Get real, Pamela, she told herself. She glanced at him and caught him studying the rearview mirror.

"Are we being followed again?"

"Nope. It's not easy to hide in Royal. In big-city traffic,

you can move into the flow of cars and get lost, but here, a tail sticks out like a heifer in a rose garden.''

''They have to be following you. There's no earthly reason to follow me.'' His eyebrow arched, but he remained quiet and she wondered what was running through his mind. She realized how little she knew about him and suspected he could keep things to himself quite well. That arch of his brow indicated he hadn't agreed with her, but why would anyone follow her?

He turned to park in front of the Royal Diner and came around to hold the door open for her. ''You're not wearing a coat. Don't you get cold?'' she asked, pulling her denim jacket closer as a gust of wind hit them.

''Nope,'' he said, draping his arm casually across her shoulders and drawing her close against his side. ''I've got you here to keep me warm.''

She smiled at him and couldn't keep from liking his holding her close against him. She was five feet ten inches, tall for a woman, but Aaron was six feet four inches and he made her feel smaller and dainty, something she rarely experienced.

He swung open the diner door and the bell tinkled as they stepped into the warmth of the café. The windows were steamed, and smells of frying sausages and eggs and hot coffee assailed her. Before they reached a booth, Pamela knew she had made a mistake in accepting this date.

Too many mornings she couldn't keep anything down, but she'd thought if she ate lightly and was careful what she ate, she would be all right, and she had wanted to be with him one more time. But, as they slid into a booth and smells of frying foods assailed her, her stomach became queasy. She wouldn't be able to eat a bite, and what excuse could she give him?

''Something wrong?'' he asked, and she flicked him a glance. Those damnable green eyes were searching her face, and she wished he couldn't read her so easily. No one else could, yet he seemed to see what was running in her mind and guess what her feelings were intuitively, and that unnerved her, too.

"I'm all right," she said, feeling worse by the minute. Why had she come? Why was he so darned irresistible to her? Sheila approached.

"Good morning, Aaron, Pamela," she said, looking back and forth between them as if she couldn't believe her eyes. "What'll y'all have? Orange juice, coffee, tomato juice, something to start? Manny's cooking flapjacks and biscuits and gravy this morning."

Aaron looked at Pamela and frowned slightly, bending his head to really study her. Her stomach was churning now. She shook her head slightly, unable to say a word. The thought of any food turned her stomach.

"Why don't you bring two orange juices and one coffee, Sheila," Aaron said without taking his eyes from Pamela.

The moment the waitress was gone, Pamela knew she had to get out of the diner and away from the smells. She needed some cold air, too.

"Excuse me," she said as she slid out of the booth and dashed for the door. Embarrassment and anger at herself for coming with him flooded her. She should have known better. Eight mornings out of ten she lost her breakfast. Why, oh why did she let him talk her into anything and everything? Her stomach heaved and she knew she was going to be sick, and if she lost it here in the diner—oh, horrors! The rumors that would start.

Rumors that would be true.

She was fumbling for the door when a long arm shot past her and opened it. She rushed outside, too aware Aaron was right beside her. She hurried away from the diner toward his pickup, grasping the door handle as she lost everything. Her stomach heaved, and embarrassment made her want to curl up and faint. If only she could!

He thrust a clean handkerchief under her nose.

"I'm sorry," she said, unable to look at him.

"You should have told me if you didn't feel all right," he

said. "Let me take you to a doctor. You might be getting the flu." He felt her forehead and to her horror, she gagged again.

"Oh, Aaron, I'm sorry," she said, wishing with all her being that she was a million miles away from here. Or that he was a million miles away. Why couldn't he have stayed in Spain!

"Stop apologizing for being sick. Happens to all of us. Want to sit in the truck?"

"Yes," she said, thankful the windows of the diner were steamed up and had curtains, and that the street was almost deserted at eight in the morning so few people were witnessing her nausea.

He opened the door, picked her up and lifted her inside. "I can get in by myself," she protested.

"You don't need to now," he answered, closed the door and walked around the pickup to slide in on the other side. "Want the heater on?"

"No. The cold air feels better."

He felt her forehead again. "You don't feel feverish, but several people in town have the flu. Doc Williams is my doctor, and I'm sure I can get you in to see him."

"No! I don't need a doctor."

"It won't hurt," he said, starting the motor, and she panicked.

"No! This isn't anything unusual and it isn't the flu. I don't want to go see your doctor. I don't need to. Just take me home, Aaron." The words burst from her because she knew how he took charge and did what he wanted.

"You've been sick before?" he asked.

"Sometimes," she said. "It passes. I don't need to see your doctor. I'd like to go home," she said, talking fast. She wiped her brow and leaned back against the seat with her eyes closed. As her stomach began to settle, she became aware of the silence. She glanced at him to find him looking at her so intently that her breath caught.

"How often have you been sick before?" he asked quietly,

and then she realized she had blurted out too much. Aaron paid attention to every little thing.

"It's nothing. I have a delicate stomach."

"Since when?"

"You don't know what I have. I need to go home," she said, avoiding answering him and aware she was being evasive, which stabbed at her conscience.

He turned and started the motor and backed out. They drove in silence, and she couldn't wait to get home and away from his scrutiny. She vowed that she would never accept another breakfast date again with him. No more dates with him, period.

He pulled up in front of her apartment complex and climbed out. At her front door she turned to him. "I'm sorry, but thanks for being so understanding."

He took the key from her hand and unlocked her door, pushing it open and waiting for her to go inside.

"Aaron, I think I need to be alone."

"I won't be here long," he said, taking her arm and going inside. He kicked the door closed behind him and slipped her jacket off her shoulders, tossing it over a chair and leading her to her sofa. "Want anything?"

"No, thanks. Really, I'm fine." She didn't want him coming in with her and she didn't like the way he was looking at her, studying her as if he were getting ready to dissect her.

"Want to sit down?" he asked her. Her uneasiness was growing with each second and the way he was staring.

She sat and moved back against the corner of the sofa, closing her eyes and wishing he would disappear. What was running through his mind?

She felt him sit close to her and she knew if she opened her eyes, she would find him still studying her. She said a small prayer that Aaron couldn't possibly guess what was really wrong with her.

"How many mornings have you been sick?" he asked quietly, and her eyes flew open.

Frightened that he had guessed her secret, she stood and

moved away from him, feeling as if he knew her every thought. "A few."

She heard him move and then his hands settled on her shoulders. When he turned her to face him, his green eyes were stormy.

"You're pregnant."

She couldn't lie and deny it. "I should never have gone to breakfast with you." The words spilled out of her and she wrung her fingers together. She wanted to deny his accusation, to get him out of her apartment, but she couldn't lie to him, so she just kept talking in circles around his statement. "I felt queasy this morning. I never could take fried food early in the day very well," she said, trying to twist away from him, but his hands held her firmly.

He bent his knees to lean down and look into her eyes with a gaze that pierced to her soul. "*Are* you pregnant, Pamela?"

Four

She couldn't answer and she couldn't lie, so she merely nodded.

"You're pregnant with my baby." His eyes widened, and the color drained from his face. "Lordy!" he whispered under his breath, looking incredibly shocked.

"Aaron, this isn't your problem. Just leave me alone and I'll take care of it." Humiliation, anger, protectiveness, all three emotions churned in her like a stormy sea as she watched his shock grow.

"I thought you said you were protected," he said.

A flush burned her cheeks. "Well, I wasn't. That's my mistake, and I'll take care of it." Anger at herself and with him fueled the fires she was suffering. She just wanted him out of her house. "This isn't your problem, Aaron." Closing her eyes, she bit her lip while all her worries about his discovery of the truth crashed in on her.

Staring at her, Aaron was shocked because, even though they were in the throes of passion, he had accepted her "yes," that night that she was protected. A baby. *Their baby.* He was stunned. Always methodical, he had planned his college years, planned his years with the State Department and, in the back of his mind, he had planned to someday marry and have a family. He had figured on a wedding before a baby.

He was shocked, but realized that this pregnancy was what had been disturbing her. He came out of his fog of surprise and looked at her. Her cheeks were flushed, tears brimmed in her eyes and she was wringing her hands together, and he realized in his momentary shock, he wasn't treating her the way he should.

"Aw, Pamela," he said, tenderness and wonder filling him. They were going to have a baby! This pregnancy wasn't the way he had planned his future, but she had to be very early in her pregnancy. They could have a wedding, and everything would be right. "Darlin'," he said, stepping close to wrap her in his arms. "We'll have a wedding right away."

"No!" she said, wriggling away from him, startling him again. She was stiff and unreceptive, and now when he looked at her, her blue eyes blazed.

"Look, I'm sorry," he said gently. "I was just surprised. I want to get married—"

"No, Aaron. We're not having a wedding. I'm the one to blame for this—"

"Well, I sort of think it took two of us," he drawled, frowning and seeing he would have to mend his fences quickly.

"No, I should have been responsible and I wasn't. This isn't your problem—"

"Pamela! Our baby isn't a *problem*," he interrupted, suddenly terrified she was thinking of abortion. "You can't harm this baby!" he snapped, wondering if he knew her after all.

While all color drained from her face, she trembled, and with relief he knew he had been wrong on that score.

"I would never knowingly harm my baby," she said fiercely, placing her hands in front of her flat tummy.

"Hell, I'm going about this all wrong," he said. "It's my baby, too, and I want to marry you."

When she closed her eyes as if he had struck her, he felt at a loss. "No."

"What am I doing wrong here?" he asked, puzzled and realizing something was terribly amiss between them. Yet she had gone out with him and she had responded to his kisses. He glanced past her at the small clock on her mantel. He had an appointment to meet his friends at the Texas Cattleman's Club soon. They'd just have to go on without him, though, because this was more important.

Her blue eyes opened and were as fiery as ever. If looks could have flattened him or sent him running, hers would have. "You're not doing anything wrong. You just need to realize that you don't have to marry me. I did this and I want my baby and I'll give this baby all the love possible, but you're not part of this."

"The hell I'm not," he said, realizing she was in earnest. "That's my baby, too."

"Aaron, did you think you'd get married someday?"

"Yes, of course."

"And you imagined a big wedding with your family and friends, didn't you?"

"Yes, I did," he said evenly. "But it's not too late for that. With the money I have we can pull a big wedding together quickly," he said, for one of the few times in his life mentioning the wealth he had inherited.

"No. You go on with your life the way you planned it. You'll find a woman who is your type, who lives the lifestyle you do and has your family's approval. When you find her, you'll marry and have your own family and you'll be very happy. I appreciate your asking me to marry you, but I knew you would do that because you're a good person. I want love in my marriage and we don't share love. No, I won't marry you."

"That's bull, Pamela," he said. "I'm back here in Royal because I wanted to be with you."

"The night we had was magic, but it was sex, and sex turns men's heads. You're not thinking about this clearly. Your goodness and your emotions are running away with you. When you calm down and get accustomed to the idea, you'll agree with me.''

"The hell I will," he said quietly. He wanted to pull her into his arms, but she had put invisible barriers between them and he could see the stiffness in her shoulders. Her chin was in the air as if she were getting ready to go into a fight, and her eyes still blazed with anger.

"I saw your first reaction," she accused.

"I was just shocked. And I wasn't thinking."

"Oh, yes, you were. Those were your true feelings."

"I'd like to kiss all those foolish notions about me right out of your head." As he moved closer, she stepped back and held up her hand.

"You're not going to! Don't you kiss me."

"Darlin'," he said gently, "you're upset and emotional and reading my feelings all wrong. This won't be a shotgun wedding."

She waved her hand. "Aaron, look around you. We're totally different. I rent this little apartment. I've hardly traveled away from Royal. You have homes all over the world—Washington, D.C., Spain, here. The women you date are sophisticated and from your world."

"I don't want to date them, and you're selling yourself short. The women I know are sophisticated and some of them want things I don't want and value things I don't value. Some of them are tough and ambitious to the point of putting that first in their lives."

"Haven't you done exactly that with your work? Aren't you very ambitious?"

"Yes, I am," he admitted, "but I don't want to marry someone who is ambitious above all else."

"You can't tell me you've never been attracted to any of the women you've known!" she snapped, sounding more annoyed with him.

"Of course, I have, but I've never found anyone who

wouldn't get out of my thoughts or who seemed so right to be with or who made me feel like a human being again.''

She drew a deep breath and looked shaken, and he felt a degree better until she shook her head. "No. I think you're getting desire and lust all mixed up. Men are driven by what their bodies want. Your heart has little to do with what is going on between us.''

"I don't—"

As the doorbell jangled, Aaron swore under his breath. "Ignore it and they'll go away," he said, but she was already walking away from him. Trailing after her, he clenched his fists and knew he was going to have a fight on his hands. He wanted to kick himself for not hiding his shock. He knew better, and no matter how shocking the news had been, never in his career had he let his feelings be exposed like that. But this was different. The realization that he would be a father ran much deeper than diplomacy and politics. His relationship with Pamela involved his whole heart and life.

He wished to hell he could take back the first moment he'd found out. He suspected his lady had already made her mind up about their baby and no matter what he had done, it would have been the wrong thing.

When she swung open the front door, three little girls faced her.

"Hi, girls."

"Can you play, Mellie?" the oldest one asked.

Pamela glanced over her shoulder at him. "Yes, I can," she said coolly. "Come inside, and I'll introduce you to my friend."

"Pamela!" a woman called.

She stepped outside, and Aaron could hear a woman's voice and guessed it was their mother. "Do you mind? Is this a bad time for them to come over?"

"No, it's fine. I'll bring them home in about an hour."

"Sure?"

"Yes, I'm sure," she answered firmly, and Aaron knew she was getting rid of him. Three towheaded little girls with large brown eyes stared at him as if he had dropped from Mars. He tried to smile at them, but he wished they would come back in an hour and let him finish talking to Pamela.

She closed the door and turned to face him, looking satisfied that she had found a quick end to their conversation. "Aaron, these are my neighbors, Hannah, Rachel and Ellen Colworth. Girls, this is Mr. Black."

"Hi," he said, and they solemnly said hi to him and then the oldest turned to Pamela.

"Can you read to us?"

"I surely can. Mr. Black was just leaving. Unless you want to stay around and listen to *Peter Rabbit* and *Goldilocks and the Three Bears.*

"We'll get the books," Hannah said, and the three of them scampered toward her bedroom.

"You do this often?" he asked, realizing she was good with children.

"They're my preschool neighbors and they like to come play. They have a new baby in the family, and it gives their mother a break."

"Mellie?"

"They can't pronounce Pamela."

"Okay, you get out of this conversation for now, but I'm not finished."

"We are finished, Aaron," she answered so solemnly that his heart clenched.

"No, we're not. I want to take you to dinner tonight."

"No—"

He was tired of the foolish arguments when he knew from her kisses and responses that there was something good and true between them. He stepped forward swiftly, wrapped his arms around her and kissed away her negative reply.

She pushed against him, but he leaned over her and kissed her hard and deep and with all the hunger, conviction and longing he had pent up in him. As their tongues tangled and clashed, she yielded to him and then responded. Knowing that at any minute the children could return and interrupt them, he raised his head.

"I'll pick you up at half past seven. All right?" He could see her coming out of her daze. Her lips were red from his kisses, her eyes burned now with different fires. His pulse jumped because there had to be more than a strong attraction between them for her to react so swiftly and intensely to him. "Say yes or I'll kiss you senseless, girls or no girls."

Pamela stared at him, knowing she had to refuse, yet knowing he was going to win this argument. "Arguing more tonight won't do you any good."

"Don't care. Is half past seven all right?" As he leaned down and his mouth touched hers, his tongue touching her lips, she twisted away.

"Yes! You know what you can do to me," she accused as he straightened and stepped away, but he kept his hand on her waist. With his other hand he touched her cheek.

"Has it occurred to you that maybe your reaction to my kisses is because of the depth of feelings between us?"

"We don't know each other that well. That first night we were together had to be physical attraction, pure and simple."

He wound his fingers in her hair and stared at her while he shook his head. "It went deeper than that or I'd be in Spain right now."

"Mellie!" Hannah called, and he glanced around to see the little girls standing a few yards behind him with books in their arms.

"I'll go now, but I'll see you tonight."

"A dinner date won't change a thing."

"We'll see, darlin'," he drawled and leaned forward to kiss her lightly.

"Now your kiss will raise questions from the girls."

He turned to go out the back door and paused when he reached the little girls who were staring at him. "What books will she read to you?" he asked, hunkering down in front of the oldest child.

"We want her to read all these. I like *The Three Little Pigs* and Rachel likes *Goldilocks* and Ellen likes *Billy Goats.*"

"Good choices. It was nice to meet all of you. I'm going now, and Mellie can read to you. Have fun."

Hannah nodded solemnly as he stood and turned to Pamela. "I'll let myself out. See you tonight."

She watched him stride through the house and she wanted to let go the tears she fought to hold back, but she couldn't cry in front of the girls. Instead, she tried to close her mind to Aaron and his proposal and his arguments. She smiled at the girls. "Ready to read?"

"Are you crying?" Hannah asked bluntly.

Pamela swiped at her eyes. "Not really. Let's sit on the sofa." She sat down and let Ellen climb into her lap while Hannah and Rachel crowded close beside her, and she picked up the first book to start to read. She was going out with him again tonight. Why couldn't she just say no and stick with it? She knew why—she thought of his hot kisses that drove every rational thought from her head. The chemistry between them was incredible, no denying that. Her mouth still tingled, and she ached with longing to just let go and give herself to him again. She longed to accept his proposal—

She stopped her thoughts from continuing down that track because she knew that kind of forced marriage would never work. Not when they were so different and knew each other so little. No matter how painful it had been, she had done the right thing. And she had to make him see that he wasn't being realistic about marriage. When the town found out about her pregnancy, gossip would begin linking her to her mother's behavior and she didn't want Aaron pulled into that ugliness.

She tried to focus on the book in her lap and forget Aaron.

Aaron entered the bar of the Texas Cattleman's Club and strode across to a private room where he joined his friends, shaking hands with his longtime friend Dakota Lewis.

"Your hand doesn't feel like ice," Dakota teased, "but I'll bet you're late because you've been with the teacher."

"As a matter of fact, I have," Aaron admitted, greeting Matt Walker, Justin Webb and Sheikh Ben Rassad. "I've been eager to get here because we have a new problem." Aaron sank down onto one of the leather chairs and stretched his long legs in front of him. "There are two investigators here from Asterland."

"Garth Johannes and Milo Yungst," Matt Walker said, sitting on a sofa and propping his elbows on his knees.

"You know about them. They questioned Pamela and shook her up," Aaron said.

"They've wanted to talk to Lady Helena, but so far, the hospital has refused to let them. They shouldn't be aggressive with these women," the rancher remarked. "Did you tell Pamela about the jewels?"

"No," Aaron answered. "Not because I don't trust her. I just think she might be safer knowing as little as possible about what's happened. I'd like to keep her out of it as long as I can."

"Good idea," Justin added with a grim note in his voice, and Aaron wondered if the physician was concerned about the safety of his fiancée Winona Raye, since she was involved as their liaison with the police.

"There's something else," Aaron said. "Two men are following Pamela. I don't know whether Johannes and Yungst are tailing her or if the men following her are hired guns." He went on to tell his friends about chasing the man who had been watching her apartment.

"Did you get a good look at them?" Justin asked.

"The one I chased is tall and thin. Then, as I hit the car, I glimpsed them. Oval face, long nose—the other looked square. It was too dark to get anything definite."

"Sounds like the investigators," Justin said. "Winona and I saw them at Claire's."

"I traced the license-tag number and it was a car stolen over a year ago, later found stripped and burned with the tag missing. A dead end there," Aaron said. "I want to know why they're following her. Do they think she was involved some way in whatever caused the forced landing? Do they think she has the red diamond?'' Aaron asked, mulling over his questions aloud. While he talked, his thoughts were just partly on the mystery. Part of his thoughts kept returning to Pamela and her news of their baby. He couldn't get her pregnancy out of his mind. He thought about Justin who was getting married and adopting a baby girl. A wife and a baby. The idea was awesome and breathtaking. He wished he could talk to Justin about how it felt to become a father, but his fatherhood had to stay a secret at this point in his life. Glancing at the doctor, Aaron realized Justin was talking, so he tried to focus on what his friend was saying.

"The women who were on the plane may be in danger," Justin said. "If the Asterland investigators are following Pamela, they may be watching Lady Helena, too."

Aaron's concern deepened because Justin was probably right. The women could be in a lot of danger. "I think we should keep a watch on the women who were on the plane," Aaron said. "I'll watch Pamela because I'll be with her anyway."

"I can guard Lady Helena," Matt said quietly, his green eyes were cold as he met Aaron's gaze. "I know Anna and Greg Hunt plan to take her home with them when she can be released, but until then, I'll stand guard."

"Jamie Morris stayed behind in Royal instead of going on to Asterland on the next flight," Justin added. "She was on her way to an arranged marriage to a member of Asterland's Royal Cabinet."

"I wonder why she stayed in town. Whatever the reason she is still here, she was also on the Asterland jet and may need protection," Aaron said. "How about you, Ben?" He looked at the sheikh who frowned. Dressed in his robes and kaffiyeh, he stood out from the rest of them.

"If she is in danger, I will do this," he replied, nodding solemnly.

"How about Dakota keeping tabs on the investigators?"

Matt asked, and all heads turned toward the tough male who was estranged from his wife. He nodded.

"Sure. I'd like to catch them following someone."

"Klimt's in a coma," Matt said. "The diamond is missing, and we're no closer to a reason why the stones were on the plane or why the plane went down."

"Someone has the missing red diamond, but evidently it isn't anyone connected officially with Asterland or their investigators wouldn't be quizzing the women so much about the jewelry they were carrying on the plane," Aaron said, remembering all Pamela had told him about their questioning.

"None of the federal investigators of the crash have come up with the reason yet for the forced landing," Justin said. Standing by a window, he stared outside. "As soon as they do, we'll know a little more than we do now."

"So we still don't know if the forced landing had something to do with the missing jewels," Aaron said.

"No, and the police are as baffled as we are about Riley Monroe's murder," Justin added. "Who killed him?"

"When we know that," Aaron said, "we'll know what they intended to do with the jewels. Was it a theft for the fortune they would bring, or were the stones intended for someone or some purpose in Asterland since they were found on the jet headed to Asterland?" He glanced at Justin. "You have them safely hidden?"

"Yep, they're behind our plaque in the front entrance hall."

"Leadership, justice and peace," Ben said quietly. Aaron knew the stones represented each of these three qualities, a mantra for the Cattleman's Club members to uphold and the words carved into the plaque.

The men sat and talked for another half an hour about various topics—how the Cowboys' football season had gone, how it should shape up next fall, until finally Aaron stood and said he needed to go.

Matt was on his feet instantly, saying he had to get to Royal Memorial to guard Lady Helena.

As they stood, before they broke up their group, they once

again went over the questions in a reminder of the problems facing them.

"We've got one murder and one missing diamond." Justin added, "The women may be in danger. We don't want anything else bad happening and we need to find the red diamond."

"See you later," Aaron said, leaving the club and already thinking about his date that night with Pamela.

As they walked outside, Matt fell into step beside him. "If those bastards try to harm Lady Helena after all she's been through—they'll have to go through me to get to her."

"I've started carrying my gun," Aaron said solemnly. "I'm worried about Pamela's safety."

"Yeah, well, now with Ben watching Jamie and Justin trying to keep an eye on Winona and Dakota following those investigators, maybe everyone will be safe."

"If I can talk her into it, I'm taking Pamela to my house tonight."

Matt arched his brow and gave him a look. "Good idea. She'll be safer there. Taking her to the ranch?"

"No, we'll stay in Pine Valley. I don't think I can get her to go out to the ranch. She's accustomed to living in town."

"It would be easier to protect her at the ranch."

"The lady is going to make up her own mind about it. That's for sure."

"Yeah, they have a way of doing that. Be careful."

"You, too. I think Pamela wants to go to the hospital to see Lady Helena so you'll probably see us tonight or tomorrow night."

"Good. Pamela's great, Aaron. I've known her a long time and a lot of people let all that crummy stuff about Dolly color their feelings about Pamela, but she's a good person and damned nice."

"I think so, too. I want to marry her."

Matt nodded. "Good."

He turned away and Aaron headed to his car. She was carrying their baby. The more he thought about it, the more awesome and wonderful her pregnancy was. She was so mistaken about his feelings. But they'd talk it out tonight. Whistling, his spirits lifted as he looked in his rearview mirror to see whether or not he was being followed.

The minute Pamela swung open the door that night, Aaron knew he was in for a battle and some fast talking. Standing stiffly facing him, she took his breath in spite of the fiery stubbornness flashing in her eyes. A simple red dress clung to her slender figure like a scarlet flame. She so often wore clothes that covered her to the chin, but nonetheless she exuded a sexy air that kept him hot and disturbed.

"This dinner date is just ridiculous," she said.

When he stepped inside, she moved back to let him pass, but he could see her reluctance before she turned to go get her coat and purse.

He inhaled her lilac perfume and looked at the satiny highlights in her hair, which swung slightly as she walked ahead of him. He watched the pull of the skirt across her hips. A zipper ran from the neck down below her bottom and he wanted to tug it down and peel her out of the dress. He knew he'd better keep his mind on the problems between them because he suspected it was going to take some of his best powers of persuasion to convince her of his feelings.

She turned to face him and folded her arms across her middle, looking challenging and stubborn and beautiful. "This is so silly for us to go to dinner. We'll spend the evening arguing."

"Well, then, we won't argue," he said cheerfully, picking up her coat. "You have to eat, so you might as well go with me and have a scrumptious dinner at Claire's and we can talk about any subject you want."

"That's just putting off the inevitable."

"It won't hurt to put it off until after dinner." He held her black coat out for her to slip into, and they stared at each other over it.

"You look beautiful," he said, his voice lowering a notch.

She seemed exasperated by his compliment and thrust her arm into her sleeve. He slipped the coat onto her shoulders and lifted her hair out of the way, brushing her nape slowly with his fingers.

"Stop flirting, Aaron," she said darkly.

"Impossible when I'm with you," he whispered at her ear and then brushed a light kiss across her cheek.

Turning to slant an angry look over her shoulder at him, she clamped her lips together. He could almost see her refusal to go out surfacing, so he took her arm and spoke quickly as he steered her to the door. "I told my brother Jeb about you. He has a second-grader, my little nephew Robby. He's having trouble with his reading. Can I tell my sister-in-law she can call you and talk to you about Robby?"

"Of course."

"They have Robby in a private school, and they've had a tutor, but something isn't working right."

"Have they had him tested for dyslexia? I'm sure they have," she answered her own question swiftly. "I can't imagine with all the individual attention, he doesn't get the help he needs."

Aaron held open the door, locking it behind them and looking around as they stepped outside. He didn't want Pamela to know he was carrying a gun now. If he gave chase to anyone again, he was going to be able to stop a car from getting away. And he worried about Pamela's safety.

He didn't see anyone lurking in the shadows, but once they were on Main Street, he spotted a tail again. Picking up his phone, he called Dakota to inform him of the black car and learned that Dakota already knew about it. As soon as he broke the connection, Pamela spoke.

"You're being followed again. Aaron, what are you involved in that someone would follow you? You're halfway around the world from Spain."

"I don't think I'm the one who's being followed."

"Not me! You're so wrong there."

"Those two investigators from Asterland were persistent in

their questions and were with you for over an hour, weren't they?"

"Yes. You think they're following me?" She twisted around in the seat to glance out the back.

"The investigators seem a likely possibility. If you're trying to see them, the men following are two cars behind us."

Turning to face him again, she settled in the seat. "I'm sure you're the one they're interested in. There's no reason to follow me."

He reached Claire's and turned into the lot for valet parking, climbing out of the car and glancing at the street, but he couldn't spot the tail and he wondered if they had turned off before the restaurant.

The maitre d' greeted Aaron and led them to a table near a quiet corner of the restaurant.

"Now I know why you aren't drinking any wine."

Reflected candlelight flickered in the depths of her luminous blue eyes that were so large, he felt enveloped in blue. "It wouldn't be good for the baby," she said quietly.

He nodded and looked up as the waiter stopped at their table. "Good evening, Miss Miles, Mr. Black," he said. "Would you like to see our wine list? Tonight we have a special French red wine."

"I'll take a glass of the red wine, and the lady will have water," Aaron replied. As soon as they were alone, he asked her, "Who's your doctor?"

"I went to my family doctor, Dr. Woodbury."

"You should have a specialist."

"I'm going to change because I got a call today from Dr. Woodbury's nurse and he's retiring. They're notifying his regular patients, so I called and made an appointment with an obstetrician."

"Good. I could ask Justin who he recommends."

"No, you don't. I'll decide which doctor I go to."

Aaron rubbed his cheek and nodded, suspecting he wouldn't get anywhere with an argument. "Who's the doctor you have an appointment with?"

"Dr. Burke."

"Ahh. Leon Burke?"

"Yes. I take it from your 'ahh' that you approve of my choice?"

"My sister knows him and thinks he's a good doctor. I've heard her talk about him. Yes, I approve."

She rubbed her forehead. "Whether you approve or not, Aaron, this is my choice of doctors."

"Sure, darlin'. Are you still planning to do substitute teaching?"

"Yes, I enjoy teaching and I can keep busy with substituting. Actually, I haven't signed up to sub yet because I was waiting for my ankle to heal. When I teach, I'm on my feet most of the day, but I'm able to do that now, I think."

"Which school will you teach in?"

He listened, steering the conversation away from anything personal while they were served drinks and later were served their dinners. At first she was stiff and remote, but gradually she relaxed somewhat, although she was still guarded. She seemed to have as little appetite as he did.

"You're barely eating. That can't be good."

She shrugged. "It won't last. I just don't feel hungry tonight."

Neither did he. Placing his fork in his plate, he reached across the table to take her hand, holding it lightly in his. "I want to marry you."

She shook her head. "Thank you, Aaron, but no. I want to marry for love. How many times have you said, 'I love you' to me? Or have I said it to you?" Before he could reply, she spoke again. "Don't declare your love now. You haven't said 'I love you' to me because you don't love me."

"I think I am in love."

"Oh, please, Aaron! You're doing what you think is right."

"No, I'm not," he replied and it hurt him to see the pain in her blue eyes. He ached to pull her into his arms and convince her to marry him.

"Aaron, I saw the look on your face when you realized I was pregnant. It wasn't joy."

"No, it was surprise," he admitted honestly. He leaned forward. "How did you learn that you're pregnant?"

"Dr. Woodbury told me."

"And wasn't your first reaction surprise?"

She gave him another exasperated look.

"Answer me, Pamela. Wasn't your first reaction surprise?"

"Maybe it was, but it didn't last long."

"Neither did my surprise. But you can't hold surprise against me when that was the exact same reaction you had."

She stood abruptly. "I want to go home."

He knew he had gotten to her on the last. He held her coat for her and draped his arm across her shoulders as they left the restaurant.

In the car Pamela sat with her arms crossed tightly in front of her. They were going back to her apartment, and she knew they would have another battle and this time the little girls wouldn't interrupt and end it. She glanced at Aaron. He could be so darned persuasive! But when she thought of the future, she knew she was right. He wasn't really in love. Never once had a declaration of love crossed his lips. It might now, but she wouldn't believe it. She just needed to stand firm and then he would go on his way and that would be that.

As he drove, she watched him. His hands were well-shaped, blunt fingers with nails trimmed short. He was handsome, intelligent, the best daddy for her baby.

He glanced in the rearview mirror.

"Are we being followed?" she asked.

"No, we're not."

She couldn't imagine he was right about anyone following her. Why would someone follow her? She didn't have anything valuable. As they approached her apartment, a muscle worked in his jaw, and her pulse raced. She knew he would finally have to come to grips with her decision. This would be their last date. He would kiss her. Anticipation made her pulse fly, but he wasn't kissing her into accepting his marriage proposal. No way would she yield on that. Longing for him stabbed her, and she wanted to reach out and put her hand in his, but she couldn't.

Instead, she hugged her middle and slid out of the car when he held the door open for her. When she took her key out of her purse, his fingers closed over hers to take the key from her.

"Aaron, why don't we just say goodbye right here and right now? It would be so much more pleasant than arguing about our futures."

He unlocked the door, shoved it open and switched on the light. "Let's go inside," he said, stepping back.

"It won't do you any good," she stated, looking into his green eyes that blazed with determination. Taking a deep breath and knowing she was going into a contest of wills and a fierce verbal struggle, she moved past him into her apartment. Stunned, she halted.

With swiftly mounting horror she stared at overturned drawers, clothing, books and papers strewn everywhere, furniture slashed and stuffing pulled out. A scream worked its way up her throat as she gasped and clamped her hands over her mouth.

Five

Aaron pushed past her, already talking to someone about her apartment on his cellular phone. He switched his phone off. "The police are on their way over here."

He placed another call and she could hear him talking quietly, telling someone else about her place. When he shut off his phone and jammed it into his pocket, he motioned to her.

"You stay right here by the door while I look around," he said grimly.

He pulled a gun out of the waistband of his trousers at the small of his back, and she stared at it in horror. She knew nothing about guns and Aaron suddenly looked different carrying a weapon. Tall, rugged, dangerous. His green eyes were angry, and fear for his safety filled her until he glanced back at her and she looked into his eyes. His gaze held the coldness and hardness of ice, frightening her. She remembered him telling her about being in the military, and she realized now she was seeing a different, much tougher side to him.

She shivered, keeping her arms wrapped around herself. Who would do this to her? Why?

Aaron disappeared into her bedroom and the lights switched on. While she waited, she looked at the slashed pillows. Someone wanted something, but what? She had nothing of great value, nothing important to anyone except her.

In seconds Aaron returned minus the weapon. He crossed the room to her to pull her into his arms, and for the moment she was glad to feel the reassurance of his strong arms.

"Why, Aaron?"

"Somebody wants something they think you have," he replied grimly. "You're shivering."

"I feel violated to think some stranger has been in here, destroying my things. I don't have any valuables."

"You'll stay at my house tonight."

"I can stay at the hotel or with my friends."

"No, you can't." He leaned back. "You don't want to endanger your friends. You may be in danger. I want you to stay at my house," he declared in a tone that ended the discussion.

Nodding, she no longer wanted to argue with him. "I'm all right," she said, moving out of his arms. "I want to look at my things and see what's ruined."

"Wait until the law arrives. Let's not touch anything else because they may be able to get fingerprints." He pulled her close again and held her tightly, stroking her head.

They waited, and when he heard voices approaching, he took her arm and they went outside to meet two plainclothes detectives who introduced themselves as Ed Smith and Barney Whitlock.

"What time did y'all get here?" Detective Smith asked, and before she could answer, Aaron spoke up.

"About fifteen minutes ago. You made good time."

"We try."

While the men talked, Pamela listened in a daze, looking at her slashed and smashed belongings. Neighbors began to call, asking if she was all right, and if they could help. She talked on the phone constantly until Detective Whitlock wanted to take her statement. Aaron righted an overturned chair for her while the stocky, redheaded Whitlock stood nearby and wrote everything down on papers on a clipboard.

As she answered questions, all around her a police crew worked, moving in and out of the apartment, dusting for fingerprints, taking pictures, searching through the rubble. When Detective Whitlock finished with her statement and his questions, he lowered the clipboard.

"Thanks for your cooperation. We'll let you know anything we learn."

"Thank you," she said stiffly, wondering whether she would ever feel safe in her apartment again.

"Why don't you get what you want to take with you," Aaron suggested as soon as Whitlock moved away. "When they leave, the police will secure your place. They're leaving someone to watch your apartment."

"I didn't know they would do that." As soon as the words were spoken, she realized why they would guard her apartment. "You hired someone to watch my place, didn't you?"

"Yes. I want to. Don't worry about it because it's no big deal. He's an off-duty cop and glad for the extra work."

"Oh, Aaron!" she exclaimed, annoyed by his taking charge, yet glad, too, that someone would stand guard.

She walked cautiously to her bedroom, once more shaken by the destruction. Her mattress was flung on the floor. It was ripped and slashed, with the insides strewn about the room. Her clothes were tossed everywhere and to her dismay, when she looked at her dresses, most of them were slashed.

She fingered one and glanced around to find Aaron watching her from the doorway.

"What are they searching for, Aaron? What could anyone think I have that's valuable? I'm a teacher with no family. I don't have anything."

"Someone thinks you do," he answered grimly.

"I'll get what I can salvage." As she looked through her clothing, she thought about all the questions the Asterland investigators had asked her, and the many times they had asked about what jewels she carried. She studied Aaron while he stood waiting patiently. He looked relaxed as he leaned against the door, but she noticed he was methodically scrutinizing her room and she wondered what was running through his mind. Then her attention returned to gathering what she could to take with her to Aaron's.

Bits of lace underwear were tossed on the floor, and she felt violated again. Anger made her shake. "I hope they catch whoever did this."

"I'm just glad you weren't home," Aaron said quietly and turned away.

Pamela gathered a few clothes that were in one piece. She wanted to wash all of her clothing, as if by washing she could cleanse them of the stranger's invasive touch.

Twenty minutes later she and Aaron left her apartment. As they walked past the yellow police tape that cordoned off the area, she saw three of her teacher friends standing in a cluster.

"Aaron, come meet my friends."

After they hugged her, she introduced Aaron to Jan Raddison, Amy Barnes and Robin Stafford. While Aaron stood quietly waiting, they offered help and sympathy for her loss. When she said goodbye, she and Aaron walked only a few yards to find more friends waiting to talk to her. It was another thirty minutes before she was seated in Aaron's car to drive away.

"You have a lot of friends."

"They were nice to stand out there in the cold to see me. And their offers of help were gracious. If I wouldn't endanger one of them, I'd stay with them."

"This is better."

"Suppose I put you in danger?"

He glanced at her. "I'd like to catch whoever ransacked your apartment."

Realizing there was a side to him she didn't know and didn't want to know, she shivered and became silent. While they rode, her jangled nerves settled until they approached Pine Valley. As they drove through the gated entrance, she thought of their first night in his house. Glancing at him, she wondered if memories assailed him also. If so, he gave no indication.

Inside his house he dropped all her things in the utility room except one small bag, and then he led her upstairs.

"Aaron, my robe was cut up."

"I'll give you one," he answered lightly. "I have a T-shirt you can sleep in if you'd like."

"Yes. I want to wash everything before I wear it. I know that's silly, but I feel as if everything I own fell into a mud puddle. Or worse."

"I figured you'd want to wash your clothes." Halfway down the hall to his large bedroom, he paused. "Being here with you brings back memories," he said in a husky voice as he brushed locks of hair away from her cheek.

"Yes, it does for me, too," she admitted. Their gazes locked and held while tension filled the moment and the air between them crackled.

"Which room will I stay in tonight?" she asked, prompting him. A muscle worked in his jaw as he took her arm and headed down the hall to the room next to his.

"I'll put you in here," he said. When he swung open the door, she entered another huge bedroom with a queen-size four-poster bed, a pale blue spread, thick cream-colored carpet and mahogany furniture.

"This is lovely. Your home is beautiful."

"Thanks. Mom's the one to thank for that."

"Once again, I'm sorry you lost your parents," she said.

"I think that's why I was more than a little upset when I heard about your plane having to make the forced landing." He set down a small bag she had packed and turned to drape his hands on her shoulders, kneading them lightly. She was aware of his touch and of his searching gaze. She longed to step closer and wrap her arms around him and feel his arms around her.

"You were tense before the break-in. You're really uptight now. Let's go downstairs and have some hot chocolate. Okay?"

Nodding, she dropped her purse, and he helped her out of her coat and tossed it on a chair. He waited while she went out ahead of him.

In minutes they were seated in his family room in front of a roaring fire with cups of hot chocolate.

"Who do you think ransacked my apartment?" Pamela was curled in a corner of the sofa with her shoes off and her legs tucked under her. Aaron sat only inches away. He had shed his suit coat and tie and kicked off his shoes. His cup of chocolate sat on the table in front of them, and he reached out to twist her hair in his fingers. Each little touch sent tingles racing in her. Even though their conversation was impersonal and about her apartment, she was aware of how close he sat, of the fact that they would be under the same roof all night. Locks of his brown hair fell across his forehead, and while she watched, he unfastened two more buttons of his shirt. In the firelight that created an orange glow, he looked too appealing.

"I don't know. Whoever trashed your apartment will just know he didn't find what he was looking for. That doesn't mean you don't have it."

She shook her head angrily. "You were right, I suppose. I'm the one someone has been following."

"I chased someone from outside your apartment last night."

Shocked, she stared at him. "There was someone watching my apartment?" Goose bumps rose on her arms. "Why didn't you tell me?"

"I didn't want to worry you. I've cautioned you to be careful. I couldn't catch him. He went over a fence and jumped into a car and drove off. There were two of them."

"I'm glad you didn't catch him. Can't you leave that sort of thing for the police?"

He gave her a level look. "I wanted to catch him, and if I see him, I'll go after him again. I want to know why you're being followed."

She sipped her cocoa and set her cup down, all the while

studying him as she mulled over possibilities in her mind. Her
curiosity rose as she pieced little things together.

"What's running through your mind?" he asked.

"You're in the Texas Cattleman's Club. I've heard rumors
about the members doing things to help people in trouble.
You're one of those members who help people, aren't you,
Aaron?"

"When I need to be," he answered.

"You've known all along that I was the one being followed.
How did you know that?"

He studied her. "It's all confidential, Pamela. Anything I
tell you can't go any farther than between us."

"It won't."

"We're concerned that all of the women on the plane are
in danger."

"Who is we?" she asked, mulling over what he was revealing and again feeling chilling surprise that she could be
in danger.

"Justin Webb, Matt Walker, Ben Rassad, Dakota Lewis.
You know some of them."

"If we're in danger, what's being done?"

"Matt is watching Lady Helena. Ben Rassad is going to
watch Jamie Morris."

"And you're watching over me," she said, closing her eyes
and wondering how she could get him out of her life. At the
same time, she was glad he was there. She thought about the
rumors she had heard about the members of the Texas Cattleman's Club, that they helped save deserving people, and she
could imagine Aaron doing this. His diplomatic background
would give him opportunity to help overseas; his wealth would
give him freedom and resources. She remembered watching
him move through her apartment with his gun in his hand.

"What's worrying you?"

She looked into his searching gaze. "What's worrying me
is how you always can read my thoughts."

"Not really. If I could read your thoughts I wouldn't have
asked what's worrying you. I would have known. But we do

understand things about each other without having to say anything. Haven't you noticed?''

"I haven't noticed that I can guess your feelings. Not like
you do with me.''

"Maybe I'm concentrating more on you," he said quietly.
"I'm fascinated with everything about you," he said softly,
leaning forward to kiss her throat lightly.

"You just can't be. I'm so plain vanilla ordinary, West
Texas born and bred," she said, barely aware of words, aware
only of him.

"And I think that's absolutely wonderful. And, my lady,
you need to remember I'm West Texas born and bred, too.''

"It's been educated out of you. There's nothing about you
that's countrified.''

"My values are," he whispered.

As she pushed him gently away, she wondered if he could
hear her pounding heart. When he stroked her throat, she realized he could feel her racing pulse beneath his fingers.

"I want you to stay with me until we catch them.''

She rubbed her forehead. "Aaron, it'll complicate our lives
more than ever.''

"No, it won't. We don't even have to talk about pregnancy
and babies and marriage if you don't want. Just stay here until
it's safe to go home. Okay?''

She nodded, wondering how many nights that would take,
and how many nights she could stay out of his bed. "I'll stay
if we won't talk about marriage.''

His green eyes were dark as he tangled her hair in his fingers. "If that's what it takes to get you to stay, fine. No talk
of marriage.''

"Aaron, I told you that I've signed up to substitute teach.
I don't want to do anything to jeopardize the safety of children. I can't imagine that I'm in danger, but then I'm shocked
that someone searched my apartment.''

"If you can afford to wait, it might be best if you didn't
substitute for a little while. I don't think you would bring any
element of danger into a classroom, but if you're a target,

maybe it's best not to take the chance. I don't think it'll be long before we learn something about what's going on. There are several of us working on it.''

"You think all of us, Lady Helena and Jamie Morris, too, are in danger?''

"Yes," he repeated. "Just be alert to everything going on around you.''

Once again she sat and studied him, piecing together questions and remembrances and what she knew about the Texas Cattleman's Club members.

"What's running through your mind now?" he asked, while his fingers continued to comb slowly through her hair and his other hand rested on her knee.

"Aaron, there's an old legend about Royal prospering because of jewels found in the War with Mexico. They were put away for safekeeping and, according to the legend, the town has prospered because of them. I always thought it was just a legend, a myth, and the jewels didn't actually exist. Now those investigators asked me so many questions, and I keep recalling a lot of questions from them about jewelry. Did I own any? What jewelry was I taking to Asterland? What valuables did I have? I told you the things they asked me.''

"Yes, you did.''

"Is the legend of the jewels true?''

He looked down at her knee, rubbing his fingers lightly over it.

"It's true," he said finally, meeting her gaze. "It's safer if most people think there's only a legend. Do you know any of the story about the jewels?''

"I've heard that old Tex Langley who founded the Texas Cattleman's Club hid the jewels that were found during the War with Mexico.''

Aaron nodded, and more questions swirled in her mind, puzzle pieces that might explain some of the strange happenings lately.

"The Texas Cattleman's Club members are the sworn guardians of the jewels," Aaron said quietly. "I wasn't going to tell you about them because I thought the less you knew, the safer you might be. Since you're getting more involved all the time, maybe you should be informed.''

''Those stones—are they safely hidden?''

She knew his answer before he gave a negative shake of his head.

''That's what they think I have? Good heavens! That's impossible.''

''Someone has one of the stones.''

''What are we talking about here? I'll keep it confidential, but is this why I've been followed?'' she asked, aghast that someone thought she had something highly valuable. ''What are these stones? Are they valuable?''

''They're damn valuable. We've already recovered two of the jewels. Justin found the emerald and the harlequin opal on the Asterland jet. There's a missing red diamond.''

''I've never heard of red diamonds or harlequin opals,'' she said, growing more appalled that someone would think she possessed one of the stones.

''The black harlequin opal is the stone of justice. It's credited as a healing stone with the power to protect its owner, not just from disease, but to give the owner wisdom. It's not as valuable as the emerald, which is two carats, but the opal holds a great deal of value because of its history.''

As Aaron talked, his fingers drifted across her nape, winding in her hair, sliding along her arm and then drawing circles on her knee. Every touch was fiery, causing a continual awareness and building the need that was already burning in her, taking half her attention from the problems at hand.

''I know that emeralds are sometimes considered healing stones,'' she said, barely thinking about the stones. ''And I think I remember that an emerald was supposed to be the gemstone of Ceres, a Roman goddess.''

''The goddess of agriculture,'' he whispered, as he brushed a kiss on her cheek.

''They're the color of your eyes,'' she added, unable to

resist telling him. His gaze met hers, and the desire that flamed in the green depths curled her toes.

"I hope our baby has your blue eyes," he said in a husky voice and her body grew taut with desire while heat smoldered in her. "Beautiful blue eyes," he whispered, rubbing her cheek with his knuckles.

His words were magical, tempting and taunting, making her long for all she couldn't have. "When I think of my baby, I think of a green-eyed, brown-haired baby boy," she whispered, unable to keep her secrets to herself.

"Ahh, darlin'. When I think of *our* baby, I see a little blue-eyed, black-haired girl."

Her heart was squeezed as if a fist had closed around it, and she tried to close her mind to what he said before she lost control of her emotions.

"Aaron, we were talking about the jewels," she reminded him, catching her breath and knowing she sounded as disturbed as she felt. "The emerald—remember. What about the red diamond?" she asked, trying to concentrate on his words, but far more aware of his hand caressing her and the tempting magic of his words. As she caught his hand in hers, he watched her intently. "The red diamond," she prodded.

"Red diamonds are rare. They've been called the stone of kings. This particular one is over a carat with no flaws to the naked eye. Its value could be enormous now. These stones were stolen and taken on board the plane for Asterland."

"How do you know the red diamond was there, too?"

"It just is a logical conclusion. All three were stolen, two turn up on the plane—the third stone was bound to be there, but in the forced landing everything was tossed everywhere."

"Everything and everybody," she said. "That landing brought out the best and the worst in people. I'm sorry Lady Helena was hurt so badly. When we first boarded the plane, I talked to her a little. I didn't know the man who was hurt at all, but, from what I last heard, he's still in a coma."

"That's right. He's an Asterland cabinet member, Robert Klimt."

"Someone thinks I have a red diamond in my possession," she said, dismayed and realizing she might be in a great deal of danger. She ran her hand across her forehead. "I don't need this."

"Don't worry. You'll be safe here."

"I can't stay shut up in your house."

"You can for a few days. We're working on this."

"Then you're in even more danger. Someone may want something from me, but the person who's doing this may just want you and your friends out of the way. Aaron, be careful," she urged, while concern for his safety overrode all her other stormy emotions.

"You *care,* darlin', a lot more than you want to admit," he said in a husky voice. His eyes darkened, and his gaze lowered to her mouth. Every inch of her flesh tingled, her lips parting because she couldn't get her breath. Her breasts were taut, and the heat smoldering so low inside her became a wildfire that raced along her veins. He was ruggedly handsome, too appealing, too irresistible. And the way he was looking at her now made her tremble. Forbidden, tantalizing, he was all she wanted.

Unable to resist, she leaned toward him and closed her eyes.

His mouth covered hers, his tongue sliding over her lower lip, touching the tip of her tongue and then stroking it while he lifted her onto his lap.

Throwing caution to the wind, she slid her arm around his neck, feeling his heart pounding in his chest as she placed her other hand against him. She twisted free his buttons and rested her hand on his solid chest. His heart thudded just as hers did. She let her hand drift lower to his flat stomach and she heard him growl deep in his throat. He was aroused, constrained by the suit trousers. She longed to just let go completely, to follow her heart and yield and love him. She did love him and she had to hold back the words because if she said them, he would, too, and his would be meaningless.

He leaned over her, shifting so she was lying on the sofa. While he kissed her, his hand slipped beneath her dress and he pulled away her panty hose, his fingers caressing her warm, bare thigh.

She wanted to spread her legs and arch her back and let him love her. Everything in her cried out for him, her body, her heart. Instead, she pushed against his chest.

Pausing, he raised his head. His green eyes were stormy and filled with scalding desire as he stared at her. "I love you," he said.

She placed her fingers on his mouth. "Shh. Stop that, Aaron." Hurting and wanting him, wanting his love and wishing he meant it, but keeping a grip on reality, she sat up and then stood.

"I should go to bed. Alone."

His darkened emerald eyes conveyed his roiling emotions. She was buffeted by his will, yet she knew the time would come when he would look at all this in a more rational manner, and be glad he wasn't married to her out of duty. He was aroused, his belt unbuckled, his shirt pushed open to reveal his muscular chest, covered in a mat of chest hair. Locks of straight brown hair fell across his forehead and his mouth was red from her kisses. He looked incredibly appealing and she found it wrenching to turn and walk away from him.

If only…

She knew better than to follow that line of thinking, but it was so difficult to resist. *If only he really did love her. If only they had known each other under different circumstances.*

Oh, sure, a small voice whispered in her mind. It wouldn't have mattered how different the circumstances. She was still small-town West Texas and he was jet-set, international man of the world. It wouldn't have mattered what circumstances. She could not link her life to his any easier than a Texas filly could link its life to a shooting star.

Picking up her discarded panty hose, she went upstairs, pausing at the top of the steps. He hadn't followed her, but had let her go.

"I love you."

His words rang in her ears, and he had sounded convincing.

She hurt so badly with wanting him. With wanting it *all*—his love, their marriage, their baby. Aaron, a father, there all the time for their child. Hurting, she clutched her middle and hurried to her bedroom, closing the door and leaning against it, feeling drained of all energy. Feeling drained of hope. She placed her hand against her stomach. She had his baby. She would always have that part of him. Tears stung her eyes, and she wiped at them furiously and moved to the bed where he had placed a large T-shirt of his and a navy velvet robe.

Gathering up the T-shirt and robe, she went to the adjoining bathroom, showered and pulled on the T-shirt, too aware that it was his. She slipped into the soft, elegant robe that was fancier than anything she had ever owned. She heard a knock, and her pulse jumped as she stared at the door.

Feeling a mixture of trepidation and eagerness, she crossed the room and opened the door.

Aaron stood there with his hands on his hips. He had shed his shirt and his trousers rode low on his narrow hips. His gaze was as stormy as ever as it swept slowly over her.

"Do you look good!" he said in a husky voice. He looked into her eyes, studying her.

"Did you want something, Aaron?"

His brow arched. "You," he said, his voice dropping still lower, and her heart thudded.

"We're not—"

"I know we're not, but I wanted to kiss you good-night."

"Oh, Aaron!" Against all good sense, she stepped forward and moved into his arms. In a deft movement that she never even noticed, he had the robe unbelted and pushed open, his arm sliding around her waist as he pulled her tightly against him and leaned over her to kiss her for all he was worth.

Aaron's pulse pounded hot and heavy as her soft curves pressed against him. Only his T-shirt covered her, and he longed to shove it away and caress her. He slid his hand beneath the shirt, running his fingers over the luscious smooth curve of her bottom, feeling her move against him. And then his hand went up to the small of her back, caressing, memorizing her.

When she pushed against him, he released her reluctantly. Stepping back, she stared at him with huge blue eyes that danced with searing flames. Her breathing was as harsh and fast as if she had run a mile. Her mouth was pouty and red from their kisses. And the T-shirt clung, revealing the taut peaks of her nipples.

He wanted her and he loved her. And she only believed half the truth.

"Good night, Aaron," she said. She closed the door, and he stared at it, wanting to kick it open and take her in his arms and kiss her until he melted every protest.

Instead, Aaron returned to his room and took a cold shower that did nothing to cool him down. As the cold spray hit him, he shifted his thoughts to her apartment. Not a cushion had been left untouched. Her wicker furniture had been ripped apart, and all her dresses had been slashed. Someone had to be searching for the missing red diamond. The Texas Cattleman's Club members didn't have it, but then, neither did someone else who had to have known it was on the Asterland jet.

This made Jamie Morris and Lady Helena incredibly vulnerable, too, but Ben and Matt would protect them.

Who had the diamond? What had happened to it in the forced landing? And the jewels had to be tied to Asterland for the two Asterland investigators to question Pamela so much about what jewelry she was carrying. The jewels were priceless, so a fortune could be gained from their possession. But because of his background, he couldn't keep from thinking of other possibilities for the money from the sale of the stones. Terrorism? Revolution? Drugs? Weapons? They had to find the missing diamond and all clues seemed to indicate that it was still somewhere in Royal. Someone thought it was in Pamela's possession.

He turned off the shower and toweled dry, climbing into

bed to stare into the darkness. He was aroused, taut and aching for her. Aware she was only yards away. He went over the entire day, the news of her pregnancy, their arguments, their date.

He searched his own feelings for her. Was it sex as she accused? He tried to study his feelings impartially, tried to sort out what he felt from what his body desired. And the more he thought about it and considered and remembered, the more he determined that he was deeply, irrevocably in love with his West Texas lady.

"Lady, I love you," he whispered into the darkness, turning to look at the door and thinking about her in the next bedroom.

He did love her. The more he searched his feelings, the more certain he became. He was head over heels, unable to get her out of his thoughts, heart-pounding in love with her. She filled this great aching emptiness in him that had grown worse the past couple of years. When he was around her, his life had purpose. Even now, with all the disagreements and turmoil between them, he didn't have that chilling desolation that filled him most of the time in the recent past. And she was so much that he admired—good with children, intelligent, sexy, caring, fun.

She would have to come to realize the depth of his feelings for her. He thought about five years from now, ten years— and he knew if it was five or a lifetime, she was truly the woman for him.

"I really love you with a love that's bigger than Texas, and, whether you let me show you or not, my love will last," he said in the darkness, and his resolve to convince her of his feelings grew.

Their first and only night together, he had taken her virginity and gotten her pregnant. From what all his friends had told him about her, she had never really dated anyone. Which meant she had never really been courted by anyone. She deserved that much. He sat up, thinking about what he could do and mapping out his plans just as he had mapped out every important move in his life.

He switched on a light and moved to his desk to jot down things he wanted to do first thing in the morning. When he was back in bed in the dark, he mulled over everything that had happened and he looked again at the closed bedroom door, thinking about her so near and yet so impossibly far. "You're my lady, and I'm not letting you and our baby go out of my life. I love you, Pamela," he said, and searched his own feelings. Would he feel the same if there were no baby?

He realized that that was the critical question. He had to get all thoughts of their baby out of his mind and look at his emotions and feelings. For the next half hour he lay in the dark, mulling over every moment with her, all his feelings, his longings. What would he feel if she wasn't pregnant?

His conclusion was the same. The more he was around her, the more he was certain he truly loved her, and the more he wanted her. No woman had ever had that effect on him. And first thing in the morning he would try to show her every way possible how much she meant to him.

He slept little and was up so early, he dressed in sweats and jogged, circling his block for half an hour so he would never be far from the house and watching to see if he could spot anyone lurking in the area. He returned, showered, dressed in jeans and a wool shirt and saw that her bedroom door was still closed. He paused beside it and didn't hear a sound, so guessed she was sleeping. Taunting images of silky long legs and luscious curves floated in his mind and, without thinking, his hand closed around the doorknob. Reluctantly, he released the knob, turned and went downstairs to start breakfast, wondering what she could eat that wouldn't cause morning sickness. It was still early, but his housekeeper usually arrived at half-past six, so he called her and made arrangements for her to come only once a week. He called the family cook with the same instructions. He wanted Pamela to himself as much as possible.

The moment the clock struck half-past seven he called the local florist at home. Since the turn of the century, the Handleys had been in the flower business in Royal, and Aaron had gone to school with Rufus Handley who ran the Handley Floral Shop now. In minutes he had ordered three dozen red roses to be delivered today.

Impatiently, he waited until eight and then made more calls while he moved around the kitchen finishing breakfast preparations.

"Good morning," Pamela said.

He turned and his insides clenched. She wore his robe and was barefoot, her skin glowing and her hair still damp. He dropped whatever he was holding, unaware of what he was doing except moving toward her. He couldn't resist going to her. He had to touch and hold her and he knew he was absolutely, irrevocably in love with her.

Six

Immobilized by the intensity of his gaze, Pamela could barely catch her breath and every thought flew out of her mind. He narrowed the space between them and a thrill curled down through her to the center of her being. There was no question he desired her, but there was a quality of something else in his expression—tenderness? Love?

It couldn't be, she reminded herself, but her pulse raced as he closed the distance and his arm went around her to pull her against him.

"Oh, Aaron, don't do this to us. It—"

There were no more words because his mouth covered hers, and he kissed her long and deep with a soul-searching passion. His hands moved beneath the robe and T-shirt until she caught his wrists and leaned away.

"Aaron, don't keep doing this to us!" she pleaded again, gasping for breath, trying to do what she knew she should do.

"I love you."

"Shh. Stop saying words you didn't say until you knew you should marry me!"

He framed her face with his hands. "I love you and I won't stop saying it because it's true. I was awake hours last night, and I searched my feelings."

"Stop saying things you don't really mean, or I'm moving out of your house. I have a friend in Midland and—"

"I'll stop," he interrupted grimly. "You stay right here at my house where it's safe."

She caught a whiff of an acrid smell. Smoke curled over the burners and a dreadful smell assaulted her, sending her stomach rolling.

"Something's burning!" As her stomach heaved, she fled. She heard swearing behind her and a clatter of utensils. She hoped he hadn't set his house on fire, but she had to run for the bathroom.

Nauseated, embarrassed again, and unable to stop thinking about the past few moments, she rushed to a downstairs bathroom. After her stomach stopped heaving, she took a clean washcloth from the linen cabinet and sponged her face with cold water.

No man had ever looked at her the way Aaron had. Just the memory heated her and took her breath. In agony, she closed her eyes and placed her fist against her heart. Why was he making this so difficult!

"Get out of his house," she told herself, but then she remembered her trashed apartment and knew she couldn't go back to it. Her stomach settled, and she belted her robe and went back to the kitchen, promising herself that she would resist him. Embarrassed by her morning sickness, she entered the kitchen cautiously. The smells had gone; a fan whirred softly above the burners, and Aaron had his back to her as he reached into the refrigerator.

Watching him, she looked at his thick brown hair, her gaze drifting down across his broad shoulders, sliding lower to his narrow waist and slim hips. He wore faded jeans and once again looked like a lot of local cowboys except that he was

Aaron. There was no way she could ever look at him and see Aaron as an ordinary man. Not once, not from that first moment of looking into his eyes across the Texas Cattleman's Club ballroom, had she ever been able to view him with the same objective manner she did all other men. And she knew she never would.

As if he sensed she was there, he turned. He held a pitcher of orange juice and he studied her. "All right now?" he asked gently.

"Yes. You're very nice about my morning sickness. I'd think it would send most guys running."

He shoved the refrigerator door shut and shrugged. "I grew up on a ranch and you see a lot of things. Birth, death, mating, fighting—it's all there and it's part of living. Sure you're all right now?"

"I'm fine. Did you burn something?"

"Yes, but fortunately, it was contained in a skillet. I tried to get all of the smells out of the room. Now, what can you eat?"

"Actually, that orange juice looks good. Sometimes this hits and then it passes and then other times, I can't eat anything until afternoon. And sometimes food looks so good, I eat and then I lose it."

"Come sit down and try out my cooking," he said, smiling with a flash of white teeth, and once again becoming his irresistible, irrepressible self.

The round oak table was set and looked inviting with cheerful bright blue place mats and colorful china. She took a tentative sip of her orange juice, aware of Aaron seated across the table from her and watching her with a faint smile.

"What do you have to do today?" he asked.

"I have an appointment with the obstetrician. I told his nurse about my morning sickness, but I don't think he can do much for it. My appointment is at eleven. Then I'll go to my apartment and see what I can do there."

Aaron shook his head. "I'll take you to the doctor's, and then we can have lunch together. I hired a cleaning crew to work on your apartment as soon as the police will let anyone go back inside.''

She lowered the glass of cold juice to the table and memories swirled in her mind of gifts men showered on her mother and her and how much she had hated having to accept them.

"Aaron, I don't want you to hire someone to clean my apartment. You don't have to do things like that for me.'' She knew she was overreacting, but she was too conscious of being pregnant and unwed, too conscious of Dr. Woodbury's reaction that lumped her together with her mother. "I don't want you to do that for me,'' she snapped.

His smile vanished and he studied her, reaching across the table to take her hand. She tried to pull away, but he held her firmly.

"What is it?'' he asked. "You're not giving me a polite 'oh, you shouldn't have' objection. I've upset you, but why? What is it?''

"I can take care of myself,'' she said stiffly, withdrawing her hand from his.

With a scrape, he pushed back his chair and came around the table. She watched him as he paused beside her and held out his hand. "Come here.''

"Aaron, we'll end up in each other's arms and at a stalemate.''

"I just want to talk. I think we need to talk because I don't understand why you're upset.''

When she stood, he picked her up, sitting in her chair and holding her on his lap. Her heart raced as she looked into his eyes. She was only inches from him and could smell his aftershave, see his clean-shaven jaw that was smooth and tan. His lashes were unbelievably thick and gave him sexy, bedroom eyes that were irresistible.

"I don't think this is a good way to have a reasonable discussion,'' she said, barely able to get her breath, too conscious of him to think straight.

"I think it's the best way,'' he said easily as if they were in an office and seated across the room from each other. He seemed undisturbed by her closeness until she looked into his eyes, and the longing she saw there was unmistakable. "My hiring help for you really disturbs you. Why?"

"I can take care of my apartment. I'm used to taking care of myself. I took care of my mother all the last years of her life and I was only in high school. I don't want you doing things like that for me."

Aaron pushed locks of her hair away from her face, tucking them behind her ear and letting his fingers trail over her ear. "I want to do things like that for you. Please let me."

She shook her head, not trusting her voice to speak. She thought of how much like her mother she had been, tumbling into bed with Aaron the first night she met him.

"Mellie," he said softly. "That's a good nickname. I'll commandeer that from the little girls. What's bothering you?"

"Nothing," she replied stiffly, aware when he drawled the nickname it sounded infinitely more personal than when it was said by the children.

"Good, then you'll let me do these things for you."

"No, I won't!" she answered fiercely. "I'll be just like my mother, sleeping with someone and then taking gifts—" She bit her lip and looked away.

"Ahh, here's what's disturbing you," he said so gently her insides wrenched. "You're not like your mother. No one could possibly think that."

"Yes, they could. Dr. Woodbury did the moment he found out I was pregnant."

"Then I'm damn glad you have another doctor," Aaron said, his green eyes turning cold. "And it might have been your imagination. Darlin', I've talked to guys I know here. Your reputation is impeccable."

"When they find out that I'm pregnant, they'll just see my mother in me. That sterling reputation will be tarnished forever," She locked her fingers together in her lap while painful memories taunted her. "Aaron, the men that came to our house...they would bring presents to her. They gave her all kinds of gifts. And they brought gifts to me to try to please her, and when I was small, she made me accept them." She met his gaze and couldn't keep the anguish out of her voice, while hating herself for spilling so much of what she had always kept hidden. "That's where I got money for my clothes. That's how we got our furniture. That's where she got her cars. Kids would tell me she was the town tramp, and they were right. But now that's all people will think of when my pregnancy shows." As old hurts welled up in her, her throat burned while she struggled with her emotions. "The first time you looked at me, I just fell into your arms and into your bed. Everyone will compare me to her and say I'm like her. I don't want your gifts!"

She started to get up, but his arms wrapped around her and he held her. "No, they won't," he answered firmly.

"Let me go, Aaron. I've lived with this. I've lived with them calling my mother all kinds of ugly names and calling me trash and such."

"That was a long time ago. You haven't heard anyone call you a name since you've grown up, have you?"

She didn't want to look at him. Embarrassment flooded her and she just wanted to be gone, out of his scrutiny, out of temptation, back to the security of her quiet life.

He put his finger beneath her chin and turned her to face him. "That was a long time ago and I'm not giving you gifts in payment for sex. I'm doing the things I want to do for my lady, the love of my heart."

"Aaron, stop it. If I married you, you know what your family would think. They'd think I trapped you into it." She wiped furiously at tears that brimmed over and spilled down her cheeks. "I can't control anything with you. Too many times now you've seen me at my worst."

"And the worst looks pretty damn good to me," he said quietly, giving another wrench to her heart.

"Stop being so adorable!" she cried, wriggling to get off his lap.

His arms tightened, holding her against him. "I want to do things for you, and wanting to doesn't have anything to do with that night. Now let me. Guys all over the world do things they want to do for women in their lives. Let me do what I want for you. And I want you always to know that it's because I love you and not because we went to bed together."

"I don't believe it."

"Just give me a chance here. We haven't had sex since that first night. If having sex was why I want to shower you with things, do you think I'd continue? Of course, I wouldn't."

"Aaron, the smooth-talking diplomat in you is showing," she said, knowing she was going to give in, yet suddenly feeling better. "Everyone will think I'm like her."

"No, they won't. For them to think bad things about you, there will have to be *men* in your life. Not just one particular man who wants to marry you. Believe me, you have a reputation for being very cool and collected." He stroked her face lightly with his fingers and his voice was so tender, she knew some of her hurts were vanishing.

"Maybe I'm too sensitive about it, but I've spent most of my life struggling with insults and men making passes and being ostracized."

"Oh, damn, darlin', I wish I could take away the hurt, but that was a long time ago and it has nothing to do with us."

"I can't turn hurts from my past off, Aaron."

"I know you can't. But what I feel and do has nothing to do with what happened when you were growing up." He stroked her head, running his fingers through her hair while he held her close. Touching the strong column of his throat, still aware of his arm holding her tightly, she took his hand to hold it in hers.

"I've never told anyone all that."

"I'm glad you told me. I've never told anyone how purposeless my life has become the past few years. But the desolation is gone when I'm with you."

She searched his thickly lashed green eyes, and he met her gaze squarely. "When I think about your lifestyle," she whispered, "I just can't believe you don't have everything you could possibly want. And I can't believe I give meaning to your life."

"I'll show you, lady. This is one Texan who knows what he wants, and I'm going to try to make it clear to you just how deep my feelings run. They're bigger than Texas, stronger than the Texas wind, as lasting as that hard-packed West Texas ground. I love you, Pamela Miles, and that's the only reason for the gifts from me."

Golden and warm, his words washed over her, melting away her hurts, and she wanted to believe them. For the moment she did. She couldn't resist him.

"You sweet-talkin' charmer," she whispered, and wound her arms around his neck, and knew he had won another round as she leaned forward to place her lips on his. She saw the one second of surprise that widened his eyes, and then his arm tightened around her, and he leaned over her to kiss her. His hand stroked her back and he wound his fingers through her hair, kissing her until she was gasping for breath and her hands were all over him. He was aroused; there was no mistaking he wanted her. And she wanted him, but she knew she shouldn't.

Aaron was the one who raised his head and shifted her away. "I want you." He ground out the words in a husky voice. "And you're going to be mine, but it isn't because of sex that I want to do things for you." He scooted her off his lap.

Standing, she pulled her robe together and realized he had stopped kissing her to try to prove to her his feelings weren't driven by sex. She suffered another twist to her heart.

Her body throbbed with need, her breasts were taut and tingled and she wanted to sit back in his lap and kiss him, but this was best. And there was no mistaking that he wanted her. He was aroused, ready. His forehead was beaded with sweat and the hunger in his eyes made her knees jelly.

"I can't eat any breakfast," she whispered. "I'll get ready for my doctor's appointment."

"Pamela."

At the door she turned as he stood. "I need to go to a meeting. I'll come back in time to take you to the doctor."

She nodded and went upstairs, mulling over all the things they had said to each other.

In spite of his arguments, she was reluctant to accept the cleaning service. It seemed ridiculous when she wasn't working, and she couldn't shake the old feelings that she was doing what her mother had done and would bring down the same reaction from townspeople. It was just a matter of time before her pregnancy was known, and then the gossip would start. If people knew she was living in Aaron's Pine Valley home, gossip would start even sooner.

After showering and dressing, Pamela meandered through Aaron's elegant mansion, looking at family pictures, studying pictures of his brothers and his sister. They all had brown hair. A brother and his sister had green eyes, the other brother, the minister, had blue eyes.

Dr. Rebecca Black. Pamela had heard about his sister's work in remote areas of the world, now in the jungles of Belize. In this picture, Aaron's sister had short brown hair and looked practical and intelligent and, judging from childhood pictures, had been a tomboy.

Pamela studied the two brothers' pictures, Jeb Black managed the family fortune and lived in Houston. "He's our hard-headed businessman," Aaron had said, describing his family.

The other brother, the minister, was shorter than the rest of the men in his family. He was Reverend Jacob Black whose reputation was international because of the money he raised and channeled into church missionary work around the world.

With his rugged features, his height and his slender build, Aaron resembled his dad.

The doorbell rang and Pamela went to a window. Before he'd left, Aaron had told her not to answer the door unless she knew for certain who it was, which had made her laugh.

"Who knows I'm staying here?" she questioned, amused by his instructions. She'd stood at the back door with him while he pulled on a shearling coat and picked up a black Stetson.

"You might be surprised, darlin'," he drawled in his West Texas accent, touching her cheek. "I like your dimples, Mellie. If someone comes to the door, before you open it, just make sure you know who it is. Now set the alarm when I close the door."

"Sure thing, cowboy," she said with a wink, and he drew a deep breath, coming back in to haul her into his arms and kiss her senseless. When he released her, he looked down at her solemnly. "You're going to be mine, Mellie," he whispered. Then he had jammed his hat down farther on his head, turned and left while she stood breathlessly watching him.

As the soft melodic chimes rang again, she came out of her reverie and experienced a swift stab of apprehension when the sight of her trashed apartment flashed in mind. Concerned, she hurried to an upstairs window and looked down at the drive. At first glance she recognized the robin's-egg-blue van with bright yellow letters, Handley's Floral Shop. With relief surging in her, she hurried downstairs to the door.

When she looked through a peephole, she recognized Rufus Handley's brown eyes and blond hair above an enormous bouquet of red roses.

"Oh, my!" She stared at the flowers in surprise and then jumped when Rufus punched the doorbell again. She turned off the alarm, unlocked and opened the door.

"Hi, Miss Miles," he said with a wide smile. She had had his little girl in her second-grade class three years ago. "I have some flowers for you."

"For me?" she asked, feeling embarrassed, amazed and chagrined all at once.

"Can I bring them inside?"

"Of course," she said, stepping back and looking at the enormous bouquet of gorgeous red roses. "How's Trisha?"

"She's great. You can't believe how well she's reading. Ms. Stafford said she's two levels beyond her grade."

"That's great!"

"Well, we owe a lot to you. You really helped her with her reading."

"She's a very bright girl and a very sweet one."

He grinned. "I'll tell Lucy and Trisha you said that. Enjoy your flowers. I'm sorry your apartment was broken into. We don't have much of that around here, so I hope they catch who did it soon. You've had some bad luck lately, with the plane going down and now having a break-in. I'm sorry."

"Thanks," she said, following him to the door and closing it behind him, knowing Royal was small enough that people still knew most everything that was happening in town. She reset the alarm and then walked back to the bouquet, laughing and shaking her head. The roses were beautiful. She pulled out the card.

To Pamela With Love. Aaron.

"Oh, no!" She let the card flutter from her hand and fall to the floor and her amusement and joy over the flowers vanished. By nightfall it would be all over Royal that she was staying at Aaron's house and he had sent her roses and signed the card "with love, Aaron."

"Oh, no!" she whispered again, embarrassment flooding her. He might as well have put banner headlines in the newspaper.

"Why did you sign it that way?" she asked the empty house. Even though she was home alone, her cheeks flushed with embarrassment. Rufus Handley and everyone at his shop would know about the card and flowers, and before long the whole town would know. Why hadn't Aaron just signed his name and let it go at that?

Her embarrassment was tinged with anger. Aaron Black had a streak of bulldog stubbornness.

He was picking her up to take her to her doctor's appointment, but she didn't want to see him or go to the obstetrician with him and add to the rumors about them that would already be flying. The sight of Aaron Black escorting her into the obstetrician's office would be more noticeable than banners waving over the town. Heavens, what talk that would start!

She should have told him no when he offered to take her to the doctor's office, but when she was with him, her thoughts were always half jumbled.

Hurrying to the phone, she called the only cab that served Royal, knowing that would be just one more rumor because she had been picked up at Aaron's house on another occasion—near dawn that first morning.

She locked up and left, going to her doctor's appointment early and calming as they discussed her morning sickness.

When she stepped out of Dr. Burke's office, Aaron was lounging against the wall in the hallway. His hat was pushed back on his head. Sunglasses were hooked into a pocket of his shirt. He had shed his coat and held it in one hand. At the sight of her, he straightened. "I thought I was going to pick you up and bring you here for your appointment."

"The flowers are beautiful."

"And another gift is worrying you. I thought we settled that this morning."

"Aaron, you signed the card 'with love.' I'm staying at your house. Pretty soon it'll be all over town. And if you had escorted me here—to the obstetrician's—what talk that would stir!"

Dropping his coat, he turned her so she was against the wall and he braced both hands on either side of her, hemming her in. He glanced around them at the empty hallway. "Look, lady. You have the most exemplary reputation in town. I know you have old hurts and I'm sorry."

"This isn't about that," she whispered, surprised by the forcefulness of his words. "It's that everyone—" She faltered over the words. "Everyone will think—"

"Will think I'm in love. That's fine and dandy. I could shout it from the rooftops because I am and there's nothing to be ashamed of or to hide about it. I love you, Pamela," he announced clearly.

"Aaron, don't!" she cried, hurting. "You don't know what you feel and you didn't say that to me until you thought we had to get married."

Aaron glanced over his shoulder again. Following his gaze, she glanced down the empty hallway as a door closed at the end of the hall.

He took her arm. "Let's talk somewhere else," he said tersely.

She walked with him out to his car. Wind buffeted her while he unlocked the car door, and she watched him look around. "You think I'm being followed again."

"Yes, I do. While we were talking, someone was at the end of the hall. I would have gone after them, but that would have left you there alone and that's not good."

She shivered and sat down in his car, watching him go around to the driver's side. He slid in and looked at her. "Marry me and we'll stop all worry about gossip."

"No. We've been over this. And you said you wouldn't talk about marriage while I'm at your house."

"We're not at my house now. I love you and I could happily spread it on billboards or in the newspaper or anywhere else."

"Don't!"

"I'm not going to because it wouldn't make you happy," he said solemnly. "But I am going to keep right on trying to get you to face the truth about yourself and about me." He stroked her cheek lightly with his fingers. "Darlin', you're getting over old hurts and I know that takes time. I can be patient because it's important."

She inhaled deeply, looking into the depths of his direct gaze and feeling that he meant every word now. Yet she was still certain he would change in time.

"What did the doctor say?" Aaron asked while his eyes conveyed a hungry intensity that made her think his mind was barely on his words.

"He said I should try to eat when I can. I've lost some weight," she said, aware of Aaron, knowing someone outside had followed her again and she should be more concerned about the danger she might be in, but all she could think about was Aaron and his declarations of love that had sounded absolute. If only she could believe him. If only, if only…

She realized he was staring at her intently. "I'm sorry. Did you say something?"

"I said a lot. What're you thinking about?"

"What you've said to me in the past few minutes."

"Good! I want you to think about what I'm telling you because every word I've said is true. Sooner or later you're going to see that I mean what I say."

"I still don't think you're giving this enough serious thought."

"Did the doc give you anything for the morning sickness?"

"No. He said that will pass after the third month—"

"That's a long time."

"It'll go in a hurry."

"Can you eat lunch now?"

"Yes, as a matter of fact, I feel starved."

"Is the Royal Diner okay?"

"Sure."

She noticed he still watched the rearview mirror as he drove. Main Street had the ordinary amount of traffic, the usual number of people walking in front of buildings, going in and out of stores, but someone out there had ransacked her apartment and slashed her belongings. Someone out there had followed her to her doctor's appointment. Someone out there thought she had a rare red diamond worth heaven knows how much. The idea chilled her.

"Aaron, where can that diamond be? Are you sure it isn't still at the landing site and all of your friends overlooked it?"

He shook his head. "That site has been searched inch by inch, by not only Texas Cattleman's Club members, but investigators and lawmen. No, it's somewhere else, and we're not the only ones searching for it."

"Why would anyone think I had it?"

"Why *not* you, darlin'?" he drawled. "You'd be the perfect cover, particularly if you didn't know you were carrying it."

"If I'd had it in my belongings, I would know it now because I unpacked everything."

"You're sure?"

"Very sure. And the clothing I took with me on the plane was in the apartment, so it's been slashed and pawed over." She bit her lip. "Whoever is searching for the diamond has to know now that I don't have it."

"Not necessarily. Someone followed you to the doctor's."

"So someone is watching your house," she said, and saw a muscle working in his jaw.

"We'll catch whoever it is."

"I don't find that reassuring. Please be careful."

He turned to give her a quick searching look and then looked at the street as he slowed for a stoplight. After parking in front of the diner, Aaron took her arm and they hurried inside.

Over hamburgers that tasted delicious to her and a thick creamy chocolate malt, she listened to Aaron talk about his life in Spain. Long after they finished, they still sat and talked until he glanced at his watch. "I have an appointment with our local attorney at four. I'll take you home unless you have somewhere else you want to go."

"Your house is fine," she said, reluctant to go to her apartment if she didn't have to.

"Good. Will it bother you to fly?"

"I don't think so, but I don't plan on any trips soon."

"How about dinner tonight in Dallas with me?"

She closed her eyes. "Aaron, you're not getting what I'm telling you."

"Yes, I am. I told you, I want to show you that you're important to me and I'm in love." He slid out of the booth and stood waiting, holding her coat for her when she stood. He draped his arm over her shoulders and she knew that everyone in Royal would be linking them together now.

Monday morning he took her back to look at her apartment. Aaron unlocked the door and put his arm around her as they entered. "I'm having an alarm installed this morning."

She turned to stare at him, but before she could speak, he put his finger on her lips. "Shh. I'm doing what I want to do. You need an alarm, and I know you hadn't even thought about getting one, had you?"

"No. I don't know that I'll continue living in Royal."

A fleeting look of pain flashed in his eyes and was gone. "All right, so it's temporary," he said grimly. "At least, for now, humor me and accept my present."

She studied him and could feel the clash of wills, yet knew his intentions had been good. "Thank you," she said, and he leaned forward to brush a kiss on her forehead.

"You're welcome. The guy should be out here in thirty minutes to install it. Insurance will cover your losses on your furniture and clothing."

"Please, Aaron, don't replace my furniture," she said solemnly.

He studied her and held her shoulders, rubbing them lightly. "I'm just trying to do things to help, not hurt."

"I know you are and the flowers are beautiful and the alarm will be very nice, but I'm accustomed to taking care of myself. Besides, I want to pick out my own furniture."

"You don't like the way my house looks?" he teased, trying to lighten the moment.

"Your mother did your house, not you. You leave my furniture to me."

"Fine, but let me at least buy you a new dress and take you out in it."

She smiled and shook her head. "I think you're incredibly used to getting your own way."

"Might be a little, but I think you are, too."

"Not like you are, Aaron," she remarked dryly, thinking of his unlimited funds that allowed him to do so much of what he wanted.

"Maybe that's what makes me so lovable."

She had to laugh then. "That and your modesty."

He grinned, touching her dimple. "If you only knew what

your smiles do for me. They chase away all my rainy days. Come on, let's see how things look."

When they entered her living room, she drew a deep breath. The cleaning service had the floors polished and things righted. The room smelled of lemon furniture polish and surfaces gleamed. Books were on bookshelves, but most tables and shelves were bare because her vases and candlesticks had been broken. Throw cushions were gone; her pictures were stacked on the floor against a wall, the frames broken, the glass that had covered them gone or cracked. The few pieces of furniture that were not ruined were in place, but the cushions had slashes in them and the apartment was not livable. She went to the kitchen and found some of her dishes and utensils intact, but most crystal was gone and much of her china, swept out of cabinets carelessly to the floor when the intruder had searched her apartment.

"I hope you do catch who did this," she said quietly.

The cleaning service had hauled away the ripped mattress and springs, so she had only a frame for a bed. Loss overwhelmed her and she ran her fingers across her brow.

"They're only things, Mellie," Aaron said gently, pulling her closer against his side. "You're safe and that's what's important. This can all be replaced."

"I know—" The doorbell rang, startling her, and she realized how tense she was. "That's probably the girls," she said, turning to answer. He caught her arm.

"Let me go to the door," he said grimly, moving ahead of her.

Seven

She moved cautiously behind Aaron. As he paused to look through the new peephole, he motioned to her to join him. When he opened the door and stepped back, Pamela faced her next-door neighbor who stood holding a casserole.

"Nancy, come in," Pamela said. "This is Aaron Black. Aaron, meet Nancy Colworth."

"We met the night of the break-in," Aaron said smoothly. "Can I take that for you?" he asked, motioning to the casserole.

"Yes, I brought you a tuna casserole. Even if you aren't staying here, you can take it with you," she said, handing the dish to Aaron.

"Thank you, Nancy," Pamela said, touched that her friend would take time from her busy schedule to help. "Come in and sit down—if we can sit," she said, smiling ruefully.

Nancy shook her head and ran her fingers through her black curls. "I have to pick the girls up. They're at their grandmother's and then we're going shopping for shoes, so I need to get them. Purchasing shoes for them will take us a while, and they'll wear out and get tired, so I have to run." She looked past Pamela at the apartment. "I see you're back in order."

"Such as it is," Pamela replied, watching Aaron returning from the kitchen. He looked so out of place in her tiny apartment. He belonged in a spacious house like his Pine Valley home. He wore a plaid shirt and jeans and she thought how handsome he looked and how full of vitality. It amazed her that he was still in her life and she in his. When she realized Nancy was talking, she tried to pull her attention from Aaron.

"So a few of us would like to have a party for you—sort of a house shower—when you can find time."

"Nancy, that's so sweet of you!" Pamela said, hugging her neighbor and deeply touched by the kindness of her friends. "Y'all don't have to do that."

"Of course we don't. We want to. You pick a time that's good, and we'll plan a party at my place. Give me a list of your teacher friends and anyone else you'd like to invite."

"That's so sweet," Pamela repeated, tears stinging her eyes. She was embarrassed by her emotional reaction. Aaron was beside her, his arm firmly around her waist, and she was glad for his reassuring presence.

"That's nice of you," he said in a deep voice, while she tried to pull herself together. When had she gotten so emotional over everything that happened? Was it hormones because of her pregnancy? Or the upheaval in her life caused by Aaron?

"We want to. Pamela is special. Particularly to us. The girls have little things they've made for you, but they'll want to bring them over to you. In the meantime, is there anything any of us can do to help?"

As Pamela shook her head, Aaron said, "Let me give you my phone number and pager, in case you should want to get hold of us for any reason." He pulled out a small tablet and pen and jotted down numbers, tearing out a page and handing it to Nancy.

"Call anytime you need to."

"I will. Let me know when you pick a date for a party," Nancy said.

"Thank you, and thanks for the casserole. We'll enjoy it," Pamela said, thinking about the freezer filled with casseroles at Aaron's house and his cook who came in once a week.

Closing the door behind Nancy, Pamela leaned against it and turned to face Aaron. "Friends are nice."

"You're nice," he said, placing his hands on either side of her. "Want to keep her casserole in your freezer or take it to my place?"

"We don't need it at your house, but I'd rather take it and eat it, so I can thank her and return her dish." It was difficult to think with him standing so close.

"Ready to go home?"

"Aaron, you're going to make it so hard to say goodbye," she whispered, knowing she ought to stay anywhere except his place.

"I hope I make goodbye impossible," he replied solemnly, looking at her mouth and making her ache to kiss him. What would one more kiss hurt? How many times would she ask herself that question? If they kissed, she knew he would stop, and if he didn't, she would stop before it escalated to reckless abandon. She couldn't resist winding her arms around his neck and pulling his head down to her. She stood on tiptoe and placed her mouth on his to kiss him hungrily.

His arms went around her, and he held her tightly, leaning over her to kiss her hard, passion flaring between them. Her pulse roared and she wanted him desperately, more every hour she spent with him.

In minutes she paused to whisper, "You're making it next to impossible, but someday, Aaron, I'll say goodbye and go. I promise—"

"Don't make promises you can't keep. I hope to see to it that you never go out of my life, lady," he whispered in return, turning so he leaned against the door while he kissed her. He spread his legs and pulled her up against him. She felt his hard arousal, his long lean body and legs pressed against her, while one hand slipped beneath her sweater and pushed away her bra, cupping her breast.

She moaned, wanting him, grinding her hips against him in need and feeling as if she was drowning in desire, knowing that minute by minute and kiss by kiss he was wearing away her resistance.

"We're not at my place now," he whispered, raising his head to look at her, locks of his brown hair falling over his forehead. His solemn green eyes made her heart lurch. "Marry me, Mellie," he said, and she felt as if all air had been squeezed from her lungs. She hurt, a pounding pain that hammered her. *Don't think about what might be.*

"Aaron, stop pushing. If I say yes, it'll be for the wrong reasons," she said, wanting him, certain that the wrong reasons were his, not hers. She kissed him to stop his words that tempted and held out glittering false hopes.

They stroked and kissed until he held her in his arms and her legs were locked around him, yet clothes were between them. He stopped and set her on her feet and moved away from her, crossing the room to stand with his back to her. His fists were clenched and she could hear his ragged breathing even above her own.

"We timed that right. Here comes the guy to set the alarm."

She straightened her clothing and hoped she looked composed as the doorbell rang. She swung it open to face a uniformed workman with a toolbox in his hand. She ushered him in, and, in seconds, he and Aaron were deep in discussion about the alarm.

She gave up and let Aaron take charge, amused and chagrined at how easily he stepped into her life and took over. As soon as the man was working, Aaron said he would leave for a meeting and he would come back later to pick her up.

She agreed and followed him to the door, watching him look around carefully as he stepped outside, and she realized that even when she forgot, he was always conscious that someone could be watching them.

When he returned two hours later, she showed him the new alarm, gave him the code and finally they took the casserole and left for the Royal Memorial Hospital where she went to see Lady Helena Reichard.

While Pamela talked briefly with Lady Helena, Aaron found Matt Walker and spent time with him.

The moment Pamela emerged from Lady Helena's room, Aaron and Matt appeared. She looked at the two of them, thinking Aaron looked as much a cowboy as Matt, but she knew he wasn't. And she thought that both she and Lady Helena had some very good protection, but how long could this go on? As she joined them, Aaron draped his arm across her shoulders and pulled her close against his side.

"I'm glad you're staying at Aaron's," Matt said, glancing past her toward Lady Helena's door.

"It's hard to think we might be in danger. Lady Helena is brave, and she has enough to go through without more troubles."

"She doesn't know I'm out here. I plan to see to it that she's protected," Matt said quietly, but his tone of voice sent a shiver down Pamela's spine and she knew he had that same toughness that Aaron did.

"We'll see you," Aaron said, moving away while Pamela and Matt said goodbye.

As they left the hospital, she looked up to see Aaron's gaze sweeping the area. She looked at the drive and the parking lot, people coming and going. She didn't see anything out of the ordinary, yet why did she feel as if they were being watched? Were they still being followed? Or was her imagination becoming overactive?

By the end of the week Pamela's nerves were as frazzled as shredded paper. She ached with longing to accept Aaron's declaration of love. She was unable to sleep and she had lost what little appetite she had. Drawn to him more each hour they spent together, she wanted him and loved him more than ever. At the same time, the gulf between them seemed vastly wider. During the past week Aaron had taken her to the Black ranch, the sprawling house set on windswept plains covered with cactus and mesquite. He had flown her to Dallas and Houston for dinners and dancing. His life was houses, jets and money. Her world was Royal, Texas, little children and, soon, a baby. Yet when she was with him, she forgot everything else. He was fulfilment, fun and a companion she could confide in. He was the dash missing in her life. And dancing in his arms this past week had brought back all the powerful memories of their first night together.

She wandered restlessly around the bedroom as she got dressed to go to dinner. After spending almost two weeks constantly with him, she was on fire with sheer desire. Now it was Aaron who stopped their kisses and caresses, Aaron who pulled away, and she knew he was doing it to show her that it wasn't sex that was driving him to declare his love for her.

Glancing over her shoulder at the baskets of flowers in her room, she wondered if Aaron had bought all of Handley's flower inventory. The house was filled with them and twice this week she had sent baskets to the hospital and a nursing home.

He flirted and teased. When they weren't kissing, he constantly touched her, holding her arm, playing with her hair, stroking her back until she burned with wanting him. By now everyone in Royal knew they were a couple. They were constantly out in public together, and she had given up trying to keep their relationship private.

She glanced at the closed bedroom door and thought of him in his big bed and drew a deep breath. Safe or unsafe, she needed to move home. This was torment and only made the inevitable goodbye more difficult.

And she knew there would be a goodbye. Her feelings hadn't changed about marriage. She wanted Aaron and she loved him, but she was sure about her refusal to marry. He hadn't changed her mind one iota about their future. Aaron was dating her because being together was good. They liked each other and the chemistry was volatile, but it took more than that for a family and a lasting marriage. All his declarations of love had come after he had learned about her pregnancy, not one word of love from him before.

Also, she wondered if she had simply become a challenge to him because she suspected he was accustomed to getting what he wanted out of life and ran across few obstacles.

She touched the diamond heart-shaped pendant around her neck, lifting it to look down at it. He had given it to her Valentine's night after dinner and dancing in Houston.

She shook her head and dropped the pendant against her bare skin, picking up a black dress to slip into. Today her friends had given her a party and showered her with gifts to replace what she had lost in the break-in. A few had teased her and asked when she and Aaron would be getting married, questions easy to fend off. Only her closest friend, Jessica Atkins from Midland, knew the truth about her pregnancy. Jessica was trying to help her find a teaching job for the coming year.

The new furniture was arriving next Wednesday, and then she would be able to move back into her apartment. Wednesday she would tell Aaron goodbye. She wondered if he would accept goodbye or if she would have to move to Midland. Yet would any distance stop Aaron's persistent courtship? He was a man accustomed to getting what he wanted, but sooner or later he would see that she meant what she said in her refusal to marry.

She ran her hand across her forehead, knowing she was doing the right thing. It still seemed right to her because she was sure Aaron wasn't as deeply in love as he thought. Should she give marriage to him a chance? Would love develop between them?

The questions plagued her more and more often now, but she always came back to the same answer. Aaron hadn't been in love until he discovered he would be a father. True love doesn't switch on like turning on lights.

She sighed and zipped up her dress. Another enchanting, magical evening that would tear at her emotions. Yet it would also be a precious pearl of memory that she could cling to when he was gone.

Each day she loved him more. She combed her hair, slipped into her black pumps and looked at herself in the mirror, turning to study her flat stomach that didn't reveal a trace of her pregnancy. She turned again, looking at the diamond heart sparkling against her black dress. Her reflection looked poised, happy. None of the hurt and anguish showed in her reflection.

She picked up her small black bag and left to go downstairs. She knew Aaron would be ready and waiting. As she paused at the top of the stairs, he appeared below and stopped with his hand on the newel post to look up at her, his gaze slowly drifting over her like a caress.

Conscious of his consuming gaze, she came down the steps to meet him. Her pulse raced because he was in a dark suit that emphasized his tan skin and green eyes, and he looked incredibly handsome.

"Hi, handsome," she drawled as she came within a couple of steps of him. She stopped because the steps put her on his level, and she could look directly into his eyes.

"Hi, beautiful," he answered lightly in return, but his voice was husky and passion burned in the depths of his eyes. He rested his hand on her waist and propped his foot on the second step where she stood, his thigh pressing lightly against her. "Ready to go eat?"

"Starving, actually."

"Aw, shucks. I thought of something else we could do that would be more fun," he said in a husky voice that made her instantly think of making love.

"I don't think so," she whispered, unable to get her voice. He wasn't doing anything except flirting and looking at her as if he would devour her, but she was melting inside.

"We could order dinner sent in," he suggested. He reached up to stroke her throat. "Hot kisses all over, letting go, doing what your heart wants—what mine wants. We could take all night, darlin', wild, hot loving." His hand slid down her back and over her bottom.

"Aaron, stop," she whispered in anguish.

"You're answering me without thinking. Why not, Mellie? Why not? You don't want to kiss?"

"Yes," she whispered and saw a flare of eagerness in his eyes. "No!" She put her hand lightly against his chest as he leaned toward her. "No. That isn't wise or what I want."

"Isn't what you want?"

"All right. I don't think we should whether I want to or not. Let's go to dinner," she whispered, but her heart pounded and she wanted to wrap her arms around his neck and let him carry her right back to his bed.

She received another one of his searching gazes, and she was certain he could hear her heart pounding. He ran his finger across her forehead and she realized she was damp with perspiration.

"Hot?" he asked, arching a brow.

"On fire," she answered, and his eyes darkened.

"How do you expect me to keep my distance when you give me answers like that? Lady, your heart wants the same thing mine does."

"Not heart—our bodies. This is physical."

"I won't buy that one. There's a lot more to it than physical attraction. Come on, I'll take you to dinner and tell you how much more," he said, linking his arm through hers and starting down the hall.

"Aaron, don't make this harder."

"Honey, I couldn't get any harder," he drawled and looked down at her as she walked beside him. "Want me to prove it to you?"

"No! Stop teasing me." A blush heated her cheeks.

"I can't resist. You're too solemn, and I know you're not always that way."

"We shouldn't even be together."

"Oh, yes, we should. Now and forever. You'll see."

"Do you always get your way? Is that where all your optimism comes from?"

"Nope, I don't always get my way. This time my optimism

comes from being right and knowing that sooner or later, you're going to see the truth.''

She shook her head. ''Where are we going tonight?''

''My brother's boat in Galveston.''

Knowing it would be another evening that would be an onslaught against her refusal to marry, she lapsed into silence.

They flew to Houston where a limo whisked them to Galveston, and they spent the evening on his brother's yacht. It was almost dawn when they returned to his home in Pine Valley. She was dazzled, so in love, and she knew she would have been bubbling with happiness if she could just let go and follow her heart, but wisdom still told her that this was all fleeting and temporary.

They kissed until both were on a ragged edge and she stopped him, hurrying to her room to spend the rest of the night in agony, wanting him, questioning her feelings over and over and still coming up with the same answers. At least this week, she was moving home and it would end some of the turmoil. It would also end his courtship that had been the most exciting, joyous, thrilling time of her life. She stared into the darkness and could see only Aaron.

Today she was moving home. Her new furniture had been delivered yesterday and now she could once again live at her own place. No matter what his arguments, no matter how persuasive, she had to stand by her decision and begin to break off this constant togetherness. It was the twenty-second of February. She had been with Aaron almost a month now. Forever. Minutes. Could she actually make the break with him and survive?

Over breakfast, looking into his green eyes, it was much more difficult to say the words that she had rehearsed more than a dozen times during the night.

''I'm moving home today, Aaron.''

He lowered his fork to his plate, leaving scrambled eggs uneaten. ''You're safer here, and I'd like you to stay.''

She shrugged. ''I can't stay here forever.''

"Yes, you can."

She raised her chin and inhaled. "No, I can't. I'm going home where I need to be. Even if we were going to marry—which we aren't—I would want to go home. I need to be in my own place."

He nodded. "All right. I'll take you home when you want to go. You'll still go out to dinner tonight, won't you?"

"Aaron, we're just postponing the inevitable. You're not changing my mind."

"I'm patient," he said, reaching across the table to touch her cheek. She couldn't resist, but turned to brush a kiss across his fingers. He caught her chin and turned her to look at him. "Why are you fighting what your heart wants?"

"Because I keep thinking ahead and know this isn't the marriage for you and I'm not the woman for you."

"Don't you think you should let me make that decision?"

She shook her head and stood, picking up her dishes to carry them to the sink. "No. One of us needs to think straight. I'll get my things as soon as we clean the kitchen."

"Leave the kitchen. I'll have someone here to clean this afternoon."

She turned to look at him. "Just like that?"

"Just like that."

She put down the dishes and left the room, and Aaron watched her go, wondering how long it would take to get her to listen to her heart and really listen to what he was saying to her. He knew she had been hurt badly when she was growing up, and old hurts were slow to mend, but he thought he was making progress. He looked at his knuckles and remembered her soft lips pressed against them when she had turned to kiss him. "Patience, man," he whispered. "Patience."

After dinner that night Aaron took her key to unlock the door to her apartment. He hadn't spotted a tail all evening, nor could he see anyone lurking in the shadows. "I'm going to look around," he said, stepping inside and turning off the new alarm. "You wait here."

Pamela hung up her coat and watched him prowl through
the apartment. Tonight they'd driven to a honky-tonk outside
Royal for some two-stepping music and barbecue. She wore
jeans and a red sweater. He was in his black boots, a black
wool shirt and jeans, and just the sight of him made her pulse
race. She was going to miss him and knew in a few minutes
he would kiss her good-night and be gone.

He came back and headed for the front door. "I'm going
to look around outside. I have your key, so lock up behind
me and turn on the alarm."

"I'm not real happy to think about you prowling around
out there in the dark."

He crossed to her and brushed a kiss on her lips. "Uncle
Sam taught me how to get around in the dark and take care
of myself. And I grew up out here with the rattlesnakes, so
I'll be careful."

She couldn't laugh at his casual remarks that were meant
to reassure her. She watched him leave and followed him,
locking the door and resetting the alarm. She paced the floor
until she heard the key in the lock and he stepped inside. It
had been thirty minutes since he left.

"All quiet on the home front," he said, tossing the key on
a table, turning off the alarm and crossing the room to sweep
her up into his arms.

"Aaron!" she cried, hugging his neck as he swung her
around.

"You look far too solemn. I liked it better when we were
two-stepping tonight and you were laughing and your dimples
were showing." He carried her to the sofa and in minutes they
were locked in an embrace. She had stopped thinking about
all the reasons she shouldn't kiss him, instead giving herself
up to the kisses they shared, because usually he stopped sooner
than she would have. This time when he did, he stroked her
hair from her face while their erratic hearts slowed, and they
caught their breath.

"Well, I wish you'd stay at my house, but if not—here we
are."

Startled, she stopped straightening her sweater and looked at him in surprise. "No."

"We're not going to argue this one, lady. You're staying here. I'm staying here. Until I think you're completely out of danger, I'm your shadow."

"Aaron, I don't have another bedroom."

"You have a couch. We're sitting on it."

"Look at it. It's not long enough for you!"

"Well, now there's another possibility," he drawled, his green eyes smoldering.

"No way!" she snapped, knowing he was teasing, yet aware he was watching her closely. "All right, just stay on the couch and get kinks in your neck and back. This is crazy, Aaron."

"Need I remind you that your apartment has been broken into?"

Her emotions churned as she had a vivid memory of her trashed apartment. Yet how could Aaron stay here in her tiny apartment? "Okay, stay. I'll get you a blanket and pillows." She left, dismayed to find she was going to have him living with her. She knew the only way she would get him out of her apartment was to go home with him. At her place, more people were going to see them together and realize he was staying there. In some ways, she preferred the privacy of his place. Reluctantly, she gathered up bedding and took it back to him.

He had shed his shirt and boots and belt, the jeans riding low on his narrow hips. Her mouth went dry at the sight of his bare chest, and she paused, assaulted by memories of how his naked body had felt against hers, how he had felt inside her.

"For me?" he asked as if nothing had changed, yet his voice had dropped a notch and he was watching her with that hawklike intensity as he crossed the room to take the pillow and blankets from her. He tossed them onto the sofa and turned to pull her into his arms. "I'll win you over," he whispered before he leaned down to kiss her, "because half of you is already on my side. Your heart wants the same thing I do. Sooner or later your head is going to listen to your heart and to what I'm telling you and hear the truth.''

"Aaron—''

His kiss shut off the world and she was lost, melting into his arms and welcoming his embrace. She slid her hands over his warm, bare back that was smooth as silk. She hated the layers of clothing still between them. Then his hands slipped beneath her sweater. Swiftly he unfastened her bra and pushed away the lace, cupping her breast while his thumb moved in lazy circles over her nipple.

Sensations assaulted her, and desire became molten heat in her veins. Moaning softly, she arched against him, wanting him, her hands caressing his smooth back.

When he stepped away, desire was blatant in his hungry gaze. "To prove a point to you, I'll wait to make love to you. I love you, Mellie, now and always.''

"Aaron,'' she said, hurting, wanting him, knowing he was as tormented as she, yet still certain she was right. "You shouldn't stay here, and we should stop kisses that can only lead to heartache.''

"I'm staying, lady. There's only one way to get me out of here.''

"Aaron, this is insane. We'll bump into each other constantly. I only have one bathroom.''

"Want to go to my place?''

"No!'' she cried in exasperation. "You'll get tired of this fast,'' she muttered darkly.

"Never as long as you're here,'' he answered with such cheer that she gritted her teeth.

Within ten minutes she had decided she might have been better off going back to his place. Her apartment was tiny and didn't give them the privacy his spacious mansion had. She yanked on her fuzzy robe, remembering his elegant navy velvet robe and headed for the bathroom only to stop when she heard the shower running and Aaron singing lustily.

Visions of him taunted her because they had showered together that first night. She ground her teeth together and rushed to the kitchen, getting down cups and fixing hot chocolate and trying to stop thinking about Aaron naked in her shower.

"Can I help?" he asked.

He wore jeans again that rode low on his hips. His chest and feet were bare and her mouth went dry. She couldn't stop her gaze from drifting down over his muscled chest tapering to a slim waist. Her gaze flew back up to meet a mocking look in his eyes as he crossed the room with deliberation. Narrowing the distance between them to inches, he took a cup of chocolate from her hands and set it on the sink without taking his eyes from hers. Her pulse drummed as he moved close. She was pressed against the kitchen counter, looking up at him. His green eyes held such blatant desire that her knees weakened. He ran his fingers through her hair and framed her face with his hands and she knew from looking into his eyes what he was going to say before he ever uttered a word.

Eight

"I've waited, Mellie. I've waited damned long so you'd have to know it isn't just sex driving me." His voice was hoarse and low, almost a whisper and his eyes sent a message that scalded her. "I want you and I love you. There's love in my heart or I wouldn't have waited. Love and respect, Mellie, love as enduring as the Texas sunshine."

"Aaron…" she whispered. She should say no. He placed her hand against his chest, and she could feel his racing heart, and she knew her own was racing equally fast.

"Feel my heart—you excite me in a way no woman ever has. I want you forever, my partner, my friend, my wife. I know this is right and good. And I know, deep in your heart, it's what we both want."

"It can't be," she whispered, his words becoming etched in her memory and her heart. She was lost, knowing she couldn't resist him this night, and that she didn't want to.

Tossing aside all wisdom and caution and reserve, she let go. "For now, Aaron, I can't tell you no." She slipped her arms around his neck and turned loose all her pent-up frustrations and longing.

Before his head lowered and his mouth covered hers, she saw the flare of eagerness in his eyes. Their tongues met and stroked and she gave in to all the impulses and desires she had fought for so long. Her hands slipped over him, rediscovering his marvelous body, lean, muscled and hard. She tangled her fingers in the mat of hair on his chest, then let her hand drift down over his flat belly.

He made a rough noise deep in his throat and crushed her in his arms, leaning over her and kissing her deeply. Their tongues stroked and then his plunged in an age-old rhythm, stopping and teasing, flicking against the tip of her tongue. She moaned with pleasure while her roaring pulse shut out all other sounds.

She pushed back to look at him. "This doesn't change anything."

"Yeah, sure," he drawled in a husky voice as he pushed her robe off her shoulders and peeled away the cotton nightie. She knew her words were only a half truth. His loving couldn't change what she thought she ought to do, but it would change the depth of her love for him. More than ever, her love for him would deepen.

"You're beautiful," he whispered while his hands cupped her breasts and he bent his head to stroke her nipple with his tongue. As he kissed and teased, his thumb drew slow circles on her other nipple and delicious sensations tormented and rocked her.

When she unbuttoned his jeans and shoved them away, her fingers shook with urgency. She pushed away his briefs and freed him, taking him in her hand.

Aaron's pulse roared, and his heart pounded violently. He knew that for tonight, she had thrown aside her refusal to love. *Now, now…* The words played in the back of his mind. *Now I can show you how I love you.* He wanted to say the words to her, but his voice failed him, and only a low growl in his throat came as her hand stroked him.

He knew she had no idea how she affected him. That she could turn him to jelly, scramble his thoughts all during the day when she was completely across town from him. He knew she didn't think of herself as beautiful, but to him, she was the most beautiful woman he had ever known. He loved her slender, soft body with its curves and feminine secrets. He loved her wanton passion, her eager responses to his slightest caress. He loved her laughter, her caring.

He was going to have to stop her caresses because he wanted to last far into the night, to make love to her until she was wild with need—until she felt the way he did. He wanted to devour her, to kiss every inch of her, stroke and love her and try to show her in a million different ways how he loved her.

And he wanted to bind her heart to his irrevocably, drowning all her foolishness and convincing her that his heart was in his words and that he had thought everything through. Damned if he didn't know his own feelings!

She was the woman for him. He didn't have a shred of doubt, and every kiss made him want her more than ever. She was a marvel to him, a mystery, as necessary as breathing for him to survive. He couldn't think about life without her. He wouldn't accept defeat in this affair that was the most important thing in his life.

In government, he had had irrevocable rejections, stalemates, severing of ties, and he knew how to pick up the broken pieces and go on with life. But not here, not when the pieces were his heart and when his life and future were at stake. Here he couldn't accept defeat. Especially not when he thought his lady really wanted the same thing he did, but was afraid to let go and trust. Old hurts tormented her and jaded her views, but she would see the truth.

Too much was at stake for him to give in to her steady refusals: their future, their baby, their lives together. This passion that was beyond his widest imaginings.

With a groan he picked her up, sweeping her into his arms to carry her to her bed. The only light was a small lamp on a bedside table that shed a warm glow over their naked bodies. He lowered her to the bed, shoving the mound of lacy white pillows to the floor as he moved to her feet. With deliberation, watching her, he trailed kisses along her slender foot and ankle while his other hand stroked her smooth leg.

Tingles radiated from each kiss and caress, and Pamela gazed into his eyes while he kissed her.

"I love you," he said hoarsely. "Every inch of you."

"Aaron," she gasped, reaching for him and tangling her fingers in his hair. She started to sit up, to try to pull him to her, but he gently pushed her down.

"Let me kiss you, Mellie. I want to kiss you all night long. I want you to want to make love as much as I want to make love."

Her heart thudded at the look in his eyes and the words he whispered to her. His green eyes held a hunger that made her feel every word he spoke was the truth. Trailing kisses along her inner leg, he moved higher to the sensitive inside of her thigh.

"Aaron," she said, her eyes closing while passion rocked her. She grasped his shoulders, tugging to pull him to her, but he continued brushing kisses along her thigh while his hand lightly caressed her, touching the sensitive center of her femininity between her legs, driving her crazy with need. He watched her steadily, while he kissed her inner thigh, the stubble of his beard faintly tickling her.

"Aaron," she cried his name again, trying to sit up to reach him, but he pushed gently.

"Let me kiss you the way I want to," he urged, and then his head dipped between her thighs, his tongue following where his hand had been, his tongue stroking, driving her to an even higher threshold of need. She moaned, losing awareness of anything except his touch while she moved against him and all she knew was his hands and his tongue.

As her hands slid over his broad shoulders, she spread her legs, opening herself to him completely, yielding and clinging to his shoulders. She wound her fingers through his short, thick hair and she arched her back. His loving drove her closer and closer to a brink.

"Aaron, please," she gasped, moving against him, on fire with need, taut and trembling.

"We've just started," he whispered. "Before this night is over, you'll want to love as badly as I want to."

"I do want to. I want you!" she cried, in a frenzy already, wanting him desperately, driven to such urgency she thought she would fly apart any minute. "Aaron!" she gasped, coming up to shove him down and move astride him, pressing her knees against his hips. She leaned down, taking his manhood in her mouth, to kiss and drive him to the same brink of desire. He lay beneath her, watching her, his hand tangled in her hair and his other hand stroking her hip. She looked at his tanned body against the snow-white comforter covering her bed, his masculinity so blatant, so marvelous.

He was so out of place in her bed and in her life. Yet how wonderful to have him here, beneath her, his hands touching her. He was bare for her, letting her kiss and touch him, explore and memorize, letting her love him as she had dreamed of each night since their first time together.

For only seconds more he let her caress him, and then she was in his arms, looking up at him as he leaned down to kiss her more hungrily than before. She wound her arm around his neck, running her fingers through his hair, her other hand resting on his waist.

Aaron cradled her against him, caressing her with his free hand, cupping the soft fulness of her breast. His mouth muffled her moan. Sweat dotted his forehead and he shook with the effort to maintain his control because he wanted to keep loving her far into the night.

"Aaron, love me," she whispered, wanting him completely.

"We've just started loving," he whispered, showering her with kisses along her ear and throat and then moving her, rolling her onto her stomach. "Let me kiss you all night," he whispered, trailing kisses on the back of her leg, up behind her knee while his hands stroked her. She moaned and spread her legs for him as he kissed her thighs and his hand slid over her bottom.

She flung herself over and pulled him down. "Come here, Aaron. You're driving me wild," she whispered fiercely, pulling his head down to kiss him as if it were the last kiss of her life.

It was almost an hour before she leaned over him, caressing him, her hand closing on his thick, hot manhood. She moved closer to trail her tongue over the velvet tip, to take him in her mouth as his hand caressed her legs and then touched the magic center of her, rubbing and driving her into oblivion again, pushing her to another brink as he had countless times during the night. She moved against him, kissing him and yielding to abandon.

"Don't stop," she whispered. "I want you. I want you…" Her voice trailed away and she gasped, her body tightening as an explosion of release came, her hips moving convulsively, and then she wanted him more than ever, desperately needing him.

She shifted, moving over him. "Now, Aaron. I won't wait."

His eyes were dark as obsidian. Glittering green turned black by hot desire. He rolled them over so she was beneath him as he moved between her legs.

She looked at him poised over her and knew she would never forget this moment. He was hard, his shaft thick and dark, springing from a mass of thick hair. Short hairs covered his strong thighs and his body glowed with vitality. Love surged in her along with a consuming physical need. "Come here, Aaron," she said, pulling on his hips, running her hands over his tight bottom, hard and smooth. She wrapped her long legs around him and tried to pull him down.

His gaze ran over her slowly. "You're so beautiful," he said roughly, lowering himself.

As the tip of his shaft pressed against her, she reached to hold him, to guide him, but he caught her hands and teased her while her hips thrashed and arched. "Aaron!"

"You want all this, don't you?" he whispered. "And it's good, isn't it?"

"Yes! Oh, yes."

Then he slipped into her, filling her slowly, hot and hard. She cried out in eagerness, her hips rising to meet him as he came down over her and kissed her, stopping her cries.

They moved together, united at last, and she relished it, giving completely, wild with wanting him. Her world narrowed to his marvelous body that drove her to a frenzy. And beneath all the passion was the knowledge that she was once again in his arms, loving him and being loved by him, united with him with no restrictions.

Eternity was now, this moment only. Thought swirled away, lost in the most urgent, primal dance. "Mellie!" Aaron cried, his voice guttural and hoarse. "My love."

"Ah, Aaron," she whispered. "How I love you!"

He kissed her as they moved together until she crashed over a brink, climaxing with a cry of ecstasy while he thrust hard and fast and she could feel the hot burst of his climax within her. And then she was carried away on another wild, swift climb into another burst of rapturous release.

Her return to reality was gradual while their pounding hearts slowed. She was aware of Aaron showering her with light kisses, holding her close in his arms. He rolled onto his side, taking her with him, while he stroked her hair away from her face. Their bodies were damp, sated with love. How perfect it seemed to be with him.

"I love you," he whispered.

"Aaron—"

"Shh." He placed his fingers on her lips. "Let's let tonight be something special like that first night was."

She tightened her arms around him and placed her head against his chest, willing to do what he wanted for now. She agreed with him to drop worries about the future. Tomorrow would come soon enough. At the moment she would take tonight like that first night as something very special and unique and unforgettable. His heartbeat was steady and strong. His arms held her close, and their legs were entwined. She was wrapped in bliss.

"You're magic in my life," he whispered. Relishing the words, she knew she would remember them always. "I've wanted this every night since that first night."

"You couldn't have!" she said, surprised and questioning.

"I did. Why do you think I came back from Spain? Why do you think you were important to me when the only time we had been together was that one night?"

She wanted to believe him, yet she couldn't. Their first night was a night of passion that they both got caught up in, and she still couldn't believe that it had been important to him. He hadn't tried to call or get in touch with her except right after the plane's forced landing.

She kissed him, wanting to keep touching him, to stay in his arms forever, wishing the moment they would have to separate would never come.

"I wish I had you all to myself, and we could stay here all day tomorrow without any interruptions. We could fly to Dallas—"

"Stop planning. No, we can't. You said we'd take tonight as something special. Tomorrow you and I both have things we have to do."

"Maybe. But I know what I'd prefer." He shifted away and stood, scooping her into his arms. "Let's try out that shower of yours again."

"Oh, Aaron!" she exclaimed, remembering the last shower with him and the lovemaking they had shared. He carried her the short distance to her tiny bathroom and in minutes they were in her shower over the bathtub, Aaron slowly soaping her up, sliding his hands over her wet skin. She took the soap from him to do the same, running her hands over his broad, muscled back, down to his smooth backside and then along his thighs. He turned to face her and as she moved up, she saw he was ready to love again, fully aroused. She looked up at him and met a smoldering gaze that heated her to her core.

He took the soap from her hands and let the spray wash

over them as he lifted her up. She locked her long legs around
him and he eased her down, sliding into her and then she was
spun away, the dance of ecstasy starting as she clung to him
and kissed him.

While he braced his feet apart and held her, he pumped and
ground his hips and knew he couldn't get enough of her in a
lifetime. With the slightest touch or look from her, he was
aroused. Being with her naked and knowing she would yield
had him tied in knots. He knew he should be sated, worn and
satisfied from their last session of lovemaking, but he wasn't.
He wanted her more than ever. She couldn't get it through her
head how much and how deeply he loved her, but she would.
She had to. If it took him the rest of the year, he wasn't giving
up because he wanted her with his whole being.

She was kissing him, hot kisses that felt as if they would
melt his teeth and his tonsils. She was fiery, passionate, totally
giving when aroused and that excited him even more.

Thought ceased and he loved her blindly, mindlessly, this
time hard and fast and reaching a roaring climax. Dimly he
heard her cries of passion, felt her fingers dig into his back
and her legs tighten around him.

His heart pounded as if it would explode in his chest and
even under a stream of water, he was sweating.

Gradually she slid down, standing on her feet while they
kissed. He couldn't stop kissing her or holding her. She was
slender and soft in his arms, her skin smoother than satin. He
framed her face with his hands. "You're beautiful."

"You're blind, Aaron, but I'm glad you think so. I'm glad
you're holding me. Otherwise I think I'd just slide down and
go into the drain with the water."

"Let's see if I've still got legs I can walk on." He shut off
the water and opened the shower door, grabbing a towel to
dry her. She took the towel from him.

"Maybe I should do this, and you should dry yourself off."

He looked at her, seeing fires still burning in her blue eyes.
"You really think so?"

She studied him, her gaze drifting down over him and back

up and she shook her head, beginning to dry him with the towel. She slanted him a mischievous look.

"Let's see what happens."

"Insatiable minx," he whispered, bending down to kiss her. He grabbed another towel and slowly drew it across her shoulders, then leaned back to look at her as he ran it so lightly across her breasts, just touching her nipples and seeing them become taut. He drew the towel down across her stomach and then over her bottom.

"Aaron," she whispered, winding her arms around his neck and pulling his head down to kiss him. They attempted to dry each other until he picked her up to carry her back to her bed where he lay down and pulled her into his arms, and they kissed slowly, leisurely, stroking each other. Within minutes fires built and urgency drove them.

Finally she sat astride him, lowering herself while he caressed her breasts, and then she leaned down to kiss him, moving with him. After they had reached another rapturous climax, he pulled her beside him, cradling her in his arms, talking softly until they fell asleep.

In the gray light of dawn Aaron came awake, staring at the pink rosebuds in her wallpaper, remembering clearly where he was and what had happened between them. He looked down at her, still asleep in the crook of his arm.

"This time you won't disappear, darlin'," he said softly. She lay with one arm thrown across his chest and her leg across him. He gently brushed her hair away from her face, and, with just the sight of her and his memories, he was aroused, wanting her as badly as he had yesterday.

He stroked her breast so lightly, caressing her soft nipple until it became taut. She moaned and stirred and opened her eyes to look up at him. He saw she was completely awake, a lazy sensuality radiating from her like heat from a stove. She wrapped one arm around his neck and raised to kiss him while her hand played over his stomach, caressing his thighs and then touching his manhood.

In minutes they were loving with all the urgency of the

night before. Aaron knew the day would intrude and end their intimacy, and he slowed, trying to prolong the moment, wanting to savor every inch of her and every moment with her.

Finally he moved between her legs, wrapping her in his arms as he entered her and her legs locked around him. While they loved passionately, he heard her crying his name. He climaxed and slowly settled, showering her with kisses, amazed how the more he made love with her, the more he wanted her.

"You're easy to wake."

She trailed kisses along his throat. "That's the best way to wake, Aaron."

"Maybe. Maybe there's some way even better. I'll show you in the morning."

"No, you won't either," she said, her fingers playing in the hair on his chest.

"Mellie, I'm going to shrivel up and blow away. You've demolished me."

"Are you complaining about what I'm doing?" she asked, raising up to look at him with wide blue eyes. A dimple showed, and she lowered her head. "Just lie back and enjoy the morning. Go back to sleep," she whispered, trailing kisses along his stomach, laughing seductively when he became aroused again.

"Wench," he growled, rolling her over on her back and moving over her with his legs on either side of her. "Two can play that game." He leaned down to kiss her, his hand moving between her legs. She gasped and opened her legs for him and in minutes they were loving again.

Wrapped in each other's arms, they fell asleep. Aaron came awake instantly at the ring of his cell phone. It was a faint sound and he slid out of bed and hurried to the front room where he had left the phone on a table. He picked it up.

"Aaron? Sheriff Escobar. You wanted me to call you when we got a report in on the Asterland plane. The feds finished their investigation."

Nine

Two hours later on Thursday morning, Aaron sat in the Texas Cattleman's Club in the private room he and his friends used. Coffee had been served and a silver urn sat on a table on a silver tray. Bone china cups and saucers with the club's gold crest sat beside the urn.

Matt Walker was the last to arrive, and, as he sat down facing them, Aaron leaned forward. "Before we get down to business—I think we should congratulate the new bridegroom," he said, looking at Justin, who grinned and accepted congratulations and a few teasing remarks.

"Winona and I just wanted a quiet wedding," he said. "We didn't want to be away from Angel," he added, fishing a picture from his wallet. When the others crowded around to look at the picture of the tiny blue-eyed baby girl, Aaron's insides knotted. He ached for his own baby, thinking that falling in love and having a baby with Pamela were the most awesome events in his life. *He couldn't lose her and his baby.* He refused to accept that she would do what she threatened and walk out of his life. It was unthinkable.

"She's beautiful," he said hoarsely, touching the corner of Angel's picture. He looked up. "You're a lucky man," he said solemnly, and Justin grinned.

"I know I am."

Aaron turned away, but he saw Matt give him a searching look.

"You went from a bachelor to a husband and father in a hurry," Ben Rassad said.

"Yes, and it's great."

Aaron thought of Pamela and their baby and could understand the sparkle in Justin's eyes. He looked happier than Aaron could recall ever seeing him, and Aaron was glad for him.

After getting refills of coffee and hearing a little about Angel, they sat down again, except for Dakota who stood beside a bookcase. "What's up, Aaron?" he asked.

"I had a call from Sheriff Escobar. The investigation about the cause of the crash is over. It was a malfunction in one of the twin jet engines."

"No sabotage?" Justin asked with disbelief in his voice.

"Nope." Aaron shook his head. "The engine fire caused some of the systems to lock up, including the landing gear, which caused the crash landing. When they landed, the electrical systems inside the plane shorted out. Liquor bottles from the bar broke and spilled—"

"And Lady Helena was unfortunate enough to be sitting closest to the bar," Matt interrupted grimly.

"Right," Aaron replied. "They think sparks from the rough landing ignited the liquor, and that's how she got burned."

"Damn," Matt muttered, rubbing the knee of his jeans idly as he stared into space with troubled eyes, and Aaron knew he was concerned about Lady Helena.

"At least now we have one bit of the puzzle solved," Dakota said, moving restlessly at one end of the room.

"If the plane hadn't had trouble, we wouldn't have found the stones," Justin added.

"We can stop worrying about who might have sabotaged the plane and why," Aaron summed up. "It's one little question answered. The other questions are still puzzling, and I think the women are still in danger. With the murder of Riley Monroe, we know someone is in deadly earnest about the jewels."

"A man tried to get into Lady Helena's room," Matt said. "I had to leave for just a few minutes, and the guy I got to stand watch was called away. He was only gone minutes. While he was gone, I came back, and another man was starting into her room. He ran when he saw me."

"Damn. Sounds like the one trailing after Pamela. Did you get a good look at him?" Aaron asked, and Matt shook his head.

"No. It was late and the lights were down in the hall so the patients could sleep. He was gone in a flash, and it was more important to check on her and stay with her than to go after him. She was asleep and didn't know anything happened. She didn't know I checked to see if she was all right. I couldn't leave her unguarded to chase him."

"Yeah," Aaron replied, thinking about seeing someone following Pamela outside the obstetrician's office and making the same decision to stay with her.

"If someone is getting more desperate about the missing diamond," Ben observed, "the risk for these women may be increasing."

"And we don't have any leads on the missing diamond," Dakota said quietly.

"You were going to keep an eye on the Asterland investigators. What about them, Dakota?" Aaron asked.

Dakota shook his head. "They've split up, so I have to choose which one I follow. So far nothing has come of it. One was behind you when you and Pamela were going to dinner but I don't know whether he was actually following you or just driving down Main. Before you turned into Claire's lot, he drove into the gas station.''

"If you can, keep watching them," Justin urged. "We need to find out who's after the women."

"We need to find out a lot of things," Aaron said.

"Robert Klimt is still in a coma. If he ever comes out of the coma, I hope we can question him," Matt said. "And there's always the possibility that one of the women might have the diamond and not know it."

"I don't think it's Pamela. They shredded everything she owned and didn't find what they were searching for," Aaron stated, remembering her apartment and clothing.

"Think that might have been Johannes and Yungst?" Dakota asked.

"Could be. Although anyone would want the jewels," Aaron said.

"I still wonder if whoever is after them intends to sell them and use the money for something else," Dakota remarked curtly.

"That's what I'm thinking," Aaron agreed.

"Perhaps in your diplomatic job you have dealt with espionage and terrorism too much," Ben said. "We know Dakota has."

"My mind may run that way because of all I've seen. The possibility exists that it's more than just the fortune from the jewels that someone is after. They may have a use for the fortune and it may be tied to Asterland. I wonder if we shouldn't call in a foreign affairs specialist," Aaron suggested quietly. Dakota's head whipped around, and he stared at Aaron who gazed back steadily.

Aaron had been overseas when Dakota's breakup came from his wife, Kathy Lewis, and he knew they both still hurt over it. A former Foreign Service Officer, Kathy was an expert foreign affairs specialist and Aaron knew she was well acquainted with Asterland royalty. She might be able to help them with their questions. Yet he could see the pain in Dakota's eyes over his suggestion.

"No need to rush into that yet," Justin said, and Aaron nodded. He didn't want to hurt Dakota, yet he didn't think Dakota had ever lost his love for Kathy, and he hadn't heard of Kathy being involved with anyone else since she'd left Dakota. He hoped they could get back together because both seemed to still be hurting, and he understood that kind of pain. He thought of Pamela and glanced at his watch, calculating the time until he would be with her again.

Dakota said, "We'll all keep searching and looking and seeing what we can learn."

"I want to talk to the Asterland investigators," Aaron said. "I think it's time we asked them some direct questions."

"If that's it, I need to get back to the hospital," Matt said, standing. The others came to their feet, murmuring reasons they had to go.

Aaron met Matt's gaze and could see the worry in his eyes. He could understand Matt's feelings because he was concerned about Pamela any time he was away from her. He had been much less worried when she had been at his house where there was a guard at the gate, a high wall, an alarm and seclusion. Her apartment complex had almost as many people coming and going as a shopping mall, and there was no security, but he knew he wasn't going to get her back to his place easily.

In spite of feeling a sense of urgency to get back to Pamela he stopped at a jewelry store to look at diamond rings. He wanted something special for Pamela, knowing she seldom wore jewelry, and that what she wore was simple. He settled on a design of smaller diamonds flanking a three-carat diamond and on impulse bought her as well a simple gold link bracelet.

He drove home to take care of some family business and to make an appointment to talk to the Asterland investigators. When he stepped into his empty house, he suffered a pang. It was the first time he'd come home since Pamela had moved out and he missed her. He looked at flowers she had left behind because there wasn't room for all the bouquets at her place. He missed her with a hungry longing that made him want to toss aside all he needed to do and go find her. He picked up the phone to call her, and the moment he heard her voice, he felt better.

"I miss you."

She laughed softly. "It's only been a few hours, but that's nice and I miss you, too."

"Can I pick you up for lunch? Say yes."

"Yes, but I have to get a haircut at three o'clock. I need to run some errands, too, so either I meet you for lunch or you bring me home afterwards to get my car."

"I'll take you home after lunch. I'll be at your house at—" he paused to glance at his watch "—at twelve."

"Sure, Aaron. I'll be ready."

"I'll be ready, too," he said in a husky voice, wanting to take her to bed again.

"Ready for lunch," she said emphatically.

"We'll see, darlin'," he challenged. "'Til then I'll think about last night."

"And this morning," she added softly. "Hurry home, Aaron," she said in a sultry voice, and heat flashed in his body.

"I'll be there in twenty minutes," he said, deciding to make some of his phone calls later.

"See you," she said softly and broke the connection.

He replaced the receiver. "I wish you could see what's in your heart, darlin'," he said to the empty room. He thought about the night and her complete abandon, her loving him as if her love for him was total. "You have to see what you mean to me," he said softly. "You have to." He thought about Justin's glow and could understand how Justin felt. To be married to the woman you love and adore and to have a precious baby would be the kind of happiness to make a man glow. And it would be a glow that would go deep, clear to the heart. "You just have to see I mean what I say, lady," he repeated to the empty room, thinking of Pamela.

"Patience, patience," he reminded himself as he went upstairs to his desk to make his calls.

* * *

Pamela had a long lunch with Aaron in which he flirted constantly and kept touching her instead of eating. He left his lunch almost untouched, just as she did, and she was giddy from his attention. She drifted through the afternoon in a daze, and as she stepped out of the shop after getting her hair cut, she saw Winona Raye only a few feet away on the sidewalk. In Winona's arms was a baby carrier, and Pamela's heart beat faster.

"Congratulations on your marriage, Winona."

"Thanks," Winona said, and Pamela saw the sparkle in her eyes and had a pang of longing that stabbed into her heart like a knife for what could never be.

She moved closer to Winona to peer into the carrier. "May I see Angel?"

As she turned so Pamela could look into the carrier, Winona smiled. "How are you doing? Did you get over your injuries from the landing?"

"Yes. I wasn't seriously hurt." Pamela looked at the baby who gazed back with wide blue eyes. "She's so beautiful!"

"I think so," Winona said softly with a laugh. "Angel is a joy."

"I know she's in her carrier, but can I hold her?" Pamela said, unable to keep the longing out of her voice.

"Of course," Winona said, setting the carrier down and bending down to unfasten the straps. She handed Angel to Pamela, who took the warm, soft baby and held her close.

"She's wonderful," Pamela said, her imagination racing away with her as she thought of her own baby. *Hers and Aaron's.* "I know you're so happy."

Winona laughed. "Here, let me give you a blanket to put on your shoulder. Just in case—"

"She's fine," Pamela said, turning the baby to cradle her in her arms and look down at her. Angel cooed and waved her fists, and Pamela knew she was keeping them out in the wind and she needed to hand Angel back. Reluctantly, she passed the baby back to Winona.

"Thanks for letting me hold her," she said as Winona quickly fastened Angel back into her carrier and picked it up.

"Anytime. Come see us and you can hold her all you want."

Pamela wanted to offer to babysit, but she knew right now was not the time to do so.

"See you," Winona said, moving on and Pamela turned away, thinking about Angel and how precious a baby was. She'd walked a few yards, starting to go to the driver's side of her car, when she saw a man leaning against the door of her car. As she approached him, he straightened up. Aversion filled her when she recognized Garth Johannes. A fedora was jammed on his head, the spiky ends of his greasy hair sticking out beneath his hat, and in a topcoat he looked square. His thick neck bulged over the collar of his shirt.

"Miss Miles. I haven't seen you in town very often in the past few weeks. Shut away with your lover?"

The question was personal, and the man was obnoxious, and she suspected if Aaron were present, Johannes would never have been so bold. His gaze raked insolently over her. He blocked her from getting into her car, but she didn't feel any fear, standing on Main Street in Royal. Anger was her only reaction.

"You're in my way."

"I just wanted to ask you a few more questions."

"I've answered all I intend to," she replied curtly. Out of the corner of her eye she saw a red pickup sweep into a parking space a few cars beyond hers. Johannes turned to look at it.

"Then I'll ask you another time," he said abruptly, and turned to hurry across the street, almost stepping in front of traffic in his haste to move away from her car. She glanced back at the pickup as a door slammed and a tall, black-haired man emerged. She didn't know Dakota Lewis very well, but they had met, and she recognized him. She guessed he had stopped because of Johannes.

"Hi, Pamela," he said easily, but his eyes held a coldness

that she wouldn't want to be on the wrong side of as his gaze
followed Johannes hurrying across the street. "Did he bother
you? I can go after him."

"No, Dakota. Thanks for stopping. He's gone now. He
wanted to ask me some more questions, but I told him I wasn't
answering any more."

"Good. Aaron's at the Wrangler Drilling Company in a
meeting. I can page him—"

"Good heavens, no! Aaron would tear up the town to go
after the man, and it's not necessary. I'm glad you stopped
though. Thanks. I'll go on home, and there's no need to let
Aaron know. I'll tell him tonight when I see him."

Suddenly Dakota's gaze flickered back to her briefly, and
amusement flashed in his dark eyes. "No deal. I'll tell Aaron
before tonight, or he'll have my neck for not letting him know
that that guy was bothering you. I think I'll see where the
creep is going. Sure you're all right?"

"I'm fine. See you later, Dakota."

He was already gone, striding across the street. She went to
her car and slid inside, shivering. Johannes was creepy, and
she really would rather Aaron didn't know about the incident
at all, but Dakota was going to tell him.

She was getting ready for her dinner date with Aaron that
evening, dressing in jeans and a red sweater, when she heard
the key turn in the lock, and then he stepped inside. "Hi
honey, I'm home," he called, and she smiled as she left the
bedroom to meet him. He wore jeans, a white shirt and his
black Stetson and her heart jumped at the sight of him.

"The cowboy diplomat," she said, crossing the room to
him and walking into his arms, her pulse jumping another
notch at the hungry look in his eyes.

"You look beautiful," he whispered, before he leaned down
to kiss her. When his mouth touched hers, desire ballooned
within her. Tightening her arms around his neck, she stopped
thinking about the future, once again clinging to the moment
loving him with her whole heart and soul.

"Ahh, darlin'," he whispered as he trailed kisses along her throat and his hands slipped beneath her sweater, unfastening the clasp to her lacy bra and cupping her breasts. She moaned softly, her hands tugging at the buttons on his shirt, and all she wanted was to be in his arms, loving him and letting him love her.

They left a trail of clothes to her bedroom, where Aaron picked her up to carry her the rest of the way to her bed, and then she was in his arms as if it were the first time all over again. Need drove her and she pushed him down on the bed, trailing kisses over his chest and down his flat stomach, down to his manhood. He caught her beneath the arms and rolled her over, moving on top of her and the sight of him poised above her made her tremble with hot desire for all of him.

"I want you so badly, Aaron," she whispered.

He lowered himself, slowly easing into her. "Never can you want me the way I want you, love. Never." His green eyes were dark as night with hot pinpoints of fiery longing. He moved slowly within her and she moved with him, her hips raising as her legs tightened around him.

While her pulse roared and sensations rocked her, she closed her eyes. All the time, she reveled that Aaron was in her arms, Aaron was loving her and she was his love once again.

They climaxed and drifted back slowly to reality. He held her close against him, stroking her and showering her with light kisses.

"I love you, Mellie," he said. "Love you with all my heart."

She closed her eyes and buried her face against his chest and hurt. Why hadn't she been careful that first time? They might have had a chance, but this way, she still couldn't believe that what he felt was anything but infatuation, passion, a relationship ruled by great sex and some fun times together. But there was more to life than that. And they weren't living in a real world, staying together at his place or at her place, neither of them working or dealing with everyday life. How could she fit into his life?

She couldn't. The answer was always the same. She couldn't see herself married to a diplomat. She had no background for his life.

He shifted and tilted her chin up, his green eyes stormy. "What're you thinking, darlin'?"

"I'm thinking some day you'll wake up and see our relationship the way I see it. I don't fit into your lifestyle, Aaron."

"You belong in my life because I want you there, not because of some set of rules."

She knew they were going to get nowhere with this argument and she turned away. "You said something about dinner."

"Sure did," he said cheerfully and scooped her into his arms, rolling to the side of the bed and standing with her in his arms. "We'll shower and go eat supper."

"If we shower together, I'll never get supper."

"You're complaining, lady?" he asked with a wicked grin and she had to smile and kiss him.

"No complaints, cowboy," she whispered. "Not the tiniest one."

Two hours later when he turned into the drive to his Pine Valley house, she glanced at him. "What are we doing at your house?"

"I'm going to show you my culinary talents."

"You have—at breakfast, remember?"

"I can do better than oatmeal and toast. How about grilled fillets of bass, caught by my own hands and now cooked by me?"

"You talented rascal, how can I resist you," she teased in a sultry voice, and he grinned.

They sat in his kitchen with a roaring fire in the fireplace and she ate flaky bites of fish and lemon-covered rice with steamed asparagus. In spite of the delicious food, she was far more fascinated with Aaron, just wanting to watch him, tall o him, be with him. He dug into his pocket and pulled out a small box to set it in front of her.

Curious, she looked at him and then at the box. She opened t and gasped with pleasure as she lifted out a gold link brace-et. "Oh, Aaron, this is beautiful! I love this! Thank you!"

He looked pleased as he fastened it on her wrist, and she :ame around to give him a kiss. His arm slipped around her waist, but she pulled away from him and sat down again facing aim. "We should eat dinner and never let this cooking go to vaste."

"Sure, darlin'," he drawled.

He held her hand while they ate as if he couldn't bear to et go of her. After she stopped eating, he set down his glass of water and studied her. While his expression didn't change, he could see that frightening coldness come into his green eyes. "What's wrong, Aaron?"

"Dakota told me about Garth Johannes," Aaron said sol-mnly. "For a while I get to take you wherever you need to ;o."

"Aaron, that's ridiculous! The man didn't hurt me. He just aid he wanted to ask me more questions, and I told him no."

"Good for you, but damn him. Exactly what did he say to ou?"

"I don't remember precisely," she said, looking away, and Aaron turned her to face him.

"You are one poor liar, darlin'. Lack of experience prob-bly causes that. What did he say to you?"

"Drop it, Aaron. It'll just make you angry."

"I'm getting more angry by the minute and imagining the vorst. I may go punch him out just because my imagina-on—"

"Aaron, don't! Please don't do something violent. He just aid he hadn't seen me around town much lately. He said it vas probably because I was with you. He told me he wanted o ask me a few more questions."

"Dakota said he blocked your way to your car."

"We were on Main Street, for heaven's sake!"

"Don't ever get close enough to him that he can grab you Promise me."

"Now you're scaring me," she said quietly, looking at the solemn expression on Aaron's face. "I have no intention of getting close to him or his revolting partner."

"Shortly before that—I guess while you were getting your hair cut, I met with him and the other one, Yungst."

"What did you think?" she asked, feeling an intrusion into the warm glow of the evening.

"Probably the same reaction you had. I didn't like them. I don't believe much of anything they said. They know you're expecting and they know the baby is mine."

"How do they know that! I didn't think anyone else knew it yet except Dr. Woodbury and now—" She stopped, remembering seeing the door close at the end of the hall when she had been talking to Aaron in front of the obstetrician's office. "The doctor's office."

"Right. They sort of tipped their own hand by saying that to me. I didn't get much out of them, but I don't trust them or like them. Dakota is watching them. That's why he was there today."

"I wasn't sure Dakota knew who I was, but I've met him before."

"He knows you. He's older than you—like I am," Aaron added dryly.

"You poor decrepit thing," she teased, leaving her dinner and coming around to sit on his lap. "Let me feel and see if you're falling apart," she said, running her hand along his thigh.

He wrapped his arms around her. "This is good, lady. Very good. And I'll show you decrepit," he said, leaning forward to kiss her.

After a few minutes she pushed him away slightly. "Aaron, I interrupted you. You were telling me about Dakota Lewis. What did you start to say?"

"Just that Dakota is trying to watch Johannes and Yungst. Until today, he hasn't seen them do anything they shouldn't

He said they usually split up, so he can only watch one at a time. They know we're watching them."

She sobered, thinking about the danger and the missing diamond.

"Stop worrying. We're safely locked away in my house, and no one is watching this place except the security guard. Now I was going to prove that I'm not decrepit and falling apart yet," he said, standing and slinging her over his shoulder.

With a squeal, she laughed as he crossed the room to the oval rug in front of the fireplace. With a flick of the switch, Aaron turned off the lights and only the glow of the fire gave them light.

"Come here, woman," he said, setting her on her feet. He had his feet apart, his legs braced, and he hauled her into his arms, leaning over her. Her laughter vanished with his passionate kiss, and in minutes she was returning kiss for kiss and caress for caress as they loved again long into the night.

As she lay in Aaron's arms with moonlight spilling over them and embers glowing in the fireplace in his large bedroom, he rolled away and crossed the room. She watched him, looking at his lean, muscular, naked body and long legs and her heart pounded with mixed emotions. She knew she had to end their lovemaking or else agree to his proposal. Yet her feelings still hadn't changed.

He picked something up off his desk and sauntered back to bed, sliding beneath the covers beside her to take her into his arms again.

"That was too long away from you."

"That's foolishness, Aaron."

He turned away and she heard a click, and then he settled back with his arms going around her again. He picked up her hand and held out a ring. "Please marry me, Pamela."

Her heart missed a beat. As tears stung her eyes, a knot burned in her throat and hurt overwhelmed her. The diamond was huge, catching moonlight and holding out glittering promises of dreams come true.

She wanted to cry out, *Yes, yes* and throw herself into his arms and stop thinking about tomorrow and the life Aaron had away from Texas and all his background and wealth. But she couldn't shut out his heritage. It was as much a part of him as his Texas upbringing and she still couldn't see herself, a plain elementary teacher from Royal, Texas, holding a lifelong fascination for the sophisticated diplomat that he truly was.

"Aaron…" she said, unable to stop the tears from spilling over. She couldn't talk and all she could do was shake her head. "No. No," she whispered. "I haven't changed how I feel. I don't think this will last. Not for you. You'll have regrets—"

"Dammit, lady, let me make that decision! I'm in love. You're everything I want and have dreamed about—"

"Oh, please, Aaron. That's not true and don't tell me it is. You're infatuated, lost in the fun and the sex we've had, but there's more to life than that. And there's your family. I know how they'll see me."

"They'll see you like I see you, and you're marrying me. They don't get a say in this decision. And it's ridiculous to worry about them because they'll love you when they meet you," he said, sitting up and letting the covers fall around his waist.

She shook her head. "I can't take your ring. I don't feel any differently. I can't resist loving you—you know that," she said, barely able to breathe or say the words and hurting all over. "I can't resist your kisses, but all the loving doesn't change my mind about the future."

He framed her face with his hands, winding his fingers in her hair. "I love you, now and forever."

"Aaron, stop! You're just caught up in the moment." She scrambled away and grabbed a blanket to wrap around herself as she stood. "I have to go home. Now."

She rushed across the room, gathering her clothes, barely aware of what she was doing, moving by rote, knowing this was what she had to do and she had brought this moment on herself by letting down all the barriers and making love with him.

She rushed into the bathroom and closed the door, gasping for breath while tears continued to stream down her face. "I'm right, Aaron," she whispered. "I know I am. When it's out that I'm pregnant with your baby, your family won't love me. Gossip will fly in town, and folks will see me like my mother. I don't want you involved in my old problems."

With shaking hands she dressed swiftly. When she came out of the bathroom, he was seated on a chair with his elbows on his knees. Dressed in jeans and a T-shirt, he raised his head to look at her. "You're wrong, Mellie."

"I can get home by myself."

"No, you don't," he said, standing. "I'll take you home and I'm staying when we get there, whether we talk or not. Lady, you may be in danger—another fact you fail to face."

He took her arm and they went downstairs to his pickup and rode in an uncomfortable silence to her apartment. She knew it was useless to protest his staying with her. Thirty minutes later as she stepped from the bathroom in her robe, he stood in the hall. He had shed his shirt and wore only his jeans, and he stood with one hip canted against the wall while he studied her.

"I know how to be patient. I love you and want to marry you. And I want to be a father to my baby."

"I have to do what I think is right for you, for me and for the baby."

"Well, you're blind to the truth. I don't see how you can think going our separate ways will be good for any of us."

"I think you're the one who's blind to reality," she said gently, hurting more than she thought was possible. "And I think we need some distance between us for a while to really think things through."

"Not while you're in possible danger," he said tersely. A muscle worked in his jaw and while he looked relaxed, leaning slightly against the wall, she saw one fist was clenched, his knuckles white.

"If you were away from me, you might feel differently about all this."

"I was away from you for a month in Spain."

"I don't want to rush into marriage. The minute you found out about the baby, you were in love. Not before, Aaron. That isn't the way it should be." She hurried past him to her room and closed the door, sagging against it, surprised he had let her pass without stopping her.

As she crossed the room, for the first time she noticed the blinking light on her answering machine. She punched the button to hear her messages and received two. The first was from Nancy, her neighbor, to tell her Handley's had left a bouquet for her and Nancy had the roses at her place. Pamela shook her head, thinking about all the dozens of flowers Aaron had sent her, the dazzling ring and life he had offered to her tonight. The next voice came on:

"Pamela, it's Jessica. They have an opening right now in one of the Fort Worth elementary schools. I know the principal—he called me to see if I knew anyone who could fill the position because they're desperate. One of the teachers had to quit in the middle of the semester to take care of her mother. They're going to fill this immediately so you need to talk to them tomorrow if possible. I've tried to get you all evening. Give me a call, no matter how late tonight."

Pamela stared into the darkness. A teaching job in Fort Worth would take her away from Aaron, and she knew it was the right thing to do. Reluctantly, she reached for the phone.

Three hours later, long before dawn, she wrote a note to Aaron. She propped it on the kitchen table and, taking great care to turn off the alarm and not make any noise, she let herself out of the apartment. She suspected she could never have slipped out at his house without waking him, but people came and went all hours of the day and night at her apartment complex and the place was never quiet like his neighborhood. A car starting up wouldn't jolt him out of sleep here.

She looked at his pickup parked next to her car and ran her hand along the door. "Goodbye, Aaron. I love you," she whispered. As she unlocked the door to her car, she glanced around, aware someone could be watching her, but at the moment, caring very little and unable to see for the blur of her tears.

She slid behind the wheel and locked her car doors, driving out of the complex before she needed to switch on her car lights. As she accelerated and headed for the highway, she felt as if her heart was breaking into a million shattered pieces that would never fit back together.

Ten

Aaron came awake, staring into the quiet living room. A faint border of light showed around the edges of the blinds. He stretched and sat up, knowing things weren't right. For the first time, he began to wonder if he would ever get across to Pamela his feelings for her.

Whatever happened, he intended to be at her side for the birth of their baby. In frustration he ran his fingers through his hair. For once in his life, words had failed him, and he had been unable to convince her about his feelings. Marriage to her was the most important thing in his life. She didn't believe he knew his own feelings. And she couldn't stop seeing herself as too country for him.

He loved the woman with all his heart. He was as sure of that as he was certain he was a Texan. Why couldn't she see it? He had tried every way he knew how to show her.

"Darlin', you're a stubborn woman," he said softly, shaking his head. He didn't want to put any distance between them. Far from it. He wanted her in his arms and in his bed every night of his life. Life was empty and cold without her. He rubbed his neck, kinked from sleeping on her short sofa. His whole life was in a kink over this woman.

He stood and stretched, yanking on briefs and jeans. He didn't want to wake her, and went to the kitchen to start breakfast, trying to be quiet as he poured orange juice and fixed himself a piece of toast. He went back to the living room to fold up his covers. He tiptoed out the front door to get the Royal newspaper and the Dallas newspaper and then he sat in the kitchen, reading. When he was through with both papers, he moved restlessly. She was never this late getting up. He glanced at his watch. Almost eight in the morning. He had appointments and needed to shower and shave.

He turned and looked at the alarm and saw it was turned off. He crossed the room to look at it closely and then started to go to her room when he noticed a note propped on the counter with his name scrawled across the front of the folded paper. How had he missed seeing this earlier?

Cold dread enveloped him as he crossed the narrow space and picked up the note. Knowing what he would find, he didn't want to read it.

Dear Aaron:
I think we need some time and distance to sort feelings out. I have friends, I have a job and I'll be very careful. Take care of yourself.

           Love, Pamela.

He let the note flutter from his hands to the counter as he walked to the window and opened the blinds. Her car was gone and only his pickup was in the carport.

Where had she gone? How long since she'd left? How long had she planned leaving him? She already had a job and hadn't told him?

He hurt with a consuming pain that immobilized him. "Dammit," he swore, worrying about her safety. He whirled around and hurried to the bathroom to dress and start searching for her.

As he drove to his Pine Valley home, he called Dakota on his cellular phone.

"Dakota, Pamela's gone and she didn't leave word where she was going. She wants to be on her own for a while, but I'm worried about her. Keep those two under surveillance as much as you can, will you?"

"Sure. I'll get a friend to help. Anything else I can do?"

"If there is, I'll let you know. Thanks."

Aaron punched off the phone. "Dammit, Mellie. This isn't the time to slip off without letting anyone know where you are or what you're doing." He prayed she hadn't been followed from her apartment and tried to reassure himself with the fact that he hadn't seen anyone following them for several days now. But if someone discovered she had gone off alone...

"Dammit," he swore again, pressing the accelerator and feeling a sense of urgency to find her as quickly as possible, not only for himself, but for her safety.

"She doesn't want you to find her," he reminded himself and grimaced. If she wanted to get off by herself to think things over, he didn't want to crowd her, but he was worried about her. And he thought they had been so close to an end to all her foolish notions that she wasn't the woman for him. Couldn't the lady see that she was the *only* woman for him?

By noon Aaron felt as if the earth had opened up and swallowed her. He couldn't find a trace of her from her neighbors, and he had to wait until school was out to talk to her teacher friends. Shortly before school was out, he went to see the principal of the school where she had taught, remembering Thad Delner from the Texas Cattleman's Club gala the night he met Pamela.

Within minutes after sitting in Thad Delner's office, Aaron's frustrations increased. The principal sat behind his desk and studied Aaron. "I remember you from the gala. I think you took her home that night, and I hear you've been dating lately.''

"Yes, sir, we have. I've asked Pamela to marry me.''

"Ah, congratulations. Pamela is an excellent teacher, a wonderful person.''

"I think so. Right now, I'd like to find her because I'm worried about her safety. I've been staying with her or she's stayed at my place since someone broke into her apartment and trashed it. She left a note that she was going to see a friend, but I'm concerned for her safety.''

"Have you talked to the police?''

"Not yet. I thought if I can find out where she is, I can talk to her myself.''

"I'm sorry, Mr. Black. I can't help you. I don't know all of her friends. My teachers' lives are their own, for the most part, once they leave my school.''

Feeling restless and knowing he was at a dead end here, Aaron stood and offered his hand. "Thanks. If you don't mind, as soon as school is out, I'd like to talk to several of the teachers who are her close friends.''

"That's fine. In about five minutes the bell should ring. If you'd like, you're welcome to wait here in the office until school is dismissed.''

"Thanks, I'll be fine.''

As soon as the building emptied of students, Aaron talked to three teachers before he found a woman named Sally Grayson who told him Pamela's best friend was Jessica Atkins who lived in Midland.

Within the hour Aaron was in his pickup driving to Midland. He had already learned Jessica had an unlisted phone number, but with the help of Dakota Lewis, he had found Jessica's address.

In Fort Worth, Pamela left the principal's office and stepped into the sunshine. It had been a little over twelve hours since she'd left Aaron at her apartment. Not long enough for any of the pain to dull. Now she had a job in Fort Worth and would

start Monday morning teaching second grade. It was what she
wanted and what she thought she should do, but why did it
seem so wrong? She hurt constantly and could barely carry
on a coherent conversation. She suspected she would never
have gotten the job except that the school was desperate and
she had come highly recommended, but during her interview,
she'd had difficulty concentrating on anything the principal
had said to her.

She hurried to her car parked in visitor parking and looked
back at the school. Only three years old and made of brick
and glass, the sprawling elementary school had state-of-the-art
equipment, and her salary would be an increase over what she
had made in Royal, yet she didn't feel anything except a deep
sense of resignation for doing what she had to do.

The morning sickness was as bad as ever, and she prayed
she could handle her nausea. Wind caught her hair, blowing
it across her cheek. Next she had a list of apartments to look
at. The sooner she made the move, the better off she would
be. She suspected Aaron would not give up easily, and when
he found her, she wanted to be in her own apartment, working
at her new job. In order to give her a little time to get settled,
she had wrung a promise out of Jessica not to tell Aaron where
she had gone.

Time to get settled and to heal. She wondered if she would
ever heal over the hurt of telling him goodbye. And why was
it nagging at her that she was making a mistake? She had been
over and over it, but everything had been so good between
them and the tempting thought of letting go of her doubts and
marrying him, giving their baby a father, tore at her.

She straightened her shoulders. "Remember his background, his life away from Royal. Get real, woman. You're
country and he is not. Maybe a bit of cowboy still lingers in
him, but he is so much else."

She looked at her map of the area and at the list of apartments, hoping she could find something close to the school.
Suddenly she was swamped with loss, missing Aaron, knowing what she was losing, and she had to lean her head against

the steering wheel while she cried. It hurt so badly because she missed him dreadfully.

She spent the rest of the day looking at apartments, none of which appealed to her, and early in the evening went back to her motel room on the Midland highway. She drove slowly and carefully, knowing that her full attention wasn't on her driving.

That night she could eat only a few bites of dinner and cried herself to sleep, missing Aaron more with each passing minute. While she kept telling herself the pain would dull with time and finally heal, the loss hurt badly, and she couldn't believe her own words.

The next morning she spent the first hours nauseated and crying. With determination, she left the motel, a list of available apartments in hand to begin another day's search for a place to live.

Late in the afternoon she made a deposit on a small, one-bedroom apartment that was sunny, filled with windows. She hoped it would be cheerful to come home to, but as she stood signing papers, she could only think how empty it looked and remember Aaron sprawled on her short sofa, his long legs dangling off. She missed him every second of the day. Missed him to distraction.

"You need to sign here, Miss Miles."

"I'm sorry," Pamela said, coming out of her daze and staring at her new blond landlady. She couldn't even remember the woman's name. Pamela took the pen and signed her name, handing over her check for the deposit.

"It's a very quiet place, and you'll have a swimming pool and clubhouse facilities."

"That's nice. Thank you," Pamela said, barely hearing the woman. She accepted a key, glancing once more at the place that would be her new home. A home for her and their baby. *Aaron's baby.*

As tears welled in her eyes, she was aware her landlady was staring at her. "Thank you," she mumbled, accepting the key and turning away before she was crying uncontrollably.

As soon as she was in her car, she jotted down the address again, certain she wouldn't remember it an hour from now. She went out to eat, barely able to get anything down, knowing the hardest part was ahead of her because she had to go back to Royal and get her things and move. And she would see Aaron.

It was dusk when she left the restaurant and drove back to the motel. She was exhausted, still hurting as much as ever. She turned the corner to her room and gripped the steering wheel in a moment of déjà vu when she looked at the shiny black pickup parked in front of her motel door.

Aaron watched her drive up, and his heart was in his throat. He had rehearsed what he would say to her, but his practiced arguments were forgotten when she stepped out of her car and stood facing him. All color drained from her face. She looked haggard, her eyes red, yet she still was the most beautiful woman on earth to him.

For the first time in his life, he had nothing to say. He felt helpless and adrift, wanting with all his heart and soul to let her know the depth of his feelings for her. He walked over to her and took her into his arms.

Pamela looked up at the tall man holding her, and fought her tears and tried to conjure up the words she knew she should say, but then he leaned down. His mouth covered hers, and words were gone while he kissed her as if he had waited years for this kiss.

"Mellie," he whispered. Shocked, Pamela tasted salty tears and leaned back to look at him, stunned that this tough, worldly cowboy diplomat was shedding tears. She looked into his green eyes and saw that he was as torn with hurt as she. It was astonishing. Impossible. A moment of revelation. Aaron, hurting enough to *cry* over her?

"You love me," she whispered.

"I've been trying to convince you of my love for the past month," he said roughly, swiping at his face. "You're my life, woman. I'm not fit for anything without you. I love you, Mellie.''

"Oh, Aaron,'' she said in awe, letting go of her doubts and fears and wrapping her arms tightly around his neck as she stood on tiptoe to kiss him. "I love you. I missed you.'' She leaned back. "You're sure? I don't know anything about fancy balls and the life you lead overseas.''

"You can learn it just like I did. You think I knew about it when I left Royal? And if you really don't want that, we can stay home. I can live on the ranch. I'm as good a cowpoke as a diplomat.''

"You'd give up your diplomatic career if I wanted you to?'' she asked, beginning to realize the depth of his love and feeling as if boulders were lifting off her heart. "Oh, Aaron!'' She threw herself against him to kiss him.

His arms banded her tightly as he leaned down to kiss her long and hungrily. He raised his head, dug in his pocket and pulled out the engagement ring. "Will you marry me?''

"Yes! Oh, yes, yes, yes!''

He kissed her again, longer this time, and then raised his head to look down at her. "We'll have a big fancy church wedding with family and friends.''

"I don't have to, Aaron.''

"I know you don't, but I want one. My family will love an excuse to get together.''

"Your family! Aaron, they're not going to—''

"Yes, they're going to love you like I do. You'll see. What do you think I have for a family—a bunch of cold-hearted monsters?''

"Of course not.''

"They're lovable like me. Now what we're going to do— we'll have that wedding and it will all be official and a big deal, but for tonight, I don't want to wait. You said yes and I don't want any cold feet or worries. I want to find a justice of the peace and get married right now.''

"Get married twice?'' she said, laughing and feeling giddy.

"Yes, darlin'," he drawled. "I'm not letting you get out of my sight until you're Mrs. Aaron Black."

"Mrs. Aaron Black," she repeated, unable to believe it and touching his cheek, feeling the rough stubble.

"I didn't shave. I had to wring where you were out of your friend."

"She promised me she wouldn't tell you, and Jessica has never gone back on a promise."

His eyes twinkled. "I did a little sweet-talking and she saw things my way."

"Aaron, you're impossible."

"C'mon. We're wasting time here."

She couldn't stop touching him any more than he could keep his hands from her while they found a justice of the peace and were married with two neighbors as witnesses. By nine o'clock they were in the bridal suite of a hotel in Fort Worth, a room with a balcony and a view of the lights of the city sprawled below, but she had eyes only for Aaron as she stepped into his arms.

"I'm not dressed for a wedding."

"It doesn't matter. You'll be undressed in minutes," he whispered as he pulled her into his arms to kiss her hungrily. "I want you with me the rest of my life, darlin'," he said, showering kisses on her throat as he twisted free the buttons of her blue shirt and pushed it away from her shoulders.

Suddenly she leaned away from him. "Aaron! I forgot! I have a job and an apartment I leased for the next six months. I have to be at work Monday morning."

"No, you don't."

"I signed a contract for the apartment, and I have a verbal contract for the job."

"Darlin', my big brother is ever so good at untangling things like contracts and commitments. We'll turn the problem of your new job and apartment over to him and he'll get you out of the deals and he'll find someone else to teach in your place." Aaron unfastened her bra and cupped her breast. "Don't give it another thought," he said in a husky voice.

She closed her eyes and moaned, the worries already vanished as she tugged at his belt. "You and these big Texas belt buckles."

"It's easy. A flick of the wrist," he whispered unfastening his belt and bending down to stroke her nipple with his tongue.

"Oh, Aaron, I love you, love you."

He framed her face with his hands, looking into her eyes. "I love you, Mellie, with all my being. Mrs. Aaron Black, my wife, my love." He wrapped his arms around her to kiss her, and she melted into his embrace, sliding his shirt off his shoulders and running her hands across his bare back.

He picked her up to carry her to bed and she clung to him, happiness filling her and a sense of everything being right once again in her world.

Epilogue

Pamela hurried across the foyer of the church.

Looking handsome in his black tux, Matt Walker stood waiting. His expression was solemn and preoccupied, but as he took her arm, he smiled down at her. "You look gorgeous."

"Thank you. Matt, I can't tell you how much I appreciate your standing in for the father I never had. The minute this service is over, you go on back to the hospital. You don't have to come out to the ranch for the reception."

"I'm going to take you up on that, Pam. Dusty Winthrop, one of my best hands, is standing watch for me."

"Miss Miles, Mr. Walker." The wedding coordinator peered at them over her glasses. "It's time." She hurried around to straighten out the train of Pamela's wedding dress.

As they began to move toward the center aisle, Pamela looked up at Matt. "You're the most handsome man any bride ever had escort her down an aisle."

Matt grinned. "Aaron can't stop grinning and he can't carry on a coherent conversation, so we need to get this over with."

As she smiled, her gaze ran over the crowd that stood and turned to face them. She couldn't believe this was happening to her. Aaron had paid for everything and heaven knows what it had cost him to pull this all together within days. Jessica was her maid of honor, and after she'd met Rebecca, Aaron's sister, Pamela had asked Rebecca to be a bridesmaid. Aaron had been right. All his family were friendly and welcoming and she knew she was going to be good friends with Rebecca who had accompanied her to the church today. When they'd arrived, the two had been alone for a few minutes.

Rebecca had hung up the wedding dress, helping Pamela with her things in the dressing room. "My brother looks like he's going to explode with happiness." She turned to face Pamela. "I'm so glad you're marrying him and you'll be my sister-in-law. I didn't know my brother had such great taste, finding someone like you."

"Thanks, Rebecca. I'm so in love with him and now I'm falling in love with his family. I only had my mother and there were always problems."

"That's over. Forget it," Rebecca said with a dismissive wave of her hand.

"Rebecca, we haven't told anyone—well, I've told Jessica, but no one else—we're going to have a baby. I'm pregnant."

Rebecca's mouth opened and her eyes widened and then she flew across the room to hug Pamela who let out her breath. Now she knew everything would be all right with his sister.

"I'm thrilled. Oh, have a girl. We need more girls in this family. I'm so happy for both of you. And I'll keep your secret. Don't worry," she said, her eyes twinkling.

The door opened and Jessica entered and the conversation changed, but Pamela felt as if another weight had lifted off her heart.

As she walked down the aisle, she looked at Aaron and joy warmed her heart. Her Aaron, the love of her life. He looked breathtakingly handsome in his black tux, but then she looked into his green eyes and forgot the wedding, the crowd, everything except the man waiting to marry her for the second time.

As Matt placed her hand in Aaron's, she looked up at him and couldn't wait to be alone with him again.

His brother officiated, and his other brother, Jeb, was best man. As she looked at Jacob Black, she could see little resemblance in the two brothers. The Reverend Jacob Black was stocky, blue-eyed and only their brown hair was similar. Aaron and his brother, Jeb, looked far more alike with their height, green eyes, brown hair and lean builds.

With Aaron, she repeated wedding vows, and Aaron slipped a gold band onto her finger. After a blessing and prayer, Reverend Black declared them husband and wife.

Aaron raised her veil and leaned down to kiss her. She placed her hand on his shoulder and kissed him briefly. He raised his head. "Race you up the aisle."

She laughed as he turned, stretched out his legs and gave Matt a high-five when he passed him. She tried to keep up with Aaron's long stride.

"You weren't joking."

"I want you alone in bed with me, darlin'. We're not staying long at the ranch, and my family knows that. Our guests can party until tomorrow, but I have other plans for you. We'll have our own party, darlin'."

"Your sister and brothers—"

"I had my visit with them during the past few days."

They raced to a limo and the driver pulled away, speeding out of Royal to the Black ranch and from the moment they settled in the back seat, Aaron closed them off from the view of the driver and pulled her into his arms to kiss her.

An hour later on the lawn behind the ranch house, Pamela stood talking to Jessica who moved away to get a piece of cake. Within moments Rebecca sauntered up. "I've told Aaron goodbye and will tell you goodbye now. My flight leaves this evening."

"I'm so glad you were here," Pamela said, meaning it wholeheartedly.

"You'll see more of me. I'm thinking of coming home and opening a practice here."

"For selfish reasons, I'm glad, but we'll be in Spain."

"He'll come home eventually. You can't keep Aaron away from Texas."

Pamela looked across the lawn as a breeze tugged at her hair. She saw her handsome husband standing with a cluster of his Texas Cattleman's Club friends and wondered if they were talking horses, football or the missing diamond. For a time, she would be glad to leave the danger and problems behind, but she knew they were having a short honeymoon because Aaron wanted to get back to Royal to help his friends. When he turned his head, his gaze met hers and she felt as if he had reached out and touched her.

Aaron turned back to his friends, looking at Dakota, Ben, Justin and Greg Hunt who had joined them as well as the fellow Cattleman members Forrest Cunningham and Hank Langley. Greg, Forrest and Hank were interested in the problems the other club members were facing.

"Matt went back to the hospital to watch Lady Helena."

"That red diamond has to be here in Royal," Dakota said.

"Pamela and I won't be gone long and then I'll be back in Royal. Dakota, you and Matt both have my pager number and my cell phone number if you need to reach me."

"Yeah, I'm sure you'll answer your cell phone on your honeymoon."

Aaron grinned and looked across the lawn at Pamela who took his breath every time he glanced at her. In a white satin and lace wedding dress, she looked regal and beautiful, but he wanted her alone and naked in his arms.

He heard his friends discussing the burned scrap of paper found at the landing site, speculating on the little they could read, but he barely listened.

"The coroner agreed to see me Monday," Dakota said, "and Sheriff Escobar has agreed. Maybe we can learn a little more about Riley Monroe's death. Ben, are you still watching Jamie?"

"Yes, I am. Not a difficult task, and I am going to say goodbye now because I do not want her out of my sight." He looked at Aaron and offered his hand. "May all happiness come to you and your beautiful bride," he said.

"Thanks, Ben," Aaron said, shaking his hand and watching his friend stride away, the long robe swishing around his legs. Aaron moved impatiently. "Excuse me, my friends, I'm getting my bride and getting the hell out of here."

They laughed and gave him congratulations and best wishes as he walked away. He told his brothers goodbye and then found Pamela, slipping his arm through hers. "I need to see you," he said, smiling at the group of friends clustered around her before he whisked her away.

"C'mon. I have a car waiting and we're going."

They rushed through the house and to the long, four-car garage. Aaron held open the door to a two-door black sports car that she had never ridden in before, and in minutes they were roaring away from the house, stirring up a plume of dust on the lane that led to the highway.

As he drove, Aaron tugged off his tie and then thrust out his hand. "Get the links out of my cuffs?"

"I think you should keep both hands on the wheel and pay attention to your driving. Do you know how fast you're going?"

"Do you know how badly I want to be alone with you and not have to concentrate on anything except you?"

She smiled as she tugged free his gold cuff link. She held his wrist and raised it to trail kisses across his knuckles.

"Maybe we'll just pull off in the bushes and I'll have my way with you right here," he said in a husky, threatening voice, and she laughed.

"Behind a mesquite in a bed of cactus? I don't think so, Aaron. You put both hands on the wheel and drive."

On the Black private jet he held her on his lap and kissed her until she pushed against him. "I'm going to change out of this wedding dress."

"Let me help."

"No! I'll be right back." She slid off his lap and he stood and retrieved a bag for her, handing it to her while his gaze devoured her.

With excitement bubbling in her, she hurried to change to a simple black sheath that buttoned down the back. The moment she returned, Aaron pulled her back onto his lap and kissed her, his hands sliding over her until she caught his wrists.

"You wait to go any farther until we're alone!"

"Monty is flying the plane. He's not paying any attention to us."

"I don't care. Behave, Aaron." She gazed into his eyes that held such scalding desire that her pulse raced.

"I need to talk to you," Aaron said while his fingers played in her hair. "I finally got my boss in D.C."

"And?" she asked, unable to tell from Aaron's expression whether he was going to relate good news or bad.

"I told them we wanted our baby to be born in Texas."

"You did!" she exclaimed, surprised because she had expected to move back to Spain right away.

"I want our baby born in Texas. Not anywhere else. So we're here until the baby comes. Then, they've offered me a position as an ambassador to a tiny, obscure country in Europe, San Raimundo."

"Aaron, no matter how small the country, that's an incredible promotion for you, isn't it?"

"Yes, it is," he replied solemnly. "What about it? Do you want me to take it or not?"

She was astounded he was asking. He seemed so forceful, so determined in everything he did and she knew this was an undreamed of promotion. "Oh, Aaron, of course, you'll take it." Tears welled up and she kissed him, feeling his arms tighten around her.

When she pushed away to look at him, she had her emotions under control. "Congratulations on your promotion. That's fantastic."

"Thanks. There's more. I thought you'd agree, so I told

them I'd take the ambassadorship, but I will retire in six or seven years because our baby needs to go to school here."

"You went to school in England. They have marvelous schools."

"You don't want to come home to Texas?"

"Of course I do!" she said, suspecting that in six or seven years, she would want to be living in Texas.

"We'll come home and settle on the ranch if that's all right."

"You have this all mapped out, don't you?" she asked, realizing he had her life planned.

"Sort of. What about ranch life? You're a town gal. Think you can take the ranch?"

"Of course I can. You'll be there and I'll love it."

"Good." He gazed out the window of the jet at the deep blue sky. "Someday I may go into politics and we'll be back in Washington, but we'll worry about that when the time comes."

"In all your planning, you better schedule in a little brother or sister for this baby, Aaron."

His gaze swung back to her, and he stroked her cheek. "I haven't ever asked you—how many children do you want?"

"I would like five. That's adding to overpopulation, but they'll be brilliant like their father and a real asset to the world. And you can afford five, Aaron."

"That I can. Five sounds grand to me." His expression became more solemn. "The Texas Cattleman's Club guys want my help, too. That's another reason not to rush back to Spain right away. We need to find that missing diamond because until we do, I think there is a lot of danger in Royal. Now, my lovely bride, it's been far too long since we kissed."

It was an hour before Aaron locked the hotel door and turned to her. Her heart thudded with eager anticipation and she ran into his arms, winding her arms around his neck and pulling his head down to kiss him. He had already shed his tux coat and now studs flew and his shirt was gone. Locks of brown hair fell over his forehead and his green eyes held fires that scalded her. "Turn around and let me get you out of that dress," he said.

When she turned, she felt his hands lock in the neckline of her dress as he trailed his tongue across her nape and started wild tingles coursing in her.

"Aaron, no!" she said, whirling out of his grasp. "You unfasten the buttons. I'm keeping this dress, too, for memories of today."

"I can get it sewed up."

"No! Promise me—"

"We're wasting time. Turn around. I'll unbutton—what, three hundred buttons—damnation!"

She laughed softly and turned her back to him. "Don't be absurd! More like twenty buttons, but you started this, so you finish it carefully."

"Sure, darlin'," he said, kissing her nape and trailing kisses lower over her back as he unfastened her dress. He tossed it on the bed and picked her up to sit down on the bed and hold her in his lap. She wore a white satin-and-lace teddy while he had on his black tux pants. As she ran her hand across his chest, his arms tightened around her.

"My love," he whispered before he kissed her. "Mrs. Aaron Black."

"Being married is wonderful, and I'll never get tired of being called Mrs. Black. I love you, Aaron, with my whole heart."

"I love you with all my heart and soul." He lowered his head to kiss her. She clung to him and returned his kisses, her heart thudding with joy. Mrs. Aaron Black. How wonderful life was! Happiness filled her along with joy for her tall, lean husband. She knew he truly did love her. "Oh, Aaron! You're my life, my family, my all."

He leaned over her to kiss her again, and she tightened her arms around him, eagerly winding her fingers in his hair and knowing her love for him would last the rest of their lives.

Aaron shifted slightly to look at her, his green eyes filled with warmth. "I'm going to spend our forever showing you how much I love you, darlin'."

"I'm trusting you will," she said, as she pulled him closer to kiss him.

* * * * *

Watch for the next double instalment of

THE MILLIONAIRE'S CLUB

*where more of the ultra-secret mission
to uncover the missing jewel is revealed in*

Millionaire Men

containing

Lone Star Knight
by Cindy Gerard

and

Her Ardent Sheikh
by Kristi Gold.

*Coming to you from Silhouette
Desire® in February 2002.*

For sneak previews of
Lone Star Knight

and

Her Ardent Sheikh
please turn the page.

Lone Star Knight

by

Cindy Gerard

It wasn't true. Not completely. Your entire life didn't flash before you when you were about to die. Only bits and pieces, odd, unrelated little snippets scrolled by like a vivid Technicolor collage—along with an extreme and acute awareness of those who were about to die with you.

While the flight crew and eleven other men and women in the charter jet bound from Royal, Texas, to the European principality of Asterland prepared for the crash landing with stalwart optimism, whispered prayers, or soft weeping, Lady Helena Reichard thought silently of Asterland, the home she might never see again. She thought of her parents, the Earl and Countess of Orion, and the pain her death would cause them.

Oddly, she thought of the tall, handsome Texan with smiling green eyes and dark curling hair who had waltzed her around the dance floor at the Texas Cattleman's Club reception just two nights past.

She'd met commanding men before. Sophisticated.

Worldly. Titled and moneyed. She hadn't, however, met anyone like Matthew Walker. With his quick, slashing smile and devastating wit, he'd been at once charming yet subtly and purposefully aloof. He was obviously a man of wealth, yet the hand that had held hers in its strong grip had worn the calluses of physical labor without apology. His polished and gallant formality had been a fascinating foil for an understated man-of-the-earth essence that had both intrigued and captivated—and left her wishing she hadn't had to leave Royal, Texas, so soon.

How sad, she thought, that she'd been denied the chance to know him better. How sad that her last glimpse of Texas would be from five hundred feet and falling. And then she thought of nothing but the moment as the jet, its left engine shooting fire, lurched, shuddered and dropped the last one hundred feet to the ground. She lowered her head, wrapped her arms around her ankles and prepared for impact....

Matt Walker was striding wearily toward the burn unit nurses' station when he spotted Dr. Justin Webb, dressed in green scrubs, heading for the elevator. "Hey, Justin, wait up."

Justin turned and scowled at Matt. "I've done admits on patients who look better than you."

Matt knew exactly what his friend saw: five o'clock shadow, badly rumpled shirt and bloodshot eyes. He scrubbed a hand over his unshaven jaw, rolled the stiffness out of his shoulders. "I'm fine. Just a long night."

Justin snorted. "More like a lot of long nights."

It had been almost two months since the plane crash landing that had resulted in Lady Helena Reichard's emergency admission to the burn unit at Royal Memorial Hospital. She had been among a group of Asterland dignitaries and a few locals—Matt's friends Pamela Black and Jamie Morris among them—who were en route to Asterland after a posh diplomatic reception at the club. Close to a full month had passed since Matt had been assigned by his fellow Texas Cattleman's Club members to stand guard outside Helena's door.

It didn't much matter that he was beat. His welfare wasn't at stake here. Helena's was. He just wished he knew who, or what, he was protecting her from.

Besides Matt and Justin, only three other club members knew the mysterious details surrounding the charter jet's emergency landing that had sent Helena to the hospital. Though luckily no one was killed, even now, two months later, it was still tough to absorb. The crash had been bad enough. But there'd also been a murder. A jewel theft. The hint of an attempted political coup involving the European Principality of Asterland.

Helena Reichard, it seemed, was stuck smack in the middle of it all; Matt understood exactly how vulnerable she was. He also understood that nothing, absolutely nothing more was going to happen to her under his watch.

"How's she doing?" he asked Justin.

After a glance toward the charge nurse who was busy on the phone, Justin steered Matt toward the sofa at the end of the hall on the pretense of privacy. Matt suspected what Justin really wanted was to get him off his feet. Too tired to make an issue of it, he sat.

"As you already know, most of her burns are second-degree and restricted to her left arm and upper leg." Justin eased down beside him. "It's that nasty patch of third-degree on the back of her left hand that's giving her trouble. We had to graft. Unfortunately, the site's been problematic."

Matt slumped back, rubbed an index finger over his brow. "Infection, right?"

Justin nodded. "It's cleared up now but it set her recovery back. Only time will tell what kind of mobility she'll regain."

Matt thought of the lovely hand he'd held in his at the Cattleman's Club reception and dance. The petal-soft skin. The slim, graceful fingers. "And her ankle?"

Justin shook his head. "That's still up for grabs, too. It's a bad fracture. Even with the surgery and the pins in place, we can't guarantee that she won't have a permanent limp."

Matt stared past Justin's shoulder to the partially open door of Helena's room. He thought of the beautiful, vivacious woman he'd waltzed around the dance floor. The woman whose cornflower-blue eyes had smiled into his with unguarded interest. The woman who had said his name in her perfect, practiced English yet made it sound exotic and made him feel extraordinary. That woman had been beyond perfection.

He didn't have to be inside her head to understand that the woman in the hospital room, though still beautiful, was now badly scarred, potentially disabled—and that here would be much more to her recovery process than knitting bones and healing flesh. And he couldn't throw off the helpless notion that there wasn't a damn thing he could do to help her.

After a long look at Matt, Justin rose. ''Look, I can cover for you for a few hours.''

''Thanks, but she's *my* assignment, not yours.''

Justin's long, measuring look asked the same question Matt had been asking himself lately. *Are you sure this is just an assignment?*

Matt wasn't sure of anything except that he wasn't ready to admit, even to himself yet, that it might be more.

* * * *

And now for Her Ardent Sheikh...

Her Ardent Sheikh

by

Kristi Gold

He had never seen anyone quite so beautiful, nor heard anything quite so intolerable.

Sheikh Ben Rassad pretended to peruse the antiques displayed behind the window as he watched the young woman walk away from the adjacent local dry cleaners.

She clutched a substantial garment covered in clear plastic—and sang in a pitch that could very well wake those who had long since returned to Allah. Ben would not have been surprised if every hound residing in Royal, Texas—pedigreed or of questionable breeding—had joined her in a canine chorus.

She sang with a vengeance, optimism apparent in her voice. She sang of the sun coming out tomorrow, although at the moment bright rays of light burnished her long blond hair blowing in the mild April breeze, turning it to gold. She sang as if tomorrow might not arrive unless she willed it to.

Ben smiled to himself. Her enthusiasm was almost contagious, had she been able to carry a decent tune.

As she strolled the downtown sidewalk, Ben followed a comfortable distance behind his charge while she searched various windows as he had for the past few moments. Although she was small in stature, her faded jeans enhanced her curves, proving that she was, indeed, more woman than girl.

Ben had noticed many pleasing aspects about Jamie Morris in the weeks since he had been assigned to protect her covertly. His fellow Texas Cattleman's Club members had originally requested that he guard her against two persistent men from the small European country of Asterland. The men had been sent to investigate after a plane en route to Asterland had crash-landed just outside Royal—a plane Jamie Morris had been on. She'd been bound for her wedding to Asterland cabinet member Albert Payune, a man with questionable intentions and connections. Jamie had walked away from the crash without serious injury or further obligation to marry. Although the suspected anarchists had returned to their country, she was still not safe. The arranged marriage had come with a price. Quite possibly Jamie's life.

Because of Jamie's ties to Payune, Ben had secretly memorized her habits in order to keep her safe. Guarded her with the same tenacity he utilized in business. Though she was a magnificent creature to behold, duty came first, something he had learned from his upbringing in a country that starkly contrasted with America and its customs.

Now he must protect Jamie from Robert Klimt, a man believed to be Payune's accomplice in planning a revolution in Asterland—someone he suspected to be a murderer and thief. Klimt had escaped not hours before from his hospital bed after languishing for weeks from injuries sustained in a crash. Obviously the club members had underestimated the man's dangerous determination, and Ben despised the fact that they had not been better prepared.

At the moment, he needed to question Jamie Morris about the crash. Make her aware that he would be her shadow for however long it took to apprehend Klimt. Ensure her safety at all costs. In order to accomplish his goal, she would have to come home with him.

Carefully he planned his approach so as not to frighten her. Yet considering all that she had been through the past few weeks, he doubted she was easily intimidated. And he suspected she would not like what he was about to propose.

But the members of the club depended on him. Little did Jamie Morris know, but so did she.

Jamie took two more steps, stopping at the Royal Confection Shoppe not far from her original location. The song she sang with such passion died on her lips. For that Ben was grateful.

She stared for a long moment at the display of candies with a wistful look of longing. Ben studied her delicate profile, her upturned nose, her full lips, but he'd never quite discerned the color of her eyes. He suspected they were crystalline, like precious stones, reminding him of his family's palace in Amythra, a place far removed from his thoughts more often than not in recent days. Reminding him of Royal's missing legendary red diamond and trusted friend Riley Monroe's murder. Reminding Ben of his mission.

Jamie turned away, but not before Ben caught another glimpse of her plaintive expression. Then she began to whistle as she moved to the curb toward her aged blue sedan parked across the downtown street. He must make his move now.

The squeal of tires heightened Ben's awareness, the bitter taste of danger on his tongue. He glanced toward the grating noise to find that a car was headed in the direction of the sidewalk, aimed at unsuspecting Jamie Morris.

His heart rate accelerated. Sheer instinct and military training thrust him forward, in slow motion it seemed. *Protect her!* screamed out from his brain.

As he reached Jamie, the maniacal car's right front wheel swerved onto the sidewalk. Ben shoved her aside, out of danger, sending her backward onto the concrete in a heap. Her head hit the pavement with a sickening thud. The car sped away.

Ben knelt at her side, his belly knotted with fear—fear that he had caused her more harm in his efforts to save her. "Miss Morris? Are you all right?"

When Jamie attempted to stand, Ben took her arm and helped her to her feet, relieved that she seemed to be without injury.

She grabbed up the bag from where it had landed next to a weathered light pole, carefully brushing one small hand over the plastic surface. "I'm okay."

Concerned over her condition, he grasped her elbow to steady her when she swayed. "Perhaps we should have you examined by a doctor."

She stared at him with a slightly unfocused gaze and as he had suspected, her eyes were light in color, verdant, clear as an oasis pool. A smile tipped the corner of her full lips as she touched the kaffiyeh covering his head. "White sale in progress at Murphy's today?" With that, her eyes drifted shut, and she collapsed into Ben's arms.

He lifted her up, noting how small she felt against him. Fragile. Helpless. Had he failed to protect her after all? If so, he would never forgive himself.

He lowered his ear to her mouth, and her warm breath

fanned his face. He laid his cheek against her left breast and felt the steady beat of her heart. A wave of welcome relief washed over him, and so did an intense need to shelter her.

* * * *

Don't forget **Millionaire Men** *containing*
Lone Star Knight *and* Her Ardent Sheikh
will be on the shelves next month.

SILHOUETTE®
DESIRE™

AVAILABLE FROM 18TH JANUARY 2002

CHILD OF MINE

COWBOY'S SECRET CHILD Sara Orwig

The only way Jeb Stuart would gain custody of his son was by proposing a marriage of convenience to the boy's adoptive mother. One huge side benefit was teaching his new wife to enjoy her own sensuality, but could *she* teach *him* to love again?

THE RANCHER AND THE NANNY Caroline Cross

Rugged John MacLaren didn't know the first thing about making a home for his motherless daughter. He needed help in the unforgettable form of Eve Chandler. She was making his daughter blossom and melting John's icy reserve…

MILLIONAIRE MEN

LONE STAR KNIGHT Cindy Gerard

Billionaire Matt Walker was not a man who walked away from what he wanted—and he wanted Lady Helena Reichard. But Helena was vulnerable, so Matt needed to protect her while he made her *his* forever!

HER ARDENT SHEIKH Kristi Gold

Sheikh Ben Rassad promised innocent Jamie Morris protection. But their passion soon ignited and when he discovered she carried his child, he was determined to convince her to be his bride! Only she could see the man beneath the prince.

ROYALLY WED

THE EXPECTANT PRINCESS Stella Bagwell

When Princess Dominique's father went missing she turned to loyal Marcus Kent. And when Dominique revealed she was pregnant, the ever-honourable Marcus proposed marriage. But was his proposal made out of love for her or duty to the king?

THE BLACKSHEEP PRINCE'S BRIDE Martha Shields

Once she was sure of his innocence regarding the king's disappearance, lady-in-waiting Rowena Wilde agreed to marry Jake Stanbury to help him retain custody of his son. But could she accept only a temporary union, when she wanted forever?

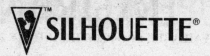

™SILHOUETTE
SENSATION®

presents a new heart-pounding
twelve-book series:

A Year of Loving Dangerously

**When a top secret agency is threatened, twelve of the best
agents in the world put their lives—and their hearts—on
the line. But will justice...and true love...prevail?**

0601/SH/LC18

SILHOUETTE® SPECIAL EDITION™

is proud to present

The Stockwells

Where family secrets, scandalous pasts and unexpected love wreak havoc on the lives of the rich and infamous Stockwells!

THE TYCOON'S INSTANT DAUGHTER
Christine Rimmer
January

SEVEN MONTHS AND COUNTING...
Myrna Temte
February

HER UNFORGETTABLE FIANCÉ
Allison Leigh
March

THE MILLIONAIRE AND THE MUM
Patricia Kay
April

THE CATTLEMAN AND THE VIRGIN HEIRESS
Jackie Merritt
May

1201/SH/LC24

SILHOUETTE®
INTRIGUE™

is proud to present

TOP SECRET BABIES

These babies need a protector!

THE BODYGUARD'S BABY
Debra Webb - January

SAVING HIS SON
Rita Herron - February

THE HUNT FOR HAWKE'S DAUGHTER
Jean Barrett - March

UNDERCOVER BABY
Adrianne Lee - April

CONCEPTION COVER-UP
Karen Lawton Barrett - May

HIS CHILD
Delores Fossen - June

Unwrap the mystery

1201/SH/LC27

1 FREE

book and a surprise gift!

We would like to take this opportunity to thank you for reading thi
Silhouette® book by offering you the chance to take ANOTHER
specially selected title from the Desire™ series absolutely FREE
We're also making this offer to introduce you to the benefits of th
Reader Service™—

- ★ FREE home delivery
- ★ FREE gifts and competitions
- ★ FREE monthly Newsletter
- ★ Exclusive Reader Service discount
- ★ Books available before they're in the shops

Accepting this FREE book and gift places you under no obligatio
to buy, you may cancel at any time, even after receiving your fre
shipment. Simply complete your details below and return the entir
page to the address below. *You don't even need a stamp!*

YES! Please send me 1 free Desire book and a surprise gif
I understand that unless you hear from me, I will receive
superb new titles every month for just £4.99 each, postage an
packing free. I am under no obligation to purchase any books an
may cancel my subscription at any time. The free book and gift wi
be mine to keep in any case.

D2ZEA

Ms/Mrs/Miss/Mr ....Initials.................................
BLOCK CAPITALS PLEAS

Surname ....

Address ....

....

....Postcode..........................

Send this whole page to:
UK: FREEPOST CN81, Croydon, CR9 3WZ
EIRE: PO Box 4546, Kilcock, County Kildare (stamp required)

Offer valid in UK and Eire only and not available to current Reader Service subscribers to this seri
We reserve the right to refuse an application and applicants must be aged 18 years or over. Only o
application per household. Terms and prices subject to change without notice. Offer expir
30th April 2002. As a result of this application, you may receive offers from other carefully select
companies. If you would prefer not to share in this opportunity please write to The Data Manager
the address above.

Silhouette® is a registered trademark used under licence.
Desire™ is being used as a trademark.